FROM THE ACCLAIMED AUTHOR OF **JIM KANE, THE OUT-FIT,** AND **THE FORESTS OF THE NIGHT** COMES THE STIRRING SAGA THAT CAPTURES THE SPIRIT OF THE SOUTHWEST THROUGH THE LIFE AND TIMES OF THE UNFORGETTABLE MEN AND WOMEN WHO CARVED THEIR DESTINY FROM A MAGNIFICENT LAND OF SANDSTONE CANYONS AND SUN-PAINTED HILLS. . . .

BEN COWDEN—Proud and passionate, he settled the score with the Briggs clan fair and square only to find himself the target of a gang of hired thugs calling themselves a posse and bearing a bogus warrant for his death.

MAUDY JANE PENDLETON—Long-legged and lovely, this Arizona cowgirl is every young rancher's dream, but she wants Ben—and she'd fight to keep him.

A.B. COWDEN—Strong, lean, and tough as rawhide, this straight-shooting rancher made his brand famous throughout the land—but how long can one family stand against an Apache scourge and a conspiracy of powerful cattle barons?

LES COWDEN—A.B.'s second eldest son, his wild streak and brooding temper made him a scrapper and brawler by nature, but there was no better man with a gun—and no better brother to watch your back.

LORRIE BRIGGS—Beneath her calico and lace, she was all Briggs and her sweet-talking charm was both a magnet—and a trap—to any man of the Cowden persuasion.

CAPTAIN FRANK MARSHALL—Armed with a fast pistol and a heavy blackjack, this special agent for the Interior has two goals: to hang Ben—and court the dead man's sister!

BETTY COWDEN—She had her mother's looks and her father's pride—and the unwanted attention of a mean-spirited, hateful man who would do anything to possess her.

DUNCAN VINCENT—Dude owner of the vast VO spread, his hired guns were trained on the one thing that stood between him and his plan to make his white-faced cattle king of the Arizona plains—the Cowdens.

CHE CHE—Solemn, mean, and mysterious, this Mexican tracker had a revenge-hungry nature that made him the best of allies—and the deadliest of enemies.

THE ARIZONA SAGA
BOOK II
THE HORSEMAN

THE ARIZONA SAGA, BOOK II

THE HORSEMAN

J. P. S. Brown

BANTAM BOOKS
NEW YORK · TORONTO · LONDON · SYDNEY · AUCKLAND

THE HORSEMAN

A Bantam Book / January 1991

ISBN 0-553-28562-9

Published simultaneously in the United States and Canada

Bantam Books are published by Bantam Books, a division of Bantam Doubleday Dell Publishing Group, Inc. Its trademark, consisting of the words "Bantam Books" and the portrayal of a rooster, is Registered in U.S. Patent and Trademark Office and in other countries. Marca Registrada. Bantam Books, 666 Fifth Avenue, New York, New York 10103.

PRINTED IN THE UNITED STATES OF AMERICA

RAD   0 9 8 7 6 5 4 3 2 1

For our friends
Fred and Helen Klumpp

CHAPTER 1

Paula Mary Cowden found herself back in school again. Her life was filled with school. Every time she stopped and realized where she was and what she was doing, she was at a desk again. She liked her studies, and she was bright enough so that she gave good recitations for her teacher, Mrs. Chance, but she hoped that someday she would look up and find herself in someplace better than school.

Paula Mary noticed the floor under her cousin Lorraine's desk was littered with scraps from lunch. Her cousin Myrtle's floor was in the same condition. Paula Mary leaned over and looked under her seat. Her floor was worse than theirs. She leaned way over to investigate the situation more thoroughly. She was upside down, her hair brushing the floor, when she realized Mrs. Chance was calling on her.

"Is that right, Paula Mary?" Mrs. Chance asked.

Paula Mary was hanging so far down over her seat that she had trouble straightening up. The whole class laughed at her. Her face was red, and she tried to smile and take the joke on herself, but she was embarrassed at being caught in another world during arithmetic. Spelling was her favorite subject; she was not fond of numbers. Now, she guessed Mrs. Chance would call on her to repeat what she had been saying about arithmetic.

"Are you back with us, young lady?" asked Mrs. Chance.

The class murmured softly with laughter.

"Yes, ma'am," said Paula Mary. Mrs. Chance disciplined

her students against going wild, and she was dead set against laughter in her school.

"Come to the front of the class and recite *The Arrow and the Song* for us, please."

"I thought we were in arithmetic," Paula Mary said, to more laughter.

"Not in this class, but I guess you could not have known, since you have found something more interesting to study under your desk."

Paula Mary slid off her seat and went to the front of the class.

"Stand on the bench and recite Longfellow's poem. Maybe that will help put your thoughts rightside up instead of upside down."

The class was very still and attentive now that Paula Mary had been singled out as an example of inattention. She climbed on the bench and began reciting:

I shot an arrow into the air,
It fell to earth, I know not where;
For, so swiftly it flew, the sight
Could not follow it in its flight.

She drew as big a breath as she could to go on with the next stanza. As she did, an audacious mouse took advantage of the stillness of the class and skittered up the aisle toward her. Paula Mary was taken completely by surprise and forgot to expel her breath to say the next verse. She froze and watched as the mouse, compelled by the scent of meat and bread, hurried deep into the crowded room.

"That's fine. Go on, girl," said Mrs. Chance.

"'I breathed . . .'" Paula Mary was still holding her breath, fascinated by the mouse.

"'A,'" prompted Mrs. Chance.

"'A . . .'" said Paula Mary.

"'Song.'"

"'Song . . .'" Paula Mary repeated.

"'Into.'"

The mouse saw the lunch scraps under Lorraine's desk, hopped into a dance, and scouted in a circle that included Myrtle's desk. He scampered into the morsels under Paula Mary's desk with such abandon that he braked and scratched the floor to keep from sliding past.

"'Into the air,'" exploded Paula Mary, overcome by mirth. Painfully, she blurted, "'It fell to earth, I know not where.'"

The class tittered, but looked puzzled and critical of her behavior. She was the only one who knew about the mouse. The mouse stood on his hind legs with his potbelly protruding, his head back, chewing—watching her with the same expression as the rest of the class. Paula Mary hugged her own belly and folded on the bench with laughter.

"Paula Mary Cowden, you are out of control," said Mrs. Chance.

Paula Mary laughed so hard the pain scared her. She pressed her face against the bench so she could not see the mouse.

Mrs. Chance picked her up by the shoulders and stood her on the bench, forcing her to look at the mouse again. "Get hold of yourself, girl," she said.

The mouse was gobbling scraps, knowing his time was short. Paula Mary, to vindicate herself, pointed at him and said, "It's the little mouse, Mrs. Chance."

The class surged in their seats to have a look. Lewis Porter, who sat behind Paula Mary, was the mouse's nearest enemy. Lewis raised off his tailbone with his largest book in both hands and slammed it down to crush the mouse. The mouse leapt out of danger, dashed in a tight circle to find direction, and skittered away under a hail of laughter. Paula Mary collapsed on the bench again.

"Get up from there, Paula Mary Cowden, and go to your seat," Mrs. Chance said.

Paula Mary could not move her legs.

Mrs. Chance seized her and sat her up. "Go to your seat, young lady."

Paula Mary realized the lady felt none of the mirth that plagued everyone else in the class. "But, Mrs. Chance, didn't you see the little mouse cutting didoes?" she shrieked. This time the class turned loose all holds and roared.

Mrs. Chance did not allow this sort of thing. She tried to hold Paula Mary straight on the bench, but the girl was so afflicted with spineless hilarity that she rolled back on her side.

"Get up, Paula Mary Cowden," Mrs. Chance ordered once again, but the girl was still heedless. Gently, Mrs. Chance lifted her by the shoulders, helped her to the door and put her outside. "Perhaps you can find your way home. You have no business here."

Paula Mary stopped laughing. The look of sadness on Mrs. Chance's face distressed her. Now she felt doomed.

"Go on home, Paula Mary. I'm very disappointed in you. Don't come back to my classroom until you regain control of yourself."

Mrs. Chance shut the door, and Paula Mary found herself alone outside the schoolhouse. She heard Mrs. Chance speak softly inside, and the class subsided again. Then her cousin Myrtle Farley resumed the recitation:

I breathed a song into the air,
It fell to earth, I know not where;
For who has sight so keen and strong,
That it can follow the flight of song?

Paula Mary began to cry. As she stumbled toward home, she heard Myrtle recite the last of the poem:

Long, long afterward, in an oak,
I found the arrow, still unbroke;
And the song, from beginning to end,
I found again in the heart of a friend.

She floundered toward home awhile, lost over the mishap and misfortune of an uncontrollable mirth. Her home was El Durazno, the Peach Tree Ranch, three miles north of town. Her father, A. B. Cowden, raised fine horses and was under-sheriff for that part of Pima County, Arizona Territory. This was September 1885.

Paula Mary was twelve and small for her age. Everybody else in her family was grown up. Her brothers, Ben, Les, and Mark, were twenty-one, nineteen, and seventeen. Her sisters, Eileen and Betty, were twenty-three and fifteen. She was related to almost every Anglo cowman on the Santa Cruz River. Her mother's people had come to Arizona from Mississippi before the War of Northern Aggression, and her father had walked away from Mississippi with nothing after the war.

Paula Mary stopped crying and began worrying how she would explain being sent home early from school. Her family did not like her to be alone on the road between Harshaw and the ranch.

In May, Geronimo had broken away from the reservation at San Carlos and was raiding ranches. This region of the Santa

Cruz, called by the Indians The Enchanted Land, was the most fertile and beautiful country on the traditional wartrail of the Apaches. El Durazno and the range upon which its cattle ran was on Geronimo's warpath. Geronimo had not been seen much, but one of his chiefs, an old warrior called the Yawner was preying on the country at will. A month ago, while the Cowdens were in town, he had raided El Durazno and scalped Betty's doll.

Paula Mary heard horses coming behind her, and she quickened her step. When the riders came abreast of her, she stretched out like a pacer.

"You're in quite a hurry, there, for a little girl," one of the riders said.

Paula Mary looked up at them. They were giving her room to walk on the road, but she was keeping to the shoulder. She wanted them to go on and leave her alone.

Dick Martin, one of the riders, was sort of a bum. For a long time, he had hung around her brothers, trying to learn to cowboy. He was not a diligent worker. He did not take care of the horses he rode. He turned out to be sort of common and worthless. She had very high standards, being a sister of the three Cowden brothers. They were the best ropers, fighters, and wild-horse riders in the whole country, by God.

"Why, it's Paula Mary Cowden, making tracks and dust toward home," Dick Martin said. "Look what we have here, Mr. Marshall, the littlest of the famous Cowdens you came to see."

The other rider was staring down at Paula Mary with eyes black as an Apache's. The hair beneath his hat was as black as her brother Ben's. Paula Mary had always been sure that her hair and her brother Ben's were the blackest in the territory, except for the Apaches'. This man's was as black. He was dressed in a pressed three-piece suit that he wore easily and comfortably. His hat was the best money could buy and set at a cocky angle so the brim slanted low across his brow and showed off the authoritative look in his handsome eyes.

Paula Mary Cowden was not much impressed by the look of authority most ordinary men assumed when they rode big horses past little girls. Her father, A. B. Cowden, could paralyze the lizards off the trees with his look. Her brother Ben could shrug his shoulders and leave dudes like this one dead in the dirt.

"This is just right," said Marshall. "Get her up on your

horse with you, Martin. We'll take her home for her folks while
we're at it."

Dick Martin rode up beside Paula Mary. Although she
heard the dude make his plan, she ignored Dick Martin.

"Come on, Paula Mary, you heard Mr. Marshall," said
Martin. "Give me your hand so I can lift you up here behind
me."

Martin and Paula Mary both knew he was being overly
familiar with her. If he did not watch himself, one of her
brothers would harelip him for even offering her a seat on the
same horse with him. As a favor to him and in order not to
embarrass him in front of his dude, she did not answer.

"Come on, Paula Mary," Martin coaxed.

The dude stopped and looked back over his shoulder at
her. "Little girl, didn't you hear the man?" the dude demanded, his black eyes glittering with temper. "Give him your
hand and climb up on that horse."

That was enough for Paula Mary. She looked around for the
best way to depart their company. She looked back and saw
Chris Wilson coming with a wagonload of ore and his twenty-
mule team. Paula Mary gave the dude a look of pure hate and
Martin another of pure contempt and ran to meet Chris. He
checked his team, and she climbed a wheel to take the seat
beside him.

"Well, well, this is a surprise," said Chris. "How did I get
so lucky as to have you for a traveling partner in the middle of
a schoolday?"

Paula Mary looked Chris in the eye and said, "I got sent
home."

Chris Wilson and Paula Mary dearly loved each other, and
she could tell him anything. Chris smiled and gave her a
glimpse of the gold way back in the shadows of his mouth. His
nasty old pipe jutted out of his face like the branch of a tree.

"Now, Paula Mary, why would anybody send you away
when they could have you with them all day?" he asked.

Ahead, Dick Martin and his dude stopped and watered
their horses at a ford where a cattle trail crossed Harshaw
Creek. Nobody was having trouble crossing the creek these
days. The climate was drouthy. The big teams and ore wagons
that traveled the road from the Harshaw Mine to the railhead
in Patagonia kept the dust roiling and settling layer on layer.

Paula Mary told Chris about the little mouse that cut
didoes, and they were both laughing when they passed Martin

and the dude. Paula Mary made sure she got to look Martin and the dude in the eye when she was laughing. Chris saw her raise her head and give them the high-hat, and liked it.

"How come you didn't let those two escort you home, young lady?" Chris asked. "Aren't two armed sheriffs enough for one little girl?"

"Sheriffs? Who's a sheriff? My papa's the only sheriff around here. That's only Dick Martin and some dude acting like he knows stuff."

Chris did not say anything more about it, but he had seen badges on the vests of both men. Dick Martin did not look so much like a bum in his suit and tie and badge. Chris looked back. Martin and the dude were coming on at a trot.

Chris stopped his team in front of the barn at El Durazno and let Paula Mary down. She waved and ran into the barn. Martin and the dude caught up. The dude was wearing a fake smile now because he was in Paula Mary's territory.

"So this is where you live, Paula Mary," he said, as though the next thing she should do was ask him to come in the house. Dick Martin knew better than to hint for an invitation like that. The Cowdens knew him too well. The dude companion ought to look at Dick's face and learn his place.

Paula Mary hurried on through the barn to the house. The dude tried to follow her. Bill Knox, the Cowden's blacksmith, stepped out and cut him off. Bill was a gruff and grouchy old giant with snow-white hair and big muscles as hard as the iron he shaped. He would not let any man ride a horse on Paula Mary Cowden's heels. He stood in front of the dude's horse like a wall.

"You can let us by," Marshall said. "The little girl promised to introduce us to her mother and father."

"Get off your horses," Bill Knox said. "Tie them outside. Water them in the corral, if you want. You can wait in A. B.'s office. The Mexican boy went to fetch him."

"We want to go to the house," said Marshall. "We're here on government business."

"He'll be here in a minute." Bill turned back to his forge.

Dick Martin tied his horse outside, went into A. B.'s office, and drank water from an *olla*, a clay pot, that swung from the rafters. He squatted in the corner of the room, a man who did as he was told. He knew Marshall was at El Durazno to cause trouble. Martin was forced to help the man because he had just been made constable of Patagonia, but he did not like doing it.

He was no great friend of the Cowdens, but he sure did not want this trouble with them.

Marshall sat down at A. B.'s desk, lit a cigar, and threw the burning match on the floor. Martin watched it scorch the oak floor before it burned out, but Marshall paid it no mind. He was poking through papers on the desk when A. B. came in.

Martin stood up to shake A. B.'s hand, watching for the warm look the man sometimes gave him. A. B. was always courteous and seemed to be waiting for Martin to do something that would allow him to like him. Well, Martin was fouling that possibility again, because he did something A. B. Cowden would live to hate. He introduced him to Special Agent Frank Marshall, of the Arizona Department of the Interior.

Ben Cowden rode into Patagonia leading a packhorse loaded with the carcasses of two of his worst enemies, Hoozy Briggs and the Yaqui. This was Hoozy's hometown, and people did not receive Ben as though he was at the head of a parade. Everybody knew one of the corpses under the tarp was Hoozy's, because Ben had told them Hoozy was dead when he came in to borrow the packhorse.

Now all he wanted to do was turn the bodies over to Dick Martin, return the packhorse, and go home. Because of Hoozy Briggs, Ben had not been home much lately. For some time before he got himself killed by Apaches, Hoozy had been doing mischief to Ben Cowden and his family. Hoozy and his Yaqui partner had been running away from Ben when the Apaches caught them and lanced them.

Ben did not like it that Dick Martin, a friend of Hoozy's, was the new constable of Patagonia. Martin was not quite as sorry as Hoozy, but he would do for sorry when Hoozy was not around. Ben paraded the packhorse all over town, by every saloon, and could not find Martin. He wanted Martin to be the one to turn the body over to Hoozy Briggs's parents. He finally saw he would have to take Hoozy home himself.

Not a sign of a Briggs was showing when Ben stopped his horse at their house in the middle of town. Rather than shout for them to come out for their son, he dismounted, tied his horses to a tree, and knocked on the front door.

He heard no sound inside the house. He went around to the back and was about to knock when he heard metal strike metal behind him. He turned and saw an elderly man lift an ax out from under a plowshare.

Ben did not think the man intended to use the ax as a tool, but as a weapon. Anytime a Briggs was near a Cowden these days, both sides dropped tools and picked up weapons. The trouble was, there weren't many Briggses left. This man was the father, but he was hardworking and not prone to mischief. His two mean sons, Whitey and Hoozy, were dead. His daughter Lorrie was somewhere on her way to new adventures after being caught in a hotel room with Pima County's self-styled leading citizen by that citizen's leading wife.

Ben knew a teenage brother of Whitey and Hoozy still lived with his parents. He looked around for him. Everybody said the poison of young snakes was the most potent. The Briggs offspring were mean as snakes, but Ben had always thought the mother and father were decent people because they worked so hard.

"Good evening, Mr. Briggs," Ben said.

Briggs did not even nod.

Ben made himself walk toward the man. Some men would rather stand away at a distance to tell bad news, but Ben thought it hurt people worse when they were told that way. He did not like the Briggses, but he did not have anything against this man, who had lost two sons in the last month and a half.

"My name's Ben Cowden," Ben said when he was decently close.

"I know who you are."

"I'm here on sad business, Mr. Briggs."

"I know why you're here. They came and told me you borrowed a horse to bring in the body of my son."

"Yes, sir. I found him in Rosemont Canyon, lanced by Apaches."

"You're one of the sonsabitches that found Whitey's body too, aren't you?"

Ben did not answer. He did not want to fight. He only wanted to hand the man his son's body.

"Now you bring me the mess that's left of another son. You're kinda rubbing my nose in it, aren't you?"

"No, Mr. Briggs. Hoozy and I weren't friends, but I thought you'd want his body back."

"No, you goddamned murdering Cowden, you wanted to parade my son's body back here so everybody'd know you finished him."

"Sir, I've done the decent thing. Will you help me take him down off the horse?"

"I will not. I won't help clean up your mess. Get it away from here before his mother comes home."

Ben went back to the front of the house. Lorrie Briggs, Hoozy's sister, was coming through the front gate with her mother and Ted, the young brother. Mrs. Briggs hurried into the house. Lorrie and the boy stared at Ben as though he was to blame for Hoozy's killing. That was all right for the father, the mother, and the brother, but Lorrie had no right to blame him. She was Hoozy's boss's mistress. Ben and Hoozy's boss were at war.

"You've got a lot of nerve, you sonofabitch," Lorrie said. "Killing my brother and then trying to dump him on our doorstep."

Ben wanted to get on his horse and go somewhere and wash. He was not handling Hoozy's corpse because he liked it. He should have let Hoozy rot on the side of the hill where he found him. "Lorrie, I didn't kill your brother. I found him in Rosemont Canyon, and I thought your folks would want him home."

"Yeah, and where's Rosemont Canyon, you bastard?"

"You know where it is, Lorrie."

"Yes, I know where it is. It's way out in the most desolate corner of the county where even God won't go. You're trying to tell me you just 'found' my brother there? How was that? What were you doing there? Much as you hated each other, how come you just happened to find him dead in a place where nobody else in the world ever goes?"

"I was after him, Lorrie. You knew that."

"Yeah, you were after him, and you killed him the way you did his partners in Santa Cruz, but you're so high and mighty, you think you'll get away with it."

Ben stared at Lorrie. She was so damned pretty, and she used to be his best girlfriend. Now she'd like to kill him.

Lorrie glanced past him at something, and Ben turned to see old Briggs come around the corner of the house with the ax.

"Mr. Briggs, please put that down," Ben said, and drew his pistol.

Briggs kept coming.

"Get him, Teddy," Lorrie said. The boy charged Ben with a pocketknife. Lorrie was wearing a joyful look. Ben fired over

Mr. Briggs's head and stopped him. The boy came on as though he would collide with Ben, slashed at him from a safe arm's length before he reached him, and ran away. He might wish he was mean and tough, thought Ben, but he'll never be a Hoozy Briggs.

Ben walked past Lorrie toward his horses. She hit him a heavy blow on the side of the head with her purse. The purse hurt so much that he thought it must be full of rocks. He recovered and warded off the next swing of the purse, but it wrapped around his head on its drawstrings and bloodied his ear. He took it and threw it into the yard as he walked to his horse.

"That's right, run, you sonofabitch," screamed Lorrie. "And don't try to dump your rotted carcasses in our front yard. Take them home and bury them in your mother's flower bed."

Ben climbed on his horse, ducked his head under the tree, untied the packhorse, and rode toward Harshaw. He would turn the bodies over to the coroner there and be rid of them legally.

"Turn tail, you bastard," yelled Lorrie. "Tell your sister Betty to throw away her teddy bear and take my brother's carcass to play with. My brother was too good a man for her when he was alive, but he's just right now."

That made Ben feel sad. Hoozy had once come sparking after Ben's sister Betty.

CHAPTER 2

A. B. Cowden did not know much about the Interior Department of Arizona, but he knew most employees of the territorial government were incompetent and corrupt as hell. The way Frank Marshall lolled behind the desk and looked at A. B. out of the side of his face was enough to make A. B. distrust him.

The man leaned forward as though he might stand up to shake A. B.'s hand, then slumped back on his tailbone when A. B. did not offer it across the desk. He kept his face profiled to A. B., pretending he was interested in something outside the window.

"Nice place you've got here, Cowden," Marshall said.

Dick Martin winced. People in that country called A. B. Cowden Mister. Calling him by his last name, as though he was some clerk in a bureau in the basement of the Interior Department, was a foolish mistake. Any fool should be able to see A. B. was a dignified man, respected by everyone who knew him. He was a leader who exerted a good influence on people. Martin did not want A. B. to think he approved of Marshall's insulting manner. He stood up to leave the room.

"Where are you going?" asked Marshall.

"Outside, to see about our horses," Martin said.

"Just squat back down there. I want you to hear this."

"Aw, you can handle it without me." Martin went out.

"Come back here, mister." Marshall uncoiled, reached the door in one stride, and threw it open, but the constable was already gone.

Marshall was a tall man. A. B. figured he was six feet six. He carried himself with a grace that came only with prime strength in a mature man. A. B. knew only two other men who moved like that, his sons Ben and Les. Mark would someday be as graceful, but he was still a gangly boy. This Marshall might be a bureaucrat, and he probably was a martinet and a bully, but he was big and powerful. His hands were well shaped and big. His head was large, his hair thick and curly, his face handsome. His arms and legs were long, his shoulders wide, his stomach flat.

He sprawled in A. B.'s chair again. "Have a seat and let's talk," he said.

"What can I do for you, Captain Marshall?" asked A. B.

"Well, Cowden, I'll tell you, I'd consider it a great kindness if you'd send to the house for some coffee and maybe a little something nice to eat. I've been riding several days, and I haven't had one proper meal since I left Tucson."

"Of course." A. B. stepped to the door and asked Gordo Soto, his stableboy, to go to the house and ask the girls to send coffee and cakes for Constable Martin and Captain Marshall. He closed the door and stepped back to the center of the room. "Anything else?"

"Have a seat. We have quite a lot to talk about."

A. B. stayed where he was. Marshall leveled his authoritative gaze on him. "Listen, old man, I can't talk with you standing over me like that. I'm ordering you to have a seat."

"Captain Marshall, I'm sure you can say all you have to say and be on your way before I get tired of standing here. Speak up and be done with it."

"Well, all right, I hope you can stand what I have to say. The governor has put me in charge of doing away with cattle theft and title fraud in Arizona Territory. I understand a warrant has already been issued for your son Ben Cowden by the county for cattle theft. You were supposed to enforce it, but it's still outstanding.

"A new federal warrant has been issued for him for the crime of murder. He recently killed two Americans in the town of Santa Cruz in Sonora. I'm here to find him and take him in. Tell me where he is, and I'll be gone."

"He's not here, and I don't know where he is."

"Old man, I'm going to camp right here on the Peach Tree Ranch until he comes home, and then I'm gonna put knots on his head and take him to jail."

"Let me see your warrant, Captain Marshall."

"Now there you have me for the time being, Cowden. We should be notified of the issuance of our warrant by telegram sometime tomorrow. I came a little early because the Tombstone marshal notified us Ben Cowden was headed this way."

"I don't abide by telegraphed warrants," said A. B. "Any crooked bureaucrat can issue a warrant that way. When I see the real document, signed by Judge Black in Tucson, my son will wear irons. Until then, go find someplace else to park."

A. B. was not carrying his pistol and his double-barreled shotgun was in the house behind the kitchen door. At that moment, he felt he might need a weapon.

Marshall drew his revolver. "You will not impede this arrest. I always know when old villains like you are about to pull a gun. Raise your hands and face the wall."

A. B. opened his coat to show he was unarmed. Marshall crossed the room, turned him to the wall, and frisked him expertly. As he straightened and stood back, Betty tapped on the door and came in with a tray of coffee and rolls.

Betty was so beautiful that almost every man, woman, and child who saw her was forced to turn and give themselves another look. Frank Marshall was no exception. The girl was in bloom. Her curly black hair, blue eyes, fairness, and carriage stopped hearts when she walked by. Frank Marshall quivered to his full height as though a cockroach had run up his leg. He put the pistol away so fast Betty never saw it. A. B. was always thankful for the good looks of his daughters, but at that moment Betty's served him better than a pistol or a double-barreled shotgun. He would rather have subdued Marshall and driven the meanness out of him some other way, though. Now he might never be rid of him.

"Papa, here's coffee and cinnamon rolls," Betty said, setting the tray on the desk. She paused near Marshall long enough to allow her father to introduce him. When A. B. did not make the introduction, she headed for the door.

"Pardon me, young lady. I'm Frank Marshall, special agent for the Interior Department of the Territory." Marshall stretched up to the last inch of his six-and-a-half-foot frame, rocked on his toes for more, showed his broad white teeth in a smile, and puffed up like a pouter pigeon.

Betty glanced at him with the same consideration she would give a broken pitchfork handle and left him standing with his teeth bared. If her father would not introduce the fellow, he must be awfully common.

"Is that creature *your* daughter, Cowden?" Marshall asked when she was gone.

A. B. poured Marshall a cup of coffee and said, "If you're satisfied you don't need to search me anymore, young man, here's the collation you asked for."

"Say, listen. I'm sorry about that. It seemed to me our talk had broken down. I don't mind telling you, I'm a careful man."

A. B. went to the door and called for Dick Martin. When he came into the office, A. B. turned to Marshall. "Our talk did not break down, Captain Marshall. You said everything you needed to say. You didn't need to pull a gun on me when I didn't tell you what you wanted to hear, though. I don't pull guns on my visitors. When a visitor pulls a gun on me, his visit is over. Have your coffee and leave."

"Listen, I'm really sorry about this," Marshall said. "Won't you please forget it? I'd like to call on your daughter. What's her name?"

A. B. walked out of the office.

"Martin, tell me the name of that girl who brought the coffee," Marshall demanded.

"That is Betty Cowden," Martin said.

"Geez. Are there any more like her? Of course not. There couldn't be another girl that beautiful anywhere else in the world."

Ben was riding up to the barn. A. B. called to Gordo and Bill Knox when he saw the packhorse. Ben dismounted and hugged his father.

"Son, what are you carrying on the packhorse?" A. B. asked.

"It's the bodies of Hoozy Briggs and that Yaqui who ran with him, Papa. I brought them here because I didn't know what else to do. I took them to the Briggses first because I thought that was the most decent thing to do, but Hoozy's folks had a fit and ran me off. I sent a wire to Harshaw asking Judge Dunn to meet us here for an inquest. I guess I should have taken the bodies on to Harshaw. I can still do it."

"No, son, we'll wait for Judge Dunn and have the inquest here. You can rest."

"Thanks, Papa."

Frank Marshall and Dick Martin came out of the barn.

"Hello, Dick," said Ben. "I looked all over Patagonia for

you when I heard you'd been made the constable. I wanted to turn these carcasses over to you."

Dick Martin lifted the tarp on the packhorse and looked at the bodies. "Who is it, Ben?"

"Hoozy Briggs and his Yaqui," Ben said.

"You kill them?"

"No, the Yawner's people killed them in Rosemont Canyon."

"What do you have there, a couple of dead men?" Marshall moved his coat aside and showed his badge. "You say you found them in Rosemont Canyon? What were you doing there, Cowden?"

"I was on my way home."

"From Tombstone? Wasn't Rosemont out of your way?"

Ben turned to A. B. "Who is this, Papa?"

"He probably has the right to question you, son. He says he's a special agent for the Department of the Interior."

"That's right, Mr. Cowden," Martin said. "He showed me his credentials before I ever brought him here. I wouldn't bring anyone here that wasn't legitimate. I hope you know that."

"I know, Dick," A. B. said. "You identified him when you introduced him. I don't need to see his credentials if you vouch for him."

"I wouldn't try to lie to anyone," Martin said.

"Well, I want to see his credentials," Ben said.

Marshall rolled his shoulders and rocked on his toes, trying to intimidate Ben.

"Well, let's see them," Ben said.

"Fella, I don't have to show you a damned thing. I'm about to arrest you with the authority vested in my good right arm."

Ben was glad the man was a talker and a bully. He would have worried about a quiet man that big. "Well, get after it if you think you're man enough," he said.

"Oh, I'm man enough, but I'd rather be nice to you. I feel a great sweetness for your sister Betty."

This brought the very blood into Ben's eye. He hit Marshall in his left eye and knocked him down. Marshall pulled his gun even as he sprawled on the ground. Ben took a step and kicked it out of his hand. It bounced off the side of the barn, and Ben skipped closer to Marshall, intending to land his next step in the man's face. Marshall's good eye widened, and he scampered backward like a spider on his hands and feet and butt. A. B. and Martin jumped in and stopped Ben from stomping him.

Marshall jumped up and examined his injuries. Ben emptied the cartridges out of the pistol and dropped it on Marshall's toe. Marshall made no sound as he holstered his pistol.

"Load it when you're ready to use it," Ben said.

"You shouldn't have done that, Ben," Martin said.

"The *hell* you say," said A. B. "He did just right. The man's been asking for a punch in the eye ever since you brought him here."

A buggy rattled up the canyon, and Judge Charles Dunn, the deputy coroner from Harshaw, appeared. John Porter, the telegraph operator and Ben's first cousin, who often served as Judge Dunn's recorder, was riding with him. They crossed the creek and pulled up in the yard, their horses shying at the bodies on the packhorse.

Judge Dunn stepped down from his rig and ordered the bodies unloaded so that he could establish their identities and determine the cause of their deaths.

"Carry them inside for this business," A. B. said. "I don't want my family or people who pass on the road to see them."

Frank Marshall drew the judge aside as the bodies were being carried in. Judge Dunn was an old friend of A. B.'s and an honest man. He looked away while he listened to Marshall. He was hard of hearing, and when Marshall was through filling his deafer ear with secret intelligence, he spoke out in his most strident and judicial voice. "Why do you keep holding your hand over your eye, young man?"

Marshall mumbled something nobody else could hear.

"What's that you say, you have foreign matter in the orb?"

Marshall mumbled again, turning his head to make sure no one read his lips.

"Ah, 'twas a fist, you say," announced the judge. "I understand that. Ofttimes fists fly on this outfit, especially when officious bureaucrats like yourself try to assert the law over the best lawman in Arizona Territory."

Marshall puffed out his chest, jutted his jaw, and said, "That old man's been fooling everybody long enough. I'm the best lawman this state will ever see."

"Young man, take my advice and don't try to prove that by fistfighting. You'll only disprove yourself again. Out here, people admire the Cowdens because they never start a fight or try to end one with words."

"I've not yet been in a fight," Marshall said loftily. "He Sundayed me."

Ben laughed.

"Enough of this," the judge said. "Remove the garments from this poor clay, and let us make the necessary decisions so we can bury it."

Viney Cowden, wife of A. B. and mother of their six living children, had called her girls out into the front yard to watch Ben's arrival. They called to him as he embraced his father. The girls were happy to see him but sobered when they saw that the packhorse was loaded with corpses. When Ben flew at Frank Marshall, Viney herded them back into the house.

Betty and Paula Mary kept watching for a chance to slip away to the barn. After dark, with the supper prepared and no one to eat it, Eileen and Viney went to the Arizona room, a screened room in the back of the house, to sew. Betty and Paula Mary ran to the barn.

The night was so dark they had to feel their way over the path, but they were guided by the light through the office window. The girls were not always allowed to see everything that went on in the barn. No proclamations had been issued that day making the barn off limits, but they knew something they were not supposed to see was going on.

The person who always protected the eyes and the ears of the Cowden girls from the barn's exotic sights and sounds was Big Bill Knox. When things the girls were not supposed to see were about to happen, Big Bill pointed to the house and sent them away. They were not allowed to look back either. Big Bill wanted them to believe they would turn into pillars of salt if they looked back. One word from him, one gesture, or a single glance was supposed to send all little girls running to mama.

The girls stood on top of a tall post under the eaves of the barn and climbed on the roof. They quietly opened a trapdoor that let out the hot air when new hay was stored in the loft. They could hear the men moving chairs out of the office and Judge Dunn talking.

They hung together in the trapdoor so Paula Mary would not be afraid. Betty whispered, "One . . . two . . . three," and they dropped into the hay. They lay still and held their breath with their faces in the hay, listening.

Judge Dunn was saying, "So, summarizing the testimony of this inquest up to now, it seems corpse number one is minus one ear. Most of us knew corpse number one in its lifetime as the clay of Hoozy Briggs, erstwhile miner of this municipality, and he was in possession of both his ears when he was last seen in Harshaw. However, the body of this inquest agrees that the evidence of advanced healing of the wound in the place of the lost ear suggests it was lost several weeks ago. It was definitely not lost so recently as to have been cut off at the time Mr. Briggs was dispatched from this life.

"One witness at this inquest, Ben Cowden, states that he saw him only three days ago, in Tombstone, with only one ear. The other ear had been completely removed somehow from the side of his head. John, am I going too fast for you?"

"Just a minute, Judge, let me catch up."

The girls waited until the judge's big voice filled the barn again, then moved to the boards on the edge of the loft. They burrowed through the hay to the boards and found cracks to look through.

Betty gave a tiny gasp, but Bill Knox, the dude, and Dick Martin were standing side by side, blocking Paula Mary's view. When they moved and unveiled the cadavers, Paula Mary could not believe her eyes. Judge Dunn was using a lot of imagination when he called dead bodies clay. She would call them two cold lumps of tattered flesh. The lumps were lying in disarray, as though cast aside, dumped, abandoned. The eyes, which had not been respectfully closed so they could rest, were unevenly open. Paula Mary saw the very pain of death on the flesh as if it remained on display after life had fled. The pain was left there to be seen after it had attacked and driven out all the feeling.

The wounds were not significant. They were only discolored punctures. The dead coldness of the clay and its disarray was significant. Paula Mary would never again entertain an illusion about lying in state as a good-looking corpse for people to pat and love, cry over, and feel sorry for.

"Furthermore," Judge Dunn proclaimed, "said Ben Cowden has testified before this inquest that he arrived at the spot where corpse number one and corpse number two lay so soon after they had been killed that the arrows were still quivering in the earthly remains, so to speak.

"And said Ben Cowden did encounter soon thereafter four indigenous Apaches who admitted dispatching said Hoozy Briggs and said Yaqui from this life. Proof of said dispatch being one little girl's ring and one gold chain the Apaches did remove from the remains and give to Ben Cowden.

"Witnesses A. B. Cowden and Gilberto Soto also testified that said gold chain and said little girl's ring disappeared on June twenty-four, 1885, from the possession of one Guilo Soto after he was murdered in Harshaw. A. B. Cowden testified that his daughter, Miss Paula Mary Cowden, told him that she saw said ring and chain around the neck of said indigenous Yaqui several weeks after Guilo Soto's murder.

"Therefore, it is determined by this inquest that Hoozy Briggs and the Yaqui Indian did meet their demise as the direct result of an unfortunate encounter with four indigenous Apaches in Rosemont Canyon in this county. This is evidenced by several puncture wounds in the clay of said victims of the encounter, to wit, one large wound in the pit of the stomach of said Hoozy Briggs, probably made by a lance or a spear, which left a four-inch wound on the surface and a tear at least eight inches deep; and two arrow wounds in the upper torso of said indigenous Yaqui, one of which was made by a conventional arrow which entered the left breast and lodged in the left shoulderblade, and another which was made by a much larger arrow which entered the center of the back next to the spine and passed through the navel, impaling the torso of the victim through and through.

"It is further determined by this inquest that examination of the clay of Hoozy Briggs brings to a close doubt and conjecture as to the identity of at least one perpetrator of what has been known in the municipality of Harshaw as the Johnson Massacre. His turning up minus an ear convinces this official body that said Hoozy Briggs participated in the murders of the three members of the Johnson family in July of this year. Evidence for this conclusion is the voiceless clay of said Hoozy Briggs, to wit, the absence of the left ear on his remains.

"One left ear was recovered after said massacre of said Johnson family from inside the mouth of one of the victims, to wit, Johnny Johnson, son of Ray Johnson, father, and Ann Burr Johnson, stepmother, one day after their bodies were found. This inquest therefore deduces that Johnny Johnson did bite the ear off Hoozy Briggs in the fray during the Johnson massacre.

"Since no other left ears have been missing in this entire county since the Johnson massacre, it is deduced that said Hoozy Briggs lost his ear while he was committing that crime, to wit, while he grappled with the Johnson boy in the act of murdering him.

"Further testimony has been given by said Ben Cowden that he and his brothers Mark and Les Cowden were on the trail of Hoozy Briggs, and they place him at the Johnson ranch at the time of the massacre. Since no one else has been placed there who has turned up minus one of his ears, this inquest must believe said Hoozy Briggs and partners unknown did commit the massacre.

"Therefore, since no testimony to the contrary is being offered or proved as to the cause of death of said Hoozy Briggs and said indigenous Yaqui by any member of this inquest, I, Judge Charles C. Dunn, do state that it is the judgment of this body that said Hoozy Briggs and said Yaqui did meet their deaths by mishap precipitated by a chance encounter with four indigenous Apaches and the condition of corpse number one does establish said Hoozy Briggs as a participant and perpetrator of the Johnson massacre.

"How's that?" Judge Dunn asked. "Does that cover it?"

Nobody said anything, but Frank Marshall shook his head.

"Captain Marshall? Do you have something to add?"

"I do," Marshall said.

"Speak, so Mr. Porter can write it down."

"I wish to cast a dissenting vote."

"Why is that?" asked Judge Dunn.

"Because everybody in the territory knew Ben Cowden was on Hoozy Briggs's trail to kill him. How can we believe his testimony that Apaches did it? No one else saw them do it. We only have the word of a man who admitted he was angry enough to kill Briggs."

"You're asking for evidence that Apaches killed Briggs and the Yaqui?"

"Yes, Judge."

"Hoozy Briggs was running like hell and did not let Ben Cowden get close enough to stick him with a lance. At the same time Briggs was killed, the Yaqui was killed by two different kinds of arrows. It's not reasonable to suspect that Ben Cowden would worry about his method of killing Hoozy Briggs. He was certain Briggs killed the Johnson family. He would have used his rifle and his pistol on him. I, as deputy coroner, am satisfied Ben Cowden certainly would never have taken the time to learn to shoot two different kinds of bows and arrows or the trouble to pack them and a lance all over the country in hopes of being given a chance to stick them in Hoozy Briggs."

Paula Mary was not sickened or shocked by the sight of the cadavers. She was greatly, enjoyably, fascinated, because she knew she was not the least bit like that clay on the floor of her papa's barn. She was glad that clay was the remains of somebody else and not Paula Mary Cowden, Esquire. Now she knew what "Esquire" meant. That had to mean all the way alive and proud of it. Now that she knew what "dead" meant, she'd enjoy being an "Esquire" the rest of her life.

CHAPTER 3

Paula Mary wanted Myrtle Farley's ring back, but did not know how to get it. She was not supposed to know it had been found.

A photographer had come to Mrs. Chance's school during the Fourth of July celebration in Harshaw and taken a group picture of the students. Myrtle had let Paula Mary wear her new ring for the picture. After the picture was taken, the ring would not come off her finger. Paula Mary caused a big scene in front of everybody before they got it off, and she was so relieved to be free of it, she lost track of it.

Guilo Soto, her classmate and friend who worked for A. B. as a stableboy, had been in charge of the basin of soapy water that was used to remove the ring. Paula Mary now believed the ring had been recovered from the soapy water by Guilo. The Yaqui and Che Che the Apache had been standing by the schoolyard watching all the goings on.

Later that day, Guilo was holding several hundred dollars in stakes for a horse race when he was stabbed to death and robbed. A few weeks later, Paula Mary saw Myrtle's ring hanging on a gold chain around the Yaqui's neck.

Now the ring had been recovered from the Yaqui's corpse, but Paula Mary couldn't ask to have it back until Ben let her know he had it. Paula Mary was glad the old Yaqui was dead. When he was alive, he had popped up and scared the peewadding out of her more than once.

She was one of the first out of bed the next morning. She

wandered toward the barn, talking to her secret friend. Since her little brother Freddie Lee had died a month or so ago, she had taken an imaginary friend. She was often alone, and since she was littler than anyone else in her family, she had decided to believe a little ghost her own size had come to walk with her and read her thoughts. She did not like to talk to him out loud because she was afraid someone would discover him, and she told him all her secrets.

She had only been making him up a few days and was still trying to picture his face. Sometimes he was a little taller than she and looked like Guilo Soto, her murdered friend. Sometimes he looked like her little brother Freddie Lee who had been dragged to death by a burro.

Her friend was about her own age, like a brother, but more like a sweetheart. You couldn't tell an ordinary friend absolutely everything, and you couldn't tell a little brother hardly anything for fear of blackmail, so her friend was more like a sweetheart who loved and trusted her, even when she was in trouble. She had been in so much trouble lately, she sometimes felt like the owls were roosting in her hair.

She heard the bellows on the forge and hurried to keep Bill Knox company. Paula Mary loved Big Bill so much, she banished her secret friend with no thought at all for his welfare.

Bill was a veteran of the Mexican War. He'd shod General Winfield Scott's horse. Mrs. Chance said General Scott was a great American hero. Bill Knox, the great hero's horseshoer, said he was a full-blown peacock.

Paula Mary slowed to a walk as she drew near the barn. Bill did not want anyone to make sudden appearances in places where horses were kept. A sudden appearance by a human could scare a horse over the top of somebody standing close to him.

She was glad she remembered that rule because Big Bill was underneath Star, Ben's big brown horse, shoeing him. Star was minding his manners and holding himself still as a boy in a barber's chair, but he could not resist rolling his eye at Paula Mary. Bill was working on a hind foot, so she made a wide circle around the horse to look at Bill's face. She would have to watch her tongue. He did not like people making useless sounds when he was shoeing a horse.

A slender curl of smoke rose from the hoof Bill held in his lap. He was pressing a hot shoe against the bearing surface of the hoof to find high spots. He lifted the shoe, examined the scorch on the hoof, and leveled a high spot with a rasp. He quickly applied the hot shoe again to satisfy himself it would fit snugly, then walked out from under the hoof and dipped the shoe in a tubful of water to cool it.

Paula Mary loved to watch Big Bill work with iron and horses. His neck was wider than his head. His head was covered with white curls. He worked in his undershirt, and his bare shoulders were thick and husky, and surrounded his neck so the lower half of his face seemed to rest on his chest. His skin was clear and rosy, and always shiny with sweat and smudged by the carbon of his forge. His eyes were wideset and the same smoky gray as white-hot steel.

Those gray-white eyes looked hard at everything first but always glanced off Paula Mary and her sisters. He seldom spoke when he was working. His voice was gruff and husky, and came from deep in the bellows of his great chest; with it, he could vibrate the barrel of a horse.

"Good morning, Big Bill." Paula Mary saw him turn his head to show he could not answer because his mouth was full of horseshoe nails.

"Hmmm!" he rumbled. He ran his hand over Star's hip and down the hind leg to the fetlock, picked up the foot, and walked under the leg so the hoof was upturned in his lap.

Paula Mary almost asked him how he was, but the query froze on her tongue. To expect an answer from a man with a mouthful of nails was silly. Questioning a man about his welfare when he was holding up a half-ton of horseflesh to drive a nail in a hoof was sillier.

Paula Mary believed she was good company for Bill because she stayed out of the way, appreciated the strength and artistry of his work, and held her tongue. He sometimes bragged to A. B. that she was one of the few people he knew who could keep quiet when he was shoeing. He kept people out of his way by ignoring their prattle. The only time he ever made conversation was when he was resting with his quart under his belt. He would not talk about his love for his work or his loyalty to A. B. Cowden, but he sometimes like to brag about the goodness of the Cowden women and often gave Paula Mary a lot more credit than she deserved.

In the summertime, Bill Knox started work at two in the morning. He stopped for an early breakfast in Viney's kitchen, but he did not pull up again until early afternoon.

The first thing he did when he left his forge was drink a half-quart of whiskey. When Paula Mary was home, it was her privilege to bring him his big lunch. After his lunch, he climbed into the hayloft and slept.

In the late afternoon and evening, he mended tack and harness, did fancy leatherwork, and made saddles while he sipped another half-quart. He ate his supper at five, then sat still and smoked his pipe. He was on his cot in the corner stall, asleep, a half hour after dark.

Now he stepped out from under Star. The horse's black hooves looked polished from Bill's handling. The buttons he'd made on the ends of the clinched nails were in straight, bright, uniform lines parallel to the shoes.

Paula Mary walked ahead to open the door as Bill led Star to a stall. He always stabled the horses inside the barn a few days when they returned from a journey. That way he could keep them from making hogs of themselves with their feed and water, and see to their grooming. He wanted to be sure they were sound before he turned them out to pasture.

Paula Mary noticed Ben's saddle was missing from its rack and asked Bill where he had gone.

"He rode out to meet Maudy." The hardness went out of Bill's eye. He loved Maudy Jane Pendleton, too. She was Paula Mary's best friend.

"Rode out to meet Maudy? He never did that before." Maudy was practically a Cowden, but why would Ben ride out to meet her?

Paula Mary heard the sound of a rig and horses and went outside. Maudy and Will Pendleton, her father, were coming down the road with Ben riding alongside. Paula Mary waved, and Will waved back, but Maudy did not. Was she mad, or what? If she didn't hurry and look up, Maudy would miss her chance to wave at her best friend.

Then Paula Mary saw the reason Maudy did not notice her. Maudy only had eyes for Ben, and that was all there was to it. Her cheeks were flushed, and her eyes were just ashining, and she was atalking to Ben, and Ben was just asmiiiling.

Will stopped the team in front of Paula Mary, and she took hold of the halters. Ben, riding Toots, got down and handed his reins to her. Before Paula Mary could even get a smile out of him, he took Maudy by the waist and lifted her out of the buggy. He just kept holding on to her and staring into her face.

"Well, I guess Paula Mary's just a hitching post around

here," she said, but nobody paid attention. She could see that the Cowden family was in for more earthquake and upheaval. The Cowdens had not been bothered with a love earthquake since the spark was struck between Eileen and Johnny Bonner. That had been a trial, with Johnny and Eileen holding on to each other and jumping into each other's eyes every time they got the chance. They were in better contact after they let go of each other than they were when they held on to each other.

Paula Mary helped Will unhitch his team. Ben and Maudy's affliction was embarrassing to watch. She pulled Ben's saddle off Toots, and it came down on top of her. She hoisted it to its place on the rack. Ben walked Maudy to the house without even looking back at his poor saddle horse or the little sister who did his unsaddling. Maudy Jane had never before neglected to wave at Paula Mary from the road, and Ben never went to the house without tending to his horse.

Horseshoes rang down the canyon, and Paula Mary's other two brothers, Les and Mark, rode into sight. They'd been at Temporal Canyon gathering cattle. She ran to meet them. She was sure these two would be glad to see her. They'd been baching in Apache land, trying to make biscuits on a smokeless fire and sleep with one eye open.

The family was all together for breakfast that morning for the first time in a long time. Viney, Eileen, Betty, and Maudy all ganged up in the kitchen to serve breakfast, and Paula Mary did not have to do a thing. She'd recently been in trouble about that but could not help being lazy. She knew she ought to offer to help, but then her mother and sisters would feel obligated to find something for her to do, and she'd only be in their way. She'd rather look at her brothers.

She listened a lot and didn't get to say much during the meal because she was the littlest person there. She knew the talk would come around to her sooner or later. It always did. Nobody was ever ignored at the Cowden table.

Finally, Will Pendleton, the Lord bless him for a saint, asked how she was doing in school. She had been hoping for a favorable time to tell her folks she'd been sent home by Mrs. Chance. Now was the time; her parents might not be hard on her in front of the Pendletons.

"Well, I didn't do too well in school yesterday," Paula Mary announced.

"What in the world happened, Paula Mary?" Will asked.

"I got sent home for laughing." The ice of December showed in A. B. Cowden's eyes. A cloud passed over her mother's brow. Oh-oh. The only one smiling and taking her misfortune with good humor was Les, and that was only because he did not give a darn about anything in the world.

"Oh, tell us about it, Paula Mary," Les said.

"Well, I was called up to recite 'The Arrow and the Song,' by Henry Wadsworth Longfellow, and the class got so still, a little mouse ran out and found my lunch scraps on the floor. He was so happy, he started cutting didoes around and around, and it tickled me, so I folded up laughing."

Everybody's face relaxed, and she knew she might survive. "I really was sorry, but I just couldn't help it. I couldn't stop. I felt awful when Mrs. Chance sent me home. Myrtle had to finish my recitation."

Her brother Ben was finally paying attention to her. Maybe now he would remember to give her the ring.

"When will you be seeing Myrtle again, Paula Mary?" Ben asked.

"At school Monday."

"I have something for her."

"I can give it to her, if you want me to."

Ben was teasing her but trying to give her the poker eye. Every single person in the family was a better poker player than he. Paula Mary could tell he was ready to fold. He knew how bad she wanted to take that ring back to Myrtle. She and Myrtle had fallen out for weeks after she lost the ring.

"I might go to town this afternoon and give it to her myself," said Ben.

"Well, I could do it for you," said Paula Mary. "That way, you wouldn't have to go out of your way to drop it off."

"You can't go to Harshaw today, Ben," said Maudy. "You have to see me off at the train."

"Where are you going, Maudy?" asked Paula Mary. "Back to Tombstone?"

"Maudy's going to visit her mother in Long Beach for a few weeks," Ben said.

"We're all going to Patagonia to see her off," said Viney. "We just decided to have a picnic down on Sonoita Creek and go to the street dance this evening."

"Can I invite Myrtle to go with us?" asked Paula Mary.

"She's probably coming to the dance with her folks," Ben said.

"Good. Then I can give her the surprise."

"Paula Mary, you just are not going to give up until I tell you what I've got for Myrtle, are you?"

"Well, if you don't want to come right out and tell me, I ought to be allowed to find out my own way."

Paula Mary acted perturbed and put on the Cowden frown. That made everybody laugh and took care of the trouble she was in for being sent home from school.

Ben reached into his shirtpocket and took out the heavy gold chain and ring. He took the ring off the chain and held it up. "Look what I found."

Paula Mary took it right out of his hand. "Why, that's Myrtle's ring. Where did you find it, Ben?" She was trying to act surprised and happy but was showing only old relief. The good poker players at the table must suspect she was guilty as hell of something.

"Honestly, Paula Mary. I didn't know you had any criminals for friends. Che Che the Apache gave me the ring and asked me if I would give it to you. How do you make friends like that? I'd hate to tell you how he got it."

"The last time I saw it, the Yaqui had it around his neck," Paula Mary said.

"Well, Che Che got it from the Yaqui. I'll swear, you sure have bloodthirsty friends doing you favors."

"Huh! They're no friends of mine," said Paula Mary. "That Che Che ought to know to stay away from me. The first time he fooled with me, Les put knots on his head, and the second time, I ran the Farleys' cart over his toe. I don't know why he'd call me his friend."

"He calls you the little wren in the tree."

"Why, he never saw me in my tree."

"Lady, cutthroats like Che Che see a lot you don't know about."

"Well, thank you for getting Myrtle's ring back. Can I be excused now?"

"You may start on the dishes now," said Viney.

Ben was watching the ring. Paula Mary had slipped it over the first joint of her middle finger and lost track of it. Being asked to do the dishes could make her mind go blank for a week.

"Take care of that ring now, little sister," Ben said. "Don't lose it again."

"Oh, I will," said Paula Mary. "If I don't lose it in the

dishwater. That's the way I lost it the first time, you know. Dishwater is bad for a body in all kinds of ways."

"Well, the sooner you get your hands in it, the sooner you'll become immune to it," said Viney. "I'll take care of the ring until you give it back to Myrtle."

Paula Mary relinquished the ring and dragged her feet around the table picking up dirty dishes. Viney put the ring back on the chain and laid it on the table.

"Oh, doing dishes is not that bad," Maudy said when she saw the look on Paula Mary's face. "I'll help you."

Gordo Soto spread the chain so the links lay flat against the tablecloth. The links were long, flat, and S-shaped.

"I know this chain," Gordo said. "See the mark of the Holy Cross on the links?" He pointed to the tiny cross engraved on each link. "The goldsmith who made this is a man named Cayetano Santa Cruz from the pueblo of Santa Cruz, in Sonora."

"I never noticed the trademark before," Ben said.

"He hasn't made many of these chains. They're hard to make, but I have one." Gordo showed he was wearing an identical chain around his neck. "Our godfather gave one to me and one to my brother Guilo."

"I have no doubt it's Guilo's chain," Ben said. "It was part of the Yaqui's share of the loot when he and Hoozy robbed and killed Guilo."

"What will you do with it?"

"Nothing," said Ben. "You keep it, or give it to your family."

Gordo opened his shirt and showed he was already wearing three chains bedecked with holy medals. He put the chain and ring around Paula Mary's neck.

"Ugh, Gordo!" said Paula Mary. "That was on the Yaqui when his flesh started rotting. Ugh!" She realized she had given herself away. Her mother and father would now find out she and Betty had watched the inquest from the loft. She glanced guiltily at Betty, implicating her.

"Paula Mary, how did you know that?" Viney asked.

The Cowdens and Pendletons pulled out for Patagonia at midmorning. Ben kept his horse by Maudy. He was proud of her. She wore a tiny flat straw hat decorated with posies that fit way up on top of the thick crown of her hair. He could not tell how she kept it on. She and her father had traveled over thirty miles from La Noria since yesterday morning, and Ben could not see a speck of dust or a sign of fatigue on her. She was pretty, and her touch was like the kiss of a butterfly, even in the dust of the drouth.

Ben knew that touch and appreciated it better than anybody. Maudy Jane had just nursed him through a month of blood poisoning and delirium.

The Cowden party went out to a big stand of cottonwoods on Sonoita Creek outside Patagonia and spread their picnic in the shade. Les and Mark gathered mesquite wood and built a fire. Ben hobbled the horses and turned them loose on the creek. A tiny stream of water was still running in the creek, even in the drouth.

When the firewood had burned down to thick coals, Les and Mark laid grills over them and put strips of sirloin on to broil. Eileen braised green chiles until the skins turned white and popped open. She peeled off the skins and ground the chiles, seeds and all, with a pod of garlic in a stone bowl called a *molcajete*. She mixed that with diced onion, tomato, salt, and black pepper for a *salza*, a green chile sauce.

The Cowdens and Pendletons swabbed the sirloin strips with salza, wrapped them in hot flour tortillas, and ate them with bowls of *frijoles charros*, whole pinto beans in thick soup.

After the feast, Ben and Maudy walked downstream to find a place to wade. Ben sat on the bank and watched her play in a pool with a school of minnows, like a child. She was only sixteen. He did not want her to go to Long Beach, California.

"Maudy, you better come on. The train is due," Will Pendleton called.

Maudy waded out of the creek, and Ben gave her his handkerchief to dry her feet. She looked for a place by him, sat down, and brushed his leg with hers. She leaned against him, hugged his neck, and gave him the deepest kiss he had ever known.

"How's that?" she said. She laughed at the shocked look on his face. "Okay, how's this?" She shook his hand two big pumps, like a man.

Ben walked Maudy back. She hugged all the Cowden women, kissed all the men, and climbed up beside her father in the buggy. The Cowdens would stay under the cottonwoods until the dance started. The train came huffing and chugging from Nogales, and Will's horses acted as though it was blowing fire in their flanks. They rolled their eyes and pranced all the way to town.

The station platform was crowded, and the train was full of Mexican families and businessmen on their way to Tucson. Will handed his lines to Maudy and went in the station to pay for her ticket. Ben sat his horse in front of the team to keep it quiet.

Ben and Maudy ordinarily would have been watching all the people go by, but they were both already too lonesome for each other to care about looking at anyone else. The conductor called, "All aboard," Will came back for Maudy and her suitcase, and there was nothing else for her to do but get on the train.

She looked back once, but adventure compelled her to hurry away and board the train. Ben tied the team and rode his horse around the platform until he could see Maudy in her seat. He sat his horse and smiled at her from time to time until the engineer blasted the whistle and moved the train.

He rode alongside at a walk, then a trot, and then a lope. Maudy opened her window, stuck her head out, and shouted, "Don't be crazy. Pull up. You can't keep up all the way to the ocean."

Ben reined in close to the car and kept Toots neck-and-neck with Maudy's window. Old Toots had as much steam as the locomotive, at least for another quarter mile. Then Maudy's hat blew off.

Ben saw the look of consternation and loss that crossed her face as she snatched for it. She grabbed after it so recklessly, she almost fell out the window.

"Oh, darn!" she shouted, but she recovered and smiled at Ben to show it was all right.

Ben did not want her to ride all the way to the ocean without her hat. He slid Toots to a stop, rolled him back on his heels, and ran to get it. It landed on the cinder track by the rails as he reached it. He ran on past the hat, turned, and spurred Toots after the train at a dead run, leaned down over his stirrup, scooped up the hat, and let Toots out in the race of his life.

The train was gathering momentum, and Maudy was so far away Ben could see only her arm waving, but he started gaining, and then Toots hit a stretch of smooth ground. He had to catch the train before it reached the Sonoita Creek trestle.

The creek would stop him, and the train would reach top speed beyond the trestle. He had a quarter of a mile.

Toots bore down and passed the observation and smoking car. People in the train were cheering. He passed the car behind Maudy, and the creek loomed only five strides ahead. He leaned over and screamed in Toots's ears. Toots coasted up beside Maudy, and Ben handed her the hat, patted the back of her hand, then rode for his life as the bottom fell out from under Toots and they flew down the steep bank and splashed in the creek.

They were a moment regaining their breath, but Ben lunged Toots over the bank and waved good-bye to Maudy so she could see he was all right. Then the train carried her out of sight.

The crowd at the station had watched his race with the train. Everybody but three men in the audience looked friendly. Frank Marshall, Dick Martin, and another big deputy were sitting their horses by the station, watching him. The big deputy started his horse toward Ben. Marshall seemed about to do the same, but he saw Les and Mark riding to meet Ben and called the big man back. Then Will Pendleton came wheeling around a corner in his buggy to join Ben.

Ben tipped his hat to Marshall as he joined his brothers.

CHAPTER 4

The Cowden brothers rode down the street in Patagonia. Ben knew he was expected to spend the rest of the afternoon with his family on the creek. Friends and relatives would be gathering there when they heard the family was in town.

Ben saw his cousins the Farley twins sitting in the shade in front of a beer garden called Los Parados and wanted to stop. Ben's brothers were reluctant to throw in with the twins. Danny and Donny Farley drank until drunk every single day they could find enough to drink.

"Maybe we ought to skip it this time," Mark said.

"Oh, come on," Ben said. "I haven't seen the twins since we ran old Yawner at Los Metates. Our troubles are over. Let's have some beer."

Mark stopped. "Mama, Papa, and the girls are waiting for us. They told us to keep you out of trouble. Papa saw Frank Marshall in town, and he doesn't want you roaming around until the warrant for your arrest is cleared up."

Les did not care a damn about warrants or anything else if he could have a drink of beer. He shrugged. "I'm with you, Mark, of course. We'll be safe if we go back to Mama and Papa, but we won't get anything but creek-water coffee down there."

"We don't need any beer," Mark said. "We can have a few drinks outside the dance this evening. Papa wants us to stay close to the family."

"Let's just have one beer and say hello to the Farleys," Ben said. "We can drink it without even getting off our horses. We haven't had a beer in so long, we're pitiful."

Mark did not argue with that. They had been riding hard and sleeping in the rocks for weeks and they needed to stop and rest at a spring. They rode under some shade trees, and Ben signaled for two pitchers of beer and three glasses.

Ben liked to sit in the shade and fill up on beer now and then, but he drank hard spirits only for medicinal purposes. He always carried an *amphorita*, a slim half-pint bottle of good mescal in his morral, his horse's feedbag, but only for revival, recovery, and medicine.

Sometimes, when he covered more than forty miles horseback in one day and knew he still must go another league, he took a swallow "to rest his horse" and himself. A swallow or two took away the weariness and dread when he was faced with traveling another four miles at the end of a forty-mile journey. A swallow or two of strong spirit helped him push on until he and his horse reached a place where they could find a drink of water, a plate of beans, and a feed of corn. He never drank strong spirits because they gave him contentment. He drank beer in the shade with his friends for contentment.

He drank most of the first pitcher quickly and greedily. Times were lean. He and his brothers had been busy keeping their cattle alive in a drouth and thinning out their enemies in a range war.

The beer found little room to do its stuff in Ben's stomach, so it escaped with glee to his head. After two glasses, he was feeling too good to leave Los Parados. The beer then made room for itself and found new hollow places Ben did not know about. Les and Mark began to marvel at the volume of beer he put away. They had seen him do legendary things horseback. Now, he sat on Toots and made two pitchers of beer disappear like a drop of sweat in hell.

He ordered two pitchers for the third time.

"You'll have to drink my part of it. I'm full," Mark said.

"Me too. I'm getting sleepy," Les said.

Ben spoke to his younger brothers with great and sincere concern. "Lie down under a tree and take a little nap, why don't you? You rode all the way from Temporal this morning. When you wake up, I'll ride back to the creek with you and take my nap. We have to be fresh for the dance tonight."

"No, brother, I like a certain cottonwood down on the creek better. It has its own little breeze," Les said.

The Farley twins were sitting under a tree in front of the Cowden's horses. Mark drained his glass and handed it down to Donny Farley.

"Ready for some more, Marky?" Donny asked.

"No more." Mark backed his horse out of the shade and rode away without another word or even a friendly look. Les grinned at Ben, shook his head, and followed Mark.

Ben did not lack for beer. Some of his friends found him there, friends who did not worry about lack of range for their stock or warrants for their arrest; friends who stayed home and tended to business and could repair to Los Parados for beer whenever they wanted to without fear of controversy.

The people in that country admired Ben Cowden because he and his family did a share of Indian fighting and actively opposed Duncan Vincent and the Pima County Livestock Association, an arm of the eastern syndicates who were trying to take over the public land.

Vincent represented a New York syndicate of railroad, oil, and packinghouses trying to control the open range and exclude the small ranchers. His syndicate owned the VO ranch that neighbored the Cowdens, Pendletons, Farleys, and Porters.

Hoozy Briggs had been Vincent's *pistolero*, a hired assassin, who had eliminated the Johnsons, another family of Vincent's neighbors. Vincent's thugs were not as effective as his political influence. One of Vincent's brothers was a U.S. senator. Another was president of the Pima County Livestock Association. None of Vincent's neighbors were ever invited to join that association.

These were the reasons Ben's brothers did not want him to sit in a public place and get dizzy on beer. They only left him because they thought he was safe among friends.

The Farley boys fell asleep back-to-back with their legs drawn up and their reins in their hands. The twins' horses were used to waiting for them while they got drunk and slept it off. They knew the only thing they had to do for the rest of the day was stand by the twins. After a while, the twins would wake up and be sober enough to feed and water them, and put them away.

Alfredo Heredia's team pulled up beside Ben. Alfredo ordered a pitcher of beer and glasses for his wife and children. Ben liked to see decent ladies like Yvonne Heredia enjoy beer with their husbands and children. The Heredias were the kind of people Ben liked most. He loved Maudy with all his heart, but nobody in her family had ever taken a sip of beer, and she would probably never use beer or tobacco as long as she lived. She did not mind if Ben drank beer. Even though her parents and brothers loathed liquor and tobacco, and thought anyone who used them was an absolute fool, Maudy seemed to like Ben's small vices.

Alfredo Heredia lived southeast of Patagonia, on the Mexican border between La Noria and the Buena Vista range. Ben asked him how the Buena Vista was weathering the drouth. Ben and his brothers had just turned out three hundred steers with their other cattle on the Buena Vista.

"Ah, Ben, you better come and look as soon as you can," Alfredo said in Spanish. "The country is so wasted it may never revive. *Es la sequedad. La requetesequedad.* The drying. The double redrying. It may be the ruination of the country. If another week passes without rain, nothing will survive."

"*Es otra plaga más, Alfredo,*" said Ben. The drouth was only one of four plagues the people of the Enchanted Land lived with that year. They also suffered from the Yawner, Duncan Vincent, and crooked politicians.

"*Y ahora hay otra.* And now we have another," Alfredo said. "We have tick fever on the Buena Vista. Some of those nice big steers you brought down from Temporal are dead, Ben. I can't explain their dying any other way. They were stronger than the other cattle, but now they're turning pale, reeling, stumbling, and dying. You better move them."

"How could we have tick fever? Did anyone bring in Texas cattle?"

"The VO turned out a trainload of steers at Calabasas. None of them looked sick, but about a week later, your cattle, Romero's, and Salazar's started dying."

"*Ay, que la*"—Ben started to say a dirty word, but looked at Yvonne and swallowed it. The lady laughed softly.

Everybody in the country, men and women alike, used the word when they felt plagued, but Ben was embarrassed. He'd better cut off the beer if he was getting so loose-tongued he would consider using an obscenity in front of a mother and her children. He looked away and swallowed again. The Heredias were not scandalized, but he thought about going back to his family in the cottonwoods.

Lorrie Briggs was coming toward Los Parados in a buggy with her father and mother. She waved to Ben and made him sit up straight on his horse. He wanted to be friends with her again, so he waved back.

Her father stopped his rig in line with other customers. Lorrie spoke to her parents and climbed down from the buggy. She beckoned to Ben and walked away through the trees.

Ben excused himself and rode slowly after Lorrie. She waited for him in a parklike stand of mesquite trees. The lower branches had been trimmed away so people could walk through the thicket without stooping. The canopy of the upper branches provided solid shade.

Ben dismounted and took off his hat for the girl when he saw her cheeks were covered with tears.

Then she laughed at Ben. "You dumb sonofabitch, you don't even know when you're hated, do you? Haven't I made it clear I hate your guts?"

Toots had a bad habit of standing too close to Ben. His warm breath was on Ben's back. In another second, he would start nibbling, and Ben would have to move him away. Ben's head was not clear, his reflexes slow, and he did not make the horse stand back.

He realized Lorrie had lured him into the thicket to make fun of him. Full of beer as he was, he should get back on his horse and leave. Then Toots spooked at something behind him and knocked Ben down. He looked up at the horse and caught a number-twelve miner's hobnailed boot flush on his jaw. The kick lifted him off the ground, and the boots started walking on him as he tried to crawl away.

Ben's ears were roaring, but he did not feel pain. His arms and legs were not serving him well.

Lorrie laughed and cheered his tormentor, yelling, "Stomp him, Bib, stomp him."

Someone else began batting his head from side to side with a logging chain. He tried to ward off the blows with his arms so he could get up, but the chain kept smashing him against the ground.

"Give it to him, Teddy," Lorrie shouted.

Ben's eyes were full of blood, and he could not see. He raised his arms again and caught the chain. He wrapped it in his arms and pulled down with all his weight. The chain was looped on the attacker's wrist, and he was not as strong as Ben. Ben wrapped the chain around his head and began to squeeze.

Lorrie clawed and pummeled at him, and screamed in his ear to make him turn loose of the chain. Ben was holding it in both hands and bearing down on the man's face. He humped up against Lorrie's little blows and squeezed harder. He thought he might strangle the man or crush his head or break his neck. The man began thrashing convulsively beneath him, and Ben knew he was almost finished. Lorrie was pulled off him and the hobnails methodically kicked him in the ribs, back, and stomach, but Ben would not stop his pressure on the chain.

Lorrie sobbed and screamed, "He's killing my little brother. Stop him! Please, please, stop him!"

Another man moved the man with the hobnails aside and said, "That's not getting it. Let me show you how to do that."

Ben's body fell away from his grip on the chain. The fight left him, and he went away into a void. He waited there a moment for his heart to stop beating so he could go on and leave the earth for good.

He was in the nothingness only a moment, then began fighting for consciousness so desperately that he moaned with the effort. The helplessness he felt when he began to regain consciousness was so hard for him to bear, he wept.

"Listen to him, the big bawlbaby," a woman said.

Ben wanted his mother. He needed a friend. Then he heard the pitiful sounds he was making and took hold of himself. He was still scared though. He had never known a beating. No horse or bull had ever wallowed him or hurt him like that. Only a lightning strike could have leveled him so completely.

"You sonofabitch, Marshall, you let the bastard kill my little brother," Lorrie sobbed. "What am I going to tell my mother and father?"

"It's regrettable," said Marshall.

"*Regrettable?*" All my *brothers* are gone."

Ben was conscious, and Lorrie saw his eyes were open.

"Stomp his eyes out, Bib. Stomp his teeth out."

Bib did not move fast enough to suit her, so she rushed at Ben and kicked him in the nose. The little foot glanced away without damaging him. Ben realized he was in irons. Shackles hobbled his feet, and manacles held his hands at the waist.

Lorrie began to wail. "Do *something* more to the sonofa-bitch. Mark him up some more. Hurt him."

"Don't worry, he'll suffer plenty," Marshall said. "He'll hang for killing Ted."

Ben thought, My God, am I a murderer now? Did I kill Lorrie's little brother?

"Get up, Cowden," Marshall said.

Ben groped ahead to find his bearings. Lorrie rushed on him with a rock and brought it down on the small of his back with both hands. The pain pierced his groin, his legs, his stomach. He retched, and all the beer came up.

"You want him hurt, little lady?" Bib said. "You think we're not hurting him? Watch carefully." He stomped Ben's fingers into the ground, and Ben hugged his hands and rolled on his stomach to protect them. Bib stomped his hamstrings, the backs of his knees, his tailbone, and the small of his back. Ben was sure his neck and head were next, but Dick Martin pushed Bib off-track.

"Damn, Bib, what do you want to do, stomp him to death so the whole town can see it?" Martin scolded. "I have to live here. Take him somewhere else to kill him."

Someone yelled, "Fight! Fight! There's a fight in the *mezquital*."

"Get him on his feet," Marshall ordered. "You'll have a crowd here in a minute. Take him to the wagon and head for Tucson. If old man Cowden tries to stop you, show him the warrant. If that doesn't keep him away, threaten to shoot the prisoner. I'll take Lorrie home and catch up with you on the other side of town. I don't want to be seen here with the prisoner."

Martin and Bib pulled Ben to his feet.

Lorrie stepped up so close to Ben that her breath was on his face. She smelled as wild as a javelina. "Hurt, Ben?" she said. "It's going to be worse, you goddam murderer. Before they're through, you'll beg for the hangman. You'll beg me and my father and mother for forgiveness, and your own father and mother won't even claim you. I'm almost happy now. I heard you moan like a woman, and I know you're afraid to die."

Lorrie went away with Marshall. Martin helped Ben walk.

"I can't see," Ben said. "Wipe my eyes, Dick."

Martin took Ben's handkerchief out of his pocket and wiped his eyes, then dabbed the cuts on his brows. Ben sighed, relieved he was on his feet and able to see.

Five men were taking part in his torment. He looked carefully into each face. Ben and Dick Martin had grown up in Harshaw together. Ben had paid him while he tried to teach him to cowboy. Bib Taylor was a miner from Harshaw, a supporter of Lew Porter, Ben's chief opponent in horse racing. The miners always bet on Lew's horses against Ben and the cattle crowd.

Two railroad section workers were also standing by, tough Irishmen. Ben did not think they had taken part in the beating. Bib, Marshall, and Ted Briggs had done the job.

The last of his tormentors was a VO hand named Campana. Ben had left him for dead after the latest battle between the Cowdens and the VO. Campana kept rattling and pulling on Ben's chains to make sure they were tight and strong enough to hold him.

A crowd of townsmen gathered around him. Most of them were young boys. He knew them, but they did not know him right away because of the blood on his face. He could barely move his feet in the chains. One of the Irishmen picked up Ted Briggs's feet, the other his arms, and they carried him away. Bib pressed a double-barreled shotgun against Ben's back.

Dick Martin held him up by one arm as they walked through the crowd. By the time he shuffled out of the thicket at Los Parados, every idle man and boy in Patagonia was there to watch the constables parade him down the street. The Farley twins were still asleep under the tree, holding their horses.

Somebody yelled, "It's Ben Cowden. Ben Cowden's killed Teddy Briggs, and they're taking him to jail."

Nobody offered to help him. Alfredo Heredia hurried his rig across Ben's front and did not even look at him.

Ben shouted, "Alfredo, bring my brothers." Wayne pushed him ahead with the barrel of the shotgun.

Ben saw his cousin Lew Porter standing on the boardwalk in front of the bank and looked him straight in the eye. Lew gave no sign he knew Ben. Lew's wife, Betsy, said, "Look, it's Ben, Lew." Lew watched the Irishmen carry Ted Brigg's body into the constable's office. He herded his wife and some other female cousins of Ben's down the walk.

"Ben, are you really a cow thief?" shouted a boy in the crowd who had always been Ben's friend. "Are you going to be a jailbird?" He limped in a half-circle in front of Ben, imitating the leg-iron shuffle.

Dick Martin was helping Ben climb into a buckboard when A. B., Viney, and the girls drove up. The Cowdens showed no expression at all when the crowd turned to look at them.

Dick Martin sat Ben down on the high seat of the

buckboard and picked up the lines. Campana untied the team and led it away from the hitch rail. Bib climbed up into the back of the buckboard and pointed the shotgun at the back of Ben's neck.

"Are you all right, son?" A. B. asked.

"Papa, I killed the boy to stop him hitting me with a log chain. I did it in self-defense."

"Mr. Cowden, Teddy Briggs was a deputy of this county," Dick Martin said. "Your son was resisting arrest when he killed him."

"Why were you arresting my son in the first place, Martin? What were the charges, and where is your warrant?"

"The main charges are murder and cattle stealing." Martin handed A. B. the warrant.

A. B. applied his spectacles and examined the document. "Who issued this? Ah, federal Judge Black. That scoundrel. Where's the federal officer in charge here? You're only a constable, under my jurisdiction."

"Bib Taylor, the man holding the shotgun, works for Judge Black," Martin said.

"Why has my son been beaten?"

"He resisted arrest."

"Did you show him your warrant? Did he know you had the authority to arrest him?"

"The constable has answered enough of your questions, old man," Bib said. "Hand us our warrant and stand back so we can be on our way."

"I'm sending two deputies after you, to be sure this prisoner doesn't try to escape," A. B. said. "Martin, I'm charging you with his safety until my deputies catch up. If anything happens to him, I'll see to it both barrels of my shotgun explode up your ass."

Dick Martin set his jaw, wheeled the team into the street, and headed out of town. Campana mounted his horse and followed. Ben took a last look at his mother and sisters. These men would have to kill him now. Nothing else would stop him from getting even. They had ruined him in front of his family.

The Farley twins appeared, and A. B. made them stand by. He wheeled his blacks and drove away with Ben's mother and sisters.

A. B. was angry at Les and Mark for not staying with Ben. He drove by Los Parados looking for them, and Frank

Marshall came out of the mesquite grove, riding Toots and showing off a handsome smile.

"Ah, you've caught me trying to steal one of your very fine animals," said he. "I caught him back in those trees. I understand Ben had some trouble. He was drunk, wasn't he?"

"Where have you been, Captain Marshall?" A. B. was not fooled by the man.

"Visiting some friends. I believe you're acquainted with them. The Briggses? They're the parents of the boy for whom we held the inquest. I was walking back from their house when this horse tried to run by me. I saw Ben chase the train out of town on him a while ago. I wasn't surprised he lost his horse. He was drunk, you know."

"Get off the horse," A. B. said.

"No, I'll leave him in the constable's pound. I don't know how long he was loose. He might have damaged property. You can claim him after the constable determines he didn't tromp somebody's cornfield or vegetable patch. You wouldn't want to go contrary to the law, would you, Undersheriff Cowden?"

Marshall winked at Betty. "Is there anything else I can do for you? Anything at all? After all, I'm a public servant."

"I know who you serve, Captain Marshall," said A. B. "I know what you've done to my son."

"I'm sure I don't know what you're talking about, venerable sir," Marshall said.

A. B. started his team. "Do as you please with the horse, but sooner or later you will have to settle with me."

The Cowden family drove away, thinking about the blood on Ben's face. Viney began to weep silently, then the girls started in. A. B. found Les and Mark back at the picnic fire drinking coffee with their uncle Billy Porter.

CHAPTER 5

"That's enough! He's had enough!" Dick Martin said.

"The *hell* he has! I have orders to break every bone in his body."

Bib Taylor had jerked Ben backward into the bed of the buckboard to stomp him some more. He looked down the road to see if Marshall was coming, and Martin picked up the shotgun.

"Taylor, I won't let you kill him," Martin said.

"What're you going to do, shoot me?" Bib said. "There comes Marshall. Give me back my gun."

Campana looked down the road at the approaching riders and shook his head. He was sitting his horse in front of the team to keep it from bolting. As a VO hand and a constable, he had to be there, but he was not taking part in the mistreatment of Ben Cowden. He had never seen a Cowden lose a fight. They did not know how to be beaten. He did not think it could be done.

Campana figured two things could happen now. Bib would kick Ben Cowden too hard and kill him, and the Cowden clan would wipe out everybody who had anything to do with it; or Ben would survive and come after them, one at a time.

The way Campana saw it, Marshall and Duncan Vincent were not winning anything by beating up Ben Cowden. This would only make the Cowdens and Porters mad. Campana would have shot him as a deer hunter shoots a buck, and nobody would have known who did it.

The last time anybody angered the Cowdens, Campana had barely survived with a lump on his head and a long sleep. His two comrades had been shot dead. Campana figured he was spared because the shooting was done in front of his sisters in the patio of their home. Campana came away from that fight thinking he'd better quit Duncan Vincent and the VO, but he stayed. What could he do? He was wanted in Mexico by the *rurales*, mounted police, and nobody else in Arizona Territory would give him a job.

"That's not Marshall," Campana said quietly. "You think that's Marshall coming?"

"Who is it, then?" Bib asked.

Exasperated, Dick Martin said, "Who the hell you think it is? Who would it be? It's Les and Mark Cowden."

"Well, so what? I've got their big brother by the throat. What can they do to me?"

"The sonsabitches'll eat us if they catch you stomping their brother, so stand away from him. Get away, or dammit to hell, I'll use this shotgun against you and join them."

"All right, I guess I can work on him later, but give me back my gun."

"All right. Do as I tell you. Hold the gun on Ben—I mean in his ear, or those two sonsabitches are going to kill us."

"Let's go then, dammit." Bib took the shotgun.

"No, we'll talk to them. I don't want to hit a bump with this buckboard and have that shotgun go off accidentally. We'll have about one minute to live if that happens."

"Shit! They can't be so tough."

Martin looked at Campana. Campana knew the Cowdens so well, he might be thinking of joining them too. Martin already felt he was a fool for taking the constable's job in Patagonia. Duncan Vincent was giving him double the constable's salary to take his side in everything, but he admired and respected the Cowdens. This beating had put him on the wrong side of them forever.

Now Les and Mark were coming, and their brother looked half dead in his custody. "Put the muzzle of that shotgun right close to the man's head and hold it steady if you want to live," he told Bib under his breath.

Les and Mark stopped their horses behind the buckboard.

"Don't come too close. This gun might go off," Bib said. One of his big feet was planted on Ben's back.

"Let him up," Les said.

"I'll let him up when you Cowdens clear out of here."

"Step away from my brother, or I'll kill you." Les drew his pistol.

"Go ahead and shoot," Bib said. "If I move my finger on these triggers, your brother's dead."

Martin saw a wild look pass over Les Cowden's face, as though he would even sacrifice his brother to kill Bib Taylor. Martin felt very sorry for himself. He could not take up with the Cowdens now unless he wanted to see Ben killed. If Ben was killed, he was on the wrong side, whether he wanted to be or not.

"No, Les," Martin said. "Be careful what you do. We have our job to do, and you have to stay out of it."

Mark rode up beside Les. "We have a right to be here and have a say in the way our brother is treated," he said. "We've been deputized for his transfer to Tucson, and we're riding with you."

"Suit yourselves," Bib said. "But if you ride with us, I'll have to hold this shotgun in his ear all the way to Tucson. It could go off accidentally."

"That accident will cause your death," Les said.

"Marshall." Campana pointed down the road with his chin. Frank Marshall was coming at a lope with two more horsemen.

"What's going on here?" He stopped Toots beside the buckboard. The two Irishmen with him were not horsemen. Their horses stopped on their front feet and humped on by the buckboard.

"Why is this prisoner covered with blood?" Marshall asked. "Who's been beating him?"

"No one, sir," Bib said. "He's been bleeding since we had to subdue him when we arrested him."

"I will not stand for abuse of a prisoner. Get your damned foot off him. Back away and let him up."

Marshall turned to Les and Mark. "And you two—who might you be?"

"We're Ben Cowden's brothers," Les said. "We've been deputized to see he gets to Tucson alive and we'll kill any man who harms him."

"Well, it looks like you arrived in time. Another mile with this miner walking on him would have been his last mile."

Martin helped Ben into the seat beside him and started the team again. Ben could think of no way to escape.

"I want to give you Cowdens some friendly advice,"

Marshall told Les and Mark when they were under way. "Even though I sympathize with Ben, I'm a lawman doing my duty. Don't try to help your brother escape. I'll fight to the death for your brother's right to a fair trial. Besides that, if you do manage to take him away from us, you'll be fugitives forever and probably never see your family again.

"Let's see if we can make it to Tucson without incident. If you cooperate, maybe Judge Black will be lenient."

"What are you doing on my brother's horse?" asked Les.

"I'm only bringing him along for Ben. He'll be impounded in Tucson until after Ben's hearing."

"That doesn't give you the right to ride the horse. In this country, nobody rides another man's horse without his permission."

"Whoa, I'm sorry!" Marshall stopped Toots in the middle of the road. "Constable Martin, stop the buckboard."

Puzzled, Dick Martin stopped the team.

"You, Mexican, stand your horse in front of the team so it won't run away while we make a switch here. You, Deputy Taylor, help the prisoner to the ground behind the buckboard."

Taylor grinned and jerked Ben over the back of the seat and into the bed of the buckboard, then over the tailgate into the road. Ben sprawled on his face, too weak to get up. Taylor snapped an iron collar around his neck. The collar was fastened to a long chain moored in the center of the wagon bed.

Les noticed how big and active Marshall was when he stepped to the ground off the horse. The man was grinning good-naturedly when he handed Toots's reins to Mark. "I was only riding the horse because your brother was in my seat on the buckboard." He climbed into the seat with Martin. "Drive on, Constable."

Dick Taylor started the team. Ben tried to get up, and the wagon jerked him down. The iron collar was loose on his neck and it jammed under his jaws as the team dragged him.

Les spurred his horse to the head of the team to stop it. The team sidled away from him and lunged. Campana rode in quickly and held the off horse by the checkrein. Martin hauled back on the lines. Mark jumped off his horse, lifted Ben by the shoulders, and dragged him toward the buckboard for slack, then helped him to his feet.

"Oh, did we start up too fast?" Marshall said. "I'm sorry. Are you ready now? All right. Drive on, Constable."

Campana was looking way off toward Mexico, and Les was standing his big horse on the team's toes. Martin was in no hurry to start the team.

"What's the matter?" Marshall said. "We ought to get moving. It's a long way to the Andrade ranch."

"My brother can't walk all that way in irons," Les said.

"Listen, I'm sorry. I don't like transporting him this way. I gave him my seat in the buckboard, but if I can't ride his horse, I'm taking my seat back. I'm not fool enough to put him on his horse. I've been warned that no chains in the world will hold him if he gets on a horse."

"Well, he can ride in the bed with the deputy, can't he?"

"I'm sorry, I don't allow my prisoners to ride behind me."

"Well, for God's sake, Taylor'll have his eye on him, and your other two deputies will be riding behind him."

"Yes, but you see, I'm the one responsible for his safety, and he'll be safer walking. That's my regulation."

"Well, I guess I don't mind if you ride his horse then," Les said. "Come on and get on him."

"No, you were right. Who am I to violate a man's rights and the code of the West in regards to his horse? It's best we abide by all regulations and customs here. The prisoner can walk. If he becomes tired, we'll apply a new regulation. He can't be tired yet. He hasn't taken one step. Drive on, Constable."

"This is goddam cruelty," shouted Les. "I won't stand for it. My brother can't keep up with a team of horses."

"Why should your brother be treated differently than any other prisoner who's been transported on this road?" Marshall said. "Your own father makes his prisoners walk. What does he call it, the shuffle? He's famous for keeping his prisoners on their good behavior by leading them along behind his buggy in their chains until they fall from exhaustion. I'm told he was the one who made the discovery it was good for men's souls to do the shuffle."

"My papa transports criminals and murderers. Ben's innocent."

"Ah, that's what they all say, yet Undersheriff Cowden makes his prisoners do the shuffle before they're even tried for their crimes."

"Come on, Marshall, let him ride."

"He can walk and do the shuffle now, Cowden. He can thank you and the code of the West for that."

"Listen, I'll give you the horse. Come and get on him. His name is Toots. I'll give you a bill of sale right now."

Marshall picked up a long supple coachwhip. "We'll see. Now, drive on, Constable. And you, Cowden, get away from the team, or I'll whip them right over the top of you. Then we'll see how well your goddam brother keeps up."

Les backed away reluctantly. Campana moved out of the way, and Martin started the team. Ben started shuffling. He and his brothers had always laughed at A. B.'s practice of disciplining his prisoners with the shuffle. Everybody figured it was only a harmless method of chastising smart alecks.

Now the shuffle was not so funny. Ben was finished after a hundred yards. He was so sore and stiff from the beating, his motors were slow starting. He resolved not to complain. He believed the only way he could help himself was by keeping quiet. Marshall's mind was made up to torture him and tantalize his brothers. The shuffle was only the start of it.

Being chained and helpless made Ben realize that his only defense would be keeping his head and being quiet and patient. His brothers were sure not helping him. Marshall could have him whipped or make him walk or drag him without raising his voice or turning his head. He was as detached about his business of torture and abuse as Dick Martin was about the lines and harness he used to drive the team.

Bib Taylor had probably lost so much money betting against Ben's horses that he would be happy if Ben left every inch of his hide on the road to Tucson. Miners knew where to stomp those hobnails when they were moving hard rock, and Bib thought he knew how to reach the bottom of a man with them. Ben did not think he was permanently injured, but Bib wasn't tired of stomping him yet.

Campana was a coyote, and if he served anybody in the world, it was Duncan Vincent. Vincent had caused a bill to be passed that gave the Pima County Livestock Association power to appoint rangers to fight cattle stealing. They carried the rank of county constable. Giving Campana a badge was like giving a crazy man a sharp new ax.

Ben tried to keep his mind off the pain of the shuffle by sizing up his enemies. He knew the only reason his father ever made a prisoner do the shuffle was to shut him up so they could both have some peace and quiet on the road. As soon as a man shut up, A. B. let him ride. He could not stand to see a man suffer when he was trying to be quiet about it.

Of course, keeping his mouth shut would not help Ben if Les persisted in mouthing off.

After the first five minutes of the shuffle, Ben's joints warmed and loosened and gave him some relief from the pain of the beating. After ten minutes, he was going on nothing but heart.

He could only go so long taking foot-long steps with a team of horses leading him by the neck. He could not keep up and he knew he could not survive the alternative. If he lost his feet, all his hide would come off on the road.

Ben applied horseman's rules to the ordeal. He would never bale off a bucking horse to save himself from pain, and he vowed to keep shuffling until his heart, lungs, and brain burst or his legs broke. He would not go to his knees voluntarily.

Then, he stumbled over a rut, and the wagon jerked him down. He could not raise his hands to break his fall, and he landed on his face. The team dragged him on his face, and the iron collar choked him and made him so desperate, he regained his feet. Dick Martin never looked back or slackened the pace.

He learned he could ignore the pain for whole minutes by looking at the mountains. They were more beautiful than ever that day. The shade under the dusty oaks would be as refreshing as deep water. Someday, when he was riding by here, he promised himself he would stop under a big oak, lie in its shade, and make up for the way he felt today.

He knew all the trails on the mountains and recalled certain boulders and trees he would pass the next time he rode them. He looked away at the Rincóns and Catalinas beside Tucson and wondered if he would live to ride in them again. When he escaped in Tucson, he would hurry into them and be hard to catch.

He fell again and could not get up. He could only roll over on his back and let himself be strangled. Marshall ordered the dragging stopped only when Les and Mark threatened to shoot the team.

Marshall allowed Ben to ride then. Dick Martin had been holding the pace down to accommodate Ben, and they still had a long way to go. Les and Mark loaded Ben in the wagon, and one of the Irishmen gave him a drink from his canteen. The

Cowden brothers were not carrying canteens. The other Irishman wet Ben's neckerchief and bathed his face with it. The Irishmen were young, and their faces seemed open and guileless.

Les was despairing. Ben was lost, wasted into a heap of bloody rags and hair. He would never be able to climb off that wagon under his own power. He looked half his normal size.

Rain clouds had been building through the long hot afternoon. In this drouth, clouds usually built slowly and flew away to rain somewhere else or shrank, turned to wisp, and disappeared.

This time, at sundown, the clouds stayed together and began to rain. Ben watched the dark shafts move across the country and pass him by, but then they grew larger, and the whole sky turned black and burst overhead. For a half hour, the world turned to water under lightning and thunder, and washed the buckboard, horses, and men toward the Andrade ranch.

At midnight, Dick Martin chained Ben to a big cottonwood at the Andrade headquarters. The tree was the lockup for all prisoners on their way to the county jail in Tucson. No protestations by the Andrades or the Cowden brothers would sway Marshall to allow Ben to sleep inside.

Les and Mark ate supper in the rain with Ben. Ben was not uncomfortable, though Marshall thought he was. He knew how to stay dry under a slicker and a big tree.

Ben's mouth was torn, and he could not enjoy supper, but he ate as much as he could to regain his strength. He maintained his silence. He ate and drank what was brought him as long as it kept coming, then rolled over against the trunk of the cottonwood. He wanted his brothers to go inside and rest.

He slept hard for a short time because the fuel was fresh and warm in his stomach, but a wind blew up and slanted the rain against his face. He awakened with his teeth chattering.

Then, his slicker was torn off him, and he sat up and was slapped, forehand and backhand, across the face.

"What *right* have you to a good night's sleep, murderer?" his tormentor said. A lightning flash lit up Frank Marshall's face.

"You've had your final night's rest, and you just ate your last meal. The rain is the last water you'll ever know. Tomorrow night, you'll be under my special care, and you'll get nothing. I'm going to hang you up and salt you down like a slab of jerky. You'll dry out so bad, the flies won't even land on you."

A flash of lightning showed Marshall holding up the first blackjack Ben had ever seen, a black leather bag filled tightly with shot. Another flash showed Ben the bludgeon was a well-manufactured contraption with a lively spring in its narrow handle.

Marshall slapped it into his hand, then slapped Ben across the ear. Impatient when Ben made no sound, he bludgeoned him on the forehead, smashed the bridge of his nose, and tapped him on the temple to demonstrate how easily it rendered a man senseless.

When Ben revived, a voice in the darkness said, "I want you to know why this is being done to you, Cowden. You see, I'm the instrument with which Duncan Vincent will rid the country of people like you. You are the rocks in his bed and sand in his shoes. He figures to make an example of you so the rest of the squatters will quit the country.

"He wants me to hurt you. You're the special one he wants me to put out of his way. Someday he'll own this whole country. He'll own stores, banks, and towns. You won't be alive to bother him. There won't be any Cowdens anymore.

"I'm going to marry your sister and live in A. B. Cowden's house. Every year, I'll make a new baby inside her. My kids will ride your horses and inherit your daddy's land and cattle. Your brothers will be dead or in prison. Your sisters will sell their bodies to stay alive. I'm going to take weeks to kill you, and then I'm taking your place so I can get everything you love and own."

With that, he walked away with Ben's slicker. Ben sat in the rain, trying to keep his teeth from chattering so loud.

CHAPTER 6

Ben and his tormentors reached Tucson at midnight in a cloudburst. Marshall dismounted and quit the party at the Porter Hotel.

The railway depot was across the street. Its dark emptiness added to Ben's gloom. Maudy had passed through there yesterday. The place must have been bright when Maudy was there. Ben's life had gone sour after Maudy Jane Pendleton went away to grace other places.

Martin, Taylor, Campana, and the Irishmen took Ben to the county jail first. When Ben's brothers went away to find a place to sleep, Marshall's gang hurried Ben through the storm to a new building on Rillito Wash. Bib Taylor and Campana unloaded him on the points of their boots, dragged him into a cell, and stomped him into unconsciousness. That stomping was merciful compared to the beating Marshall and Taylor gave him at daylight the next morning.

Marshall and Taylor paced themselves so they were never in danger of tiring of their chore or missing the mark with the blackjack and hobnails. Marshall called his blackjack, Black Beauty.

The iron doors slammed shut and shook the floor under Ben's ear when Marshall and Taylor left. Ben waited for his pain to subside. He was in a strange new jail. His brothers would have a hard time finding him.

He'd been in the county jail many times as a visitor because A. B. was in his twelfth year as undersheriff of Pima

County. The county jail was more homey. The inmates kept each other company. Ben was alone. It would never do for him to squall for mercy. He was so far inside thick new walls and separated by so many doors from the outside, nobody would ever hear him. He could not hear anything but the ringing in his ears.

Black Beauty looked tiny in Marshall's hand. He wielded it as well with his left as he did with his right. He knew how to strike nerves without dulling the pain. He could drop it on the bridge of the nose without breaking bone. Ben's ears looked like potatoes. Marshall had beaten on them until they split open. He claimed he split them as a favor to Ben, to keep the blood from turning to scar tissue and giving him cauliflower ears. He also liked to tap on Ben's kneecaps so Ben would think they were split.

Ben's hands and fingers were broken from protecting his head against Black Beauty and the hobnails. All his muscles were swollen and stiff. Black Beauty would never fray in Marshall's large, clean, well-manicured hands. Marshall never hit anything that would scuff it.

The place was well swept and mopped, but the walls showed evidence of the treatment desperate characters like Ben received. Ben's new blood was spattered on top of old brown blood. He would have to bleed a lot more to match the quantity of old blood.

Thirst reminded him he must replenish the moisture in his reservoir. He was so thirsty he did not see how he could bleed much more without running completely dry. He would not ask for water though. Asking for water would not get him a drink, but a routine distribution of water might get him one. He would be left out of the routine if he reminded Marshall and Bib he needed water.

Ben knew how to go without water, but he had not been given a drink since he left the Andrade ranch. He stretched out to sleep. The longer he could sleep, the longer he could do without a drink.

He was awakened by an old Mexican named Severiano Flores. Severiano was an ex-deputy of A. B.'s. Ben watched him mop the aisle between the cells with his head down. Ben remembered when Severiano was a horseman sitting up straight on a big brown horse like Ben's horse Star. He had been much admired in the county. Then his wife and four children died of diphtheria before his oldest child was ten. Now he had not been sober in ten years.

Now he only sobered up enough to swab the jails. The jailers always locked him inside with the prisoners. He was as expendable to the jailers as the lye soap he used on the floors. His job was to clean the jails and keep them free of lice and fleas. No one ever thought of him unless they found a louse.

Ben did not believe Severiano would talk to him and cure his lonesomeness or take a message to A. B. He was so used to holding his peace after two days, he did not think he could speak to Severiano. He did not think Severiano would know him anyway. Ben saw him often when he went to the county jail with A. B., and he never showed any sign of recognition, though he sometimes tipped his hat to A. B. Everybody figured the loss of his family had crippled his mind.

Ben decided not to ask him for a drink of the mop water. Ben had known thirst all his life. He could undergo many hours of thirst on hot days when he was riding between springs, working cattle. He and his brothers only carried canteens in country they did not know or when they expected a firefight. No one could be as thirsty as a man in a fight or fighting a fire, unless he was being bled too.

He could hear thunder, but he could not see or hear the rain anymore. The cells were windowless. The thirst squeezed a moan out of him, and to cover it, he said, "Severiano, please," in Spanish. Severiano held the sweep of his mop for an instant and looked at Ben. Ben saw he was crazy as hell. He smiled a silly smile and went on swinging his mop from side to side.

"*Tengo mucha sed,*" Ben said, trying not to beg. "I have a lot of thirst."

Severiano was *molacho*, toothless. "I don't have the key, Benjamin. I also am a prisoner until they decide to let me out."

"You know me? You remember me?"

"Of course, Benjamin. You are Campana's son. I know all the *presos*, the convicts, in the county, no matter which jail they put them in."

"I'm Cowden's son, not Campana's son."

"Ah, you don't fool me. I know a Campana when I see one."

"*Paca acabarme de chingar!* To damned well finish me off—the old coot thinks I'm a Campana."

"Sooner or later, you all end up here, or in the county."

"Who is this jail for? What kind of people do they bring here?"

"The *mastodonte*, the big mastodon, beats his prisoners here, and when he's through, I help him carry them out."

Dick Martin came in, carrying a canteen. Ben ignored him and kept talking to Severiano.

"You must make a lot of friends in these places, Severiano."

"Yes, I do. I'm the only friend they have in here. I don't hurt them, and I help carry them out."

"Ben, I've brought you some water," Martin said.

Ben only looked at him.

"I insisted on seeing you. I still work for A. B. He'll want to know how you're being treated. Is there anything you want me to tell him?"

"No."

"I haven't wasted my time bringing you water, have I? I know you must be thirsty as hell."

"I already had a drink."

Martin's face was gloomy. "I guess I have to believe you if you say so."

"Believe it."

"Ben, I'm trying to help you. I'm still your friend. I haven't hurt you, have I? I'll never be the one to hit you, no matter if it means losing my job."

"You've got some job."

"I've managed to fool Captain Marshall and Mr. Vincent. They don't know I'm your friend, Ben."

"You're a smart feller."

"Do you want this water or not?"

"No."

"I've gotta go. Is there anything you want me to tell A. B.?"

"Tell him hello."

Martin laid the canteen inside the bars of Ben's cell and pounded on the iron door. Ben watched him go through a short chamber and a second iron door, and heard him go through the wooden outside door. He scrambled for the canteen, uncapped it, and drank three swallows. The water was fresh. He went back to his corner and sipped again. He had more sense than to guzzle it. He hoped nobody would disturb him in the half hour he would require to slake his thirst.

He heard the doors and knew he would not be allowed to

drink his fill of water. He kept sipping when he knew he might as well be guzzling.

Marshall and Taylor came in with Duncan Vincent and his brother Royal Vincent. Taylor unlocked Ben's cell and took the canteen away from him. He poured the rest of the water into Severiano's bucket. Ben could still taste the sweet life it carried. Tears for his drink of water burned his eyes, he longed for it so much. It had given him at least enough wetness for one tear.

"Well, here's your thief, Mr. Vincent," Marshall said. "Cowden, where did you get that canteen?"

Severiano perked up and grinned as though the name of his best friend had been called.

"The Mexican must have have brought it to him, Captain Marshall," Bib said.

Marshall's eye fell on Severiano. "Take that Mex in the office and question him. I want to know how this prisoner got a canteen of water."

Bib grabbed Severiano's frail old neck and carried him out like a suitcase. He left the doors open all the way to the office.

"Now, Cowden, speak up and answer questions if you want to be treated well," Marshall said. "Or stand by for another good whipping."

Ben looked at the wall across the room.

"Cowden, I'm sorry our disagreements have deteriorated to this," Duncan Vincent began. "However, as newly elected president of the Arizona Live Stock Association, I have you exactly where I want you. As soon as you confess to stealing my cattle, we'll get you to a judge."

Vincent turned to Marshall. "Can he hear me? Are you sure this is Ben Cowden? I don't recognize this man, and he doesn't seem to know me either."

"We're doing what we can to change his name to Mud, but he's Ben Cowden, all right, " Marshall said. "He's just another spick to me. That's a fine family indeed. The old lady and half the kids look spick, or Indian. The rest of them look white. The old man must be a pretty active old bull to have that many kids around that all look different."

"Stick to the point here. I'm not interested in his origins. I'm telling you, I don't recognize him."

"I'm not surprised. We're doing such a good job, his own mother wouldn't know him. However, he's Ben Cowden, son of A. B. Cowden."

"I might recognize him if he stands up. Stand up, will you, fellow?"

Ben stared at the wall behind Vincent. Marshall pulled Black Beauty out of his hip pocket and smacked it into the meat of his great palm.

Vincent glanced at the sap, and his expression did not change. The blackjack was just another tool. "Get him on his feet," he ordered.

Marshall smacked Ben on the side of a knee. The sap never glanced off its targets. The shock in Ben's knee made him roll on his side. Marshall leaned close to him, fixed on his target, and gave him a tap on the tailbone that made his legs quiver. "Stand on your feet like a man."

Ben climbed up and stood with his back to the wall. Marshall stuck his nose an inch from Ben's face. "You did that real well," he said. "I must not be doing my job. You're still able to stand under your own power."

"Stand aside, Captain Marshall," Vincent said. "I want to look at the man."

Marshall moved away. "Step up close to him, Mr. Vincent," he said. "His hands are manacled, and he can't raise them above his waist. You have him exactly the way you said you wanted him."

"We'll see," Vincent said. He stepped forward and peered into Ben's face. "Yes, I recognize him now. Good work, Captain. Now we're getting somewhere."

"I told you I'd deliver him to you, and here he is."

"Remember, I don't want him killed. I want him to stand trial, but I don't want him defiant at the trial. So when you think he's ready, we'll take him to Judge Black and get this trial thing started. Ease up on the face and ears. I want him degraded, but I don't want people to see he's been beaten like a dog. I want them to think his hangdog look's caused by the guilt he feels for being a cow thief."

"Leave it to me, Mr. Vincent. I can break any half-breed like this one and make him like it."

Vincent laughed. "How can you make him like it?"

"I'll crack the sonofabitch in such a way, he'll love me like his own mother when I stop."

"Cowden, are you taking this in?" Vincent said. "Do you understand what this man has in store for you? He's going to hurt you. This is my contribution to the war you declared against me. You said your whole family would fight me, even your women. Well, this man does my fighting. He'll defend me against your women too.

"Remember when you drew the line? This was the way you wanted it. I've defeated you, but I'm not satisfied. You will be disgraced. This man will send your sisters out to make their living with men behind the barns."

Ben was looking past Duncan Vincent at Senator Royal Vincent's nose. Senator Vincent was pale and shaky. Duncan Vincent stepped over to block Ben's gaze. "Understand me, Cowden? You're alone, and you're going to hurt so bad, you'll pray to God for permission to die."

Vincent turned to walk away. Ben launched himself off the wall and sank his teeth into the back of Vincent's neck.

Vincent's flesh was soft and delicate. He was not a strong man, though he was tall and wide. He was not accustomed to any kind of pain. His knees buckled, and his eyes and mouth opened wide with surprise when he realized he was caught in Ben's jaws.

Ben drove Vincent's face into the floor. He opened his jaws and took a bigger bite, and pulled. He chewed for better purchase and wrenched his head from side to side. Black Beauty put an end to that.

He awakened to blackness. The place was usually dark, but a hatch in the iron door was sometimes left open so the guard could peer at him. If the next door, into the office, was left open, light filtered into the cellblock. Ben could not see one glimmer of light.

His mouth was dry as a seed bin, pieces of Vincent's shirt were caught in his teeth. He chewed the threads to moisten them so he could spit them out. His teeth were sore from pulling on Vincent's neck.

Ben heard the sound of a match being struck and saw a face in the flare. A man was smoking a delicious-smelling cigar in the next cell. Each time he drew on the coal, his face was lighted. Ben was too dry to miss the company of his pipe and tobacco.

"Ever ask yourself, 'What am I doing here?'" a young man's voice said.

Another voice said, "Yeah, lately I've been doing that all the time."

"Me too, ever since we got caught moving those calves."

"We were dumb, moving them the way we did. That

constable tracked them right to our doorstep. We wouldn't have had any trouble if we'd used a wagon."

"We were dumb to try to be outlaws in the first place."

"We'll know better how to do it the next time."

"Huh! I imagine the Live stock Association'll make sure there's no next time."

"What can they do to us? We're just kids. They can't eat us."

"They can eat us, I think."

Ben thought, This must be the Interior Department's jail, and Marshall is about to give them some school on how to stop being a cow thief. He slept.

He was awakened by the sound of the boys being given their thumps. At first, Ben thought the two Irishmen must be using pick handles on them. The boys sounded as though they were being killed.

Blessed light poured through the cell door. One of the Irishmen was making a sham of beating the boys. The boys bellowed like bull calves being dragged to a branding fire, but they were grinning and having fun while the Irishman pounded on a mattress with a pick handle.

"How are you feeling, Mr. Cowden?" asked the other Irishman.

Ben only looked at him.

The Irishman unlocked Ben's cell and walked in. "Would you be wanting a drink of water?"

Ben was too thirsty to refuse. The Irishman swung a big section hand's canteen off his shoulder and uncapped it for him. Ben took a big swallow.

"I have to take it with me when I leave, but we'll be here awhile."

Ben smelled the water to absorb it that way too. He filled his system with its delicious wetness. Marshall and Bib might come any minute and take it away. That might be their plan, to tantalize him with a taste and then take it away again. They had nothing to lose by giving him water. They could come in anytime they wanted and kick it all out of him.

His shrunken belly filled up before his craving for the water subsided, and he knew he had drunk too much. The sham beating and bellowing of the boys subsided, and the Irishman came back and squatted close to Ben.

"Don't lose hope," he said. "Me brother and I do not hold with these beatings. We've been talking to your brothers, and they know where you are. They're watching for a chance to free you. Keep the faith."

Ben was not keeping faith with this Irishman, that was a damned cinch. He gave no sign that he heard him. He handed back the empty canteen.

"Do you hear me, or have the beatings addled your brain? Are you here or away on the nod?"

Ben could not help smiling. What the hell, he had to trust somebody.

"Ah, that's better," said the Irishman. "At least I know you understand me and you still own the teeth for a smile."

An irrational mirth hurt Ben's ribs, but he could not keep from laughing.

"That's fine," said the Irishman. "Don't try to talk. I can see you're all right. My partner and I will be helping your brothers free you before long."

He took back his empty canteen and squeezed Ben's shoulder. Every time anyone laid a hand on him, it hurt. The Irishmen locked up and left, but they left open the hatch so the prisoners could have some light.

The boys stood up and walked around. "Those seem like decent fellers," said one.

"When you look at what's been done to the feller in that other cell, they're damned decent," the other boy said. "Hey, feller, how're you doing?"

Ben remained silent.

"I'm Billy Stiles. My partner here is George Smiley. We're in for stealing cattle. What're you in for?"

Ben thought, What the hell, I can't help myself by not talking to these boys, and I need some company. "Do you boys have any water?"

"A whole barrel of it," Stiles said.

Ben climbed to his feet and dragged himself to the door of his cell. Smiley dipped a cupful out of the barrel. The barrel was wrapped in wet gunny sacks that absorbed dampness through the water-soaked staves. The barrel was dark and heavy, and was brimful of cool, clean water. Smiley stopped at the bars of his cell and looked across the aisle at Ben. "How'll I get it to you?"

"Never mind." Ben walked back to his corner and sat on the floor. He had nothing but a chamber pot in his cell.

"Say, I know who you are," Billy Stiles said. "George, you do too."

"Do I?" Smiley said.

"You know who he is?"

"Well, who?"

"He's Ben Cowden, remember? I heard that guy say his name, but I recognize him now. He's the one who owned the horse that won the San Juan's Day race. Hey, feller, me and George here won some money on your horse that day. What was your horse's name? Was it Pete? Something Pete?"

"Prim Pete," Ben said.

"That's *right*. See? I'm *right*, you're Ben Cowden."

"Naw, Ben Cowden's a big good-looking man, a lot taller that this feller," Smiley said.

"No he's not. This is him."

Ben closed his eyes, wanting to rest.

"So, what you doing in here, Cowden?" Stiles asked. "I always thought you were one of the down-country hoi polloi. Who did you kill?"

Ben heard an iron door open. Then he heard the hobnails coming.

CHAPTER 7

Frank Marshall dismounted from the noon train in Patagonia with Dick Martin. They walked to Martin's house and saddled his skinny gelding so Marshall could ride to Harshaw. Martin called the horse Hoozy because he had been a gift from Hoozy Briggs.

Marshall had a good excuse for visiting the Cowdens. Riding Martin's dink would show them he needed a good horse. He wanted the Toots horse he'd taken from Ben Cowden.

Paula Mary Cowden was in the highest branches of her walnut tree watching him when he arrived at the Cowdens' barnyard at sundown. Gordo Soto was sitting on a saddle blanket with his back against the barn, splicing a broken *reata*.

"You, Meskin, take this horse," Marshall ordered as he stepped off. Hoozy was so weak that he almost fell over when Marshall's weight came to bear on the left stirrup. He brought up a hind leg to keep himself from falling and stepped on Marshall's toe. Marshall still had one foot in the stirrup when Hoozy pinned his other foot to the ground. Gordo Soto took Marshall's reins as Hoozy crumpled Marshall's toes.

Marshall did not cry out, but Gordo could hear his teeth grinding. Marshall could not get his left foot out of the stirrup or move his right foot off the ground because Hoozy was leaning against him while he stood on his foot. Marshall tried to shove him away, but Hoozy only shifted enough to bear down on another group of toes. He rotated the hoof over the toes and ground all the shine off Marshall's calfskin boot.

Gordo peered around Hoozy's head at Marshall's face, holding the horse so he could not step off Marshall's foot.

"You dumb spick, lead him up. Move the damned dink off my foot," gritted Marshall.

Gordo, under stress from hearing that Marshall disliked him because of his nationality, started Hoozy off the foot, stopped him, then started him again. Marshall struck out at Hoozy and caused him to drive off the offending hoof. This shaved off Marshall's big toenail inside the calfskin boot.

Marshall moaned and cursed and pounded on the horse to free himself. Gordo had all he could do to hold the horse in place. Finally, Marshall turned loose all holds and let himself fall to the ground. Gordo turned Hoozy so he could walk on the man's legs, then led him over to the shade and tied him.

Marshall was slow getting up. He rolled over to his hands and knees, and lifted his sore toes off the ground and let them touch, lifted them and let them touch again, and moaned and grunted as the great pain ebbed and flowed inside his boot. Gordo hurried away to do his chores.

Bill Knox walked unsteadily out into the light, full of his noontime whiskey. He took one look at the well-dressed dude on his hands and knees, moaning and grimacing with pain, and went back inside to crank the bellows on his forge.

After a while, Marshall limped into the barn and perched heavily on Bill Knox's anvil. "Good afternoon," he said, panting. He wiped his brow and neck with a clean handkerchief and examined it to see how much it was soiled. Bill was heating a steel bar, the first step in making a new horseshoe.

"How's about sending the Mexican to tell the man I want to see him in his office?" Marshall said. He knew A. B. was in Tucson trying to find Ben.

Bill Knox walked to the anvil, holding the length of white-hot iron in his tongs. The iron was so hot it was almost melting. Little flashing sparks jumped off it like fleas. Marshall did not move until he felt the heat and realized Knox would lay the hot iron in his lap if that was what it took to move him. He limped away to the back door and looked up at the house. He could smell the Cowden supper.

"Is that biscuits I smell?" he asked, when Bill stopped hammering.

"There's biscuits in Harshaw," Bill said.

"You think a fellow could buy supper?" Marshall asked.

Bill returned the iron to the coals and cranked the bellows. The back screendoor of the house slammed, and Betty Cowden came toward the barn, carrying a tray.

Marshall watched her walk carefully down the path. Her face was so soft, the downcast gaze so innocent, that Marshall felt she must barely disturb the rocks under her feet. She raised her eyes at the door, and the sight of him surprised her.

"Oh, my," she said, and smiled.

"Good evening, young Miss Pretty." Frank Marshall swept his hat off his head. Betty slipped close in front of him through the door. Gordo, his hair combed wet, his sleeves rolled up, his face and hands washed, held a stall door open for her.

Betty carried the tray into the stall the two men shared for living quarters. She held the tray in one hand and spread a clean white cloth over a table. She set the tray down and arranged places for two.

"Bill, aren't you ready for supper?" Betty asked.

Bill Knox glanced at Marshall.

"You come on now and have your supper. I'll take care of your visitor."

Bill looked Marshall in the eye. "He's not my visitor."

"Oh?" Betty turned to Marshall. "Are you here to see my papa?" She knew who he was. His handsomeness was startling to a girl who had only been out of Harshaw Canyon a dozen times in her life. She had seen him lose a touch of it when her brother punched him in the eye. She did not let on she knew him from a traveling salesman though.

"I'm afraid I've come at an awkward time, Miss Cowden," Marshall said. "You see, I traveled all the way from Tucson today to buy a saddle horse from your father. I haven't seen anybody but these two workmen, and they don't seem to know anything about Mr. Cowden's whereabouts."

Bill Knox measured Marshall the same way he would gauge a shiny piece of steel that would not take a temper and went to his washstand.

"Well, no, my father's not here, but maybe my mother can help you. She can't sell you a horse, but she'll make sure you don't leave here afoot."

"Oh, I can wait for your father. When do you expect him?"

"Not until tomorrow, but we're about to sit down to supper, so you can join us and talk to my mother. Maybe Bill has a horse you can ride until my papa comes home."

Marshall smiled at Bill's back and caught himself being nice. He could not help himself. If he'd been born with a tail, he'd be wagging it. A minute later he was standing in the Cowdens' front room being introduced to Betty's sisters, Eileen and Paula Mary. Then Viney came into the room in a cool hurry, and he knew from experience that she had rushed into her bedroom to make herself presentable for him.

He always commanded the attention of strong, reserved matriarchs and beautiful girls. He knew he was a fine-looking man. All he ever needed to do to have anything he wanted from women was get past the damned men who protected them like that mean blacksmith.

The Cowden women would have been more impressed if Frank Marshall was not so conceited. Viney had hurried to straighten her hair for his benefit, but she did that for everybody, even the Farley twins.

Just because they were nice to him did not mean the Cowden women would become his conquests. Paula Mary was the least impressed. She already knew the dude. The Cowden brothers were the kind of men she and her sisters liked. The Cowden men were not as tall, but they were broader-shouldered and better-looking than this dude. No matter how much charm he showed, he would always be pale and creamy to the Cowden girls until he showed how well he sat a horse and turned back a steer.

The ladies were hospitable because they liked to have company for supper when the Cowden men were gone. Bill Knox and Gordo sometimes came for supper, but they were not conversationalists.

Frank Marshall began entertaining them with stories of the opera and other music he had enjoyed in San Francisco. Viney and Eileen dreamed of going to San Francisco where A. B.'s brother's family lived so they could see the opera.

Betty wanted to go too, but to watch the ships head out for China. When Marshall found that out, he told stories of his two trips by ship, from San Francisco around the Horn to New Orleans. Paula Mary watched Betty turn into a little doughy girl with eyes so soft who nestled her little butt aboard that ship and made the whole voyage with Marshall.

Paula Mary would rather be in her walnut tree watching Hoozy-the-horse step on Marshall's toes. She knew him for the dude he really was. He might be able to ride a ship around the

Horn, but a little dinky horse could make him throw himself down in a practical swoon.

Betty must not have noticed he was only kind of a big white rat. You could tell Betty a travel story, and she was yours—at least until you got to the end or you got boring.

Paula Mary had seen Marshall coming, so to speak, before anyone else did. So when he gave her that smile that looked like sugared clabber and saw she didn't like it, he dismissed her as though she did not count at all. She was happy to let him think that. She would watch him and tell Bill Knox and her brothers what she saw.

Paula Mary figured people saw Marshall's black eyes and thought he was deep and hard to understand, maybe even mysteriously mean. Then he clobbered them with his smile and made them think he was good and friendly. He was mean, all right, but only about as deep as a shovelful of creek water and about as hard to understand as a cock's crow.

After supper, Betty showed him into the front room, but he placed himself so he could charm the ladies through the door while they cleared the kitchen. When he took a stogie out of his vest pocket, Betty hurried to him with a match. She struck the match for him and stood awful close to him while he drew at the flame. She never offered to help with the dishes, but sat on the other side of the door so he would not feel left out, or something.

That worried Paula Mary. Betty was a good hand, and all kinds of work came easy to her. Paula Mary did not like to see her quit work so she could hang on every word the dude uttered.

Eileen wore a constant blush on her face. That was dangerous, because she had a fiancé. For four years, Johnny Bonner of Benson had been braving a hundred-mile ride through Geronimo's warpath twice a month to see her. He'd already run down three or four good horses getting past the savages to her, and now she let this big chunk of a dude put her in a constant flush. Dudes should not be allowed around a ranch when the women were there alone.

"Let's put conversation aside for a moment and talk business, ladies," Marshall said, "I want to buy the horse you call Toots."

This brought the Cowden women back to real life in Harshaw Canyon. Toots was too splendid for anybody else. He made the women remember the merry day they'd spent with the men, riding with Maudy to the train. A pall fell on the room. This man had taken Ben away, and now he wanted his horse. The three things most important and personal to a cowman were his country, his women, and his horse. All of a sudden, this man showed up with plans to replace Ben Cowden in the country by charming his women and taking his horse.

The Cowden women gave Frank Marshall the look they saved for a rat turd in a bowl of rice.

"I hope I haven't touched on a sensitive subject," Marshall said easily. "I know you folks are in the business of selling horses. I figure you're like I am. When I'm in business, everything I have is for sale, and since the horse has already been confiscated, you might welcome a buyer for him. Am I mistaken?"

Betty went to the sink and began drying dishes. The blush left Eileen's face. Viney did not show it, but Paula Mary knew her distress. The women had begun to enjoy Marshall, but now the fun was gone. Marshall could see that these women were all of the same stock, never mind the jet-black hair of Viney and Paula Mary, the reddish-brown hair of Eileen and Betty. The girls were full-blooded sisters and daughters of the same mother and father. There wasn't a hair of difference between them when they thought someone was trying to unhorse one of their men.

Marshall was careful not to look at any of them. He kept his manner easy, as though he did not notice their disapproval. One face bothered him because it did not turn away from him. Paula Mary's gaze was as unwavering as a crouching wildcat's a second before she pounces. Looking at her, he could believe wildcats would tackle anything from a house cat to a grizzly. She stared until she was sure he knew her great disdain, and then looked away.

"I guess I'm wrong. I thought you'd welcome the chance to make a sale since the horse might be confiscated if Ben is found guilty," Marshall said. "He is for sale, isn't he, Mrs. Cowden?"

"That I could not tell you, Captain Marshall," Viney said.

"I can't believe you won't deal with me, Mrs. Cowden. I'll pay you better money for the horse than I would Mr. Cowden. And please call me Frank, will you?"

Viney turned her back to him and folded her tablecloth.

"Well, I just meant there must be something we can do. I haven't wasted my trip, have I?"

No one answered him.

"Mrs. Cowden?"

"I don't know what you consider time well spent, Mr. Marshall," Viney said. "However, if you expect me to tell you the horse you mentioned is for sale to you, you are wasting your time. The women in this family don't make horse trades. If you want to buy that horse, you'll have to speak to my son Ben."

"Oh, the horse is Ben's? Where is he?"

The Cowden women went on with their business.

"Hasn't Ben been home yet?"

Eileen turned to him. "He has not. Our papa's gone to Tucson to look for him."

"That puzzles me. I looked for him in Tucson. I thought he'd been released to return home."

Marshall put on his most sincere and concerned face, the look of a leader of men with compassion for all. "You know, ladies, another reason I came here was to get to know Ben Cowden's family better. I am a special agent of my government, and my duty is to prove the innocence as well as the guilt of people suspected of crimes. I believe Ben is innocent, and I mean to clear him."

Viney paused in her business and examined a strip she would have to mend on the hem of the tablecloth. She sighed, and Marshall believed he was bringing her back into his confidence.

"Where do you think our brother is, Captain Marshall?" Eileen asked.

Marshall could see these women were quick and enterprising when it came to working a man, plying him for information. He would have to be a lot more careful with them. He needed to convince them he was their ally in seeking fairness and justice for Ben Cowden.

"For the life of me, I don't know where he could be," Marshall said. "But, believe me, if anybody can find him, I can. You see, as a special agent, I spend all my time in the field. I don't usually follow up on what happens to suspects after they're in custody. You can be sure I'll find out what happened to your brother, if I have to use every bit of the power I'm granted from the capital, in Washington."

He looked to see if Betty was impressed. She was gazing thoughtfully out a window over the sink and giving him her profile. She might be an innocent young thing, but she had the ancient instincts of a pretty girl and knew he was looking at her. She knew he wanted her and thought she was laying a new trap for him with that profile.

A shout was heard from down the canyon, and Betty looked out the back door. She arched her back and posed for Marshall with one foot off the floor. She knew how to move a man by making pictures he would remember. If she kept this up, he would have her under his thumb in no time at all. Before long, he would make her need him for her very life, and she would think it was all her own idea.

Ignoring Marshall but still posing for him, Betty said to her mother, "It's the twins, coming from Patagonia."

The sisters trooped self-consciously out the door in front of Marshall. It was almost time for him to gloat. They, by God, were *all* wooing him. He looked so good to them and boasted such great connections with important people in the world that they were beginning to depend on him.

"The twins?" Marshall asked, without looking at Viney. He assumed Viney was hanging on his every word. When she did not answer, he turned to her.

Viney was a wise bird who was always brave, quick, and defensive around her nest. Any man might come hunting her chicks.

"The Farley twins, my nephews, Captain Marshall." Viney held the back door open for him.

He heaved himself out of the chair. He was stiff from riding the dink fifteen miles from Patagonia, and he was positive his toes were broken. He tried not to limp because he did not want to have to explain it, but a grunt of pain escaped him. Viney noticed he was in pain but did not seem to care.

He made it out the door and waited for her, but she shut it behind him and turned back into the house. Now he did not know how he was going to get back into the house. He dearly wanted to be asked to stay the night. He did not know how he could ride that dink on to Harshaw that evening and look for a place to stay.

He followed the girls around the corner of the house. Surely they would invite him to stay.

The Farley twins were sitting their horses and joking with the girls. Their faces were young, freckled, and open. Nobody in the world would have known they had been drunk most of the day and all the night before and would be drunk again tonight and tomorrow. They looked sober, rested, and relaxed. Their smiles disappeared when they saw Marshall.

"What's he doing here?" asked Danny Farley.

The girls turned uneasily to him, as if they were not sure he would give a satisfactory answer.

"Hello, I'm Frank Marshall." He tried not to limp as he moved to shake hands with the twins. He could not look awkward. He might be withering inside with pain, but he could still look good for the girls. The twins wiped their right hands on their chaps after shaking Marshall's hand.

"Captain Marshall says he's going to clear Ben of all the charges against him," Eileen said. She did not say it as though she was proud to know such an influential man. She said it as though she would believe it when she saw it.

"That's funny—he's the one who arrested Ben and beat him up," Danny said.

"Yeah, he didn't have to come all the way out here from Tucson to tell you what he can do for Ben," Donny said. "He could have sent a wire. He uses the wires a lot."

The Cowden girls watched Marshall closely. He said, "I came here to see if I could buy a horse, and I will see if I can clear the man of charges."

"What horse is that?" asked Danny. "The one you confiscated after Ben was beaten half to death?"

"I don't think Captain Marshall was the one who did that, Danny," Eileen said. "He only came out to buy Toots."

"Why would he offer to buy the horse?" Donny asked. "He's already confiscated him."

"Now that's not true," Marshall said. "The horse is in the county pound. If he's not sold to me, he'll be returned to Ben."

"So, if you already have the horse, why don't you just deed him to yourself, like all the rest of the crooked lawmen do when they want to steal a horse?" Danny said.

Marshall stared at Danny for a long moment so the boy would see that he was too big to be called a horse thief. "I'm a special agent of the government, young man. I don't use my authority for my own profit. I'm going to brag right in front of these ladies and tell you I'm a good law officer. I've been sent to this territory especially by my government to correct abuses of power. Ben Cowden's case is my first, and if I say I'll clear him, you can be sure I will."

"You're long-winded enough to be a government dude,"

Donny said. "I might even believe the rest of it, but I happen to know you beat hell out of Ben Cowden."

"Wait a minute. I admit Ben was beaten when he resisted arrest, but are you saying you saw me do it?"

"You were in on it. We saw you ride his horse away."

"You didn't see me beating him though."

"Well, no, *we* didn't see you, but other people did, and they told us about it."

"I would not have allowed Ben to be beaten. I'm not that kind of a man. I settle most of my disputes in court, but I can fight man-to-man. I don't order gangs to fight for me.

"Let me tell you something. If I was you and believed somebody ordered a gang to beat up my favorite cousin and steal his horse, I'd look him up and tear his head off. Well, since I'm the man you're accusing, get after it. Come on and fight me, one at a time, or both at once—it makes no difference to me."

Paula Mary was scared. She did not want anything to happen to the twins. She did not doubt for a minute that Marshall could hurt them the way Ben was hurt.

The twins would not look at each other. Danny said, "We didn't say we saw you do it. One of the Heredia boys told us you did it."

"Well, if you believe that, you'd better do something about it."

Paula Mary knew her cousins would now probably decide to try to beat the man to death before they went on home for supper. She looked down at Marshall's feet, not sure which one was the mashed one. She thought about it and was pretty sure it was the right one, the one that got down off the horse first. The right boot was the scuffed one. So she walked up to Marshall and said, "So *you're* the one took my brother to jail, are you?" and she stamped her foot on Marshall's sore toes.

Marshall's black eyes glazed with the shock of it, and his anger almost broke bounds, but the impact of that little foot was so great, it froze him in place. For a moment, he was a statue.

The Cowden girls took his incapacity to mean he was completely unaffected by Paula Mary's featherweight attack. They laughed merrily. The sight of their tiny sister trying to harm a giant by stamping her foot on his toe was ludicrous. The twins almost fell off their horses laughing. Marshall saw they were not laughing at him. They laughed because they thought they could see no meanness in him and were relieved of their doubts about him. He was not there to hurt anybody, after all.

Marshall threw back his head and laughed as hard as he could—and gloated. From now on, the Cowden girls were his to work, use, and handle like prize livestock.

CHAPTER 8

Ben dreamed he was lying on his back on a bed of leaves in Temporal Canyon, watching the tops of the cottonwood trees. The stream of mountain water was only a few feet away. The dry summer was over. A breeze fanned his face and moved the cottonwood limbs overhead. The leaves had all turned yellow.

Ben sighed, and the cool, fragrant air he breathed was like a drink of water. Now that he was dreaming, he could roll over and drink from the stream. He was so dry. He needed to drink his fill this time. He did not want to be dry when he awoke.

The iron doors in Rillito jail slammed, and Ben awakened. He was back, but the hobnails could not make him forget the good places. Those hobs could kick down a cottonwood but could not keep Ben down. He sat up against the wall and tucked his knees under his chin.

Ben refused to eat. He had decided he could beat Marshall and Bib by not eating. They could torture him and keep him alive by giving him water only a drop at a time, but he could disappear right in front of them by not eating. They could not torture him if he was not there.

He dumped his food in a pile and let it stink. At first they thought that was funny; it would be fun to make Ben eat it. They tried that and failed. They piled more blows and kicks on him, but they could not make him eat or ask for a drink.

Bib came in with two new prisoners. Ben never looked at his tormentors. They had him where they wanted him, so his only weapon was not to look at him, to act as though their presence was insignificant. When he could lay hands on them or shoot them, they would gain significance and he would look them in the eye.

Bib shoved the new prisoners into Ben's cell. "Here's some Mexicans to talk to, Cowden," he said. "See how nice you're treated in our hotel?" He swung the door shut and went out.

Smiley and Billy Stiles did not raise their heads off their bunks. Mexicans did not deserve their attention.

The Mexicans sat down on the floor to rest and seemed grateful for a cool and shady place. That was one advantage for the prisoners. The walls were made of double adobe, a foot thick and plastered with calcimine. They were hard to perforate or move, but they kept out the heat. Heat would have made Ben more thirsty, but his tormentors did not like to work in the heat. Breaking Ben Cowden was turning into hard labor.

Ben went back to Temporal Canyon, this time on a good horse. His tormentors could bring him back, but they could not unhorse him. So far, his will remained strong, and he was showing them his heels.

"Benjamin," one of the Mexicans said. "*Mi amigo?* Aren't you my friend Ben Cowden?"

Being called a friend in Spanish was like a tonic to Ben. To him, Spanish was the language of mankind's love. He recognized the *vaquero* Martín Roblez, son of a Sonoran rancher who was a friend of A. B.'s. The last time Ben had seen Roblez, he was a soldier in Gabriel Kosterlinsky's Mexican Cavalry. A big soft tear welled in Ben's good eye and splashed on the floor between his heels.

"Why have they beaten you, Benjamin?" Roblez asked. "This is a horror." Ben's appearance afflicted him with outrage. That was the Mexican way. Even the most humble vaquero presumed his show of outrage could alleviate a wrong when no other remedy was at hand. Roblez made Ben smile.

"*Que horror* no?" Ben said. "How do you think *I* feel?"

"But Benjamin, who did this?"

"The enemies of my family, friends of your *Comandante* Kosterlinsky."

"But Kosterlinsky is your friend. I've seen you laughing and drinking with him."

"He was my friend, but not anymore."

"Benjamin, he's no man's friend. My friend here with me is Jacinto Lopez. We are part of the group of *amontinados*, mutineers, who turned against Kosterlinsky at Cananea. Your army captured many of us in Yuma. Lopez and I were caught in Calabasas. Kosterlinsky's coming for us today."

"He's coming to this jail?"

"Yes, probably."

"Why would he come here personally for two deserters?"

"Ah, because we're not deserters at all. We mutinied. We refused to sack the Gabilondo hacienda near Cananea for him."

"Why was he sacking Don Pancho Gabilondo's hacienda?"

"Greed, man. We were supposed to be in pursuit of the Yawner when we rode into the hacienda. Kosterlinsky demanded that Don Pancho provide fresh mounts for the troops. This time Don Pancho refused him. He had furnished Kosterlinsky with fresh horses on five previous occasions, and none were returned.

"Don Pancho called Kosterlinsky a *robabestias*, a horse thief, who was making a business of selling the horses he borrowed from the ranchers. We all knew it was true. Don Pancho said he and the other ranchers did not mind contributing a few horses from time to time, but Kosterlinsky was abusing the privilege. The Yawner was a hundred miles to the north of us.

"So, after he turned us away, Kosterlinsky thought about it awhile, then came about and ordered us to prepare to attack the hacienda. Twenty-one of us mutinied. We disarmed Kosterlinsky and the troopers who remained loyal to him, and set them afoot."

"Why is he coming to get you? He could send a sergeant and a corporal."

"He's applied *la ley de Fuga*, the law of flight, and killed every man he captured. He doesn't want a single one of us to return to testify against him. I figure he'll set up machine guns and put us to flight at Sahuarita. There's a flat by the river where we could run a mile and never find cover from a firing squad."

"How did they catch you?"

"Kosterlinsky put out a reward for us and published our names in the Nogales newspaper. We betrayed ourselves when we used our own names and asked for work at the railroad section house at Calabasas."

"Do you have any water, Roblez?" Ben asked.

"They gave us a drink outside. Don't you have any water?"

"No."

Roblez moved close to Ben. "Never mind. Tonight you will drink beer."

"Water would be fine."

"No, I mean we're not alone. Five of our comrades were not captured, and they followed us here. They will free us."

"Good for you, Roblez."

"Good for you too, Benjamin. You're going with us."

"We'll see."

"No 'we'll see' about it. You're going with us."

"All right. I hope so."

"*Eso es!* That's the way to talk, man. That's the *jinete*, the horseman, I know."

"Hey, what're you guys saying in the lingo over there?" Billy Stiles said. He was standing against the bars of his cell.

"Do you understand Spanish?" Ben asked.

"I know *taco, tortilla, burro, caballo, huevo, culo.*" He laughed. "*Caca pedo.* How's that? What was he telling you to make you grin. Let us in on it."

"A Mexican joke. I can't translate it."

"What did those Mexicans do?"

Roblez moved away. Ben lay down and turned his back to Stiles to shut him up. He was suspicious of Stiles and Smiley. They never stopped questioning him.

"Come on, Ben, tell me something. Ask them what's going on outside this damned jail. What'd they do?"

The iron doors slammed, and Ben heard the hobnails coming again. Bib Taylor ushered Royal Vincent and Gabriel Kosterlinsky into the cellblock. The last time Ben had seen Kosterlinsky, he came close to shooting him. Kosterlinsky had been wearing the uniform of a lieutenant in the Mexican Army then. He was wearing the duds of the rurales, the Sonora rural mounted police, now. He was wearing the *sombrero de ala*, the great sombrero with a brim like a wing and a crown like a mountain peak, and the tight brocade trousers and jacket of the *charro*.

Kosterlinsky swaggered down the aisle between the cells ahead of Vincent, and Ben saw he was half drunk. His hair was in his eyes, and he was trying to look mean. He was about as mean as a sand lizard with his tail bobbed. The leather *barbiquejo*, the wide leather throat-latch of his sombrero, was pulled tight under his lower lip, and the sombrero was on the back of his head. He must have come here straight from the bar where he'd caught a roaming shoeshine boy, for his boots were freshly shined. He would not ride far from any bar today. Ben could guarantee that. He knew Kosterlinsky better than any other gringo alive.

Kosterlinsky's eye fell on his former minions. "Caught, you *cabrones. Atención!* You will come to attention at the sight of me, you grubworm sons of your disgraced mothers! You sons of obscene perpetrations! You will assume the formal posture of attention and prepare to die!"

Kosterlinsky dragged out his pistol and pointed it at the chamber pot. Ben had seen him do that before. He liked to use his pistol as a pointer when delivering instructions to his troops. He often tried to make his point by tapping an inattentive soldier between the eyes with the barrel, but every time he tried to aim it, the barrel stuck awry out of his fist as though bent. The only way he would ever hit anything would be by ricochet.

Ben smiled and thought, Thank God I didn't kill him in Santa Cruz. It's so good that evil sometimes lodges in the heart of a real fool like Kosterlinsky and is not monopolized by serious, smart, calculating men. Good has a chance, after all.

Roblez and Lopez yielded to their humble natures and slouched to their feet before their commander.

"Delinquents!" Kosterlinsky accused them. "I promise you, this day you will go to your God without benefit of the sacraments."

The miscreants' eyes were fixed on infinity, an inch above Kosterlinsky's head. Ben realized he'd learned to do that from Mexicans. The mutineers made themselves impervious to Kosterlinsky's ranting that way.

Kosterlinsky tried the door of the cell, then turned to Bib Taylor for the key. "May I go in, please?"

Bib shook his head and pointed toward Ben. "There's another prisoner in there."

Kosterlinsky forgot his rage and allowed his eye to fall upon Ben. "Ah yes, who is this?" That was the kind of man he was. He would postpone the castigation of his peons to allow himself a moment of curiosity. Ben's beard was a week old, and his face was cut, swollen, and bruised. Kosterlinsky did not recognize him.

Senator Royal Vincent said, "This man represents a faction of murderers and cattle thieves who prey in the territory. We will hang him as an example to his kind. This one's been particularly active in the region bordering your state, Colonel Kosterlinsky."

Kosterlinsky peered into Ben's face. "Then, I should know him."

"Yes, you should know Ben Cowden, from Harshaw."

Kosterlinsky threw back his head and shouted with laughter. "Benjamin, my very good friend! But you are mistaken, Senator. You must have the wrong man. I know this man. He is vicious with his enemies, but certainly no thief. Senator, anyone who tells you Ben Cowden is dishonest is a liar."

Senator Royal Vincent was disconcerted. "This surprises me. I thought you'd be pleased to see this man disgraced."

"Oh, I'm glad to see him in chains, but he's not disgraced, by any means. You can't disgrace a man like him. He must do that himself. And what kind of fools are in charge of this jail? They've been beating him? If you want him out of the way, you have to kill him."

Vincent colored. "I believe he resisted arrest and was apprehended with considerable force and injured in the process."

"Well, you are fools to beat him and then let him live. I know him. He'll be the death of you. My advice to you? Kill him now, this minute. Don't let him get up from that corner."

Ben flexed his legs and arms, making ready to move. The iron doors were being left open all the way to the outside. Alive or dead, one way or the other, he was going out.

The two Irishmen came in, unlocked the other cell, and ordered Stiles and Smiley to their feet for their hearing with Judge Black. They waited a moment while the boys found their hats and buckled their belts, then marched them out. When he reached the chamber between the two iron doors, the Irishman who was behind the boys turned and looked Ben in the eye, nodded, and swung the door all the way open. He left the other iron door open too. Ben could see all the way out through the front door. He stood up and began pacing his corner of the cell.

Kosterlinsky was talking to Ben and feeling his alcohol. Right now, he did not want to take his men into custody. He wanted to go back to the bar. It was too late in the day for him to leave town and stop his drinking, gambling, and playing the bigshot.

He would not leave town with prisoners until early some morning, if he went at all. More likely, he would send a sergeant and a squad of troopers to take the mutineers out into the brush and shoot them. Now that he was on a *parranda*, a binge, he would not leave town until all his cash was spent.

Severiano came in to sweep and mop the vacant cell. Ben stood by the bars, his back to Bib, and watched him.

"Benjamin, you are a just man. What do you think I should do with these two sons of obscene penetrations?" Kosterlinsky asked. "You should know the grief they've caused. They are the embarrassment of all Mexico."

Ben paced across the cell to his corner.

"Mr. Taylor, let me into the cell a moment. I feel like a fool out here shouting. I need to question these men."

"How'll you handle it when they knock you down, Colonel?"

Colonel? Ben thought, How'd the worthless son of a gun get to be a colonel? The last time I saw him he was a cavalry lieutenant, running away from the Yawner as fast as he could and disgracing himself.

"What can they do? They're chained from head to toe. Anyway, they wouldn't dare oppose me. They mutinied against me, and now they regret it. They know how I deal with delinquency."

"Suit yourself, Colonel," said Bib. "You, Cowden, get over in the corner and stay there. Now, Colonel, stay away from Cowden. He almost bit Duncan Vincent's head off the other day."

Kosterlinsky halted. "He did? Ben Cowden bit somebody?"

"Jumped your partner from behind, took his neck in his teeth, and shook him like a rabbit."

"Is that why Duncan won't see anyone?" Kosterlinsky turned to the senator. "Is that why he is locked in his hotel room?"

"One of the reasons," the senator said. "He wasn't injured badly, but he needed a rest."

"He needs a rest, all right. Cowden scared the shit out of him," Bib said.

"You mean my friend *Cueva de Vaca*, Den of a Cow, might bite me if I go in there?"

"Don't worry about it," Bib said. "After the schooling I gave him, he can't even bite his food."

"You sure? I happen to know the man is vicious when he's

angry. Have you made him rabid? If he's gone mad, I won't go in there."

"Don't worry about it. His teeth are so sore, he can't even bite his lip."

Kosterlinsky walked into the cell, leaving the door open. Ben felt reckless enough to feed Bib and the senator some chain and try to get out. He slouched against the wall and kept his head down. Kosterlinsky braced Roblez and Lopez against the wall.

Ben took a deep breath. He would take short choppy steps and move like a fool. Severiano rattled his broom against the bars, looked Ben straight in the eye, and shook his head. When Taylor turned to see why Severiano was making noise, he bumped the bars with the broom again, sweeping the floor between them.

Ben relaxed. Taylor had not seen the signal. The old fellow had risked a lot doing that. Bib had already made a track across Severiano's face with the hobnails when he thought he gave Ben a drink. He'd kill the old man for warning Ben.

Ben stood hipshot against the wall. He looked at the ceiling above Kosterlinsky's head. Bib, Kosterlinsky, and the senator were all watching him, *waiting* for him. Had they opened the doors to tempt him to escape? That was it. Ben's enemies were inviting him to run.

The senator would be a good witness when it was determined that Ben was killed trying to escape. What could justify Ben's attacking a senator, a jailer, and a representative of the Mexican government? How in the hell could Ben ever escape while dragging all the chains? They counted on him being desperate and gutsy enough. They wanted to kill him and save a trial. With men like A.B. on his side, Ben might be exonerated.

Ben slid down the wall and let his head rest against his doubled legs. He would not try it without his brothers. Sometime when he could have Les and Mark by his side, he would feed his tormentors the chain and break away.

He took himself back to Temporal Canyon and the yellow leaves by the cool stream. He lay on his stomach and drank. He raised his head and watched the droplets fall from the brim of his hat.

He heard chains bouncing and awakened to see the Mexicans jogging in place to Kosterlinsky's double-time cadence. He did not see the hobnailed boot until it struck him under the eye. His cheek gushed blood.

Bib kicked at his ribs, and Ben caught the foot, tangled it in his chains, and jerked Bib off his feet. Bib kept stomping him with his heels. Ben held on to the foot and regained his feet. He tried to do some stomping of his own, but his feet were chained only a foot and a half apart. Bib was much stronger and he put Ben back on the floor with a kick against the side of his knee.

Bib stood up and circled Ben, grinning. Ben was all kicked in. His reflexes were gone. He was too slow, his hands too broken, to defend himself. Bib feinted at his head. Ben ducked, and Bib came down with both fists on the back of his neck.

The next blow might have killed Ben, but it never landed. A. B. and Ben's brothers burst into the front office. The two Irishmen were there with loaded shotguns and orders to kill Ben when he came through, but they were intent on watching Bib finish him off. The Cowdens banged through the door with cocked weapons and surprised them.

A. B. held a paper in the face of an Irishman. "This is an order by Superior Court Judge M. O. Best, giving me the authority to move Ben Cowden. Where is he?"

The Irishman did not look at the paper. He was looking at A. B.'s six-shooter. He pointed into the cellblock. "He's in there, and he's in trouble. You better hurry."

Les charged past his father through the iron doors. He saw Bib Taylor hit Ben on the back of the neck. Senator Royal Vincent was in Les's path, so engrossed in supervising the end of Ben Cowden that he did not know the Cowdens were upon him.

Les rammed Senator Vincent in the small of the back with his head, bounced his face off the floor, and ran over the top of him. He charged through the cell door and met Kosterlinsky coming out. Kosterlinsky had decided to run for his life but did not know which way to go. Les leveled him with one wild look. The colonel threw himself down, covered his head with his arms, rolled onto his face, and did not look up until it was all over.

Les raised his rifle, crushed Bib Taylor's head, and left him spastic for the rest of his life. After that blow, Bib Taylor always cried when he tried to tell people how much he hated the Cowdens. No one ever felt sorry for him because no one could tell whether tears or slobbers were running down his chin. He always sounded like a calf bellering, anyway, whether he was weeping or asking to be helped to the outhouse.

Ben's heart rejoiced, and his head cleared more with every step he took out of that cell. He did not stop to see if he could help his cellmates. Roblez and Lopez were chained together and chained at the hands and feet, the same as Ben. They tried to follow, but A. B. stopped them at the door while one of the Irishmen handed over the key to Ben's chains.

"Take us with you, Ben," Billy Stiles said. He and George Smiley were sitting on a bench, looking like waifs begging for a home.

Ben did not have a thought for anyone but himself. He hurried out with his father and brothers, and mounted his horse. A. B. had reconfiscated Toots from the compound for Ben, and he mounted a big sorrel called Colonel. A. B. usually drove a rig wherever he went, but Ben figured he preferred Colonel that day because he was helping his son break jail.

A. B. did not hurry away from the jail but headed across the Rillito River toward town. Ben wanted to hurry into the Rincón Mountains, the nearest high ground, and be above the pursuit. Ben and his brothers knew those mountains well, and their deep-hearted horses would outrun any posse in the country.

"Where are we headed, Papa?" Ben asked. "Shouldn't we go east?"

A. B. did not look at Ben. "No, son I have to turn you over to Sheriff Perkins."

"You're not taking me to another jail, are you, Papa?"

"Yes, son, I am. The best way for us to fight is in the courts. A legal battle will end the war without the killing."

Ben followed along and tried to swallow. He almost fainted. He lost his sense of direction for a time, and Toots was herded along by his brothers' horses. He recovered and stopped his horse.

A. B. stopped Colonel. "Are you too hurt to ride?"

"No. I can ride, but I can't go with you."

A. B. waited.

"I'll never go inside another jail as long as I live."

"It's wrong for you to run, Ben."

"If it is, so be it. I'm not going back in a jail."

Mark was on the verge of tears. Les's face was flushed except for two tiny white patches twitching at the corners of his mouth.

"Papa, when you mounted Colonel, I thought you were going to run with me," Ben said. "Did you change your mind?"

"No, I rode Colonel to get around town easier when I was looking for you. I couldn't have crossed the Rillito in a rig."

"Oh, I thought we were all running together."

A. B.'s blue eyes were clear and unwavering as the sky. "Where will you go, son, so I can tell your mother?"

"I'll let you know, Papa. Don't worry."

"Well, I guess I don't blame you. I know you've been through a lot."

"Good-bye. I'm sorry."

"Good-bye, Ben."

Ben rode toward the Rincóns.

A. B. rode Colonel down the street. Mark and Les hurried to catch up with him.

"What do you think Mark and I ought to do, Papa?" Les said.

"You better stay with me. One outlaw in the family is enough." A. B. was rueful.

"Maybe I better go with Ben. I don't think he can ride far, beat up as he is. I'll be there to help him when he wears out and decides to turn back. He'll want to come back when he realizes how bad this makes you look as undersheriff. You'll be in a lot of trouble for letting him go, won't you?"

A. B. smiled underneath his great gray bushy mustache. "I won't be in any more trouble than my two deputies."

"Me and Les just better go and bring Ben back," Mark said.

"We can't do that, boys. He's flown the coop. We have to think of your mother and sisters."

"What shall we do next, Papa?" Mark asked.

"We better go by the office and give Sheriff Perkins our badges," A. B. said.

CHAPTER 9

Ben hurried Toots east through the saguaro forest toward the Rincóns. He and his brothers often helped Uncle Jim Porter catch wild horses and cattle there. He knew the trails and water holes, even some lion dens. Uncle Jim set his hounds on lions that killed cattle and set traps to catch mustang horses and ladino cattle when he worked the Rincóns.

Uncle Jim Porter was Viney's brother. He often changed countries and occupations. In those days in 1885, he was resting and recuperating from his wild side by working as telegraph operator in Harshaw.

Ben would have felt better if he could have come away with his hat. His brothers had returned him his horse, saddle, and slicker, but he had not recovered his hat and brush jacket. He headed for Red Tank, a water hole on the Tanque Verde ranch.

He was already home. He was as comfortable in the Rincón Mountains as he was in his father's house. He was mounted better on Toots than any lawman in the country ever hoped to be mounted in his life. The only horses in Tucson with a chance of catching him were being ridden by A. B. and his brothers, and they would not be coming after him, not even at the point of a gun.

Ben took stock of himself. He was bareheaded and wearing a torn shirt. He would sunburn on his forehead and on the places where his shirt did not protect him. His hands and fingers were broken, and he was bruised and cut from head to toe.

A handkerchief A. B. had given him to hold on the new cut on his cheek was soggy with blood. Paula Mary would never be able to wash it clean. A. B. gave Paula Mary a dime for washing his handkerchiefs because, he said, her hands made them fragrant.

Ben knew he could get away from Frank Marshall's beatings, the sheriff's pursuit, even the army, if he could gain some time to rest. He would never be caught because of being hungry, weak, thirsty, broken, or penniless. He might be caught because he was so tired that time seemed to stop between Toots's steps. He needed a safe place to stop, rid himself of his thirst, and rest. He needed corn for Toots.

He rode up a steep switchback trail off the desert floor and knew he was making a target. He stopped once to look for pursuit and then hurried on to climb that first hill. Once he was off the switchback, he would be out of sight of town. That part of the trail could be watched from the courthouse steps all the way downtown.

Ben topped the hill and saw the place where he would finally get his fill of water. The Red Tank was a round iron reservoir that caught spring water. Ben's hands and legs started trembling when he watered Toots in the spring and hobbled him by the tank. Clean fresh water would be dripping out of a pipe into the tank.

The spring was husky, and a healthy stream of water was pouring through the pipe. A tomato can with a wire handle was hanging on the pipe. Ben filled the can with deliciously clear water and slid down with his back against the cool shady side of the tank to drink it.

As he sipped, he stared at the outline of his cheeks on the surface of the water in the can. They looked full and fat and babyish, young cheeks in repose being given water again. They needed water every day of their life but had not been getting it.

Ben drank a can of water and made himself wait a moment before he stood up to get another. He heard horseshoes strike rock on the trail below the tank. He filled his can, sat down, sipped, and waited. The rider could not see Toots because of the tank, and he would not see Ben until he came around it for a drink.

The approaching horse nickered, and Toots raised his head. Toots was a nervous thoroughbred. Getting along as a cow horse kept him too occupied to worry about other horses.

He might look away at another horse when he ought to be looking at a cow, but he was never interested enough to nicker; he was not the kind who was always lonesome for other horses. A nickering horse could get a man killed.

He was intolerably flighty and dangerous on rocky trails because he scrambled and lunged when he crossed smooth rock. He never stood still. He would rather stamp his feet, chew his tongue, wiggle, and aggravate. He wasted his own energy and made Ben tired, but at least he was not lovelorn for other horses.

Toots raised his head, flared his nostrils, and nickered.

"Dammit, Toots," Ben said.

Toots shuffled out from behind the tank and began nodding hello to the other horse. The rider came around the tank. Ben knew him, a sometime sheriff's posseman named Bill March who also tried to work as a cowboy. Ben did not know how good a posseman he was or how serious he was about chasing criminals, but he would never in his life be a cowboy.

He couldn't be much of a posseman either. He was so busy appraising Toots, he did not notice Ben sitting underneath him almost close enough to bite him like a rattlesnake. His horse shied away to keep from stepping on Ben and showed the man Ben was there.

"Oh, howdy," he said. "I was admiring the animal so much, I didn't think to look for his rider."

Ben held the can in front of his face and sipped water, hoping he would not be recognized. This son of a gun had never seen him without his hat. His week's growth of beard and the lumps made by the hobnails and Black Beauty might disguise him, but the brand on his horse would mark him as a Cowden to any man in the country who knew good horses. He would never make it into the Rincóns without a witness now.

March still did not look at Ben. He must not think Ben amounted to much. Ben hoped the man was dumb about brands and horses too.

"Your horse?" March asked.

"Yes."

March looked at A. B.'s S-dot brand on Toots's hip. "Good-looking horse. Whose brand is that?" He did not wait for Ben to answer but went on circling and coveting old Toots.

He stopped in front of Ben, his face turned aside, studying the horse. "I . . . know . . . that brand."

Ben remained silent, waiting to see if the man would

recognize him and know about him breaking out of jail. March was riding a black horse branded with the TV of the Tanque Verde ranch. He dismounted and petted Toots's muzzle. His horse stretched his neck and sniffed at Toots's parts.

"Where'd you get him?" March asked. Ben offered him the drinking can. He refused it and took down a canteen to fill under the pipe. He walked behind Ben, so Ben stood up.

March looked at his face. "Hell, I know you, don't I?"

"I don't know you," Ben said.

"Sure. That horse is an S-dot. You're a Cowden, from Harshaw. How are you?" He offered his hand, and Ben shook it. "I should say what the hell happened to you, I guess. Damn, is that blood on you all yours?"

"Every drop."

"What happened?"

"I fell off the bed."

March did not hear him. "What's that? You fell off your horse? He's a tall one to fall off of, isn't he?"

Ben did not like anybody to think he would fall off his horse but decided to let March think so. It would be worth the shame of it if it helped him make it over the Rincóns without anybody coming after him. March was less likely to talk a lot about meeting somebody who fell off his horse than somebody who was beaten by his jailer.

"Are you all right now?" asked March. "Want to come down to headquarters and doctor up? I work on this outfit. I can lend you an old hat and a shirt. When did it happen?"

"Just happened. I'm headed for town. I'll reoutfit there."

"Well, listen, there's all kinds of old clothes laying around our bunkhouse. All kinds of sizes of fellers lands there from time to time, and some leave in too big a hurry to pack."

"Thanks, I'll be all right until I get to town."

"Say, I don't suppose you'd trade horses with me, would you?" March laughed at himself for asking the question.

"Aw, I wouldn't want to take advantage of you. This one wakes up in a new world every day."

"Don't blame me for asking. I thought there might be a chance you were mad enough at him to trade him off. Stranger things have happened."

"I've seen a lot of days I'd give him away."

"How'd he hurt you?"

"Stubbed his toe."

"Damn, he really mashed you, didn't he? What'd he do, hit you in the face with the top of his head?"

"That's where I got hit—right in the face, all right."

"Well, sir, I better get going. Cook'll have supper ready about the time I get in, and he's cranky as hell. I don't want to make him mad. You're welcome to come down for beef and beans."

"No, thanks. I'll drink some more water and be on my way."

March mounted his horse and rode out of sight around the tank. Ben stayed where he was until he heard him start down the switchback trail, then headed Toots up the trail toward Vaca Springs.

Toots covered the ground smoothly in a long, stretching thoroughbred walk. Ben reminded himself that he would probably push old Toots a lot in the next few weeks, but he did not need to feel sorry for him. He would just be getting even for all the times Toots had aggravated him by stamping his feet and fiddle-patting the ground when Ben needed him to stand still. Besides that, Toots loved to travel. He would love it if each new day put him in a whole new country.

On a high point on the trail above the Tanque Verde headquarters, Ben stopped to look for his pursuers. He saw only one horse lazing in the middle of the corral. Nobody was coming up the road from Tucson yet. The posse would stop at the ranch to ask if anybody had seen Ben. March would immediately forget trying to be a cowboy and turn into a posseman again so he could point the way to Ben like a bloodhound.

Ben went on, hungry as hell. He wished he'd eaten his food in jail. He had learned a lesson. A man had a responsibility to eat. He needed his strength to escape. A man should be what the cowpuncher called a "good doer," like a good horse. Food put a man to work when he needed to work. A horse that wouldn't eat couldn't work. Like Bill Knox said, "A man who doesn't eat can't fart. A fartin mule will never tire, and a fartin man's the man to hire."

Thunderheads had been piling up behind him and now closed over the mountain above him. He watched a rainsquall sweep down off Spud Rock on top of the mountain. The storm burst down the side of Spud in a torrent, full of lightning. The water it dropped would flash down the washes. Ben would have to be careful crossing them. A flash flood might gather him and return him to Marshall's jail.

The shaft of the squall turned white and descended toward him. He heard the sheets of hailstorm inside it and hid with his horse in a thicket of white oak as the storm swept over him. Toots's head was sheltered in the branches, but his butt was in the open. Ben ducked under his slicker and rested against the downwind side of the biggest tree trunk. Toots did a tap dance when the hail started bouncing off his rump. Ben's other horses would let him sit underneath them in a storm. Not old Toots. Toots would have treated him as bad as Bib Taylor, and he wasn't even mad at Ben.

Lightning sheared through the storm on all sides of the man and horse. The hail of ice passed over and swept downhill. Ben came out from under his slicker to watch the invincible lightning blasts douse on the slopes, barely scorching them.

After the storm, Ben felt strong again, as though cleansed and renewed by the rain and lightning. He would take rain and lightning anytime anyplace he could get it, and he knew better than complain about flood and firestorm, he knew the complaint of drouth so well.

The storm wasted the last of the light. The twilight was all that was left of the day. Toots's mane was washed and hanging kinky as a girl's, and his step was fresh again. Nearing Vaca Springs, just below the timberline, Ben passed the corn crop of a *ranchería*. The crop was fenced with piled oak and manzanita brush that had been cut when the field was cleared.

Before he reached the spring he shouted *"Huuuaaah!"* to announce his coming. His voice box hurt. His lower lip split when he opened his mouth to holler.

He did not dismount at the spring. He would not get off his horse unless someone welcomed him. A sturdy old ramada with forked oak *horcones*, the pillars that held up its roof, was still in the spot Ben remembered. He had not been here in two years, but he knew Casimiro the Yaqui would be working the ranchería if he was still alive.

"Casimirooo," Ben sang. *"Aquí tienes un amigo!* Your friend is here." He was grateful for the silence of the mountain. He did not have to shout to be heard. He was unable to shout or to enunciate his words.

"Ooh! Is it you? *Si es.* Yes, it is. It's Benjamin." The Indian stepped out of the brush. He was barefoot, carrying his rawhide huaraches in one hand and a long machete in the other. A naked child, a girl about seven, was with him. He took her hand, and they stepped across the rocks of the stream toward Ben.

"Get down, Benjamin. *Ay*, what an animal you're riding. He's of the *cría*, the offspring of the horses of your father?"

"Yes." Ben stepped down. The little girl's face and limbs were beautiful, her hair and eyes primal black. She hugged Casimiro's leg and peered around at Ben. Ben winked at her with his good eye, and she smiled a straight, white, happy smile.

"Well, look, this time I have a sample of my own stock to show you," Casimiro said. "This creature is my granddaughter."

Ben shook Casimiro's hand and offered his hand to the girl. She did not take it, but she was completely unafraid and only being coy.

Casimiro avoided staring at Ben's face. "I don't know how I recognized you. I knew the brand on the horse. Come on. I have all the herbs I need to cure you."

"You have a good crop of corn, Casimiro. I'm surprised. The rest of Arizona is in a drouth."

"*Sí, Benjamin*. This mountain caught rain on days when dust clouded Tucson's streets. Here, unsaddle under this tree, and I'll bring corn for your *bestia*, beast."

Ben watered Toots but left him saddled and hobbled under the oak. Casimiro gave the horse a basket of dried corn and a *manojo*, a bundle, of cornstalks. Then he brought out a jug of mescal to sip while he and Ben relaxed and watched Toots eat. Ben saw the child had put on a dress and was preparing supper at a fire under the ramada.

"Why don't you unsaddle the animal?" Casimiro asked.

"I won't stay long. I'm going over the *puerto*, the pass, tonight," Ben said.

"But why? The trail is washed slick. Wait until morning. Eat, rest through the night, and then go. What are you after—cattle, lions, horses, what? Did your horse fall on you?"

"Casimiro, I only want to remain free. I'm being pursued."

"But who is pursuing you? How can this be?"

"The law."

"Your father?"

"No, my father's enemies are in authority now. They held me *preso*, in the jail. My father helped me escape."

"Ah, then you're in full flight."

"Yes, and soon they'll know the direction I've taken. I was seen at the Red Tank by that Bill March. He knew the brand on my horse. He knows where to pick up my tracks, and he'll lead a posse here."

"Ah, well, I'll *desviar* them. I'll detour, dismay, and confuse them, and send them away shaking their heads."

"I want you to hide from them. They'll beat you for the fun of it. They like to hurt people."

"Ah, well, they're not coming right now. My Casimira is making supper. We'll wash your wounds and fill you with hot tortilla. That little girl's tortillas are mirrors of her face.

"Don't you have a hat? You left in a hurry, eh? Ah, how nice to talk to a friend. My little Casimira is beautiful and can do everything, but she does not talk. What do you think of the mescal I made? I think this *trago*, drink, is very much indicated for the renewal of our friendship, don't you?"

The braised ear of corn Casimira gave Ben was so sweet and juicy, it made Ben's teeth ache. She also gave him a barbecue of porcupine meat with potatoes, garlic, onions, and red chile. The meat fell off the bones when Ben picked them out of the *olla*, the pot. Ben had never eaten more tasty meat in his life.

Casimiro and Casimira cleansed Ben's wounds and applied *yerba del pasmo* paste to them, a good herb remedy. The touch of his friends was so comforting that Ben fell asleep before they finished doctoring him. They rolled him onto a mat of woven beargrass and covered him with a goat-hair blanket.

Ben heard his friend say his name. Casimiro was squatting nearby in the firelight. He spoke softly. "I think your pursuers know where you are, Benjamin."

"Are they close?"

"No, but they've lighted a bonfire at the Tanque Verde ranch. I never saw that before. Your enemies are probably grouping there to come after you."

"Well, I have a good head start. If I go now, they'll never catch me. I'll top out on Cowshead Pass in an hour. After that, I'll have it all downhill."

"We've prepared your provision." Casimiro handed Ben a hat of woven beargrass. "My little creature fitted it to your head and made it while you slept, and you never knew it."

The hat was still wet from the weaving and fit comfortably on Ben's brow. The ends made a fringe around the brim, but the hat was tightly woven and would shed water and cool his head in the sun.

Ben liked his hat, and he thanked the girl and shook her hand.

Casimiro handed him a morral. "In here you have food and medicine for yourself and your horse." He made a bedroll of the blanket and mat. "Take this for your *cama de piedras*, bed of rocks. Throw it away when you find a good one." Then he handed Ben a *bule*, a gourd that held a half-gallon of water, slung in a rawhide net and stoppered with a corncob.

Ben was in such a weakened state, he began to weep. Casimiro quickly covered his shoulders with a blanket. "I'm sorry," he said. "I know your emotion. Sometimes a man can endure hardship better if he has no comfort at all."

Ben tightened Toots's cinches and shook Casimiro's hand.

"One more thing." Casimiro handed Ben a large packet wrapped in a wide, tough green leaf and tied with stems of the same leaf. "Here is tobacco. This is my own *macuzi*—grown here, dried here, and ground by my little creature. Inside the packet you have *hiesca*, oak punk, for starting fires, a shard of flint, a knife I made from an old file, and a thick sliver of pitch pine for a *tizón* to make flame. You know how to strike the back of the knife to the flint so the sparks will light the hiesca, don't you? You'll have fire this way. You also have dry corn leaf for making *cigarros*."

Ben reached down and shook the old man's hand again.

"*Que Dios te bendiga*. God bless you and your family," Casimiro said.

"God bless you," Ben said. He headed Toots up the dark trail through pine forest toward Puerto Cabeza de Vaca, Cowshead Pass. The smell of pine was fresh after the rain. The trail was dark enough to distract him from his feelings for a while until a nearly full moon rose on his side of the mountain to help him. After a while, he saw the posse's bonfire at the Tanque Verde ranch.

He was in a bad war, but he was not losing anymore. He was coming back. Vincent had managed to cut him off from his family, but he was free in the country and riding a good horse. No man could hurt him until he was ready to do battle again.

The afternoon Ben had stopped to drink beer with his brothers at Los Parados was the first time in many months he relaxed. He was only twenty-one, the age when most men were learning how to have a good time. Lately, Ben had known nothing but work and worry.

He never complained about work. His work gave him a lot of fun, and he would not trade it for all the good-time fellowship in the country, but now that he was cut off from his work and his folks, he had to find a way to be happy again. A man needed to laugh once in a while. He hoped the fun of being a young man in the country—courting, dancing, and drinking beer with his brothers and friends—was not over.

He was not going to run away like a whipped dog. He would hide himself, stay in the country, and do as he pleased. The first thing he wanted to do after he got away and found a safe place to rest, was win a horse race. Months ago, he had agreed to match Prim Pete against a horse owned by a cattleman in Tombstone. He wanted to win that race.

He wanted to renew his life. He did not like it that he'd worked all his life only to be gathered in by Vincent and kicked down so low that he had to take an old Indian's tortillas to survive.

He stopped Toots on Cowshead Pass to let him blow. The horse barely took a long breath after that hour's climb. Marshall would never catch him now. He could rest a few hours. Marshall would have to recruit a hundred men to corner him, now that he'd gained the pass. He could run downhill and outdistance any posse in any direction he wished.

He left the trail and rode along Cowshead Ridge southwest. The ridge dominated the country and gave him several miles of easy traveling on high ground while his pursuit rested through the night. The posse faced a four-hour climb to Cowshead Pass tomorrow. The tender-assed little townsmen better get up early.

Ben rode an hour on an easy, gradual climb to the highest point on the ridge. He hobbled and unsaddled Toots, and gave him his morral with a measure of corn. He spread his saddle blankets and grass mat on the ground for a pallet, used the inside of his saddle for a pillow, covered himself with Don Casimiro's blanket, and lay down.

He was free in the country for good. The sky had cleared, and he could see a million miles of other worlds shining at him. He settled into a deep sleep.

He dreamed Maudy was smiling in his face, her breath on his cheek. Her eyes were laughing because she'd tricked him into loving her, but he was laughing about that too. Her eyes said, "Be careful of my next trick. It might be so much fun, you can't stand it." She gave him a portion of love every time he looked at her. She put his hand on her bare arm, led him off his bed of rocks, and said, "Now you come right over here and sit down with me. I have us some hot tea." He walked by her side, her hair warm and fragrant with sunlight.

Birds were singing their hearts out, and horses were moving, and he knew it was too late to be sleeping, but he could not rouse himself. He wanted to be back in his dream, but flies buzzed at his face. The sun was drawing the chilly wetness out of the ground.

He sat up, wide awake and alarmed. Horses were near. Toots was gone. He whirled and stood up. Toots had only moved a few steps so he could see off the ridge and was looking toward the sound of the horses.

Ben thought. Don't go crazy. They don't know you're here, or they wouldn't be making noise. Be careful, be deliberate. Saddle your horse, roll your bed, get moving, and don't fumble.

He bridled Toots, saddled him, and pulled the slack out of his cinches. Toots was "cinchy"; he could not be hurried in the morning. Ben could not cinch him up tight and climb right on without having a wreck. He turned him around and led him a few steps, then cinched him tight enough so his saddle would not slip when he mounted. He would have to ride him awhile before he could cinch him up tight. If he baled him up and squeezed him off with the cinch, Toots would think he was being cut in two and throw himself over backward.

Ben listened to the horses move up the mountain. He tied the blanket roll behind his saddle, pulled down his beargrass hat. "*Nombre sea de Dios.* In the name of God," he said and mounted.

Toots moved eagerly out from under the tree. Ben could not see the horses. He rode down the opposite crest of the ridge from the horses, toward a gap where he figured they would climb out and cross the ridge. They would want to stop for air when they topped out.

If Ben was going to run, he wanted to know what he was running from. He hid near the gap and tightened his girth cinches to the last hole. Now he was ready for any race any posse wanted to run.

The leaders of the horses reached the gap and stopped, and

Ben moved to get a look at them. The horses, a band of mustangs, were standing still as statues on the skyline, watching something down the mountain. They heard him, saw him, and ran. They did not run back the way they had come though. Someone bigger than Ben was behind them because they ducked their heads and ran toward him, then veered past him through the gap and down the side of the mountain.

Ben wondered why the mustangs had not turned back when they saw him. He rode to the gap and looked down the other side. A deep canyon ran from the gap to the desert floor. Ten riders were coming alongside the canyon toward Ben. The posse was still at least five miles down the mountain and had not started up the steep hard climb to the top of the ridge. It would take them three hours to reach this spot.

As Ben started to follow the mustangs' tracks off the mountain to hide his own, a big ladino steer came through the gap, running from the posse. He took one wild look at Ben, bulled his neck, lowered his head, and hooked at Toots with his horns. Toots shied out of his way, and he lunged off his front feet, hooking the air. Still on the fly, he threw a number nine in his tail and skittered down through the jack pine after the horses.

Ben laughed at him. He knew he was on the right trail now; he was in among the wildest of the wild mustangs and ladinos escaping the Tucson posse. Now, if he could turn into a complete ladino like that red-and-whited-spotted steer and keep his horns sharp, he would stay free. Stock became ladino after they were taught by men that men were bad. A ladino always kept an eye out for men and stayed away from them or hooked them down and ran right over them when they got in the way.

CHAPTER 10

Ben rode south out of the Rincóns onto the McClintock range. McClintock was overpopulating the country with thousands of steers. His big business was causing a hardship for his neighbors, Mexican families that ranched in the country along Pantano Wash. Their mother cows were starving for feed and water because the more active steers were beating them to it. Ben had not seen many native cows when he was high in the Rincóns, but he saw that plenty of McClintock's steers branded *Mc* had thrown in with the ladinos. Those cattle would be hard to gather in the fall.

Ben crossed the El Paso–Tucson railroad track by the broad, sandy Pantano Wash. A narrow stream of muddy water was running in the wash beside dangerous bogs of quicksand. He rode along the bank, looking for a firm place to cross. He rode inside a thicket and found a stock trail that descended into the wash. An old cow belonging to his friend Federico Escalante was stuck in quicksand in the middle of the wash below the thicket. She was buried up to her brisket in front, and her hind quarters were bogged clear to her tailbone.

Lice and swarms of files were picking her bare, and her hide was in tatters. She had been in the bog a long time; sand was dry on her back, and her tail had swept a deep swath in the sand behind her. She did not have much future.

The cow was still alert enough to roll an eye at Ben. She was going mad. Her eye showed pure hate. She menaced Ben weakly with her broad horns and lowed angrily because she could not reach him. She was dying of thirst. Her muzzle was in mud, but she could not drink. She was bogged down three feet short of the running water, her nose dry and cracking, her nostrils full of dried mud. She opened her mouth to bellow, and her saliva was gummy, drying. Well, Ben knew how *that* was.

He rode Toots as close to her as he could without bogging Toots, cast a loop over her head, and fished until he closed it around her horns. He rode back to firmer ground, wrapped the tail of his reata around his saddle horn, and started Toots. The bog made a sucking noise that sounded as though it was trying to keep her with its last breath. Then her limbs slid out, she rolled over on her side, and Toots sledded her easily away from the bog.

Ben dragged the cow to dry ground and rode back to her. He reached down past his stirrup and took his loop off her horns. Her eye looked so mean, he preferred to be on his horse when she got up.

She did not try to get up. Her eyes rolled back in her head. When Ben tugged his loop off her horns, her head slumped back limply. She did not seem to be breathing.

He knew better, but he was afraid the new violence he had done to her by stretching her out of the bog might have taken the last of her energy. He did not see how he could help her or revive her if he stayed on his horse. He wanted to get her up on her feet before he left.

He dismounted and held his horse beside her. He kicked a horn and rattled her head against the sand, and saw she was at least breathing, but she did not show him even an eyeball. He picked up the lousy tail, twisted it, and let it fall. She would not try to help him. He left his horse, walked out of the wash to a creosote bush, and broke off two short, smooth sticks. He walked back to the cow, stood on the bush of her tail, placed a stick on each side of it, squeezed the ends of the sticks together on the tail, and began rubbing them up and down along her tail briskly enough to start a fire.

The fire began as a spark in the eyes. The orbs came back into focus and turned red. She reassembled her soggy, rickety remains, bellowed, and came rambling to her feet. She turned to put out the fire, saw Ben Cowden, lowered her horns, and charged.

Ben laughed and ran to lead the old sister away from his horse. He took the trail up the bank, hoping she was too weak to follow. She stumbled and went down to her knees when she tried the bank, regained her feet quickly, but stopped there. Now she stood between Ben and his horse.

Ben laughed while he got his breath back. He gloried in the way he could move without Marshall's chains. He burst clods off the cow's head to make her go on about her business. She shook her horns, turned away from the bombardment, and saw Toots obediently standing ground hitched where Ben had left him.

Toots knew enough about mad old cows to watch her. When she fixed on him, his eyes widened, and he began to lose his sense of discipline. He did not feel so securely hitched to the reins on the ground.

The cow menaced him with her horns, lowed angrily, and pawed the ground to show she meant business—weak, soggy, and lousy as she was. Ben threw clods at her to distract her from his horse. He sure did not want her to hook Toots or run him into the quicksand. She shook her head, lifted her tail like a scorpion, thrashed it about, squirted manure at Ben, and would not be distracted.

Toots began to tremble and braced way back on his hind legs but did not leave his ground hitch. The cow tired of her bluff, tossed her head once more, turned, and trotted jerkily away, forgetting about Ben and his horse.

Ben was coiling his reata when he heard the train coming from Tucson. He forded the wash and hurried away to hide. His pursuers might look down to watch the train and see him. He dismounted, smoked his tobacco in corn leaf, and watched the train go by.

He rode up the bottom of Davidson Canyon for an hour to keep out of sight. He emerged at the Tucson–Tombstone road and saw a rig coming, loaded with people. He hoped the people were friendly, but they were too far from town to be a threat to him. By the time they reached someplace where they could report Ben, he could be in Mexico.

Ben stopped Toots at the side of the road to wait for the wagon. The driver glanced at Ben's beargrass hat and his torn and blood-spattered shirt, and almost drove on, but then he looked into Toot's brand and recognized him, hollered to stop his team, threw up his hands, and said, "My God, it's Ben Cowden. We're being held up. Dammit to hell."

The driver was Red Shepherd, a Tucson liveryman. The expressions of the townsmen told Ben they'd heard he'd become a desperate character. He was reminded of the way he must look to them. He grinned at the townsmen, and they threw up their hands too. The passenger beside the driver reached for the sky so violently he knocked the driver's hat off. It tumbled over the dash and made the horses dance as they kicked it back and forth between their feet.

"Wait a minute," Ben said, laughing. He was forced to speak softly because his voice hurt his throat. Besides that, his lips were so swollen, his jaws so sore, he was unable to enunciate. "Put 'em down. I'm not armed. Nobody's going to hurt you." He stopped talking to recover from the pain it gave him.

"What did he say?" one of the townsmen in the back asked. "Did he say to get on with it? What does he mean?"

"I think he said he was armed, but didn't want to hurt us," the other townsmen in the back said. "Did he order us to get down?"

Ben was puzzled. The townsmen were talking to each other out of the corners of their mouths and staring at him, their hands in the air. He glanced behind him to see if someone else was holding a gun on them.

The driver had thrown his lines down in front of the dash, and the ends were on the ground under the team. The hat was making the team nervous. Ben took hold of the lead shank of one of the horses to keep them from running.

"Get down," he ordered the driver. "Pick up your lines."

"For God's sake, don't shoot," the driver said. "This team'll run at the sound of a gun."

"How'm I gonna shoot you?" Ben asked, exasperated. "I haven't even got a gun. Get down and pick up your damned lines."

"My God, if we make him draw his gun, he's gonna *shoot* us," said a townsman.

"Is *that* what he said?" another townsman said.

"All right, all right," said the driver. "We're getting down."

Ben did not know it, but Red Shepherd was half deaf. He often drove for his customers. His passengers looked to him for leadership. They were sure Ben was a road agent, and they did not need to understand every word he said to comply with what they were sure he wanted. They were not going to rile him by asking, "Huh, what did you say?" They wanted to be very, very sure they did not try his patience.

"I don't have a gun," Ben said, trying to put the travelers at ease, once and for all.

"All right, all right." Red picked a rifle off the floorboard and tossed it down on the road in front of Toots, stepped down from the wagon, and retrieved his lines.

Ben shook his head and picked up the rifle without dismounting. He was careful not to point it at the townsmen. He waved the barrel back and forth, as though giving a command. All three passengers reached inside their coats and showed brand-new pistols, cartridge belts, and holsters. They unbuckled them and threw them down beside the wagon.

Ben waggled the barrel again, and the men threw their carpetbags down on the ground beside the pistols and belts. A worn gladstone bag with fancy saddle carving on it and a Mexican sombrero remained at their feet. Ben kept hearing a sound like a rifle cocking over and over. He searched for the source and discovered it was being made by Red Shepherd's chattering teeth.

"Why are your teeth chattering so loud, Red?" he shouted, so Red could understand him.

Ben and his father and brothers had used Red's livery barn when the man first came to Tucson but quit patronizing him when they suspected him of cheating on the amount of hay and grain he said he gave their horses. They also suspected him of spreading lies about the quality of the Cowden horses and diverting clients that were headed the Cowdens' way.

"J-just a little n-nervous, B-Ben," he said. "Th-that's all."

"What's the matter, don't you like me anymore, Red?" Ben's talking mechanism was working better.

"L-like you plenty, Ben."

"I guess you don't, Red. You didn't even say hello."

"H-hel-lo, Ben."

"You were so busy nominating me for a road agency, you forgot to say hello, didn't you?"

"Yes, B-Ben."

"You felt you had to remind me of my business in case I forgot who I was, didn't you?"

"Yes, B-Ben." Red was almost blubbering, he was so sad that he was being held up.

"Well, you better relax. You're doing fine. You've made me a present of your weapons. Are you going to give me your money too?"

"I s-sure w-wouldn't refuse you anything, B-Ben."

"Well, if you don't mind making me a gift of some of your

money, I'll take it, but only if you promise to let me pay it back."

"Y-you don't have to pay it back, B-Ben. Don't even m-mention it. Don't even *think* of paying it b-back."

Ben rode closer and looked into the wagon. The Mexican sombrero was like the one Kosterlinsky wore. It was light tan and made of good felt. "What's this in the wagon? Glory, glory, would you look at that?"

"That's a Mexican hat," said one of the townsmen.

"I see it is," said Ben. "Where did you get it?"

"Red's taking it to somebody in Tombstone."

Ben leaned down from the saddle, picked up the hat, and tried it on. It fit perfectly. "I wonder if you'll loan me this hat too," he said.

Red was in better control of his teeth now, but his lips stuck together between his words. "Of course, B-Ben. I don't think anybody'll m-mind."

"I sure need a hat." Ben handed the hat to Red. "Put the money you're lending me in it if you want to. Count it, and I'll give you a receipt."

Red took a handful of bills out of his wallet and dropped them in the hat. "There's a little over three hundred dollars in there," he said without stuttering at all.

"Take it out and count it for me," Ben said.

Red counted it and put it back. "Three hundred and sixty dollars."

The passengers stepped forward with handfuls of bills and coins for the hat. Ben borrowed paper and pencil from Red and made out and signed IOUs for the money in the hat.

"My lord, where were you taking all that money?" Ben asked. "Don't you know it's dangerous to carry that much cash? A real road agent might have come along and killed you for it."

"We're headed for the horse race in Tombstone," said Red. "That money is our stakes in the race."

"What horse are you betting on?"

"McClintock's horse."

"Well, this is just right, then. I'll take your bet right here, and if Prim Pete wins, I won't owe you anything. How's that?"

"That's fine, Ben. Anything you say. You don't have to pay it back if you lose, either."

"Then I can't lose at all, can I?" Ben said.

"Gosh, no. We're only glad you're so good-natured about it all."

"Well, hold on to that IOU. If Prim Pete loses, I'll send your winnings." He looked at the clothes on the townsmen. Not one of them was his size. "What's in the gladstone."

A townsman opened the bag and showed Ben a supply of men's clothes. "That's fine," Ben said. "Hand it up here. I'll borrow that too." He hung it on his saddle horn by the grips. "Hand me those pistols and belts too."

He strapped two belts around his waist and one across his chest. He dropped his beargrass hat on the ground, put on the sombrero, and adjusted the chin strap.

"Can I have this?" Red Shepherd asked, picking up the beargrass hat.

"Sure," Ben said.

"I want to save it for my grandchildren, now that I know I'll live to see them."

"Show them an honest ledger and quit chiseling at your livery, and you might live to see them," Ben said. "Got any water?"

"Yes, we do," said one of the townsmen. "Want some?"

Ben handed down his *bule* for him to fill. When that was done and the gourd was hanging on his shoulder, he said, "I guess you fellers ought to be on your way."

Red and his townsmen climbed back into the wagon.

"Get going," Ben said. "Have a good trip."

When the wagon was out of sight, he threw away his old shirt and put on a nice linen shirt he found in the bag. He rode onto the Empire range and headed for the Whetstones. He stopped in the middle of Empirita Wash and watered Toots. The stream surfaced out of bedrock and ran a quarter mile across the sand before it sank out of sight in the sun. Nothing grew beside that stretch of the hot little stream. It ran flat and shallow under the sun and over the bleached rock and sand, magnifying the rock and staying wet enough only to keep Toots alive and replenish Ben's bule. In the bule it would cool and become a real drink.

Ben climbed out of the wash to a high point and looked back. His pursuers were hours behind him. His tracks were plain where he had pulled the cow out of the bog, but they would have to track him all the time now, and they would never catch him by tracking him. The Rincón Mountains had channeled him down a certain trail for a while, but nothing was channeling him now.

At sundown, he struck for high ground on the Whetstones.

The posse would stop in the foothills and would not try to follow him after dark. They could not see his tracks without torches. He did not stay on a main trail, often changing direction away from his pursuers. He stayed high so they would know he could ambush them any time. With these tactics and by taking to the mountains every night, he would leave them so far behind he would have time to hide his tracks.

With the last light of day, Ben stopped on a mountain and dismounted to examine his back trail. He knew these mountains too. The Cowden brothers worked cattle from the Santa Catalinas north of Tucson to the Sierra Madre east of Magdalena, Sonora in the south; from the Baboquivaris in the west to these Whetstones and the Huachucas in the east.

He watched the smoke rise from the posse's cookfire. He wondered if Marshall was with them. He bet he was not. Marshall was a tenderfoot with a delicate ass. He worked best over drinks and cigars with the politicians and knew how big a target he would be in an ambush. He was not dangerous unless he could wield Black Beauty or charm a politician.

Ben wanted to lure him to a battleground where he would have to be horseback. He wanted to have the advantage next time he faced Marshall. He would keep doubling back until he caught Marshall at a disadvantage. If Marshall kept sending posses, Ben would keep running up behind them to see if he joined them. The thing to do was to let the posses think they were closing on Ben from time to time. Make them think they were about to catch the jaguar and count his spots. Then Marshall might come arunning.

Ben rode all night. When the posse got on his trail the next morning, it would never know from one hour to the next whether he was waiting in ambush, headed east, headed west, or headed south.

At dawn, Ben rode into the yard of his uncle Billy Porter's house on the Babocomari ranch. Toots was showing fatigue. If he was not broke of his pattyfooting now, he would never be.

Ben stopped Toots in the middle of the yard and said, "*Buenos días, Tío* Beely." Uncle Billy opened the front door and looked closely at Ben's face under the Mexican hat before he recognized him. He motioned Ben to ride around the house to the corrals, then went back inside.

Ben unsaddled Toots at the saddlehouse. The horse's belly was gone, but he had never weakened. Maybe now he would learn to keep that belly full and those feet still.

When Uncle Billy joined Ben, he was carrying his rifle, but his pipe was lit. "Your horse looks like a gutted snowbird," he said. "I've had my eye on that colt since you first broke him, but I've never liked his snake belly. He's got no barrel. I wonder if he's ever going to fill out so your saddle will stay on."

Ben wondered if Uncle Billy knew he was an escaped jailbird.

"He looks bad, all right, but he's seen a lot of country since last Sunday," Ben said.

"I know how much country he's seen. Your uncle Jim came by. He said you'd made a trip to Tucson under government escort. Looks like you had a little trouble convincing them they were holding the wrong man. You don't look too good, but at least you're still grinning."

"I might be grinning, Uncle Billy, but I'm sure not happy."

"Well, I can imagine you're not."

Ben put away his saddle and came out of the saddlehouse with the pistols, the rifle, and the gladstone. Uncle Billy looked at the weapons and shook his head. "You look like a Mexican mutineer, but I guess you've become kind of a mutineer."

"I guess I have, Uncle Billy." Ben opened the gladstone.

"Come on to the house. Your boy cousins are wrangling horses, but your girl cousins are fixing breakfast, and your aunt Mary's waiting to give you a hug."

"I want to clean up before I go in the house." Ben reached in the gladstone and pulled out clean socks and underwear, a pair of gabardine trousers, a linen shirt, and a short, tight waist-length brush jacket of *gamuza*, a tough, suedelike calf leather.

The trousers were reinforced for a horseman with gamuza sewn on the inside of the thighs and the seat. The duds were sturdy, made for a man who lived horseback. He found his cousins' bathtub and soap, and went to the horse-trough with a bucket.

"You're going to bathe?" Uncle Billy said.

"Yessir, I don't want Aunt Mary to think I've become too evil to wash."

Uncle Billy's family was the same size as A. B. Cowden's. Uncle Billy was brother to Viney Cowden. His three boys were the same age as Ben and his brothers, his three girls the same age as Eileen, Betty, and Paula Mary. Aunt Mary Porter was A. B.'s sister, so she was Ben's blood aunt as Uncle Billy was his blood uncle. The boys, Ahira, Joe, and Will, were out gathering their remuda of horses that would be used in the general roundup of the country that would begin the seventeenth of September.

Ben walked through Aunt Mary Porter's kitchen door dressed as a Mexican charro, the clothes fit him as though tailored for him. His relatives looked at him as though he was a stranger. He had not shaved his mustache, but had trimmed it so it hung in a thick inverted V down both sides of his mouth. He ducked his head when he came through the back door and smiled shyly at the looks on the faces of his relatives.

"Well, say hello to your nephew from Sonora, Aunt Mary," Ben said.

"Oh, Black Man," said Aunt Mary, using her nickname for him and hugging him. She had called him that since the summer he spent with the Porters when he was eight. His cousins were all blond and freckle-faced, but Ben's hair was coal-black, and the sun turned him dark as the heart of mesquite.

Aunt Mary and the girls all went to work serving Ben his breakfast. No one said anything about his arrest or asked him about his treatment in jail. They could see the scars of the beatings, see by the way he moved and the anxious look in his eye, that he had been imprisoned and hurt and now would never allow himself to be caught again. They could see he had dodged blows that could have caused his death, and they said to themselves, Woe to the sonofabitch who chained and beat Ben Cowden.

The Porters and Cowdens were frontier people who knew about cruelty. They did not use beatings in their dealings with men or animals but were capable of hurting bullies who lived by intimidating people with threats and beatings. They were sorry Ben had been beaten because they knew it sullied his goodness in a way that only a beating could. They did not pity him though. They pitied the sonsabitches who had beaten him. They knew Ben, or the Porters, would someday take a double of a rope to them.

Ben ate his breakfast, took himself into his cousin Melvina's bedroom, and collapsed on the bed. The girls pulled off his boots and covered him with a blanket, but he did not know it.

He did not awaken until late afternoon when he heard his brothers ride in with their remuda for the general roundup. He heard their shout and for a moment thought he was home.

He sat up, completely disoriented. Even his clothes were strange to him. He walked out to the back porch and drank a dipperful of water from the olla, the clay pot, hanging in a rope cradle under the roof. Here, a small breeze always blew, and the olla was always in shade. The water saturated the earthen pot and cooled by evaporation.

Les and Mark were talking to his aunt and cousins in front of the house. He went back into Melvina's bedroom and strapped on one of the new pistols. He walked out the front door. His brothers glanced at him when he appeared, but neither recognized him. He could see them dismiss him as some visitor from Sonora they did not know.

Ben pulled down the brim of the sombrero and walked to his brothers. "*Hola, hermanos Cueva de Vaca*. Hello, the brothers Cow Den," he said. The setting sun was at his back. Les and Mark were completely fooled; they could not place him. Ben stopped between their horses and let them see only the top of his hat while he shook hands with them.

Les was acting friendly because he figured he should know this man. Mark was a quiet boy who always kept his own counsel and did not care if he remembered everyone he met. He shook Ben's hand and looked from Ben's hat back at his horse's ears, waiting for Ben to get on out of the way so he could listen to his Aunt Mary.

The girls saw that Les and Mark did not know Ben from Porfirio Diaz, president of Mexico, and started giggling. Ben headed toward the barn, turning back once to smile at the girls.

He caught a fresh saddle horse and a packhorse out of the Cowden remuda. He was leading them out of the corral to saddle them when his brothers caught up. Mark opened the gate for him. Les took one of the horses from him and led him through the gate. When the horses were tied at the saddle-house, the brothers embraced Ben.

"Boy, you sure fooled us. I never would have guessed that big Mexican who came out of the house was you," Les said.

Mark remained silent and studied Ben. Ben did not pause. He was leaving. He began saddling the packhorse.

"Where are we going?" asked Les. "Mark and I were fixing to find a place to unroll our beds, but we want to go with you."

"One of you can go to Aunt Mary's pantry and bring me a stock of chuck if you want to," Ben said.

"I'll go," said Mark. "How much chuck do you want?"

"About a week's provision," Ben said.

"For the three of us?" asked Mark.

"No, Mark. Only for me."

"We're going with you, aren't we?" asked Les.

"No, brother. Why would I want you to do that?"

"Mama wants us to be together."

"Not this time," Ben said. "I've got a pack of townsmen on my tail."

"What about Prim Pete's race? You have to be there, don't you?"

"Of course, brother. I broke jail to run that race. Why do you think I wouldn't let Papa take me to that other jail?"

"Well, can't we stay together until after the race?"

"That would be a lot better, wouldn't it?"

"Shall I bring enough chuck for the three of us, then?" Mark asked.

"All right," said Ben.

"I'll catch fresh horses for me and Mark," Les said. While he fussed around with the horses, he kept his eye on Ben. Finally he asked, "Was that really the reason you wouldn't let Papa take you to the county jail?"

"What other reason could a man have?" Ben asked.

Les was peeved. "You refused to go with Papa just so you could see your horse run a race?"

"Why sure, brother. A horse race is one of life's main events. What the hell fun would life be if we weren't even allowed to run a horse race?"

CHAPTER 11

The Cowden brothers headed toward the Whetstones. Ben was riding a brown horse, a top horse he called Star. He stayed behind his brothers and led the packhorse.

At dusk, the brothers saw the posse's campfire. Marshall's men were making an early camp. The brothers rode toward the fire and overtook a cowboy on his horse, dragging part of a dead oak tree with his rope. Les and Mark rode ahead to talk to him. The cowboy looked back when he became aware of them, and Ben was surprised to see he was George Smiley.

"Dragging in some firewood?" Les asked.

"You bet."

"Can we help?"

"Naw. I'm only dragging it to that swale over yonder."

"We'll ride with you."

"Sure, come on."

"We're the Cowden brothers from Harshaw."

"I know it. I'm George Smiley. I saw you when you went in the Rillito jailhouse for your brother."

Ben watched Smiley for menace, defiance, or antagonism and saw none.

"I didn't see you," Les said.

"You looked right at me. Me and my partner were sitting in the office."

"I remember now. You asked us to take you with us. Hell, you got away on your own, didn't you?"

"No, we weren't in jail. We were only visiting. We never

let out a peep. You fellers looked like you meant business."
George Smiley kept smiling.

Ben knew Smiley and Stiles had asked to go out with him
and knew why Smiley was denying it now. They worked for
Marshall and had been in jail to spy on Ben.

"I thought I heard you ask Ben to take you with him," Les
said. He knew damned well Smiley was lying. He remembered what he remembered. Smiley might as well know he
was not a fool.

"No. Say, which one of you caved in Bib Taylor's head?"

"Caved in his head? I just conked him with my rifle."

"You stove his head in. He's not expected to live."

Les was taken aback. "Oh, he'll be all right, won't he?"

"No he won't. He's in a coma. The doctor picked slivers of
bone out of his brain."

"I wonder how that happened," Les said. "I didn't think I
conked him hard enough to break an eggshell. I only wanted
to stop him from putting his boots to my brother."

"Oh, don't get me wrong. He deserved what he got. He
stomped his hobnails on Ben's head three or four times a day.
Now, he's paying for it. He's nothing but a vegetable and may
never come to."

Les and Mark fell in beside Smiley, their horses eyeing the
tree as it scraped along behind them. Ben stayed back.

Smiley turned in his saddle and looked at Ben. "Who's this
riding with you?" he asked.

"Aw, that's only Juan Valdez," Les said. "He's about as
much company as a fence-post."

Smiley turned again as though to watch the dragging tree,
but he kept trying for a look at Ben's face. Ben hid under the
brim of the sombrero. Smiley was being more than curious. In
that country, a man did not stare long at another man unless he
was looking for a fight. Ben adjusted his pistol belt, and Smiley
faced quickly to the front.

"Big for a Mexican," Smiley said. "How many of you
Cowdens are there?"

"Just three."

"That one back there's kinda *corriente,* kinda common-
looking, but he's big enough and has the shoulders to be a
Cowden."

"Big and dumb," said Les. "Can't get two words out of him
all day."

Mark smiled back at Ben as they rode into the swale where

the posse was camped. Ben recognized the posse horses he'd been watching on his back trail picketed in a juniper thicket on the edge of the camp.

Billy Stiles stepped forward to shake hands with Les and Mark. Ben rode past his brothers and stood away with his back to the camp and well out of reach of handshakes. He was a Mexican, did not speak English, and was probably not welcome anyway.

The Irishmen, John Maher and Dave Langley, shook hands with Les and Mark as though they were old friends. They had met in a saloon in Tucson when Ben was in jail. Bill March, of the Tanque Verde ranch, was the only other man Ben knew. The other five were townsmen. Nobody bothered with Ben. No Anglo cowboy would be caught dead in a Mexican's clothes in that country, so the posse would never in a hundred years believe Ben would dress like a Mexican rural. Ben's mustache was also *puro Mexicano*.

Then George Smiley announced to the posse, "Well, fellers, I didn't bring you the jailbird himself, but I brought you the two Cowdens who let him go." Ben made ready to fight.

Les flushed, but he kept his head. "You're damned right we let our brother go. We had to. Our own father couldn't hold him. Our order from Judge Best gave us the authority to take him to the county jail, but he broke away from us."

"He wouldn't have fought his own brothers if they'd tried to hold him," Stiles said. With the posse at his back, he figured he could talk big and bully the Cowdens.

Les would not argue with any man. "We'd have had to kill him to stop him. I wouldn't kill my brother for any sonofabitch. What's it to you? Are you the law?"

Stiles saw he was in danger of being called a sonofabitch and tired as he was, backed down. "No, don't get riled. We're just interested."

"Well, get uninterested," John Maher said. "Why question the man about his brother? That's the sheriff's business, not ours."

"You're the posse chasing our brother, aren't you?" Les said.

Stiles also saw he better not admit he was trying to hound Ben Cowden. "Hell, no. What makes you think that? We're rangers working for the Pima County Live Stock Association. We're here to represent the association in the general roundup." The rest of the posse kept still, waiting to see if Les believed Stiles.

"I heard the Live Stock Association's 'rangers' are deputized," Les said. "Is that right?"

Most of the rest of the posse was made up of young men under twenty-one, townsmen who were finding they were out of their element. Every one of them probably thought he was a good hand with a gun in town, but this pursuit of a native through his own mountains had already worn them out.

Ben felt a hundred years older than the boys in the posse. Three days' sun had been too much for them. Their lips were splitting, their noses peeling. The Irishmen were so sore from riding, they could barely sit on the ground to drink their coffee.

"We're not sheriff's deputies," Stiles said. "We're constables."

"Who pays you—the county or the association?"

"I don't know," Stiles said. "Does anybody here know who pays us?"

"No, we don't," Maher said.

"Well, we have to go on and make camp in the Whets. We'll see you when everybody comes together at the roundup. I'm glad you fellers aren't after our brother."

"We are, too," Smiley said.

"I'm mostly glad for your sakes. He's a dead shot. The sonsabitches in the jail beat him up awful. He'll be waiting for a chance to sit them on his front sight, one by one, and shoot their asses off." Les stared at Stiles, then at Smiley.

"We'll pass it on, Mr. Cowden," Stiles said.

The Cowden brothers rode on without fear of pursuit.

Billy Stiles watched the Cowdens ride away, glad to see them go. The posse's coffee was running out. Marshall had not given his rangers time to pack beds and provision. He had been in such a hurry to dispatch a posse that he ordered the Irishmen, Stiles, and Smiley to go as they were. They were only carrying the food they'd been able to buy as they hurried out of Tucson. Marshall had made Stiles and Smiley turn in their valuables when he placed them in jail, so they were broke. They borrowed tobacco from the Irishmen. Marshall did not even give them time to find canteens so they could carry water.

Luckily, Senator Vincent had provided five other young men who knew the country, and they recruited Bill Marsh at Tanque Verde. The Irishmen would have lost themselves in the Rincóns. They spent a lot of time trying to keep up or resting on their stomachs in deep hideaways of shade. Stiles and Smiley spent that same time looking for them and keeping them on Ben's track. Stiles, Smiley, and the Irishmen kept their camp apart from the other better equipped and better provisioned rangers.

The other rangers knew they would not catch Ben Cowden, even if the great horse he was riding broke a leg. Cowden could get farther faster on a three-legged horse than the posse could if they changed horses three times a day. They wanted to turn around and go home now.

"Look at them two, riding off with a Mexican," Stiles said, watching the Cowdens disappear. "Have any of you seen their sisters? Damn, if I had sisters that beautiful, I'd sure stay home. If I lived in the same house with those girls, you'd never catch me riding off to the Whetstones with an evil-looking Mexican."

"I've seen their sisters," John Maher said. "They are pretty."

"Pretty? They're beautiful. Now, if we could find a way to put the run on these other two hairy-legged brothers and get them out of the way, I'd go get that Betty Cowden."

"Why do you need to get rid of the brothers?" asked Maher. "Isn't she an eligible girl?"

"Not eligible for the things I want to do."

"I thought you and Smiley were toughguys. How could a brother's disapproval stop you from courting a girl?"

"You don't know the Cowdens. You'd have to kill them to get to their sisters."

"You might as well face it, Stiles; the Cowdens are too tough for us, and their sisters are too good for us," Maher said. "I've ridden as far as I can go. I concede the chase. I'll never be present at the capture of Ben Cowden as long as he's horseback."

"Damn, I sure thought we'd catch him, beat-up as he was," Stiles said. "He must have changed horses somewhere. How could he ride across those mountains at night and disappear the way he did without killing his horse? My horse was through yesterday morning."

"Langley and I are not looking forward to the morrow,"

Maher said. "We're not used to horses. We're used to carrying railroad ties and driving spikes. I can run with a crosstie faster than I can run on a horse."

"Maybe we ought to go to Tombstone and change horses," Stiles said.

"Yeah, let's do that," Smiley said happily. "We can look for Cowden at the horse race."

"That's right—Cowden's horse is running tomorrow," Maher said. "I'm flayed, drawn, and quartered by a damned horse a hundred miles from my bed, and Ben Cowden, my quarry, is probably in a Tombstone bar taking bets on his racehorse. I wish I'd killed him when I had the chance. I might have felt remorse awhile, but that would have been pleasant compared to the agony I feel in my ass and the cup of pain that awaits it on the trail tomorrow."

"What if Marshall's in Tombstone?" Smiley asked. "He ain't gonna like it if we go in without his man."

"We can tell him we tracked Cowden to Tombstone," Billy Stiles said. "The truth is, since we have no idea where he is, he's as likely to be in Tombstone as anywhere."

The Cowden brothers were near Perry Pass in the Whetstones. They always tried to learn everything they could about traffic that preceded them in a narrow channel like Perry Pass. Ben dismounted, knelt, and bowed over the trail; he struck the back of his knifeblade to a flint, and caught a stream of sparks in the *hiesca*, oak punk, he held in the palm of his hand. He made a spark glow in the punk so he could see the trail, the glow close to his hand. The flare of a match could have discovered the brothers to an enemy. Ben saw that so many Apache feet had used the trail in the past few hours that he could not count separate tracks.

"I didn't want to go to Perry Camp anyway," Ben said. "Can you imagine what that would be like tonight? We'd open the door to the cabin, and twenty javelinas carrying lances would run over us."

"Aw, they wouldn't be inside the cabin, would they?" Les said. "We'd never reach the door. They'd cut our throats when we rode into the sycamores below camp."

"Well, we won't be able to sleep there tonight," Ben said. "We might as well ride down to Tombstone. We'll arrive at a good time. Everybody'll be drunk or asleep."

"Um, um, um," said Les. "I was all ready to roll in my blanket, javelinas or no javelinas."

Mark laughed softly. He was happy they were going to Tombstone. His girlfriend, Garby Burr, lived there. He liked her a lot and did not get to see her very much.

CHAPTER 12

The horses stirred in the corral and awakened Alfredo Heredia an hour before dawn on September 16. He sat up on his cot in Prim Pete's stall. This was the day of the race, no time to lie asleep on his ear while something menaced the horses. People who wanted Prim Pete to lose might try to make sure he did not run well.

Alfredo sat still and listened. Everyone in town knew he was training Prim Pete at the Pendleton barn. Prim was Tombstone's horse. Alfredo rode him down the main street every afternoon at sundown, the time the race was to be run. Prim was used to the rowdy Tombstone crowds now. Nothing in that town would surprise him, unless it was the sight of John McCue's heels. John McCue was his opponent, a Texas stud. The race was for $10,000. The Cowdens would bet another $10,000 in small bets on the street. Alfredo figured if Prim Pete lost, it would break the Cowdens. That was one reason he ate his meals when Prim ate his and slept on a cot in Prim's stall.

Alfredo picked up his rifle and went quietly to the open barn door. The nights and days were hot, so he kept the big doors open to let in the breezes. The corral was dark. He listened as the horses settled down. He was used to their normal rustling. He knew when a cranky horse made a rush on another and snapped his teeth off his hide, then scrambled to dodge the answering kick. Those normal sounds were not the ones that made him go to the door with his rifle. The sound of all the horses moving together from one side of the corral to another made him suspicious of an outside menace.

Alfredo waited until the horses were standing quiet and at peace before he went back to his cot. He had guarded the racehorse all night. Now he wanted to sleep until daylight so he would be fresh when he rode in the race. He was as edgy and fit as the horse. He thrilled clear to his toes every time he realized the day of the race was at hand. He needed to relax awhile so he could make a hand.

He was deep in slumber when he heard Ben Cowden growl, "*Buenos días.* Good morning. What is this—you now feel you must sleep in the very center of the horse herd?"

Alfredo sat up as though the barn was on fire. "*Ay, Benjamin!* You scared me. But how can you be here? You're supposed to be running from a *gentío,* a crowd, of sheriffs."

"Is this the way of the *caballerango,* the master horseman—to sleep with his charge and trust in God he won't be stepped on?"

Alfredo shook Ben's hand. "But don't you know everybody in town is watching for you? They say the only reason you escaped jail was to be here for the race. People are betting as much money that you'll show up here today as they are betting on the race itself."

"I had to come. How could I disappoint the Tombstone sports?"

"You'll never disappoint anyone, Ben, not even your enemies."

Mark came in with Ben's saddle.

"Now that I'm an outlaw, my brothers do all my work. They're so afraid somebody'll see me, they won't even let me unsaddle my horse."

"I agree with your brothers. You must not be seen. A reward has been posted for your killing or capture."

"Who's putting up the reward?"

"The Livestock Association."

"Ah, my enemies. How much?"

"Three thousand dollars."

"Ah, a premium. That's good. I'm prime ribs. My day has finally come. Me and my horse are the main event in Tombstone."

A young woman dressed in widow's weeds came into the barn. She glanced at Ben and smiled before she addressed Alfredo. "Uncle, your breakfast is ready."

She shook hands with Ben's brothers without taking her eyes off Ben.

"Do you think you know this man, Margarita?" Alfredo asked.

"*Seguro que sí.* I sure do."

"No, you don't. This man might look like someone you know, but you do not know him. I present José Bravo, the horseman."

Margarita laughed and shook Ben's hand. "Enchanted, Don José."

Ben felt his luck was returning. Margarita was the eldest daughter of Don Juan Pedro Elias of the Maria Macarena ranch in Sonora. Don Juan Pedro and the Cowdens shared the Buena Vista range, east of Nogales. Margarita had been widowed in June of that year by Apaches. The Cowden brothers had found the bodies of her husband and brother only a few minutes after they were killed. They also found her little son and carried him home alive.

She looked thin in her weeds, fragile. Her face and hands were pale and clear as china against the black garments. Ben never traveled far from his country on the Santa Cruz River, and he was not a ladies' man. He did not know much about anything but his work, but he trusted his eye for a good-looking horse and a beautiful lady. The most beautiful women he had ever seen were in Sonora. This lady was better-looking than most other women or girls he had known.

"Is your family well?" Ben asked her.

"All well," Margarita said. "But my mother died soon after my husband and brother were killed."

"I heard. I'm sorry."

"Thank you." Margarita's look was frank. She liked Ben.

"Margarita, let's go to the house and ask your father if his old friend José Bravo, *el jinete*, the horseman, resembles Ben Cowden," Alfredo said.

Margarita quit looking into Ben's eyes, and he felt a loss.

"Take my brothers, Alfredo," Ben said. "I'll wait here. Your house is probably being watched."

"My friend, you have to eat."

"Send me a plate. I'll wait in the loft."

"Nonsense."

"José Bravo," Les said, laughing at the alias. "You go visit the Sonorans, and we'll have breakfast with the Pendletons in the other house, where we can watch the town."

"That might work," Ben said.

"It will work," Alfredo said.

Ben walked to the house with Alfredo and Margarita. Margarita was tiny, but she was Ben's age and already a mother and a widow. She would probably have to wear the weeds for the rest of her life and take her mother's place in her father's household. She would oversee the raising of her father's grandsons and watch her father's waistline. She already wore a settled look that told Ben she was resigned to sleeping alone the rest of her life. Now she could go out and look any man in the eye and haggle over the price of horsefeed, and no one would worry about her. Ben would. She was too pretty and too good to dry up and become a tradesman.

Don Juan Pedro Elias gave hospitality to everyone who came to the Maria Macarena. The Elias hacienda was a fort that he offered as a haven to his neighbors during periods of Apache raids.

The Elias vaqueros were not against branding a Cowden maverick if they saw he was getting so big and fat, he might go to waste. The Cowdens tried to police their own mavericks and were not averse to policing the Elias mavericks too if they saw them going to waste. Big juicy mavericks that were accustomed to hiding and getting away from vaqueros were a blight on the range. Other cattle learned their bad habits. They were like weeds in a vegetable garden, using water and room the mother cows needed for raising their calves.

The laws did not cause friction between good neighbors when the neighbors observed the unwritten laws of neighborliness. The Cowdens and Eliases would not eat each other's unbranded yearlings or branded two-year-olds. They would not steal calves from each other. They would not drive off their neighbor's breeding stock. They would not monopolize the feed and water. They protected their neighbor's stock when they were alone with it and worked together with their neighbors during the *rodeo*, the roundup.

By law, a "maverick" was any unbranded calf that was weaned from his mother and able to make a living on his own. A yearling often ran unbranded with his mother long after she had weaned him and given birth to another calf. Good cowmen left their neighbors' unbranded yearlings alone or branded them with their neighbors' brands as a favor.

Newcomers were writing laws that complicated the unwritten laws. People like Vincent introduced bills in the legislature that called any unbranded calf over six months old a maverick, even though a calf was still running with his mother when he was six months old and any cowman could see whom he belonged to. Vincent and his crowd introduced the bill so they could legally thin out their neighbors' herds. By the new law, any unbranded calf over six months became property of the territory. The ranger-constables of the Live Stock Association were policing this law.

Now, because of this new law, cowboys defined a maverick as "somebody else's calf that you get your brand on first." Ben was glad to run into Don Juan Pedro because he wanted to talk to him about reports that Vincent's rangers were prowling the Buena Vista. Vincent and the Yawner kept the Cowdens so busy warring that they were not able to husband their cattle as they should. Cowden cattle were scattered over a million square miles they shared with neighbors as different as Don Juan Pedro Elias and Duncan Vincent.

Don Juan Pedro Elias's hair was white, his mustache a trim white line under his nose. He was dressed the same way Ben was dressed, in tight trousers reinforced by suede and a short charro jacket. The trousers were extra long so they would not crawl up his leg when he was on his horse. The waist-length *chaquetilla* was adorned with silver buttons. He wore a bright white shirt with a colorful butterfly tie. Ben was not wearing the tie. Enough was enough.

Don Juan welcomed Ben with a warm Mexican *abrazo*, the formal embrace with pats on the back, then crumpled Ben's broken hand in both his own. "Your mustache makes you look older, Benjamin. Reports have it that you are a fierce rogue. What did they teach you in jail?" He examined the scars on Ben's face. "Are you ruined for life? I don't think so."

"I'm the same man, Don Juan Pedro. I'm still only a vaquero with work to do, if I can ever get to it. Lately, I've allowed my enemies to keep me away from it."

"You come and stay with me at the Maria Macarena. I want you with us. You can help me deal with Kosterlinsky. Do you know Duncan Vincent is financing that man's *sin vergonzadas*, his shamelessness, now?"

"I know Vincent has not paid Kosterlinsky his share of the money they stole from Walter Jarboe, the Kansas cattleman."

"Vincent must pay Kosterlinsky immediately. Kosterlinsky owes my brother-in-law Gabilondo for horses he confiscated and sold. The government in Hermosillo has ordered Kosterlinsky to pay or go to prison. Gabilondo has him by the throat. You might have heard that Kosterlinsky's troop mutinied when he ordered it to sack Gabilondo's ranch."

"How can Kosterlinsky make Vincent pay him?"

"Kosterlinsky could have Duncan Vincent arrested if he decided to testify against him about their partnership in lawless activities along the border."

"How does Vincent intend to transfer money to Kosterlinsky?"

"He will have to send it on a wagon with an armed escort. Kosterlinsky is making him pay in *alazanas*, the gold coin of Porfirio Diaz. Vincent will have to buy the coin up here and transport it to Kosterlinsky's headquarters in Santa Cruz."

"Where can he buy alazanas?"

"Ah, there you have me. I only know he can't send it down any other way."

"Vincent spends a lot of time in Tombstone. He can buy alazanas from the gambling halls. A lot of Mexican gold is gambled here."

"You're right, Ben."

"I am right. I'm going to get that gold."

Ben sent his brothers to town to watch his enemies. He did not think the law in Tombstone would bother him if he did not start a public turmoil. Rowdy people would be swarming in Tombstone that day and Weldon Rutledge, the town marshal, would be too busy to bother Ben.

Ben bathed and shaved in the barn, and rode Alfredo's horse into town. He heard a newsboy hawking his name in the headline of a new edition of *The Epitaph*. He bought a paper from the printer's devil at the back door of the press.

The owner of the paper was Ben's friend George Giragi, but Ben did not want to see him. He liked being in disguise in plain sight of people he knew. He did not hide his face, trusting his duds would shield him. Americans did not look closely at Mexicans. The big hat stood out like a mountain peak covered with snow in the middle of the desert, but people did not look at it. People's glances slid over him as though they would feel better if he was not there. He was a big Mexican.

Ben's face and hands were toasted from the sun as brown as an Apache's. Before Bib Taylor scarred him, his skin had glowed with the reddish tinge of a healthy young Indian. He was outdoors as much as any Apache, and his hair was as black. He, Paula Mary, and Viney were the black-headed Cowdens, though Paula Mary and Viney's complexions were clear and light. Ben's skin was dark as the heart of mesquite because he had spent few days of his life out of the sun. His eyes were blue, but half of the Sonora ranchers had blue or green eyes. He looked like most of the Anglo-Indian natives of the Santa Cruz River country in southern Arizona and northern Sonora.

The Cowdens and the Porters swore they had no Indian blood. However, Ben and Paula Mary often looked wonderingly at each other and saw an indigenous strain that was as plain on their faces as it was on the old Yawner himself.

Ben tied his horse in the newspaper's shed and went to a store to buy a carton of tobacco and a new briarwood pipe. He had sure been missing his pipe since Lorrie Briggs and company waylaid him in Patagonia. He went back to the barn behind *The Epitaph*, climbed into the seat of Giragi's buckboard, stoked and lighted his pipe, and read the newspaper.

The lead story gave Red Shepherd's account of his "running gun battle with Ben Cowden." The story was sympathetic to Ben because the editor was Ben's friend. The story also gave details of the range war that had begun between the pioneer ranchers, represented by Ben, and the eastern syndicate, represented by Duncan and Royal Vincent. The Vincent faction was made up of easterners who, *The Epitaph* alleged, were "predators more dangerous to the people of Arizona than Geronimo, the Yawner, and the Mexican mutineers all put together."

Another story was an account of a robbery of the Barth Mercantile in which a dozen new rifles and a thousand rounds of ammunition had been taken. Ben reminded himself that Jake Barth was a friend who would sell him provisions without turning him in to the law.

The buckboard seat became uncomfortable, so Ben walked across the street to the Palace Hotel. At seven, the lobby was deserted. Ben sat behind his newspaper in a corner to watch the lobby. His easy chair was only three feet from the door to Duncan Vincent's office.

He was reading about the latest claims of the snake-oil and patent-medicine companies when Doris Vincent came down the stairs and headed for the front desk. Watching her move made Ben feel good. The way she moved inside layers of clothes made Ben think old Vincent must enjoy watching her get around when she did not have to wear clothes.

Vincent seemed to have it all his own way in the woman

department, with Doris as his mate and Lorrie Briggs his mistress. This lady was handsome, dignified, and well bred, and Lorrie Briggs was a rompin-stompin beauty.

Ben had been here in this lobby the day Doris Vincent caught her husband cohabitating a corner room upstairs with Lorrie Briggs. The lady had shown a lot of heart and bottom that day. Ben was not qualified to say that her bottom was big in size, only that she had courage and stamina like a good horse and would not back down in a scrap—the other kind of sound bottom.

On that occasion, Doris Vincent had produced a pistol and put Vincent to flight in front of the whole town. She must be living with him again, though. Ben did not think she would be here unless she was with her husband.

"Are there any messages for us, Dale?" she asked, showing Ben her delicate profile and the desk clerk her smiling eyes and strong, pretty teeth.

Dale grinned with all his might and seemed to crackle like gravel under a wheel as he jumped to attention. She glanced at Ben to see if he noticed the effect she was having on the poor man. Even as she wielded her power, she had a sweet, vulnerable look in her eye that Ben liked. That vulnerable look came out of her good nature, and she could use it to level a man.

She looked toward Ben to see if she might level him too, but her gaze flinched away from his hat as from a pile of dirty laundry. Dale told her she had no messages, and she wheeled gracefully and strode out. Ben could tell by the quick little twist she gave her hips with each step that she knew he and Dale were watching her.

Duncan Vincent, Marshall, and Kosterlinsky met her on the veranda, tipped their hats, and came on into the lobby. Billy Stiles and George Smiley were behind them. The posse boys must have killed their horses in their hurry to get to town. The trail to the saloons was not nearly as hard to cover as Ben Cowden's.

Vincent and his gang headed straight for Ben, and he tightened his grip on the pistol he held under the newspaper. He decided to shoot the big bully with the blackjack first, but the whole entourage veered past Ben and went into Vincent's office. Ben relaxed. Thank God for Mexican hats.

Ben was glad to see Vincent and Kosterlinsky. He hated Marshall's every feature and had no regard at all for Billy Stiles and George Smiley, but he enjoyed the sight of Vincent and Kosterlinsky. He was concerned for the welfare of those two old bulls. He wondered how they were doing. Vincent didn't look too good, and that did not make Ben as happy as it should. His trouble might only be minor, though. Doris was probably giving him major harassment over his affair with Lorrie Briggs, but that would not do him in completely, only make him look worn.

Vincent was talking in the office. Ben did not like the sound of his voice. His face looked as if it belonged to a wise, kind man, but his voice had a mean and ridiculous edge to it.

Ben hated that anybody as mean as Vincent was running the Live Stock Association and often gave advice on Arizona land and cattle matters to the policymakers in Washington. Every bit of advice he gave was bound to cause Ben trouble.

Ben heard Vincent's helpers dragging something heavy across the floor of the office. Stiles opened the door, looked around the lobby, turned back into the office, and said, "Nobody out there but a Mexican."

Marshall stepped up and looked at Ben. Ben felt like a rattlesnake, waiting for him to come in range so he could bite him, but he knew he must learn to hide and wait if he was to hurt his enemies in this war.

Marshall yelled, "Hey, you Meskin. Go cantina now." He waved his hands to shoo Ben away. Ben kept his head down, as though trying to sleep, but he stirred the newspaper aside so Marshall could see the pistol. Marshall backed up three quick steps and shouted for help. "Hey, you, flunky. Yeah, you, Dale. How come that Meskin gets to sleep in the lobby?"

"The gentleman doesn't seem to be disturbing anyone, Captain Marshall," Dale said. "He's only reading his newspaper."

"Gentleman? Get him out of here. Hell, he's holding a pistol on his lap."

Ben shielded his face with his hatbrim as Dale came from behind the desk to talk to him. He knew Ben well because he was a regular customer in the hotel.

"Excuse me, sir. Could you please find someplace else to sit?" Dale said to the Mexican hat.

"Of course," Ben said.

Dale sighed with relief. "Thank you, sir. I consider it a big favor."

Ben walked out and sat in a rocker at the end of the veranda. A VO hand brought a team and wagon to the front of the hotel and waited. Billy Stiles and George Smiley came out carrying a heavy, ironbound chest. Marshall and Kosterlinsky followed and helped them lift the chest into the wagon, then climbed on with the driver and drove up the street.

Ben thought, Well, there go my golden alazanas.

CHAPTER 13

Ben watched the wagon head down the street, meet another rig, and turn up a side street. A. B. Cowden was driving the rig that Marshall had passed. He stopped his matched black horses in front of the hotel to unload Ben's mother and sisters.

Marshall's wagon came back around a corner into the main street, and the driver pulled up behind A. B.'s carriage. Marshall signed for Stiles and Smiley to carry in the Cowden luggage and jumped down with Kosterlinsky to help the Cowden ladies off their buggy. A. B. held his lines and glared at Marshall.

Ben could see A. B. did not like Marshall squiring his family. Ben didn't mind. He enjoyed watching Marshall and Kosterlinsky show off their manners to the Cowden women. They were practically on their knees and not doing themselves a bit of good.

The girls looked beautiful. A. B. always went out of his way to show them off, so he should not be surprised they were getting attention. He always put his own carriage and team on the train when he brought his family to Tombstone so his ladies would have their own rig.

Stiles and Smiley went into the lobby with the Cowden luggage. Marshall took charge of Viney without even saying hello or looking back at A. B. To his credit, Kosterlinsky shook A. B.'s hand before he walked up the stairs with the girls.

Ben turned away so his family would not recognize him. His mother and sisters disciplined themselves to look straight ahead when they were in public and never showed curiosity about other people's faces, but he knew they saw a lot out of the corners of their eyes. He might as well have been another pillar holding up the veranda roof, because none of them even looked his way. A. B. drove on to tie his team behind the hotel.

Ben knew he was doing the right thing now. His own family did not recognize him. He did not plan to go near his parents and sisters. The posse was undoubtedly searching the town for him and watching to see if he would contact his family.

Marshall was trying to worm in close to his family. The girls were a match for him though. He evidently was not immune to their good looks.

Stiles and Smiley came out of the hotel and sat next to Ben on the veranda. "You suppose that box is full of gold?" Smiley asked his partner.

"It's heavy enough to be gold."

"You suppose we better get in the wagon and sit on it?"

"We can watch it from here." Stiles was grumpy. "I'll be damned if I'll sit in the sun in a wagon with my chin on my knees like a flunky and wait for that damned Marshall to give me more orders."

"Where do you suppose they're sending the strongbox?"

"I don't know. Mrs. Vincent's taking it somewhere."

"On the train?"

"No, we're loading it on a coach with Mrs. Vincent's stuff. I know that because I've been told I'm going, too."

"Are you going to guard Doris, or the box?"

"Somebody has to carry the lady's valises and packages, tell the driver when she wants to stop, and make sure nobody bothers her when she goes behind the bushes."

"I wouldn't mind being Doris's personal bodyguard, myself." Smiley sighed. "That's a handsome lady."

"That's a talky boss-lady," Stiles said. "She don't look so handsome when you're in your tenth hour listening to her go on and on about the Daughters of the American Revolution."

"I hope I get to go. I'm a good listener."

Marshall appeared at the door. "Well, good listener, get in that wagon and squat on that box before it leaves without you."

Stiles and Smiley jumped in the wagon. They were sitting on the box, back-to-back, their chins on their knees, when the driver drove away.

Marshall looked around for witnesses and his eye fell on

José Bravo in the rocking chair. Ben moved his head slightly to watch some people going by in the street, just another Mexican taking in the Tombstone sights. Marshall stalked back into the lobby.

A pretty girl in a white dress and gloves, a pink-and-white hat, and parasol came up the stairs with Mark. He was wearing a new hat, oxford shoes, white shirt, and baggy dress trousers, and looked as happy as a javelina in a flower bed. The girl was Mark's sweetheart, Garbie Burr. They crossed the veranda and went into the lobby without noticing Ben.

Ben left the veranda and went down the street to the Barth Mercantile. He knew Jake Barth well, so he avoided him. He bought canvas Levi's, boots, and a hat. He bought a pair of Texas spurs and a pocketknife, a canvas brush jacket, a blanket, and other gear and foodstuffs he needed for a long stay away from home. He bought two canvas warbags for carrying his goods and waited for the clerk to tally his bill of sale.

A man stepped close to him to examine a jar full of jawbreakers. Ben gave him room, and he and Che Che the Apache recognized each other at the same moment. Che Che grinned at the surprise on Ben's face. Then they both laughed softly, the Indian way. Che Che was also disguised as a Mexican, a peon. He reached up and rubbed the lapel of Ben's suede jacket between two fingers.

"Now I know how to surprise you, Jinete," Che Che said. "I only need to catch you afoot. *Prestame un diez.* Lend me a dime."

He nodded toward a handful of banknotes in Ben's hand. At the moment, Ben felt more partner than enemy to this Apache. He was not a man to hate his enemies entirely. The wolves were his enemies because they preyed on his cattle and would eat the family colts if given the chance. They would probably even eat his sisters, but that was within the natural order, and he did not hate them when they were not bothering him. Che Che was his enemy, but only as a natural predator who was not bothering him at that moment.

The Cowdens somehow found neutral ground on which they and the predators with which they shared the country could get along. They tried to leave one another alone. The Cowdens buried their enemies but did not kill the enemy young. The Cowdens had won this Apache's respect, and Ben had reason to respect him. Arizonans and Sonorans usually lusted for Apache blood, yet here was an Apache asking Ben for a loan so he could buy a dime's worth of jawbreakers.

Ben gave Che Che a dollar and then told the clerk to add a quarter's worth of jawbreakers to his bill. When the clerk handed him his packages, he gave the jawbreakers to Che Che. The Apache took the candy, grinned ferociously, and walked out.

Ben packed his warbags with the packages. He did not even look for Che Che when he went out on the street. The Apache was not foolish. He would not give anyone the chance to discover him in a town full of people who would hang him on sight.

By ten, the saloons and gambling halls were bulging with revelers. Ben rode back to the Pendleton barn and changed into his new clothes. He did not want to disappoint the sports who had gambled that he would show up in Tombstone that day. He did not want to be recognized in his José Bravo clothes. He wanted to save them as an ace-in-the-hole for disguise.

He packed his Mexican clothes in the warbag and climbed into the hayloft to rest. He was sore, His ribs were so bruised, he could not take a full breath. His hands were losing some of their swelling, but they hurt when he tried to use them in the most ordinary way. He slept awhile and awoke when a crowd of gamblers came to watch Alfredo and Prim Pete get ready for the race.

When he was alone in the barn again, Ben caught Star and Moose, the packhorse, and put them away in stalls inside the barn. His supplies were light, so he saddled Moose and packed him so he would be ready to go. He did not saddle Star. He gave both horses a feed of grain, mounted Alfredo's horse again, and rode back to town.

The finish line of the race was drawn across the main street between the newspaper office and the Palace Hotel. Ben tied Alfredo's horse in the shed behind *The Epitaph*, and joined the crowd at the finish line. His family was sitting on the Palace veranda, and Marshall was still with them. Viney and A. B. were not dealing with him at all, and the girls were wearing looks that said they were allowing him to stand by like a big fat fly, but he was going to get swatted if he buzzed too close.

Marshall was trying to woo Betty, but Ben was not worried about her. Cowdens usually gave as good as they got in the wooing department. Betty would never fall for a sonofabitch.

Sonsabitches only pleased her when they danced barefoot in the cholla cactus. Marshall had bragged to Ben about the damage he intended to do the Cowdens by violating Betty, but he would have to get over his weakness for her to accomplish that.

Every once in a while, Marshall stepped out in front of the Cowdens, as though he felt they needed him to entertain them. The Cowden he happened to be addressing might answer him with a word or a nod, but he was mostly answered with the Cowden stone-eye. He could talk big and look sincerely into their faces, but he could not make the stone-eye in any of them come to life for him unless he got so close he spat on them.

The jockeys were parading the racehorses in the street. Prim Pete was a pretty, clean-legged, blood bay, and as calm and gentle as a good horse who spent most of his life doing quiet work with cattle ought to be. He was in the best shape of his life. A deep claret showed in the heart of his bay coat, and a golden sheen highlighted the curves of his neck and hips in certain light. Alfredo rode bareback, his knees thrust inside a wide strip of cotton cloth tied around Prim's girth. The cloth was tight over Alfredo's thighs and calves, his feet trailing.

John McCue was a tall dun horse with a red mane and tail and zebra stripes on his legs and ears. He had a long, feral hammerhead and lean, smooth muscles. Ben could see he was not a good keeper, not comfortable with his training, eating, and resting. His flanks were lean, and he was carrying no barrel at all. He stood two hands taller than Prim, and he held his head three heads taller. Way up there in the big hammerhead were two small mean eyes. His jockey was a tall, skeletal Texan with hands the size of meat platters who spoke as gruffly and meanly to everyone around him as he did to the horse. Ben could see John McCue had become a racehorse because running away in front of a crowd of people was the best thing he would ever do. Prim Pete ran because he loved it, and he still had not reached his peak at doing all the good work he could do.

Ben decided he'd better not tempt Tombstone to discover him until he was absolutely ready to leave town. He walked down the street to the Continental Bar. His friend Ray Aragon owned the place and usually served as its bartender. Ray would not be surprised to see him, would not tell anyone Ben had been in his bar until Ben was long gone. People would believe Ray when he told them Ben had been there, and that would decide the bets.

Les Cowden and Uncle Billy Porter were the only customers in the bar. Les was feeling good. He looked up, saw Ben, and said, "Well, desperado, what did you do with José Bravo?"

Uncle Billy laughed but said nothing.

Ray looked through the door to see if anyone was following Ben, then shook hands with him. "Les, hush, or I'll take away your beer," he said.

"He'll never hush," Uncle Billy said.

"Why should I hush? Everybody knows my brother's a fugitive and his life's probably ruined. He can't even come into a friendly saloon without risking his life. If he's going to get caught, and he will be caught someday, it might as well be now, so I can go down with him."

"Well, it'll happen quicker'n you think if you keep announcing it," Uncle Billy said.

"Just be quiet, Les," Ray said patiently as he poured Ben a glass of beer. Ben lifted the beer to the light so he could watch the bubbles give themselves up to the foam. He loved the miracle of each little bubble materializing in the bottom of a glass of beer. He tasted the foam, then refreshed himself with the first swallow. The beer was cool as rain and refreshed him the way a walk in the evening after a rain did. He liked the smells and the shade in the Continental Bar. The pine sawdust on the floor was freshly watered down and smelled like the ponderosa forest in the Rincóns had smelled the night Ben ran free after the rain.

He sat with his back to the wall at the table with his brother and uncle. He patted Les on the arm. Les was like a horse loose with the saddle on. He needed to kick loose awhile, even though he was cinched up with awful responsibilities.

"I'm glad to find you doing the right thing, brother," Ben said. "You can't go wrong drinking a little beer."

"That's all he's doing, just drinking a little beer," Uncle Billy said. "He's not harming anybody."

"Look at my brother, Uncle Billy," Les said. "Does he look like a man with only a short time to live? No. He's not worried, either. Every coward in Arizona wants to kill him, but does that worry him? No."

Ray posted himself at the door. Ben sipped beer and looked at his brother's face. He couldn't stop people wanting to shoot him or take him to jail; he could only try to keep it from happening. At that moment, he did not give a damn about anything other people were trying to do to him, but that was because he always felt reckless before a horse race. When he saw one of his horses walk out on a racetrack, he knew the race was on, the time for training and worry finished, the wager met and relinquished to the stakeholder. The only thing left to do was to turn loose his racehorse, let him run, and have no fear that anything would come apart.

Ray Aragon caught Ben's eye to warn him, and then Weldon Rutledge, the town marshal, came through the door.

"Good evening, Ray. Big crowd," Rutledge said.

Ray followed the marshal toward the Cowdens.

"I was told I could find Les Cowden in here," Rutledge said, addressing Uncle Billy. Uncle Billy nodded toward Les.

"I'm Les Cowden," Les said.

"You're Ben Cowden's brother, aren't you?"

"Yes, sir. You know it well enough."

Ben motioned for Ray to bring more beer. "Marshal, would you like a beer?" he asked.

"I don't believe so," Rutledge said. He might as well have been talking to the empty beer pitcher. Ben wondered what he had to do to attract attention in Tombstone.

"We're having a little beer. If you won't have any, what else can I do for you?" Les said.

"I'm glad I located you. I hear your brother might come here for the race."

"Marshal Rutledge, that's the truth."

"Well, I've never met him, but I hear he's no trouble-maker."

"That's right. He doesn't put on horse races to make trouble."

Rutledge turned to Uncle Billy. "Uncle Billy, if you see him, please tell him for me that we appreciate his staging the race here in Tombstone, good as it is for business."

"I'll tell him, Weldon."

"However, I sure don't want to see him."

"I can understand that."

"There has been no warrant issued for his arrest in this county, yet."

"We'll tell him."

"But that doesn't mean I want him here."

"We understand."

"I can understand the man wanting to see his horse run.

He's bet a lot of money, and after all, a man who raises a running horse ought to have the privilege of seeing him run. That might be the only pleasure the race gives him. His horse could lose."

"That's right," Uncle Billy said. "One of the horses always loses."

"Please tell him to leave as soon as he can after the race." Rutledge turned to Ben. "Will you please help these gentlemen do as I ask, young man?"

"Of course," Ben said, and he reached out to shake the man's hand.

Rutledge shook offhandedly. "No lawman wants to see a war start in his town."

Ray arrived with a fresh pitcher of beer.

"Let me buy this to thank you for helping me." Rutledge laid down his money and went out the door.

The Cowdens and Uncle Billy sat quietly for a moment. Ray brought them a *botana* of corn tortillas and fried *machaca* jerky with diced potatoes, onions, and green chile salza.

After they ate the snack and drank the beer, Uncle Billy said, "Well, fellers, we better go. It's about that time."

Les and Uncle Billy went out, and Ben paused to offer Ray his hand. "What do I owe you for making me feel at home, Ray?"

Ray ignored the hand. "Nothing," he said. "You don't owe me anything for the beer, either."

"I'm sorry. I thought Les already paid you. How much was it?"

"I already told you. You don't owe a thing, but do me a favor, will you?"

"Sure, Ray, anything."

"Don't try to come back. You're not welcome here anymore."

Ben straightened. "What did I do, Ray? What's got you pissed off?"

"Look, you're not fooling anybody. You've disgraced your family. Everybody knows you're a murderer. I'm like the marshal. I don't want to see your face around here. I don't think anyone else does either."

Ray turned away to his chores.

"You're wrong, Ray. I'm not a murderer. My family's in a war."

"Yeah, well, don't bring your wars around people who are trying to live decent lives, if you please."

Ben was so preoccupied with the rebuff that he could not see where he was going when he walked out of the saloon. He'd been turned away by a friend. Well, he would have to stay away from his friends. If he could not go near his own family, why did he think he could camp on other people? If he did not exempt saloons or gambling houses because they catered to outlaws and decent folks alike, then he could at least stay out of his friends' saloons. Until this war was over, he had no friends and no family.

Ben looked up. He was standing at the end of the street. The whole town seemed to be congregated in a knot at the finish line.

Ben stepped back into the shadow of a building. He was uncomfortable and befuddled by the beer. He should not have wanted it so much or drunk it so fast. His recklessness had put his head in a fog and given Ray Aragon an opening to hurt his feelings. Well, he could write that friend off. Ray had made it easy.

Ben's family was still at the hotel. Kosterlinsky had joined Marshall. Stiles and Smiley were nowhere to be seen. They were probably guarding the strongbox. Ben wondered where Marshall's Irishmen were. Duncan and Doris Vincent were standing on a balcony above the hotel veranda with their daughter, Dorothy, and other ladies and gentlemen.

Ben's family's faces were full of fun. The Cowdens and Porters enjoyed a horse race more than any other contest in their world. Ben and his cousins put on at least two races a year, and even his enemies appreciated them. He didn't run horse races only to please the gamblers and advertise his papa's horseflesh, though. He ran them mostly for the joy they gave him. For him, racehorses came nearer flying than any animal born without wings.

The race would be started lap and tap. That is, the horses started running about twenty yards before the starting line. The starter stood on the line and judged if the horses were positioned for a fair start when they passed him. If he could see no daylight between them, he would yell "Santiago!" and the race would be on. If he could see even an inch of daylight between the first horse and the second when they crossed the line, he would call them back and try again.

Ben looked across the street and saw Lorrie Briggs staring

at him from the veranda of the Grant Hotel. She recognized him, her mouth fell open, and she took a great gulp of air to scream.

Ben looked toward the starting line, asking sweet angel Gabriel to intervene and start the race soon. The horses were lined up and walking side by side away from the starting line.

Lorrie screamed, "There he is! It's Ben Cowden!" Her voice was young, clear, and strong, and turned the head of every person on the street. When they were all looking at her, she pointed straight at Ben and yelled, "It's Ben Cowden, my brother's murderer!"

With Lorrie pointing him out as a murderer, all of a sudden Ben *felt* like a murderer. His family's faces were in agony as they turned toward him. Uncle Billy's expression was calling him a dumb son of a gun for letting himself be discovered. Marshall located him and reached for his pistol. Kosterlinsky was still searching the crowd for him. Ben saw the crowd was endangering itself by turning its back on the horses to look at him. A ton of stampeding horseflesh would be coming down that street at any moment, and the crowd was in its path.

Ben looked up the street at the horses. The starter called the riders back, and they turned their horses' heads toward each other to let them run toward the starting line.

"*Do* something, somebody!" Lorrie shrieked. Several men started across the street toward Ben. Some of the women held their men back.

Prim Pete and John McCue were at a dead run toward the starting line.

Lorrie Briggs was raging. She snatched a pistol from the holster of a man standing beside her and rushed toward Ben, cocking and pointing it with both hands. The crowd scattered away from her and left a clear path for the first bullet she discharged at Ben. It missed and disappeared inside the good, dark, prosperous smells of the Barth Mercantile, lodged in a feedsack.

Prim Pete and John McCue crossed the starting line, the starter shouted "Santiago!" and the race was on.

"Get back!" Ben shouted to the crowd. He ran toward Lorrie, waving the people off the street. "The race is on! The horses are coming! Get back!"

He was stuck in Lorrie's sights. If he stepped out of the path she had cleared between them, she might shoot into the crowd. Three men tried to lay hands on him, but Lorrie let fly another round, and they skittered away from him.

The horses were cruising like juggernauts through Tombstone. Ben could see the power in their outlines—their muscles stretching, their breath exploding with every stride, the whips gesturing to the sky, the heads bobbing side by side, hooves soaring off the beaten surface of the street, muzzles straining toward the finish.

The crowd began to move back off the street.

"The horses!" Ben shouted again, and to a man, the crowd became aware of the horses and scampered off the finish line.

"Ben Cowden, you sonofabitch," Lorrie shouted.

The horses tore across the finish line, and the jockeys lifted their heads to stop them. Ben drew his pistol and fired in the air to slow the horses and clear the street.

Then one of Lorrie's bullets plowed into Ben's foot and knocked him down. Baring her teeth and screaming, Lorrie ran at him to finish him while she had him down, and John McCue sideswiped her. The pistol went off and flew away into the crowd. Her scream stopped abruptly in mid keen, and she sprawled out cold, on her face.

Ben got up and hobbled toward Prim Pete. Alfredo stopped the horse and turned back, saw Ben, and rode to him, smiling. "Did you see? We daylighted him. I saw the sunset between Pete and the other horse when we crossed the line."

Ben grabbed Prim's reins. "Give him to me, Alfredo. *Me descubrio la pinchi vieja desgraciada.* The damned disgraceful woman discovered me to the whole town."

"*Cómo?* What?"

"For God's sake, man. Give me the horse."

Alfredo's eyes went round, and he skinned off Prim Pete. Ben swung on him, walked him through the people, and gave him his head.

Prim Pete had summoned all his strength for the race, and he was still blowing. Ben let him clatter out the main street, but as soon as he was out of sight of the street, he circled back and dropped into a canyon to skirt the town back to the Pendleton barn.

The barn was deserted. He carried Les's saddle to Star's stall because his was on Alfredo's horse behind *The Epitaph.* The horse was not in the stall. Moose was in his stall, still saddled, packed, and ready to go. He counted noses. Les's horse was gone, and so was Mark's mare. He began to feel desperate as he searched the barn and corrals for the horses. He looked in Star's stall again and squeezed the boards and groaned with rage that his top horse had been stolen. He heard men shouting, so he threw Les's saddle on Prim Pete, led Moose out of the stall, mounted, and headed out of town.

Night was falling, and that was in his favor. He would not have to run his horses if he could hide until twilight was gone. He stopped in Mesquite Canyon and hid in a thicket. He needed to water Prim Pete, but that could wait until after dark. The road to Santa Cruz was just above his hiding place. He would wait awhile and see if Doris Vincent's coach came by.

He was not afraid he would be caught. Not a man in the country could outrun him horseback, and nobody was quick enough to shoot him before Prim Pete could carry him out of sight.

The foot Lorrie had poisoned with lead was a bulging, bloody sight. The new boot was punctured and torn where his little toe ought to be. The swelling in his foot had reduced the bleeding to a drouthy seep. He swung his foot over the saddle horn and tied his new neckerchief tightly around the boot.

A lot of traffic was leaving Tombstone on the road to Santa Cruz. Every wagon and team, every horseman that came down the road, appeared for a moment above him. Some of the people on saddle horses were in big gangs, like posses in a hurry.

Just before full dark, Ben saw Doris ride by in a coach with an armed escort. Two hours later, when traffic diminished at suppertime, Ben rode out of the canyon and hit a course parallel to the road. He hit a high trot and overtook the coach an hour later. He made a wide circle and passed it, then waited at the mouth of a canyon to watch it go by.

Four of Kosterlinsky's rurales rode ahead of the coach as advance guard. Ben was surprised to see Red Shepherd driving the coach. He guessed Red had rented it to Vincent and Kosterlinsky, and the cargo was so precious, he was driving it himself. Four rurales were horseback behind the coach, one of them leading Kosterlinsky's white saddle horse.

Ben let the coach go out of earshot, crossed the road, and hit a high trot. He passed the coach, got ahead of it, and returned to the road so he could see his path in the dark. Red was driving at a gentle pace that showed he was planning to go all the way to Santa Cruz and all the way back to Tucson without a change of horses. Ben could go on ahead and have a rest before the coach caught up.

Ben's foot was throbbing, but he was content. He was riding the best horse in the country and was free to do as he pleased on the Camino Real, the road everybody called the Royal Highway. He had everything he needed to become a successful highwayman.

CHAPTER 14

Ben decided he would not assault Kosterlinsky's whole squad of rurales. He would try to capture Kosterlinsky. If he could get his hands on him, Kosterlinsky would squeak as if the owls were upon him and let go the strongbox.

Ben was miles ahead of the coach when he rode into the cottonwoods at the head of the Santa Cruz River. Red would not try to come down the narrow, winding road off the Canelo Hills to the river until daylight. Ben could rest several hours.

He unrolled his bed and slept in spite of the pain in his foot. He rose at dawn, grained his horses, and cooked himself a breakfast. Then he sat down to see about taking his boot off so he could doctor his toe.

He saw he could not save his new boot. His foot was so swollen he had to cut it off. José Bravo's Mexican bootshoes fit him loosely, and their elastic, ankle-length tops would accommodate a bandage.

Lorrie's bullet had obliterated his little toe. Only shreds of bone and flesh remained. Ben would have to operate on himself. His mind was made up not to ask his relatives for shelter or care.

He sharpened his knife on a smooth rock, stropped it on his belt, washed it in hot water and lye soap, and trimmed away the remains of his toe. He washed the wound, smeared it with carbolic salve, and tore up one of José Bravo's clean shirts for a bandage. He covered the stub with a pad, bound it lightly, and put on the bootshoe.

Travelers had long used this cottonwood park on the Santa Cruz River below the Canelo Hills to rest their horses. This road was centuries old. Americans used it now as a route to the port of Guaymas and a winter route to California. The road passed near the VO ranch headquarters. The town of Santa Cruz was fifteen miles south of the VO. Teamsters always stopped in the park to rest in the shade while they checked harness, wheels, and brakes before or after they negotiated the steep Canelo Hills grade.

At midmorning, Ben heard the coach coming and realized he only had a half hour to wait before he committed highway robbery. People would turn away from him even more now for assaulting a coach that carried a woman. He might even have to shoot somebody. He did not want to do anything vicious or cowardly, but he wanted to win his war with Vincent. He might be called vicious for taking that strongbox from a dozen men, but nobody could say he was cowardly.

He grained his horses, packed Moose, saddled Prim Pete, and mounted. He waited in the closest willow thicket downstream from the park, gambling that he knew the first thing Kosterlinsky would do when he stepped down from the coach. He hoped the man had spent hours in the coach with Doris Vincent without relief and would have to go behind the bushes and pee.

Red wheeled the coach into the park and began unharnessing his six-horse team. Rurales set to work unsaddling their horses, leading them to water, and graining them.

Doris Vincent enlisted Stiles and Smiley to help her lay out a picnic spread for an *almuerzo*, the midmorning breakfast customary in the country. People in that country hurried out to work in the coolness of early morning with only bread and coffee for sustenance, then came in for almuerzo at midmorning. Dinner was the meal taken after noon. Doris would be home at the VO that day in time for dinner and siesta.

Kosterlinsky edged away from Doris, on one foot and then the other with the discomfort of his bladder, as he ordered his rurales to find a good tarp on which to lay the almuerzo. When he thought no one was looking, he headed toward Ben's thicket.

Ben congratulated himself as he watched his enemy and friend come toward him. The man almost always did what Ben expected him to do. Ben sometimes even liked him for his predictability. If he had not known him so well, he would have killed him long before this. Kosterlinsky could make any man angry enough to kill him.

Gabriel Kosterlinsky stepped into Ben's thicket, looked back to make sure nobody was looking, and unbuttoned his trousers. He caught sight of a potential peeker, moved deeper into Ben's hiding place, and almost backed into Prim Pete. He gave a great sigh, straightened as his water began to run, and touched Prim Pete's muzzle with his shoulder. He felt the horse's hot, moist, whiskery breath on his shirt, and then Prim nipped him gently with little nuzzlings and flappings of his lips.

"Huuugh!" said Kosterlinsky with a terrified intake of breath. He spun as fast as any man could move with his water running, recognized the face of the man into whose grasp he had fallen, said, "*Ay, Dios mío, no!*" cut his water, and whirled to run. He took his first pounding steps in the brush with both hands still trying to close his fly.

Ben's reata sang over Kosterlinsky's ears, whipped his neck, and closed on his throat. Kosterlinsky's feet kept going, but his head stopped in midflight and was the first part of him to strike the ground. He jumped up to run again, his eyes opaque and unseeing, an animal strangling in a snare.

"Whoa, Gabriel, whoa," Ben said quietly, soothingly. He did not want to strangle the man, only choke him a little until he calmed down. A loop around the throat-latch was such a dependable calmant. Ben administered it often to mean and panicky cattle and horses. It was the only thing to use on a runaway Kosterlinsky, so when Kosterlinsky kept endangering them both by thrashing about and shrieking for succor, Ben put a little more squeeze in his loop and allowed momentary strangulation to set in.

Kosterlinsky's eyes returned to focus and gave Ben a pleading look. Ben gave him slack, and he slumped to his knees. Ben rode up to him and tugged gently on the loop to make him look up, and he started as though he might try to stampede again.

"Now, Gabriel, don't have another fit," Ben said. "Listen to me, if you can."

"Don't kill me," Kosterlinsky said.

"I want to, Gabriel," Ben lied. "But I won't do it right away, because I need you today."

"All right, you—uh, Cowden, I'll do anything. Tell me."

"I like you, Gabriel. You didn't even think of drawing your pistol to do me harm. You're a good man, Gabriel."

"Of course I didn't draw my pistol, Cowden. I don't want to die. Here, take it. I surrender."

"I don't want your pistol, Gabriel. Leave it in the holster. I'll just point my pistol at your head. If you do me wrong, I'll shoot you through the brain. I don't care if I do it in front of your squad, in front of the lady, or in front of your mother. You don't want me to do it, do you?"

"But my poor mother is in Guaymas. How could she witness my murder?"

"Only a figure of speech, Gabriel. I thought you had a good sense of humor."

"Na, ha, no. Not today."

"All right, let's go back to the coach. We have a lot to do and a long way to go today."

"But how can I allow my squad to see me with this reata around my throat? This can't be done. This is embarrassing to me and dangerous for you. What if my squad shoots you without thinking?"

"I'll risk it. Look, I'll tie the reata hard and fast on my saddle horn. If your loyal squad does its duty and shoots me, my racehorse will be free to run away and drag you to death. I'm tying you up close so he'll kick you in the head the first jump and you won't feel it when you come apart in the rocks, the cholla, and the brush."

"No, no, take the reata off the horn. On my word of honor, I won't give you any trouble."

"I know you won't, because if I get shot, or lose control of my racehorse, you're dead. Let's go."

Billy Stiles and George Smiley were on their best behavior because they did not want Doris Vincent to stop smiling at them, giving them gentle orders, and gesturing for them with her pretty hands. The boys' heads were down over the picnic spread, their backs to Ben.

Mrs. Vincent turned, recognized Ben, and the smile froze on her face. This was not acceptable at all. Mrs. Vincent was preparing a beautiful picnic almuerzo, and this was a bad time for Ben Cowden to ride up. She looked at the rurales, smiled uncomfortably, and decided to put up with the interruption with as much propriety as possible.

"Boys, stand up and turn around," she said.

Stiles and Smiley wore nice smiles like Mrs. Vincent's when they turned around, until they saw Ben.

"Now, stand fast, boys," Ben said. "I can't miss at this range, and I don't want to spread your gizzards all over Mrs. Vincent's picnic. I don't want to kill this Mexican, either. Shoot me, and Prim Pete'll drag him from here to Harshaw before he stops."

Stiles and Smiley managed their don't-give-a-damn looks, but they did not move. "Damn," Billy Stiles said. "Captain Marshall will put us in jail for sure, now."

Ben made Kosterlinsky order his rurales to leave their weapons in the coach and sit at Mrs. Vincent's picnic. When everybody was seated, Ben said, "Red, don't be lonesome. Put up your shotgun and join the picnic."

Red Shepherd came out from behind the stage, propped his shotgun carefully on the dash, and walked, head down, to the picnic.

"Well, this is mighty decent of you, Mr. Cowden," Mrs. Vincent said. "Will you come down off your horse to carve the bird?" She uncovered a roast turkey and the necessary cutlery.

"Gabriel and I won't be having any turkey," Ben said. "A cup of coffee'll do." He ordered everyone else to eat, in English and in Spanish.

The rurales began feeding themselves, but Red Shepherd, Stiles, and Smiley only stared sullenly at Ben. Mrs. Vincent was still standing, defying Ben with hands on hips.

"You better have something to eat, Mrs. Vincent," Ben said. "Some food might improve your disposition."

"No, and I won't take orders from you. I'll tell you right now, if this is a holdup, you won't get any money from me. I never carry money, and I doubt these poor workingmen have any."

"Señora, please, don't provoke the man," Kosterlinsky said. "He does not want your money. He means you no harm at all. He's here to rob me. If you anger him, he'll kill me, too."

"Oh, I doubt he'll harm you, Gabriel," Doris said. "I don't believe Ben Cowden is vicious."

"Mrs. Vincent, Gabriel and I will have our coffee now, please."

Doris Vincent laughed. "Sugar?"

"Oh, yes, both of us like sugar in our coffee, don't we, Gabriel?"

"All I can think about is this reata around my neck,"

Kosterlinsky moaned. "What if somebody rides up and decides to shoot you for the reward? I know how fast this horse can run. Nobody will be able to catch him to stop him from dragging me."

"Think about it," Ben said in Spanish. "But be a man, or you'll frighten the lady. My poor horse is scared of hysterical women."

Mrs. Vincent poured two cups of coffee and kept her back to Ben as she sugared them. He knew what she was pulling. She was not in the mood to make him feel good. She handed him his coffee, and when he tasted it, he gave no sign that it was awful. She had filled the cup half full of sugar.

"You know, I thought I saw you in the lobby of the Palace yesterday morning," Mrs. Vincent said. "Now I'm sure of it."

"What makes you so sure?" Ben asked.

"Nobody in the whole state of Arizona has eyes as blue as yours in that dark face. I'm sure I saw you sitting by the door of my husband's office. Was it you?"

Ben did not want anyone to know about José Bravo. "I'm afraid not. Don't feel bad, though. People probably thought they saw me in Tucson and Patagonia yesterday, too."

"I could have sworn it was you."

Kosterlinsky's rurales finished eating and went to saddle their horses. Red, Stiles, and Smiley led the six harness horses into place and hitched them to the coach.

Ben was beginning to suspect he might not have to shoot anybody. There was some advantage to being known as a murderer, after all. He hoped nobody called his bluff. Mrs. Vincent was the only person there who suspected he was not a killer.

"Why are you doing this, Ben?" she asked.

"You'll be able to resume your journey in a few minutes."

"Our lives will go on as if nothing happened?"

"That's right. You'll be be home for supper."

Ben ordered the strongbox brought down. Red, Stiles, and Smiley handed it off the stage and placed it at Ben's feet.

"Open it, Gabriel," Ben said.

"Oh, I don't have the key," Kosterlinsky said. "That's Duncan Vincent's box."

"It's only some ore samples from the Mansfield Mine that Duncan wanted me to take home," Mrs. Vincent said.

"Gabriel and I know it's gold. Everybody else in the

country knows it, too. Open it, Gabriel, or do you want me to choke you like a burro in front of this lady?"

"Ah, I remember, I do have a key," Kosterlinsky said. His hand shook, but he produced the key quickly and unlocked the box. He stepped away without opening the lid.

"There's no gold in that box." Mrs. Vincent laughed. "It's only carrying worthless rocks."

"Open the lid so we can see."

Mrs. Vincent opened the lid and revealed a stash of gold coins nestled in the bottom third of the chest. In the nature of gold, the heavy mass of coins seemed to be fusing together, settling into one piece, as individual grains of placer settle and fuse together to become a nugget. Mrs. Vincent caught her breath. "What in the world?"

"Alazanas, Mrs. Vincent. You're Duncan's courier for the fortune he and Kosterlinsky stole from Walter Jarboe."

Doris turned her back on everybody, walked away, and sat under a tree. She searched for a handkerchief and held her head as though afraid something would spill out of her eyes if she tilted it.

All the men were sorry for her. Ben did not think any of them, not even Kosterlinsky, would have sent his wife out into the country with that kind of baggage. She did not deserve it. On this trip, she had treated everybody equally well, with respect, good humor, and magnificent, openhanded courtesy.

Ben asked the rurales to bring Moose and set his panniers down by the strongbox. He ordered Stiles and Smiley to count the coins by the handful and divide them equally in the two panniers.

Kosterlinsky ordered his men to break camp for Mrs. Vincent, load everything on the coach, and bring him his horse. After the boys hung the panniers on Moose and lashed the top load under the canvas manta, Ben told them to get on the stage with Red Shepherd. Red wheeled the coach around and stopped for Mrs. Vincent.

"I'm staying," she said quietly. "Just send a rig back for me from the ranch." She had been laid low by Vincent's callous endangerment of her life. She was the only one he had fooled when he sent the gold in her coach.

"But we can't leave you here, Mrs. Vincent," Kosterlinsky said. "How would we explain it to Duncan?"

"The same way you'll explain how I would have been killed if someone besides Ben Cowden robbed your damned coach."

Doris Vincent was angry. "Now, you damned ass, tell your men to get the hell out of here. I mean what I'm saying. I'm not traveling another step with you."

Ben sighed. He did not blame her for not wanting to go on with Kosterlinsky, but she could not be left behind. "Gabriel, tell your sergeant to give Mrs. Vincent his horse."

"How can I do that?" Kosterlinsky whined. "The man needs his horse to survive in this country."

"He'll survive by riding the stage." Ben jerked hard on Kosterlinsky's reata collar for the first time since he first caught him. "You'll survive as long as I don't lose my patience. Your sergeant has a better chance to survive than you do. You're not going with the coach, either, Gabriel. You're going with me."

Kosterlinsky ordered his sergeant to help Mrs. Vincent mount his horse. The sergeant spurred his horse to her side, dismounted, crushed his hat to his chest, and helped her on the horse.

Ben looked closely at the sergeant's thick head of gray hair, sweeping mustachios, and *ojos jalados*, the large slanted Indian eyes that were feral as a wolf's but altogether human. He remembered the man but could not communicate openly with him. He was an old friend from Ben's childhood, and Ben knew by the hidden looks he'd been giving Ben that he was still a friend. He did not want Ben to show recognition. Kosterlinsky would stand any man against a wall and shoot him if he suspected him of being the one who told Ben about the alazanas.

"Board the coach and be on your way, Sergeant," Ben said. "I'm keeping your colonel. Don't look back. Travel at a decent pace and don't stop until you reach Santa Cruz." Rafael Cano was the sergeant's name. *El Guero Cano*.

"I understand," the sergeant said without looking at Ben. He climbed into the seat beside Red.

Ben grinned as Stiles and Smiley took seats on their cracker butts, their chins on their knees, on top the coach. "Drive on, Red," he said. Red started the horses. Stiles glared at Ben, but Smiley smiled when his butt began to bounce on the flat top of the coach.

Red wheeled the team onto the road with the escort of disarmed rurales. Ben followed with Mrs. Vincent and Kosterlinsky. Kosterlinsky's white horse would have been pretty in a parade, but as a saddle horse he was silly. He sidled and pranced as though he was being watched by an audience of thousands. He threw froth from his bit, pat-pat-patted the road with his front feet, danced high with his hind feet, and broke into a sweat.

Ben fell far behind the coach as it crossed the open San Rafael Valley. When it rounded a bend out of sight, Ben herded his companions off the road, crossed the river, and rode up a deep canyon. When he climbed out of the canyon, the coach was making dust miles away across the valley. Ben and his companions stopped to watch the cavalcade and let their horses blow.

Ben said, "Gabriel, you can go now. It's too late in the day for you to overtake your rurales and bring them back for me. You don't want to give me a chance to strangle you again, do you?"

"No, Ben. You can let me go. I promise I'll never bother you. I'm ruined, but you needn't worry that I'll try to prosecute you."

"Don't stop for anything until you catch up to the coach. Your white horse will attract attention, and I hate to think about the many desperadoes at large who would love to catch you out here in the open."

"Listen," Mrs. Vincent said. "I think I heard shots."

"Ah, my horse Plata is of fine Arab blood. I'll catch the coach in no time at all."

"Quiet, Gabriel!" Ben held up his hand.

Shots were being fired near the coach.

"What now, for God's sake?" Kosterlinsky said.

"Somebody's attacking the coach," Mrs. Vincent said.

"Nooo. How could that be?"

Ben and his captives climbed to higher ground so they could see the coach. A band of big-hatted riflemen had stopped it in the bottom of a swale. The attacker's horses were being held under a hill by one man, and the rest were pouring rifle fire into the coach. The two lead horses of the six-horse team were down.

"Aw, hell," Ben said. "They've been ambushed, and I made them put their weapons in the coach."

"No, man. Surely they armed themselves before now," Kosterlinsky said. He unstrapped the lid of a leather case on the swell of his saddle, took out a field glass, extended it, and focused it on the coach. "But it would not have mattered if they were armed. They've been ambushed. They're all down." He handed the glass to Ben.

Loose horses of downed rurales were fleeing an open side of the swale. Red and the boys were running after them and falling behind cover to fire back at the bandits. They had a chance to escape the ambush because the horses were headed for the corner of a fence where they might stand to be caught.

Ben offered the glass to Mrs. Vincent, but she did not want to look. Ben could see the massacre well enough without the glass. When there was no longer any answering fire from the coach, the assailants stopped firing at the fleeing Americans, and two of them stood up, drew their pistols, and walked carefully down to the coach. As they reached each fallen rural, they fired a bullet into his head. The splat of the bullet striking a skull dulled the report of each close pistol shot. Ben saw one of the rurales raise his hand to the sky before the coup was given.

"The sons of their fornicated mothers!" Kosterlinsky said. "Those two killers were comrades of my men. That's Jacinto Lopez and Martín Roblez."

"The men who were in jail with me?" asked Ben.

"The same."

"I thought you gave them *ley de fuga* and made targets of them."

"I did."

"Well, what happened?"

"Well, they got away." Kosterlinsky had tears in his eyes. "Now they've come back to haunt me."

"It looks to me like they haunted El Guero Cano and his squad more than you," Ben said.

"Can't you do something, Ben?" Mrs. Vincent asked.

"Not now. All the damage was done in the first volley."

"I guess we should thank you for saving our lives."

"We have the Lord our God and his angel Ben Cowden to thank," Kosterlinsky said.

"Gabriel, you lead a charmed life," Ben said. "You can walk away from this disaster with a whole skin now. I ought to cut off your finger to remind you not to bother me again."

"Listen, I know that ambush was for me," Kosterlinsky said. "They could not have known about the gold. They wanted to assassinate me."

"Hell, Gabriel, everybody in the country who had eyes and ears knew about your alazanas. You could not have advertised it better if you'd published it in the *Arizona Star*."

"Nevertheless, I've narrowly escaped death, again."

Ben and Kosterlinsky watched the bandits ransack the coach, unhitch and unharness the sound horses, and give the coup de grace to the wounded horses.

"They sure like to do that, don't they?" Ben said. "That puts the cure to their consciences, no, Gabriel? I bet you're the one who always does that."

The five bandits rode away, leading the harness horses.

"When we were in jail, Roblez told me you killed all the mutineers," Ben said. "Did new ones grow from the stumps of the ones you mutilated?"

"As I told you, Roblez and Lopez escaped. The other three are part of a new crop of bandits."

At that moment, Stiles and Smiley, riding rural horses, burst from behind a hill and ran at an angle away from the path of the bandits. The bandits waved, laughed, and screamed high, wild calls of ridicule, like Apaches. They sat comfortably on their horses like ordinary vaqueros after a hard, fulfilling day's work in the pasture, laughing, smoking, and pacing toward home.

"Where's the other man?" Mrs. Vincent asked. "There was another man."

"Red Shepherd, the driver," Ben said. "He either couldn't catch a horse, or he's down."

"Do something, then. Those bandits are headed straight for him."

"If it's all right with you, Ben, I'll stay with you and Mrs. Vincent until it is safe for me to return to Santa Cruz," Kosterlinsky said.

"Aren't you going to do something for that man?" demanded Mrs. Vincent. "He must be hurt, or he'd be running with Billy and George."

"Mrs. Vincent, whatever his condition, he won't suffer. Those men will administer a merciful coup."

"Then you're going to sit here and let them kill him?"

"Ma'am, we might as well be in Tucson for all we can do to help poor Red. He's snakebit and has about three minutes to remember his prayers."

"If I were a man, I'd do something to save him. Give me a gun, and I'll show you it can be done."

"Lady, be thankful you're sitting here and not down there with Red. If I let you try to help him, you'll be in real danger for the first time today."

They heard the shot that killed Red Shepherd then. Ben

sighed. Doris Vincent began to weep, and Kosterlinsky bowed his head and crossed himself. Ben lifted the reata gently off Kosterlinsky's neck and patted him on the shoulder when he saw the man was crying.

"Why are *you* crying, Gabriel?" Ben asked.

Kosterlinsky only kept weeping.

"I know, you're relieved it wasn't you they gave the coup de grace, aren't you?"

Kosterlinsky nodded, nodded, nodded. "*Sí*" he said, sniffling wetly like a child.

Ben dismounted, helped Mrs. Vincent off her horse, and walked her to the shade of a tree. He reached inside his panniers and took out his coffee pot, his pouch of coffee, and three cups. He poured gold coins that had accumulated in the pot back into the panniers. He built a small fire with dry oak and leaves, and put on water to boil. He sat under another tree away from his captives and looked at the Cano brand on the blaze-faced black horse Mrs. Vincent was riding. He liked all those Canos. They were good stock, good people, and good hands with cattle. He stoked and lighted his pipe.

CHAPTER 15

Ben did not like his prospects. He was stuck with his captives. He could not send Kosterlinsky away, alone on that white horse. The horse stood out like a storm cloud in a clear sky. To turn a man out in that country on a white horse was to advertise he was fair game. Ben would have to adopt him like a child, take him by the hand, and lead him home.

He was now responsible for the lady too. He supposed the best move he could make in his war was to turn Kosterlinsky and Vincent's wife loose in the country together. They could comfort each other while they waited for the mutineers to execute them, the Apaches to butcher them, or to starve in the wilderness.

Ben decided he was some road agent. He should hurry away by himself and hide the loot. Instead, he saddled himself with his enemy's wife and cowardly accomplice.

The sun was setting. Ben had kept his captives and horses under the trees all day, mostly to hide that white horse. He was not worried that the mutineers would look back and see him or a posse would catch up and chase him, but he did worry about the likelihood of Apaches watching him from the high points.

"Oye, Ben, where do we go from here?" Kosterlinsky had been talking nonstop. Ben was relaxed, his mind shutting out Kosterlinsky's voice and concentrating on the trail ahead. He noticed Kosterlinsky had unsaddled his horse, not the best thing to do if he wanted to keep up with a man on the run.

"What do you call that horse, Gabriel?" Ben asked.

Kosterlinsky brightened. "Bucéfalo is his real name, but sometimes I just call him Plata, Silver." His horse was another of his vanities, like his manicure when he could get one. White horses were almost as hard to find in that country as manicures because horsemen did not want them and did not trade in them. Kosterlinsky must have looked long and hard, and paid a lot of money for this horse that Ben would not give a nickle to own.

"How does that translate into English?" Ben asked.

"Bucephalus, I believe. That was the name of Alexander the Great's horse."

"Alexander who?"

"Hah, not Alejandro Prieto, that's for sure. Alexander the *Great*, man."

"Who is that, Gabriel?"

"A great Macedonian general and ruler."

"Macédonian?" Ben smiled. "Is that the place down by Guaymas where your mother lives?"

"No, man, it's a country between Asia and Europe. Don't you know your military history? I thought all good horsemen knew about Alejandro el Magno and Bucéfalo."

"What did Alexander the Great and his horse do that was so great?"

"They conquered the world horseback before Alexander was even twenty years old."

"And that horse you're riding is like the one he rode?"

"As far as I can tell, he is the very image of Alexander's Bucephalus."

"Must not have been much of a world."

Mrs. Vincent smiled to herself.

"Why do you belittle my horse, Ben?"

"I'm not belittling your horse, Gabriel. A horse is only as good as the man who rides and trains him. It's not altogether your horse's fault he is silly, high-stepping, and unthinking. It's not his fault he's a walking *blanco*, target. That's what he is, you know. A student of military strategy like you should be able to see that he's a very large, plain target. What made you choose a white horse—you, a cavalryman who will have to ride him into battle? Your own word in Spanish for *target* is *blanco*, white. Now, even though you're my enemy, I can't cut loose from you, because you're a big target. I have to shield you from the predators like a woman."

"You don't have to shield me, Ben. I'm not a woman. I do my own share of fighting."

"No, dear God, no. Don't wish a fight on us. I don't want to fight with my arm amputated, or with you on my flank, Gabriel."

"I know you have a poor opinion of me, Ben. I'm not fooling myself that we can be friends again, but I trust your decency and know you'll let me stay with you until I can return to my headquarters safely."

Ben tapped the ashes out of his pipe, not ashamed of ridiculing Kosterlinsky. What the hell, the man was his enemy. If he couldn't shoot him, at least he ought to be able to embarrass him.

"After all," Kosterlinsky was saying, "I don't believe that is too much for one honorable man to ask of another, even though we are enemies."

"Of course it isn't, Gabriel. I apologize." Ben lifted the lid off the pot to see if the coffee was still hot. "Don't worry, we'll stay together. We'll have some more coffee, and then we'll go."

"I accept your apology. Where can we go at this hour? It will be dark in an hour."

"We'll be a long way from here by midnight. We'll camp then."

"Midnight? Man, are you mad? I can't ride until midnight, and you should not require Mrs. Vincent to do so."

Ben poured coffee in their cups. "Gabriel, you can go, or you can stay. You're not my captive anymore." He took a jar of pinole, dry cornmeal mixed with brown sugar, from his morral. "Here, Gabriel, pinole, a late collation for you and Mrs. Vincent."

"No, thank you," Mrs. Vincent said, applying an extra measure of fine manners to her smile.

Ben mixed pinole with water, drank it in three swallows, and was through. A breeze blew in from the southwest. He hoped they would not have wind. He could not dodge Apaches with a wind in his face. He would have to take these two greenhorns to high trails. They could not keep up with him running on level ground, so he would go slow and take them high. He would climb to a Porter camp in the Huachucas. None of his pursuers knew that country as well as he did. Up in the Huachucas, he could hide and watch or run the chasers in circles until their tongues hung out.

He made ready to leave and looked to see what Kosterlinsky was doing. The colonel was resting, smoking a cigar and looking way off toward Mexico as though he might never see home again.

Ben and Mrs. Vincent mounted and rode away. He did not want to leave Kosterlinsky alone in the wilderness, but if the man wanted to ride with him, he'd better learn to get moving. After awhile, Ben stopped a moment and saw him coming a half-mile back. Ben was climbing toward the high trails of the Huachucas on a route that gave him concealment. Kosterlinsky was taking a shortcut across the open to catch up. That's what Ben got for riding off and leaving him. He did not have sense enough to stay off the skyline. Ben had not taught him a lesson by leaving him behind; he had risked discovery by the Yawner or Jacinto Lopez.

Mrs. Vincent caught up and stopped. She was making a game effort to keep up and did not seem worried about anything but saving her horse. Her face looked girlish, and some of her girl's freckles had appeared. The strong lines of her face had replaced the weak ones Ben disliked. She seemed eager to help Ben. He had expected her to be sullen and uncooperative; instead, she was showing courage, stamina, and good style.

Kosterlinsky acted as though he was the woman of the party. For the rest of the *jornada*, the journey, to the springs on the crest of Hijo de Pedro Peak in the Huachucas, Ben held up and waited for Kosterlinsky so he would not lose him. He kept him in the track so he could not stray to the open where he might be seen.

They topped out on Hijo de Pedro Peak after ascending a long, rocky, narrow ridge. Ben stopped to let the horses blow and saw the light of a fire on Huachuca Peak. That could be the campfire of some very audacious humans or the remnant of a lightning strike. Ben had seen no lightning that day.

From that spot, the trail descended gradually into the basin of Hijo de Pedro Springs under the peak. The trail was easy to follow, through a wide, parklike pasture. Lightning strikes started fires that burned out the underbrush, pine needles, and other debris of the forest every time it grew thick enough to catch fire. The lower limbs of the ponderosa pines had been burned off by lightning fire, and only the crowns were left on the trees. Nature was keeping the trees fireproof that way, preserving the forest by burning its own debris.

This was the time of day Ben liked best, the time when he

found himself riding into camp after coming a long way. He felt safe in the heart of Arizona. He felt no soreness or tiredness now, except for his foot, because only a pleasant one-mile ride separated him from his rest.

He stopped and waited for Mrs. Vincent and Kosterlinsky again. Mrs. Vincent was so talkative in her own society that Ben was almost overjoyed when he saw she could keep her mouth shut in the country. She gave no tiresome, soulful sighs. She did not blame her horse for her discomfort and made no complaints. She even seemed to be enjoying herself.

Ben brought out his amphorita of mescal, uncorked it, and handed it to Mrs. Vincent. She did not ask what it was but lifted it and took a swallow. She did not gasp and make a fuss about the awful burn and taste of the stuff, though he was sure it must not be agreeable to her. She seemed to welcome the effect of the spirits as he hoped she would. He took a swallow. He liked the green and spiny taste of Arizona mescal. The taste made him think of the daggers of maguey sprouting out of Arizona dust after a rain.

"I saw a light way over on our right before we started down," Mrs. Vincent said. "I don't see it anymore."

"I saw it too," Ben said.

"Who could possibly have a fire up here?"

"Might be an old snag burning from a lightning strike. Sometimes they smolder for days."

"But mightn't there be someone else up here?"

"Yes, but the fire you saw was over on another mountain in this range, and it looks closer at night than it really is."

"Who could it be?"

"Oh, it could be Apaches, or it could be those *amontinados* that attacked your coach."

"Could they also be friendly?"

"No. Anybody who was friendly to us would be sleeping in a cold camp and wouldn't show a fire."

"Why wouldn't white people have a fire?"

"White people are prey when they come into these mountains."

"We're prey?"

"Yeah."

"Why did you bring us here?"

"I'm hunted in the towns, on the roads and in the valleys. They might catch me down there, but not up here."

"How will you prevent our being caught by Apaches up here?"

"We'll have to listen, watch, and stay downwind from trouble. Haven't you been doing that, Doris Vincent, Daughter of the American Revolution?"

Mrs. Vincent laughed softly. "That makes sense."

Kosterlinsky caught up. "How much farther?" he asked, for the fifth time.

"Only a little way, Gabriel." Ben handed him the amphorita.

"What is it, mescal? Well, now we're getting somewhere. Ay, come to me, baby."

Kosterlinsky turned up the slim half-pint flask and sucked on it so hard, Ben could hear the mescal roil and splash inside the bottle. Ben had finally found something Kosterlinsky could do in his imitation of a man. The amphora was empty when he handed it back. At that rate, the half-gallon jug in Moose's pannier would not last very long. Ben used spirits for medicine and for *el estribo*, the stirrup drink, to ease the stress of the trail. He had not packed it these many miles so Kosterlinsky could guzzle it like water.

When he reached the camp on Hijo de Pedro Mountain, Ben and his companions sat their horses a few moments on the edge of its clearing, listening for enemies.

Bucéfalo was so still, he could have been lighting-struck. He found level footing for the first time since night had fallen, and his structure settled in peace. His head hung low. Kosterlinsky's quirt, big spurs, and twenty mariachis could not have made him prance.

The camp was sheltered by tall pines and equipped with a good cabin, a saddle shed, and a corral on a clear stream of water. Ben led his companions to the corral and dismounted. He unsaddled Prim Pete, left him in the corral, and walked Mrs. Vincent to the cabin. He struck a match to a knot of pitch pine by the door to light his way inside. The place was clean and undisturbed, and the Porters had left some provision in the cupboards. He unpacked Moose, carried his outfit inside, then went back to the corral to make sure Kosterlinsky did not leave the gates open and let their horses out or dump the saddles where the horses would step on them or the rats would gnaw on them.

The cabin was downwind from Huachuca Peak where Ben had seen the other fire, so he built a fire in the cabin's small stove and put on the coffee water. He split up his bedroll so he and his companions would each have a blanket and rolled his mattress out on the rawhide cot for Mrs. Vincent. He fried jerky, onions, and potatoes together, made tortillas on the stove lid, and fed everybody.

Kosterlinsky ate his meal and fell asleep sitting against the wall. Ben washed the dishes and put them away, then went outside with his pipe and tobacco. Mrs. Vincent followed and sat beside him on a long bench Uncle Jim Porter had split out of a pine tree and laid along three level blocks.

Ben lit his pipe and sat in silence. Useless conversation was dangerous. He had known Mrs. Vincent to use it all the time back in her own society, and he hoped she did not try to start it here. She'd do better to listen for their enemies and enjoy the silence.

"Ben, I don't want to be a bother—I know I'm safe as long as I'm with you, but how do I get home if something happens to you?"

"Head down off the mountain that way." Ben pointed in the darkness to the west.

"Look, I can't see anything but dark night and tree trunks."

Ben pointed his finger under her nose. "Keep traveling toward tomorrow's sunset, stay on top this mountain, and you'll be able to see the VO from up here. Wait until the afternoon, when the sun starts down, and follow it home."

"You're going to take me home, aren't you? I hope you don't plan to keep me up here forever."

"Mrs. Vincent, as much as I hate to, I guess I'll have to take you home."

"Please call me Doris."

"I guess I'll have to take you home, Doris."

Doris laughed quietly. "You mean you wouldn't want to keep me?"

"I want to see you safe at home, because if I don't, I'm a criminal. I'm convicted if I keep you and in danger if I don't. I might even have to sneak by your husband's thugs to see you safely home."

"Why don't you just leave me here and let me take my own chances? I'm sure you can find a way to notify Duncan to send somebody after me."

"I could do that, but I better not."

"I know what you're doing for us, and I'm grateful. I know Gabriel is, too."

"That makes me feel good."

"It's odd that you consider yourself responsible for my safety. I'm really an anchor around your neck. My own husband never lets me be an anchor; he only keeps me for my money and my father's influence. It's my money that pays the wages of men like Frank Marshall and Hoozy Briggs. Oh, yes, I know how dirty your war is becoming."

"Don't you think you ought to be resting? I do."

"Yes, I know, I talk too much."

Ben remained silent.

"Can I sit here awhile if I keep quiet?"

Ben figured she could do anything she wanted to. He could not tell her what to do; she wasn't his wife. He did not want to tell her that, though, because she might start thinking he wished she was his wife.

He sat still and puffed on his pipe, trying to keep his lips from popping on the mouthpiece. Doris started wiggling, doing something with her clothes. Ben was sprawled on the bench with his back against the cabin wall, his legs spread wide and his feet stuck out. His right leg was on Doris's side, his sore foot was on the other, safe from her squirming.

Doris's leg brushed against Ben's, and she kept wiggling. Ben could barely see her outline when she moved. The rustlings she made, the sounds of the little breaths she was taking, and the tickling little touches against his leg were seducing him.

Finally, she leaned back with a relieved sigh and stopped wiggling. "At last," she said. "It's off. It's *finally* off." She took a deep breath. "Oh, that's good."

"What in the world came over you, Doris?" Ben asked.

"Give me your hand." She took Ben's hand in the dark and pressed it against her side. He tried to free his hand, but she caught his other hand and placed it on her other side. His fingers took hold of her lean waist, between the swell of her hips and the swell of her breasts. His hands remembered them when he drew them away.

"You couldn't see what I was doing," Doris said quietly. "I took off my corset. You can't imagine how good that makes me feel."

Ben did not dare say a thing about that, but he was happy he had his hands back, she could have been undressed when she sought his hand.

Doris was quiet for a while. Finally she stood up. "You

often in the camp of the enemy, and he always looked prosperous when he came back.

The Yawner still used him trustingly, but Che Che no longer felt close to the band. Lately he thought more about his gentle Mexican mother. He remembered that she had died a captive of these uncles. Because of her teaching, he recognized the cruelty of the Apache—and his own cruelty. Che Che had adapted to the use of cruelty, and it served him well, but it was not enough to make him a completely trusted nephew of these uncles. More and more, though free to come and go, he felt he was a captive like his mother.

The rifles were passed around. No one spoke while they were examined, but Che Che knew what the uncles were thinking. The rifles were so new, the ammunition so plentiful, the horses so fine, someone must have given them to Che Che.

"Rifles, rifles, rifles," Chato said. "Rifles enough to arm even the women and children of this band. *Sobran rifles*." Che Che was never anything but a Mexican to him, and he enjoyed speaking to him sarcastically in Spanish. "Too many rifles. What can we do with them? We don't even know if they shoot straight. Who can waste the ammunition to see if they shoot straight? Not us."

"They're supposed to shoot straight. They're new," Che Che said.

"That doesn't show me they do," Chato said.

Che Che found a basket of tortillas by the fire, sat with his back to a boulder, folded a tortilla, and ate half in one bite.

"Who gave you these arms and horses?" Pablo asked. "What did you have to give for them? Which uncle will you deliver to the Americans?"

Che Che ate the rest of the tortilla.

"How does a man find such horses? Who will come after them?"

"I stole them from El Jinete. As you see, they carry the brand we have seen on his cattle at the spring of the Javali and the spring of the Apache. It does not matter who comes after them. They can outrun any horses that come. I brought them for you, uncles."

The Yawner never seemed to close his eyes. His mouth was a slash that split the lower part of his face. His broad cheekbones shone in the firelight. His eyes were set in straight slits in his head, like healing wounds that glittered with tiny red points from his fire.

"Your uncles thank you," the Yawner said. His wide mouth stretched into a fleeting semblance of a smile. The Yawner never opened his mouth, even for yawning. His mouth was wide as a rattlesnake's and as tight and lipless as one who was accustomed to swallowing, every small warm creature that chanced by. "Pablo, you are the uncle who can have the gelding," proclaimed the Yawner. "Chato, you have the mare. I'll have the brown." He was joking. The whole band owned the horses. They would be used for their strong backs and then eaten, one by one.

"You would have done better to bring more ammunition and fewer rifles," Chato said. "We have rifles enough. We need ammunition for raiding. In our raids we always find rifles, but seldom find ammunition."

Che Che picketed the horses away from the fire. He would let them graze and water during the day. He had watered them at a spring before he rode into camp. He went back to the fire, picked up another tortilla, and took himself away to a place in the rocks to rest.

CHAPTER 16

Paula Mary knew she ought to give Myrtle Farley her ring, but she just could not do it. She felt she had a right to keep it awhile. Che Che the Apache had killed the cutthroat Yaqui for it and told Ben to be sure and give it to the Little Wren in the Tree. Paula Mary was the one he called the Little Wren, not Myrtle.

Myrtle was at El Durazno for a two-day visit. Paula Mary had decided to wait for an absolutely perfect moment to return the ring, but it had to be a moment when Myrtle's happiness would further her own. As yet, she had not felt magnanimous enough to give it up. In the meantime, she kept it out of sight on its chain around her neck.

The little girls were playing in Paula Mary's cave on the cliff above her mother's backyard. Paula Mary's dog, Gyp, panted with his tongue dripping beside them in the shade. They could see a lot of other people had used the cave for shelter. The walls were charred by campfires, and the dirt was full of ash and carbon.

The girls' safe perch was higher than the peach trees in the orchard, higher than the top of Paula Mary's house and Bill Knox's barn. Digging in the charred ground was easy; the dirt was as dry, cool, and fine as sifted flour in a bin. The only lumps they encountered turned out to be bones, flint, and pottery shards. They were having a party for their dolls with Paula Mary's seven-piece tin tea set. They used a jar of water to make mud tortillas and decorated them with flint, bones, and little colored beads they found in the dust.

The girls also kept a lookout on the traffic that came down the canyon road from Harshaw or up the canyon from Patagonia. They could see Bill Knox at his forge, Gordo Soto feeding stock, Viney hanging stockings on the clothesline, and Betty and Eileen shaking rugs.

They were being quiet because they could hear everything everybody else in the canyon was saying. Sometimes they heard things they were not supposed to hear. If no one discovered them, they might hear more.

Chris Wilson's twenty-mule team rattled his ore wagon, into sight down the canyon. Paula Mary and Myrtle were keeping track of the number of ore wagons that went by and trying to remember the names of the drivers as they approached, before they could see their faces. Paula Mary wished she was on her branch in the walnut tree that hung over the road so she could pepper the mules with sticks, but Myrtle was afraid to climb trees.

Paula Mary could spy faces better from the cliff than she could from the walnut tree. She had no close foliage to bother her, and she could see a lot farther up and down the road. She watched Chris go by and did not let him see her. She liked to surprise him. He always looked for her because she was likely to be watching him and hiding, but giving him a chance to spot her. When she waved to let him see her, it was as though she had ambushed him. Paula Mary considered herself as good an ambusher as any Apache. Her best ambuscades were laid from up in the boughs of the walnut trees. Chris and his mules never survived those.

This time she was glad she had not revealed herself to Chris because right behind him came Frank Marshall riding Dick Martin's little dink of a horse called Rosy. Paula Mary marveled at how ridiculous he looked on Rosy, a man so big and elegant, a horse so skinny and shabby. Rosy was too small to carry a man that size. He was even smaller than the horse Dick called Hoozy, but she could understand Marshall not riding Hoozy after the horse tromped his toes and crippled him the last time he came to call.

Rosy was always in a state of suffering, his big eyes teary. Now, carrying this giant was giving him the running spurts. His stool was so loose that a constant stream ran between his legs, but he kept doing his best to get on down the road with his cargo.

Paula Mary wished she could have Rosy. She'd show that Dick Martin how to make a pretty horse. Fat was the prettiest color of a horse. The first thing Paula Mary had learned about horses was that they needed to eat all the time to be presentable.

Frank Marshall must eat big. He was long-legged, broad-shouldered, and fleshy, which was why he looked so good. He was a good doer. He made sure he kept his strength up. Almost anybody who ate good looked presentable.

If Rosy had been six inches shorter, Marshall's feet would drag the ground, and Rosy would not have been able to drag them out past the Patagonia town limits. As it was, they just cleared the ground, and the little horse wobbled and staggered under the bulk upon which they hung.

Paula Mary was thankful Rosy would get to rest when Marshall headed him into the Cowden barnyard, but she sure was not happy to see Marshall's cocky face turn her way. Gyp started barking, and the girls ducked their heads. "Hide, Myrtle," Paula Mary said. "I don't want that man to see us."

Paula Mary raised up until she could see Frank Marshall from behind a bush. He dismounted by the barn and tied Rosy. He did not go into the barn, and Paula Mary knew why. Bill Knox was not one to make him feel welcome, and Marshall didn't want to waste time with Bill that he could spend with Betty.

"My Lord, there comes that Frank Marshall," said Eileen, down at the house. Betty mumbled, scurried into her bedroom, slammed a dresser drawer, then the bathroom door. Why she got so high behind for that big dude was more than Paula Mary could figure. He even shadow-rode when he walked.

The Cowdens called egotistical men shadow-riders. A shadow-rider was somebody who could not keep his eyes off the shadow he made on the ground when he rode horseback. Some men made an absolute vice of the way they had to see how they looked on their horses by watching their shadows.

Frank Marshall was doing it now as he walked from the barn to the house. Paula Mary wondered why he thought he could worm his way into her family, but here he was. The Cowden ladies were never inhospitable to anybody, so now they had one minute to fix themselves up. They felt they had to fix themselves for everybody who came to visit. They'd probably fix themselves up for the old Yawner if they heard he was on the way.

Frank Marshall certainly walked in a stalwart manner. He did not limp at all now. Paula Mary smiled to herself. Rosy had probably tried not to step on Marshall. He was dumber than little Hoozy. She bet Marshall would never ride Hoozy again.

Gyp barked and barked at the man. Horses didn't like him. Dogs didn't like him. He stopped and looked up at the cave. Paula Mary ducked and pulled Myrtle down.

"Hello, Paula Mary," Frank Marshall called cheerily.

Paula Mary did not move except to breathe against the ground.

"I saw you, girl. Wave if that's you."

Paula Mary gave him no sign, and he went on to the house. Eileen met him at the door. He was smart to come when A. B. and the boys were gone. Les and Mark were working the roundup. Since A. B. had resigned from being undersheriff, he'd gone to Phoenix to see if he could put his teams and rigs to work hauling freight. Frank Marshall was taking advantage of the absence of the Cowden men to come wooing Betty.

Nobody ought to come out to a ranch like this and go right in the house when women were there alone unless he was a close friend or relative. He probably thought the Cowdens considered him a friend now, since he had calmed the crowd in Tombstone when the sight of Ben turned it into a mob. Even A. B. admitted the man handled himself well that day.

A. B. did not like it when Marshall told the crowd that Ben's family was there, though. Some of the loudmouths turned the crowd ugly about that. The crowd was so thick, Paula Mary, Betty, and Eileen had not been able to do a thing when Lorrie Briggs shot Ben and knocked him down. The family could only press close to A. B. and stand its ground.

Paula Mary did not feel like playing in the cave anymore. She and Myrtle picked up their dolls and walked down the hill. She had told Myrtle all about Frank Marshall, and she wanted to prove to her that he used perfume, like a woman.

The girls dipped a drink of water out of the olla on the back porch. They were both sweating, and Paula Mary thought Myrtle smelled like a puppy dog. Gyp stopped at the back door to wait for them when they went inside.

Frank Marshall was already holding forth in the front room. Eileen, Betty, and Viney were sitting up straight in their chairs, their ankles crossed and the Cowden expression of stone on their faces.

"Ah, it's the littlest Cowden." Frank Marshall beamed. "Who is this other pretty child?"

"This is the little Farley girl." Paula Mary minced. "The very littlest one, here all little and cute for you to pat on the head."

"Paula Mary, that's no way to speak to a visitor," Eileen said automatically. The eldest sister could be counted on to say something that ought to be said, no matter what.

"Anyway, as I was saying," said Marshall, "from now on, the Interior Department will be policing these local land disputes. I've come to see what I can do about Ben's trouble. I think I can settle this argument between the Cowdens and Mr. Vincent."

Marshall was patiently, gamely wooing the Cowden women again. Paula Mary could have told him he would have to do it every single time he came to El Durazno. If he showed up when the boys or A. B. were there, he'd never even get to talk to them.

Then Paula Mary saw that Marshall's smooth manner was only a glaze he put on like bay rum so he could move in and give the Cowdens bad news. He said, "I'm sorry none of your menfolk are here, for I've come to warn you about some terrible new developments in this range war. It seems Ben assaulted a coach that was carrying Duncan Vincent's wife home the day after the horse race. According to survivors of that assault, Ben killed Red Shepherd, the driver, and five Mexican rurales who were guarding the coach."

Viney made a tiny involuntary sound.

"I know this comes as an awful shock to you, Mrs. Cowden, but that's not even the end of the story. Your son also kidnapped Mrs. Vincent and Gabriel Kosterlinsky, the colonel of rurales who accompanied her. No hope is being held for their survival."

Viney recovered. "Why, Captain Marshall, my son wouldn't harm that woman, or anybody else. Who says he did these things?"

"Two rangers for the Arizona Live Stock Association who were part of the guard managed to escape and bring back word of the assault."

"Are you telling me that men who were supposed to protect Mrs. Vincent allowed my son to kidnap her? Are you saying people were killed and a woman was kidnapped, but they ran away? Who are these men? How could anyone believe a word they said?"

"They are just two boys named Billy Stiles and George Smiley who were sent to do a man's job and failed. They're being questioned extensively. It does seem doubtful that Ben's gang would kill all the seasoned rurales and the driver, yet allow the two most inexperienced guards to escape, doesn't it?"

"You can't make me believe my son led any gang to commit murder."

"I know those boys pretty well. They're inexperienced and young, but they're not liars. They've been unswervable in their testimony."

"You might think you know them, but I know my son. You're being lied to, Captain Marshall."

"Well, a very, very systematic search has been organized for Mrs. Vincent and Colonel Kosterlinsky. General Carbo has been contacted in Hermosillo, and we expect his cooperation if the search takes us into Mexico, but to tell the truth, nobody expects to find them alive.

"I'm not going on the search, because I want to see if I can contact Ben. I'm sure when he hears of these charges, he'll want to come in and clear himself. Maybe he can help us bring the real criminals to justice. My best course is to stay in this region where I can keep in touch with the searchers and with Ben's family.

"It occurred to me that the best way to get in touch with Ben is by sending his brothers out to find him. I'm sure I can convince them to do it, and they're obviously our best chance of bringing him in peaceably. Are they here?"

"No, they're on the general roundup on the Babocomori, my brother Billy Porter's range."

"Ah, that's right, but are you sure they went on the roundup? Could they possibly have been part of the gang that assaulted the coach? These are questions that come to mind. I hope your sons were not a party to this heinous massacre."

"Heinous are the charges, Captain Marshall."

"Perhaps, but I'm here to ask these questions and to see if I can help put an end to this range war."

"You won't find anything here that will help you put an end to the war. You should be talking to Duncan Vincent about that." Viney rose from her chair.

"I would like to rent a horse and buggy, Mrs. Cowden, if possible."

"I'm sure Mr. Knox can help you."

"Would you allow the girls to take a ride to Harshaw with me? I need to go in, send a telegram, and find a place to stay. How pleasant it would be if the girls could go."

"That's entirely up to them, Captain Marshall."

"Why, that's most generous of you. I'll take Betty."

"You won't take Betty without taking somebody else. I want everybody back for supper at dark."

Paula Mary wanted to go. She was as curious about Frank Marshall as she was about snakes and corrupted sores. She had suspected this dude suffered from corrupted sores from the first day she laid eyes on him, and she wanted to know where he hid them.

Betty's one weakness was that she loved to go for buggy rides. She did not have to like the person who invited her to go; she'd go anytime, anyplace her mama would let her go. Having Paula Mary and Myrtle along was plenty enough protection.

"Myrtle and I'll chaperone," Paula Mary offered. Marshall gave her a look as sour as a vinegarroon's. Betty showed no expression at all. She was as good a poker player as A. B. She and Mark were alike, never showing how they felt, even when their feelings were high. Marshall the shadow-rider probably thought she was tickled to death for the privilege of being seen with him in Harshaw.

"After you, ladies," Marshall said, gesturing toward the door. Betty went into her room for a shawl, and Paula Mary and Myrtle ran out of the house and down to the barn.

Bill Knox ignored Marshall when he asked to rent a horse and buggy. As far as he was concerned, Frank Marshall could wait until after the forge cooled. Betty asked Gordo Soto to help her, and together they hitched the dun mare Scotty to a buggy. She climbed in front with Marshall and Paula Mary and Myrtle sat in back as Marshall headed toward Harshaw. Bill never looked up from his forge.

Scotty was a classy zebra dun. Everything she did came easy for her. She was Betty's favorite, a natural beauty who never seemed to work hard or get tired. She was smooth-moving and lighthearted and always accommodating when she was needed. She did not even seem to mind being caught and harnessed at feeding time.

Taking a drive behind Scotty was so pleasant that Paula Mary forgot about looking for corrupted sores on Frank Marshall, and Betty even smiled at him a time or two. Paula Mary thought Marshall was sitting too close to her sister, but Betty never seemed to mind how close she had to sit by anybody, didn't mind touching somebody or being touched. She was like a horse that way; like a good horse, she only minded people when they took advantage of her and became overly familiar, sat too close to her on purpose. Horses were only friends with other horses. Mark was Betty's only matchless friend, and he never got familiar with anybody.

The evening was cool, the country still dry, the spotty summer rains long gone. The sound of the buggy echoed in the canyon, making Paula Mary feel nicely on the go. The evening was the best time to take a drive. Long hard drives started early in the day. Evening drives were just for fun because they always ended by suppertime.

Paula Mary was happy that her family was not giving Marshall its trust. The thing to do was to keep their eyes on him, go for rides with him. That would not be enough to protect themselves for him though. After all, he was not just a dude. Most dudes were harmless if a person was careful enough not to be under them when they fell off their horses or tripped over a horse turd. Paula Mary knew Frank Marshall was not harmless. She kept trying to tell everybody he was rotten, but everybody kept telling her to be quiet. Her family would rather be nice to him and keep him in sight so they could watch him better. A patient attitude was a great Cowden family trait, but sometimes it made Paula Mary want to throw herself down in a violent fit of frenzied impatience.

Paula Mary could be patient if she wanted to be, but she would rather make things erupt, especially corrupt things. She wanted to see Frank Marshall's whole head erupt off his shoulders.

Marshall drove into Harshaw, circled the town pond, and turned down the street in front of the stores, saloons, and hotels. He swung Scotty around in the middle of the street in front of Vince Farley's saloon and stopped her in front of the Sonora Hotel.

"Do you and your sisters want to come in with me?" Marshall asked Betty. He did not look at Myrtle and Paula Mary. Paula Mary was sure he didn't want her to come in with him; he knew, sure as his butt was fat, that she did not like him. The shadow he watched might make him think he was a lady-killer, but Paula Mary would never become a casualty. His butt was too fat.

"I want to go in," Paula Mary said cheerily and looked Marshall in the eye when he turned toward her with the superior smile he always used on her.

"I need you to do something more important, Paula Mary. Will you please sit up here and hold the lines so Scotty won't go off and leave us? Would you do that for us?"

Ordinarily, Paula Mary loved to sit in the driver's seat and hold the lines, but a big dude with a fat butt should not think he could give her things to do.

"I'll hold Scotty," Betty said, trying to take the lines from him.

"Oh, no." Marshall smiled in her face. "I need you to go into the telegraph office with me and introduce me to your uncle Jim Porter. Will you do that for me?"

Betty didn't say a word. She just climbed down off the buggy and left Marshall planted on his big butt. Paula Mary knew Marshall had probably wanted to lift her down by the waist in front of everybody on the hotel veranda.

"Dammit, kid, get up here and *hold the horse*," Marshall said, gritting his teeth.

Paula Mary climbed into the front.

"Sit down, so you can take the lines, girl."

"Hand me the lines and get down, sir, so I can sit on the driver's side." Paula Mary looked down her nose at him. He sure was a dude. She took the lines and said, "Hooo, Scotty! Whoaaa!" keeping her stance and steadying the mare as Marshall climbed off the buggy. The mare was too honorable to try to go anywhere when someone was climbing down off the rig, so Paula Mary was only putting on a show.

"Attagirl, Paula Mary, hold that wild ol' thing," shouted a voice she knew. She looked up and saw Chris Wilson sitting on the hotel veranda with a group of grinning teamsters. She waved at them and took her seat on the driver's side.

Betty was already halfway up the hotel stairs. She greeted the teamsters and went in the lobby ahead of Marshall. While Betty was in sight, the teamsters couldn't see anything else in the world.

Myrtle climbed into the seat beside Paula Mary, and they watched the people of Harshaw go by. Harshaw was booming. Silver was being mined and hauled around the clock. The town's twenty-seven saloons stayed open day and night. Cavalry soldiers drank whiskey next to teamsters, cowboys, smugglers from Mexico, gamblers of all nationalities, railroad men, and hurdy-girls.

The girls loved to watch these people go by. The Cowden and Farley girls were hardly ever allowed out on the street at this hour; never, never allowed to sit and stare on the street at dark. Paula Mary was under orders not to look to the right or to the left when she walked down this street to and from school. She bragged that her folks would be astounded at the things she had seen out of the corner of her eye. Now she was getting to listen to the sounds coming out of the saloons, watch the people glut themselves, and smell the beer and whiskey fumes that mingled with mesquite smoke from supper fires.

Two bareheaded workingmen dressed like railroaders in canvas trousers with galluses over their undershirts walked up to Scotty. They were carrying beer.

"What you doing down there with our little sister, Paula Mary?" asked Danny Farley from the veranda. Paula Mary waved. Danny and Donny, Myrtle's twin brothers, were in their cups as usual, but not yet falling down. She turned away so she would not invite a shouting conversation.

"Yeah, what are you doing with our little sister?" said one of the railroaders standing in front of Scotty. He spoke into the mare's ear with his hand cupped over it. Noble person that she was, Scotty did not even waggle her head.

"Mister, please don't pester my mare," Paula Mary said. "She's gentle, but if you scare her, she might scatter this buggy all over the street." Young as she was, she knew the difficulty of handling horses when drunks pestered them.

"Aw, the little girl's scared her horse'll run away. Would you run away, little horse?" the man asked Scotty.

"These two look like little Irish girls, don't they, Dave?" the other railroader said. "Are you little Irish people? Are you Irish atall?" Both men were standing too close to Scotty. She squirmed and shifted in her harness and looked back at Paula Mary to see if everything was all right.

"No, John, they're not Irish. Irish girls're good girls. These girls're Cowden girls."

"We are too Irish girls," Myrtle said. "And you get away from our horse."

The one called John leaned on the dash in front of Paula Mary. "You're common little sluts, is what you are. Little

Cowden sluts. Little Cowden whooores. That's what you are. You're already out here on the saloon streets getting your directions for when you get bigger. Or do you think you're big enough now?"

Paula Mary looked up at the veranda. "Chris," she called, but Chris was busy talking. "Danny? Donny?" she called, but the Farley twins were too busy passing the jug.

The man called John did not have a mean face. Paula Mary would never have believed he could say such awful things. She shut her mouth.

"What's the matter, baby slut? Won't anybody come save you?"

Paula Mary only knew one other thing to do. She jerked the buggy whip from its slot on the dash, shouted, and lashed Scotty across the hip. John snatched the whip from her so roughly that he hurt her shoulder. The man named Dave held Scotty in her tracks. Paula Mary's shoulder hurt so bad, she lay down on the seat and moaned into the cushion. John took the lines away from her, leaned over, and kissed her sloppily beneath the ear, then reared back and laughed as though he'd tasted blood. Paula Mary straightened, bawling with pain and anger.

"Oohhh," John said with mock compassion. "Is the little slutty huurting?"

"*Baaaw!*" Paula Mary bellowed, mad as a rabid heathen. Her fingernails were tough from digging dirt, and she raked them down the length of his face, poked him in the eyes, clawed the skin off his nose, and stretched his lower lip off his teeth.

"You there! What's the meaning of this?" Frank Marshall shouted from the top of the veranda stairs. John let go the whip behind the dash and stepped back with both hands on his eyes. Paula Mary clubbed him on top of the head with the handle of the whip.

John looked up to protect himself, and Betty Cowden flew into his face, using teeth and claws like a wildcat. The surprise and fury of the attack bowled the man off his feet. He jumped up like a prizefighter and slapped Betty to the ground. He stepped in to punish her at a more measured pace with his boots.

Frank Marshall bounded in front of him and thrashed his fists upon his face. Paula Mary was surprised that a man as big,

agile, and muscular as Marshall did not know how to fight. He
hit like a girl. Now, if her brother Les had smitten the man, he
would be bleeding on the roof of the hotel.

Paula Mary started Scotty, to move her out of range of the
fight. The other man made a grab for the lines, and Paula Mary
made him see stars with the butt end of the whip. She lost her
temper then because all of a sudden she remembered that
these two railroad bums were the Irishmen she'd seen leave
Patagonia with her brother Ben the day he was arrested.

She ran Scotty up the street, turned her around without
slowing down, pointed her back down the street, and laid on
the whip. Marshall saw her coming, stopped whaling on John,
and jumped up the veranda stairs out of the way. He was
nimble as a cat when he had to be, when he was fraidy.

The one called Dave had his back to her and did not know
he was in danger until Scotty was upon him. When Scotty was
three jumps from hitting him, he saw her coming, leaned
back, dug in, and ran straightaway down the street.

The one called John was still batting his eyes from Marshall's thrashing when he whirled to see the buggy bearing
down on him. He stumbled backward, the mare bumped him
down, and the wheel traversed the length of him.

Paula Mary chased the railroader called Dave to the end of
the street and turned the buggy around again. Myrtle's face
was wild with glee. "You going to run over that other one
again, Paula Mary?" she shouted.

Paula Mary wanted to run over Frank Marshall. She had
done more damage to that John with her fingernails, whip, and
buggy than that phony Marshall had done when he laid his big
hands on him.

Paula Mary stopped in front of the hotel and glared at
Marshall. John was still sitting in the street, holding his head.
The Farley twins, Chris and his cronies, and Uncle Jim Porter
were standing beside Marshall. Betty was between Danny and
Donny Farley, crying on Donny's chest.

"You're a helluva man, Frank Marshall," Paula Mary
shouted. "Letting your railroad rats hit my sister. What good
are you, anyway? I know they work for you."

"Now, Paula Mary, you subside," Uncle Jim said. "Captain
Marshall did all right." He gave Marshall a congratulatory pat
on the shoulder. "I saw the whole thing."

All the drunks nodded their heads except the Farley twins.

Those two were too drunk to do anything but stand still so Betty could lean on them.

Marshall moved Donny aside, put his arm around Betty's shoulders, and walked her to the buggy. He handed her up into her seat, boarded, took the lines, and shoved Paula Mary into the backseat with Myrtle.

"I'm taking this girl home to her mother," Marshall said.

He wheeled the mare around and headed out of town. Betty slumped against him, still crying softly from the sting of the slapping.

"Yeah, our great protector," Paula Mary said. "Both those rats're on your payroll. Is that why you weren't able to skin your knuckles on them?"

"You're talking silly, little snip," Marshall said. "If you hadn't started a fight with those men, nothing would have happened. Don't try to put the blame on somebody else. You've been spoiling for a fight all day."

"Yeah, and you and I both know why, don't we?"

"Just shut up. I want to get this girl home."

Paula Mary shut up. She was glad she'd taken care of business with those hoodlums. Her only reminders of the fight were a sore shoulder and wet cheeks.

The rider was standing his dark horse in the orchard when the buggy came into the yard. The dog was barking at him, but he was in a safe place, well shielded by the trees and the darkness. He could see all he needed to see. The mother and the oldest daughter were setting the table for supper in the kitchen. He ought to know where to stand his horse and not be discovered. This was not the first time he had been here at night.

To feel more secure, he backed his horse deeper into the orchard where he would be more hidden but still able to watch the path from the barn to the back door. He turned the horse away from the house so the white star on his forehead and his eyes would not reflect the light.

After awhile, the two girls walked to the house from the barn. Both girls walked as though they were hurt. He saw their faces well as they walked past the kitchen window and again as they went through the back door. The light shone on swipes of tears on their cheeks. The sight of sadness in their gentle faces touched him. Nothing else had ever moved him like that.

He would have liked to go in and asked what he could do

to cheer them, but he did not belong here. He did not seem to belong anywhere. He was lonesome. He started the dark horse away from the orchard, having seen what he came to see—how little wren was doing.

CHAPTER 17

"Now, Ben, I have to take off this last little splinter of bone," Doris Vincent said.

Ben was lying on her cot with his foot on the table, and Doris was doctoring the stump of his toe. The toe had been giving him so much pain that Doris demanded to see it. She had trimmed the flesh with Ben's stock knife and removed loose fragments of bone. Now she applied Ben's wire pliers to a splinter that was still attached to the stump.

Ben watched her hair. She used combs to keep waves of thick brown hair from flowing over the fancy column of her neck, the gentle slope of her shoulder. The combs seemed buried in luxury. He concentrated on one stray, damp tendril of hair that curled around her pretty ear while she performed this last torture on the remains of his toe. He heard a soft little snip, and the splinter came off.

"Now I'll sew it up, and you'll have a stump you can live with," she said.

Doris's temples and upper lip were damp with perspiration. Her eyes were liquid. Ben had always considered her gaze cold and hard. He had never identified the color of her eyes because they seemed to mirror an impersonal disposition. They were an extraordinary silver-gray and now seemed warm, concerned, and loyal. Her lustrous hair had been piled on without a mirror and adorned her in an innocent, youthful way.

The sun had brought new color and tiny freckles to her face

because she was not used to staying outside without a hat. Ben had been concerned during the long ride that she might faint, but now he could see she was strong and handy as any outdoor woman. When she had carved off shreds of his skin and flesh and daubed the blood away so she could see what she was doing, Ben was the one in danger of fainting.

"Can you hold still a little longer?" she asked. "Am I too rough? Would you like to rest?"

"Better finish it while you've got me down," Ben said.

"Fine. I'll be through in one minute. I'm good at this part."

Every time Ben spoke, a grunt escaped him, as though it had been lying imprisoned in a knot in his stomach. More grunts were down there, waiting to escape.

Doris doused the stump with mescal, daubed it, and took a threaded needle out of a washpan full of hot soapy water. She laid the needle and thread in a cup and filled it with boiling water from a kettle on the stove. She laid a strip of tarp across her lap, rested Ben's heel between her legs, and began sewing the stump.

Ben's foot was comfortable. She gripped his heel between her legs to steady his foot. The bottom of his foot rested against her soft abdomen. The warmth of her body thrilled him and brought high color to his face. He was so comfortable and the woman so gentle that he wished she would never finish.

Deft as she was, she finished quickly, tied a knot on the stitches, and cut the needle loose. She swabbed it with unguent, bandaged it, held his foot gently in both hands, and smiled at him. "Finished. Did I hurt you very much?"

"I'll swear, it felt good," Ben said. "You have the touch of a saint. If I could leave that foot where it is, I'd be well in an hour."

"Rest it on the table until it stops throbbing. I'll see to the beans now. I hope you can get your boot on."

"I have to. I need to ride out and look around."

Kosterlinsky stuck his head in the door. "Can I come in now? Are you through with the surgery?"

"You didn't have to go outside in the first place, Gabriel," Doris said.

"Ahh, yes I did. It makes me ill to watch surgery."

He walked with mincing steps to the table, like a pilgrim approaching a shrine, to look at Ben's foot. He hugged his chest with arms crossed, a look of reverence on his face.

"What's the matter with you, Gabriel?" Ben asked.

Kosterlinsky bent over the foot. "Ah, the stitching is beautiful, no? A real work of art. What's that I smell?"

"I rinsed it with mescal after I washed it," Doris said.

"No, no, no," Kosterlinsky scolded. "That was wrong, wrong, wrong. The spirit should be taken internally. You only waste it when you pour it on the outside of the poor man."

"Pour us a little swallow for a remedy, then," Ben said.

Kosterlinsky lifted Ben's amphora and was about to empty it in one draft.

"Whoa!" Ben said. "Get two cups for that. We'll take it in sips, by God."

Kosterlinsky stopped the flask on its way to his mouth. His upper lip was already curled to accommodate the bottle.

"Put some of it in the cups, Gabriel," Ben said. "You can guzzle all you want in a saloon when it's not so hard to get."

"Yes, but will I ever see another saloon?"

Doris laughed. "Don't despair, Gabriel. I'm sure you'll make it back to your saloons and bordellos sooner than you think."

"Ah, if I could tell you about the luxury of some of the places I know."

"Well, don't be bashful. Tell me."

Ben put on his bootshoe, picked up Kosterlinsky's spyglass, and went out as Kosterlinsky began telling Doris about a pleasure palace he knew in Cuernavaca. Ben saddled and rode out to watch his neighbors. From the riding and spying he had done in three days on this mountain, he knew two other parties of outlaws were hiding in the Huachucas. One was on Huachuca Peak, and another was staying in the Porter camp in Lyman Canyon.

He climbed the rocky pinnacle of Pedro Peak at sunrise and watched the country come alive under the sun. He saw traces of smoke and smelled the campfires of his neighbors. He saw a troop of soldiers leave Fort Huachuca. He watched it file up the slope of the mountain toward him. The Apache scouts with the troop would soon find his tracks. He'd better move, and he could not leave his gold up here because the scouts would find it.

Ben did not hurry back to camp, but he did not want anything to delay him now. His foot felt better, and he was ready to move. Kosterlinsky was still telling Doris about the fleshpots when Ben walked in and told him someone was finally on the way to save him.

"But who would come to save me, Ben?" Kosterlinsky said. "I'm in no danger, am I?"

"A troop of soldiers is coming up the mountain. You and Doris can go home with them."

Doris put a stick of wood in the stove. She was like a mother swallow building her nest, the way she kept improving the cabin and making it homey for Ben and Kosterlinsky.

"You're both safe now," Ben said. "You've been good prisoners. Thank you for being partners instead of enemies."

He began gathering his outfit.

"Which way will you go, Ben?" Doris asked.

"Oh, well, I'll decide that when I get on my horse."

"May I go with you?" Kosterlinsky asked.

Doris looked back and forth between Ben and Kosterlinsky, as though afraid she would be left behind.

"Why do you want to go with me, Gabriel?" Ben said. "You better stay here and wait for the soldiers. If you go with me, I might lose my patience and shoot you. I'd hate to do that."

"No, Ben, you won't shoot me, don't worry."

"Well, you're awful damned sure of that."

"I want to go with you."

"All right, Gabriel, why?"

"Why? Why would I want to go with the troopers? They're on patrol and probably looking for a fight. I'm a soldier too. They'll expect me to fight if they ride into a skirmish. They're under orders and won't feel obligated to take me home. I'll have to ride my ass off and eat hardtack and raw jerky until they can drop me off. They won't have mescal. They won't have a blanket for me. I'll spend the duration of their patrol with them, listening to them cuss in Gringo. No, I want to go with you."

"You have to stay here with Doris, Gabriel. We can't leave her alone."

"What if they don't even come to this cabin? What then?"

"You can ride out and meet them. Don't worry about finding them; they'll see your horse."

"I want to go with you too, Ben," Doris said.

"Don't worry, Doris. You and Gabriel won't have long to wait. The soldiers will be here by noon."

"I'm not afraid to wait for the soldiers, but I'd rather you took me back to the ranch."

Ben could see he'd turned out to be a *helluva* road agent, the way he allowed his hostages to hold him up and argue with him. "Doris, what could be better for you than a military escort to your front door?"

"Don't you see? If you leave me here, Duncan can say you abandoned me in the wilderness to die. If you take me back to the ranch, he won't be able to say you kidnapped me or intended to kill me."

"That's right," Kosterlinsky said. "Same with me. I'll be a witness that you returned Mrs. Vincent safely to the VO."

"None of that will do me any good if you slow me down so much I get caught. I'm not going back to any jail, even if I have to shoot you both to keep from worrying about you. I've got to keep moving."

"We won't slow you down," Doris said. "We'll do anything you say."

Ben hoisted his bed and panniers, and headed out the door. "Well, I guess I can't stop you, but if you're coming with me, you better get amoving. God, I'm dumb. Lord save me if anything happens to you."

Ben headed south through thick pine forest. Every once in a while, he climbed a high point and looked to see if his neighbors on the Huachucas were also traveling. He made good time with good concealment, staying high on the cordon of the range. An hour before sunset, he reached the south slope above the big flats he would have to cross to reach Mexico. He decided to wait where he was until dark. He would use the twilight to make his descent and wait until full darkness to cross the open flats.

Ben sat in a pile of rocks on a ridge and accommodated his sore foot so it would stop throbbing. Kosterlinsky and Doris were close below him, resting quietly in the shade.

He heard the murmur of a deep voice. The voice was too close below for him to see the speaker. Another voice answered the first.

Ben made a sign to warn his partners. Doris was already holding her hand up to keep Kosterlinsky quiet. Ben crawled along a shelf and found an opening in the rocks where he could look through brush and see the trail below. Apaches were filing onto his trail in full march toward Mexico.

Ben admired their soundless pace as they strode downhill. They carried their loads in morrals, their water in bules, and they were eating *bellotas*, black-oak acorns, on the march. They would probably stop on the edge of the flat until dark as Ben had planned to do.

These Apaches were running from the same troopers Ben was fleeing. By now, the army must be on both their tracks. The whole troop would not be after Ben, though, unless its orders were to hunt him down. The cavalry was more likely to be after these Apaches. Ben needed to get off mountain trails and down on the level where he could run and have the advantage in horseflesh. He needed to rid himself of his charges.

The Apaches were nearly out of sight. Ben could see a head bob now and again as they disappeared down the mountain. Seeing Apaches this close was like seeing a pack of migrating wolves. A man always got to see them when he did not want to. These last glimpses were of creatures who would soon disappear as if they did not exist—until they fell on somebody again.

Ben climbed down off the point, mounted Prim Pete, and headed west, backtracking the Apaches. He skirted Huachuca Mountain and reached Lyman Canyon in full darkness. He found his way on the mountain by instinct. The darkness was so complete that he had been on the trail along the edge of Lyman Canyon awhile before Moose made him sense the open space of the chasm by snorting softly and veering away from his right. Prim was also lowering his head and keeping his nose to the right. The canyon was so deep, its walls so sheer in places, that a horseman had better not try to move along it in the dark. A horse could take one step too many on the edge of the rim and not touch ground again for a hundred feet.

Ben could barely see Kosterlinsky's white horse in the darkness. The horse was like a haze or film on his eye. Doris was between Ben and Kosterlinsky; he could not see her black horse, but he sensed his warmth. That warmth might be Doris's too. His discovery of Doris's warmth bothered him all the time.

Ben dismounted and felt the ground ahead to find the trail. He took out his oak punk, a sliver of pitch, his knife, and flint, struck a spark, and made it glow in the punk. He blew flame into the pitch pine, raised it and found the trail. He put out the light when he discovered the brink of the canyon only three feet away.

He climbed back on Prim, gave him his head, and went on. He knew that was dangerous with the cliff edge so close to the trail, but he had to keep moving. He had to cross the San Rafael Valley in darkness to reach La Noria unseen. He could hide through the day at La Noria, leave his partners there, and ride into Mexico after dark.

He stopped above the Porter cow camp that lay in the deepest part of Lyman Canyon. No Apaches would ever camp there when they could use a peak like Huachuca to hide and watch. Ben figured the mutineers must be there. Kosterlinsky rode up beside Ben.

"How much farther, Ben?" he asked.

"You have to be quiet, Gabriel, but you'll be happy to know we'll keep going tonight and you'll be home tomorrow."

"Is that *right*?" Kosterlinsky said, too loudly.

"Well, no, Gabriel. We won't make it if you don't keep quiet. The people who want you more than anybody else in the whole world are right down there in the bottom of this canyon. You could probably hit their cabin with a rock from here."

Kosterlinsky whispered, "Are we near a canyon?"

"Use your ears, Gabriel. Can't you hear those trees moving in the breeze below you on the right?"

"Ah, yes, I think so."

"And do you hear a sort of moaning below the sounds of the trees?"

"Maybe. Yes, I think so."

"That's the amontinados snoring. If that snoring stops, it will mean they heard you and are coming to see who woke them up. Imagine what they'll do when they find out it was you."

Doris laughed softly.

"Now let Doris come up here behind me. You stay back so they'll shoot you first. And keep old Bucéfalo right behind Doris. If you get too far off the trail on the right, you'll fall in the canyon, and you won't hit bottom until sunup."

Ben gave Prim Pete his head again. They left the Huachucas behind them and crossed the Santa Cruz by the time the *guía*, the guiding star, that rose to herald the new day, showed itself in the east. They followed the river through the San Rafael Valley and stopped in Will Pendleton's yard at La Noria before the first glimmer of dawn.

Ben expected Juan Heredia to be there with his family. The kitchen lamp was already burning. Juan was always there. "*Buenos días*," Ben said in a low voice.

The front door opened, and Will Pendleton showed himself in the light. "Good morning," he said.

Ben smiled in the darkness, happy his friend was home. "Will, it's Ben," he said.

Will remained silent.

"Ben Cowden, Will."

"I know who you are," Will said. "Who is that with you?"

"Your neighbors, Mrs. Vincent and Colonel Kosterlinsky."

"You don't say."

"Yes, Will." He could tell Will Pendleton was another one who believed he had turned outlaw. "Is it all right with you if I water my horse and give him a feed of grain before I go on?"

"Suit yourself. I don't have to know what you do, do I?"

"Yes, you do. You're my friend."

"I don't have to know what you do, friend, and I don't want to know."

"All right, but these people want to stay here until daylight so they can get back to their homes."

"They can do whatever suits them. If they want to come in, the coffee's on the stove."

Doris and Kosterlinsky dismounted. Ben took their horses and headed toward the corral.

"Hello, Will," Ben heard Doris say.

"Hello, Mrs. Vincent. Come in."

For the first time in his life, Ben had trouble finding his way across the yard at La Noria in the dark. He knew this yard as well as his own, but he tangled the horses in a clothesline and ran up against a corral fence with no idea which way to turn.

Will Pendleton had treated him worse than a stranger. People in this country customarily extended hospitality to strangers.

Ben wondered why he should have to beg Will Pendleton for hospitality. He and his brothers had been fighting Will's battle against Duncan Vincent as well as their own. The Cowdens were shedding all the blood, sweat, and worry to keep Vincent from taking ranches away from people like Will Pendleton.

Ben did not care if Will Pendleton never lifted a hand against Vincent. He and his brothers would do all the fighting. He fought for Will's rights because he loved Maudy. He loved all the people Vincent was trying to break and run out of the country.

Uncle Billy Porter was another one who was sitting back and letting the Cowdens do all the fighting. Uncle Billy had three big sons of his own. His reputation had not suffered one bad word. His sons went on about their business of building their herds. They were welcome on any street, could go to all the dances, and ride into any yard at any time of the day without being turned away.

Pendleton had shipped Maudy Jane back to Long Beach to visit her mother, hoping she would like it out there and decide to stay. He had shipped his wife and smallest daughter to Long Beach months ago because of all the killing Duncan Vincent and the Yawner were doing. Will did not mind availing himself of Viney's hospitality at El Durazno now that he'd shipped his wife away to a safe place, but he felt he could be righteously indignant over Ben's part in the war.

Ben let Prim Pete move down the corral fence slowly until he found the way to lead the crowd of horses away from the clothesline. Someone was milking a cow in the stall next to the saddlehouse.

"*Buenos días,*" he said, figuring Juan Heredia was doing the milking.

"*Buenos Días, Ben,*" Maudy Jane Pendleton answered.

"Maudy, Maudy, I thought you were in Long Beach."

"Well, no, I came home."

Ben unsaddled the four horses and put them in a corral with feed and water. Maudy ambushed him and kissed him when he returned to the dark saddlehouse.

"Now, what's all this about you killing people, robbing stages, kidnapping women, and terrorizing Mexican colonels?" Maudy asked.

"It's not true."

"Why does everybody say it is?"

"The mutineers were the ones who slaughtered Kosterlinsky's guard when they attacked the stage. Mrs. Vincent and Mr. Colonel Kosterlinsky were with me, and I just turned them over to your father."

Maudy took Ben's hand as they walked to the house, and he kissed her again before they went inside. He wished he could stop with her awhile. He felt doomed never to have all of Maudy's kisses he wanted.

Will did not stop Ben from coming in the house, but he did not like Ben so much, now that he was in trouble. Doris and Kosterlinsky had told him the truth, but he still wanted Ben to beg for his friendship.

Doris was acting her role as Daughter of the American

Revolution. She carried Ben's coffee to him, brushed hay off his shoulder in a proprietary fashion, and allowed her hand to linger on his shoulder in an awfully familiar way. Ben knew and she knew that she had no right to do that. None of her attention to Ben was lost on Maudy, and that seemed to be the way Doris wanted it.

Doris also assumed her usual role of acting superior over her countrified neighbors. She wanted people to know that she could take charge of good things better than anyone else. If she was the biggest lady in the house at breakfast-time, the kitchen was hers. If there was a big man in the room, he was hers too.

She took over Maudy's kitchen. After she served Ben his coffee, she began ordering Maudy around, using her to make an artistic creation of breakfast for Ben and Kosterlinsky.

Now *that* was something a woman did not do in that country unless she wanted trouble. Maudy was only a young girl, but she would not stand for anybody trying to use her as a maid in her own kitchen. Maudy helped her willingly at first, but when Doris started fluttering around Ben and letting her gaze linger on him as though she owned him, Maudy began watching her with a mean look on her face. Doris told of her stay on the mountain with Ben and Kosterlinsky, and how completely *gentlemanly* Ben had been at all times, how brave about his misfortune, how strong and uncomplaining when she trimmed and sewed the stump of his toe.

Maudy already knew how Ben acted when he was sick or hurt. She could have told Doris a thing or two, but she would not talk to the woman. The worst part of Doris's new treatment of Ben was the way she made her eyes go all soft and big when she looked at him, like a mare's right after she'd been bred to her heart's content. Ben knew what Maudy thought about that. She would be wondering what the woman had really been doing with Ben all that time she was supposed to be kidnapped. Doris acted as relaxed and happy as a rich, spoiled woman who had just come back from a week at the spa.

Will finally tired of listening to Doris, turned to Ben, and said, "What made you come down, if everything was such a paradise up there on Hijo de Pedro?"

"I saw a troop of soldiers head my way from the fort," Ben said. "We rode off the south side toward Mexico and almost collided with a band of Apaches going the same way."

"What were Apaches doing there?"

"Why, running from the soldiers."

"Why didn't they scalp you on the spot? Have you made friends with the Yawner too?"

Ben felt sick about Will's antagonism. He did not want to answer. To be polite, he said, "No, Will, they didn't scalp us because they didn't see us. I had climbed into some rocks to look around and heard them just as they struck the trail."

"Heard them, you say?"

"I heard them speak, and they were so close I could hear them crack bellotas with their teeth as they walked away."

"Which way were they headed?"

"South on that route that passes Los Metates, where we fought the Yawner."

"When did you report it?"

"Well, now is the first chance we've had to tell anyone about it."

"Why're you telling me and Maudy? There's whole communities down in Mexico who would appreciate it a whole lot more."

"Hell, Will, we just got here. We traveled as far and fast as we could."

"It seems to me you should be telling somebody besides me."

"All right, Will, what do you want me to do?"

"Seems to me there's three things you have to do. Ride to Santa Cruz and alert those people; wire Harshaw and alert those people too; and then go back and find those troopers, and volunteer as a scout."

"In the first place, if those Apaches intend to raid Santa Cruz, they're doing it right about now, and there's not a damned thing I can do to stop it. As for the army, it's closer to Santa Cruz by now than I am. If their scouts are any good at all, and I know they're damned good, they picked up the Apaches' tracks before dark last night. They sure don't need me. I'd only be putting myself back in jail."

"Seems to me that's the only course for you to take—if you're innocent."

"I'm innocent, but I'm not going back to jail to please any man."

"Sure you're innocent. So are all the rest of the mutineers, bandits, and road agents in this territory. You're all innocent and misunderstood."

"The mutineers are in Lyman Canyon," Kosterlinsky said. "Ben knows where they are. He also has the gold off the stage."

Ben glared at him. Kosterlinsky had the face of a third-grade tattletale.

"How do you explain that?" Will said.

"That gold belongs to Cowden Live Stock Company and to Walter Jarboe."

"You can just turn it over to the authorities and let the court decide who it belongs to," Will said. "You better get on your horse."

"I'm getting on my horse," Ben said. "But it won't be to run to the authorities. I'm fighting a war. Funny thing about it, it's your war too."

"Don't try to put any of it on my head," Will said. "I'll have no part of it. Furthermore, if you don't report the presence of these Apaches and bandits right now, don't ever show your face around me again. As far as I'm concerned, this is your only chance to put yourself on the right side of the law. If you don't take it, you must be guilty of everything they're saying about you."

"You're wrong about this, Will," Doris said. "Ben won't remedy anything by turning himself over to the army. My husband has trumped up a case against Ben, and the state and federal governments are on his side."

Ben was already gone. He went straight to the corral and saddled his horses. He stuck both hands down in a pannier and felt the gold coin to see if it gave him compensation. When he looked up and saw a figure in a dress coming toward him, he hoped it was Maudy so he could say good-bye, but it was Doris.

"Where are you going now, Ben? Please don't go. Stay and rest. Give me a chance to change the dressing on your foot. You can wait here while I go to the sheriff with the truth. I'll get the governor to grant you amnesty."

Ben did not answer. He finished packing Moose and stepped close to Doris to untie Prim. She took his hand, put it all the way around her waist, and leaned against him to be kissed.

For a road agent, he sure was being kissed a lot. What the hell, why not? He *liked* all the kissing that seemed to come with a road agency. He brought Doris in close and kissed her for all they both were worth.

"Oh, Ben, take me with you," she said.

He heard a light footfall and looked up. Maudy was standing ten feet away, watching him.

Now if that wasn't the worse kind of luck. He'd been completely innocent of wrongdoing for days, and the first damned time he did something that was not exactly down the straight and narrow, Maudy was right there to catch him.

CHAPTER 18

Maudy walked back to the house, not going too fast or too slow, not hanging her head or dragging her feet, but not looking back. Ben could tell by the way she moved that she was thinking of leaving him behind for good. He needed to run and catch her and try to explain this new trouble he was having with females getting too close to him in the dark, but he did not have time.

Doris Vincent could not have put the run on Maudy any better. Getting caught kissing a married woman made Ben feel bad enough. Her liking it so much that she begged him to haul her away made him lose his desire to kiss her face ever again.

Prim Pete wavered along, not wanting to leave his breakfast. Ben was so stunned that he could not bring himself to spur the horse and make him line out. He recognized that he suffered from a malady A. B. Cowden called Woman's Dolts. A. B. laughed about the way little females sometimes sent men down the road stumbling blindly and shaking their heads. A woman could jolt a man into confusion with a look, a word, or the way she set her head and swung her hips when she walked away and left him. His eyes could be open, but he would not see where he was going because the woman had distracted him by her irrationality, desirability, possessiveness, complete independence, and resourcefulness with one jolting word, look, touch, or gesture. A jolt of the dolts left a man tired and embarrassed, and this was not the right way to be if his enemies were close upon him or he had to pick up a shovel, saddle a horse, count cattle, or clean his pistol.

Ben's luck was so bad these days, two women had seen fit to dolt him at the same instant. He was lucky he could find his way in a safe direction away from there.

The dolts began to wear off as soon as he left the corrals of La Noria behind. He had just ridden into the cottonwoods by the Santa Cruz River when Will's lion hounds started baying. He looked back and saw a gang of riders pull up in the front yard. He stopped in a thicket to watch.

Every man in the gang was a VO hand and wore a constable's star on his chest. Campana, Billy Stiles, and George Smiley were in the front of the pack, and the two Irishmen were in the rear. Ben knew Campana was responsible for bringing the gang this close to him. He thought like a cowboy native to the country. He knew how to pace himself, his horses, and his help. Horses and men might all drop dead one minute after the job was done, but Ben did not doubt that Campana could do a better job of coming after him than any other man in the country.

Will Pendleton was standing on his front stoop, listening to an angry Stiles. Campana turned away and rode slowly across the yard, looking at Ben's tracks.

Doris Vincent stepped up beside Pendleton to talk to Stiles. Campana walked his horse toward the barn. Ben hit for the south at a lope, feeling like a jockey at the start of a race. Moose came along with his great stride. He could easily keep up with Prim Pete on a long flight. He could not keep up when Prim sprinted, but Ben did not figure on sprinting to stay ahead of his pursuers. They could never catch him now, unless Prim stepped in a hole.

Ben headed uphill toward the Patagonia Mountains and passed within a mile of the VO. He did not slow Prim and Moose until he crossed the open San Rafael Valley and entered the oak forest on the slope of the Patagonias. This last five-mile uphill sashay would test the air of the VO horseflesh.

He stopped in the oaks to let his horses blow. The gang was three miles behind him, and whether they knew it or not, they were beaten. From now on, he would change direction erratically in the brush, and his pursuers would have to slow down to track him. He hurried on.

An hour and a half later, he rode into the oak, and sycamore shade of the Mowry camp the Cowdens shared with the Farleys. He tied Moose and Prim away from the water, climbed over rocks with his panniers so he could not be tracked to the top of the cliff, and let himself down into a fissure on its brow. He buried the coins in the fissure. He wiped out his sign and climbed down over the rocks again. As far as he knew, he and the Farley twins were the only ones who knew about that crack in the face of the cliff.

He wiped out his tracks from the rocks to his horses with a sycamore bough, he packed his panniers again, and left the place. He had only taken fifteen minutes to hide the gold. Campana was a half hour behind him. He rode for ten minutes back toward his pursuers, wiped out fifty yards of his tracks so the gang would not know he had gone to the Mowry, then hit for Mexico at a high trot.

He left the oaks behind and started across the open Buena Vista range he shared with the Eliases, the Romeros, and the Salazars. He rode along the bottoms of the washes to keep out of sight. At dark, he doubled back into the Patagonias. He topped out by the Washington mining camp and looked back. Campana and his gang were still headed across the Buena Vista toward Santa Cruz.

Ben rode into the Ojo Azul camp the Cowdens shared with the other ranchers on the north of the Buena Vista range. He unsaddled his horses, and after they had cooled, he watered them and fed them corn.

He walked down to Washington Camp and went into the saloon. He was plenty hungry, and, running alone, he wanted to be seen in some places so he could be safe to stay in other places.

The saloon was run by Dutch Goethal, a German immigrant who made his own beer. Ben loved that beer. Every man in the saloon was a miner, and most of them had lost money betting against Ben's racehorses at one time or another. Dutch always bet on Ben's horses and won his neighbors' money. Ben hoped Dutch would not turn him away before he could have a meal.

The saloon was full of smoke, loud talk, and dirty bodies. Miners were not an observant lot as a rule. They were tough, hard as the rock they broke to make a living, brave, and quick to fight with their fists. They were not dangerous about fighting with knives or firearms, but they liked to break heads with their bare hands.

Miners worked so hard pulverizing rock and moving it

away in the dark all day, they came to the saloon only to sit comfortably awhile and slake their thirst. Ben caused no stir when he walked in.

He stepped up, rested his foot on the brass rail under the bar, rested his back against the wall, and watched to see if somebody would recognize him and start a row. The free lunch was beautiful. Great blocks of white Sonora cheese and *panelas*, fresh curd cakes, roast beef, baked ham, fried chicken, chile salza, and *pan bolillo*, round crusted buns, were laid out on the bar in quantity, with mustard, pickles, and pigs' feet.

Ben ordered a growler of beer and paid for it with a golden alazána. Dutch was a tall heavy man with a gruff way of speaking. His hands were big, meaty, and pink, like the pigs' knuckles in the big jar on the bar. He recognized Ben but showed little sign of it until he saw the alazána.

"How are you, Dutchy?" Ben said.

"I'll tell you," Dutch said, jabbing a big finger at Ben's chest. "I . . . am . . . fine . . . and . . . I . . . do . . . not . . . wish . . . trouble. I will not even say your name, because someone might hear me."

"Don't say it, then."

"I don't want you here. I . . . don't . . . wish . . . trouble."

"Put that coin in your pocket and be quiet, then. You can keep the coin if you allow me a little food, peace, and quiet. I only want some bread, cheese, meat, and a growler."

Dutch looked at the coin. "All right." He handed Ben a large plate. "Eat, drink, and be gone."

Ben straightened to help himself to the lunch. He was seeing spots in front of his eyes, ready to faint from hunger. He'd risked his life to come to Dutch's beer and food, and the sight of it buckled his knees.

A big young miner stepped in front of him, blocking him from the lunch as though he was not even there. He wore a constable's star. "I'll have a mugga beer," said he. He glanced out of the corner of his eye at Ben and began piling food on a slab of bread.

"You *are* a mug," Ben said.

The constable glanced at him again, decided he could not believe his ears, and stacked a half-dozen sardines on top of the rest of his feast.

"A big, ugly mug," Ben said.

The constable turned to face Ben. "You talking to me, friend?"

"Good, you can hear. You're such a pig, I thought you must have filth in your ears."

"Say, do I know you?"

"I've never laid eyes on you," Ben said.

"I'm Constable Don Cannon."

"Never heard of you."

"I'm constable in this camp, friend."

"You're a pig."

"You're trying to pick a fight with me, aren't you?"

"You mean you'd take time off from slopping your big, ugly mouth to fight?"

The constable laid down his lunch and licked sardine oil off the heel of his hand.

"No trouble," Dutch said. "No fighting."

"Pig," Ben said. He stood with his back against the wall, relaxed.

The constable roared and lunged at Ben's throat with both hands. Ben deflected his arms with one hand, drew his pistol with the other, and pounded the cylinder and barrel down on top of the man's hat. The constable grunted and dropped on his knees. Ben flipped the hat off with his pistol barrel and hit him hard enough to imprint the Colt trademark on the top of his head. Constable Cannon measured his length beside the brass rail, his fist in the cuspidor.

Ben heard somebody say his name, and he looked up at the saloonful of miners. Everybody in the room was looking at him. He held up his beer mug with his pistol still in his hand and took a drink off the edge. He was so hungry and thirsty he was shaking. He picked up a panela cake, took a bite, and started chewing before anything else happened to keep him from it.

He had not eaten in so long, his jaws were stiff, and his saliva made them ache. The panela was salty. He needed salt. It was also cool, smooth, and refreshing on his tongue. Most of all, it was nourishing and tasty. He swallowed and chose more food for his plate. He laid the plate on the bar and leaned against the wall so he could watch the room.

Dutch brought Ben another growler and told him a miner from the other end of the bar was paying for it. Ben recognized the man as one who always lost money betting against Ben's racehorses. Ben raised his mug to him and drank all the beer.

"Good for you, Ben," the man said. "Our constable needed his head broke. He's been thunking on his neighbors too much."

Several other men raised their glasses to Ben, then went back to their drinks, dominoes, and cards. The man who had bought the beer walked up to Ben, holding his mug in both hands.

"Some of us are glad to see you here." The man was callused and muscular from busting rock with a double jack.

Ben finished chewing. "I'm glad too. I was about to starve to death."

"We know about the war you're fighting against Vincent. He's run a lot of miners off their claims. I'm one of them."

Ben did not have anything to say about that. He'd never looked to a miner for help and never considered he might be on the same side as the miners.

"Most of us are strangers in this country. It's good a native like you is taking our side against Vincent. I imagine you feel bad, being kept away from home because of this range war. Most of us had our own claims, but Vincent turned us out to work for wages in mines owned by his syndicate."

"I didn't know Vincent was in the mining business."

"Hell yes he is. Him and his brother the senator work for a syndicate that's lobbying in Washington for mining interests."

"Well, well."

"You'll never have to worry about the law bothering you here. Your father was a good undersheriff for us. We want him back, and anytime you want to come here, we'll hide you if you want us to."

Constable Cannon stirred and whimpered. Ben knew how he felt. Getting knocked out didn't hurt, but reviving from a knockout sure did.

The miner squatted by the constable and helped him sit up. He wiped blood off his face with his handkerchief. Ben was full of beer and lunch, and ready to go.

"I have to go now," Ben said. "I hope your constable isn't hurt bad."

"Don't worry about him," the miner said. He straightened and offered Ben his hand. "I'd like to shake your hand before you leave. I'm Don Cannon. I've been a friend of your friend George Morris, the miner, for a long, long time."

"I thought the constable's name was Don Cannon."

"It is. He's my son. If he wasn't so ornery, I'd jump you for splitting his head. However, since I saw why you did it, I can only hope he wakes up smarter."

"Well, I hope he's all right."

"Where are you headed now, Ben?"

"I've been thinking of turning myself in to the sheriff," Ben lied.

"Is that the smart thing to do?"

"Yeah, I'm tired of running."

"Well, you must know what you're doing."

"I do. Good-bye."

Ben went out the door. He thought, Now wouldn't I be a brilliant dude to traipse on back to jail? Wouldn't Marshall and Black Beauty be glad to see me?

He rode out on the Harshaw road so he would be hard to track in the traffic to and from Washington Camp, hoping Campana would go back and look for him at El Durazno. Then he doubled back and put up for the night at George Morris's cabin on the edge of the Buena Vista.

George was another miner Vincent had dispossessed. He was one of Betty's suitors, or used to be. He was out of favor these days. He had been at El Durazno sparking Betty in his fashion a month or so ago, and he'd put his foot in a new batch of fudge Paula Mary had set on a stoop to cool. He had not been very popular with Paula Mary after that.

Ben spread his bed under George's favorite tree. The weather was cooling. Lightning flashed on the horizon over the desert by the Sea of Cortes in Sonora. George's camp on the slope of Lone Mountain was a good lookout for the Santa Cruz river valley. Ben did not waste much time looking or thinking. He went into a coma the minute he stretched out under his blankets and tarp.

He dreamed of branding big fat mavericks and chasing wild ladinos in the brush. He dreamed of the little wrens, his sisters, and the way they sometimes came up behind him and gripped him by the shoulders.

He awoke an hour before dawn and built a fire, made coffee, and cooked himself bacon and biscuits. He broke camp and rode away toward Macarena before sunup.

He rode through the Buena Vista unhurriedly, confident his pursuers were miles away, looking for him on another trail. He was a cowboy again. He had not been on the Buena Vista for two months or more. He and his brothers had turned some big steers out here in the spring, hoping they would grow, fatten, and gentle down.

The Buena Vista had caught some rain. However, after two hours riding, Ben did not see one steer belonging to the Cowdens, their neighbors, or the VO. Evidently the VO and Kosterlinsky had taken every single steer.

In the past months, people had reported seeing VO cowboys and Kosterlinsky's soldiers and rurales driving steers off the Buena Vista toward Santa Cruz. Ben saw plenty of breeding stock and calves belonging to the Cowdens and their neighbors, but not a solitary steer.

He was on the foothills of the San Bernardino Mountains when he rode on to a fat Hereford cow belonging to the VO, her three-month-old heifer calf trotting alongside her. A big two-year-old maverick heifer, the spitting image of her except for being larger, was also with her.

Ben felt so good he started whistling in a quiet, tuneless way. He had paid himself in gold for the cattle Vincent stole from his family, but that was not enough compensation. Now he would compensate himself some more.

He hobbled Moose, tightened his cinches, shook out a loop, and rode to get ahead of the cow. She threw up her head and started trotting for the San Bernardinos. She had not raised a fat two-year-old maverick by letting herself be caught out in the open like this. The new green feed had attracted her away from her steeper, more hidden haunts. Ben got in front of her, and she stopped with her head high, straining to see her way past him, thinking hard about how to escape without losing her calf or her life.

Ben only wanted to show her he could slow her down if he wanted to. She did not need to think she could outrun him. He reined Prim Pete aside and let her go on toward the mountains she craved. As she and her brood streamed by, he spurred in and stood his loop in front of the calf so she could stick her head in it. He tied her down, the cow bawling and pawing dirt a safe distance away. He unsheathed Casimiro's knife, earmarked the calf with the VO's earmark, and let her go.

He had not earmarked the calf as a favor to Vincent. The calf's mother was a ladina and likely to escape the roundup. The calf was as likely to escape branding as the two-year-old had been. Now, when VO cowboys spotted her from a distance and she was going away in a hurry, they would let her go because she was earmarked, and the earmark would make them think she was branded. When the calf was ready to wean, Ben would look her up, catch her, brand her with a Cowden brand, trim the earmark to a Cowden earmark, and take her home. Ben had "sleepered" the calf.

He charged the maverick heifer next, swinging his loop and smiling. He lived for this. His happiest dreams were filled with the running and catching of big fat wild unbranded livestock. Both the VO cow's heifers were daughters of native bulls, the common longhorn Spanish stock that had been in the country for centuries.

The maverick heifer could run. She knew how to get away. She was headed for the San Bernardinos with a good head start, stretching out so far and jumping so high that Ben could see her clean white underbelly, her fat navel, and her sparse little titties airing themselves off the ground. She was far enough ahead of Ben that the first time she dropped into a wash, she thought she could cut sharply at a right angle from him and get away like a coyote.

Ben expected that. When he didn't see her running straightaway across the wash, he looked down and saw the deep tracks she had made when she hit the bottom and turned down the wash.

He was glad he was riding a racehorse. When next he saw her, she was flying over arrowweed downhill. He caught up with her in two hundred yards, but she turned sharply and ran up the bank to leave the sandy, weedy bottom. He topped out with her, and she fell into the wash again.

Before he dropped after the heifer, something made him look over his shoulder. The VO gang was coming toward him across the Buena Vista. He did not even think about pulling up and letting the heifer go. He drove on, snagged her horns in his loop, fairgrounded her, and stood her on her head in the sand. He jumped down and tied her while Prim was still dragging her like a dog. He gathered wood, lit a fire, and put on his running iron.

He climbed the bank and saw the gang coming on at a walk about three miles away. They were walking because they did not know Ben was so close. He laughed at himself for doing what he was doing with his hangmen only three miles away. He slid back down the bank to the heifer.

His iron was still not hot enough to brand her. He did a loving, artistic job carving A. B.'s earmark on her ears. He loosened his cinches, cooled his horse's back, reset his saddle, and gave his iron more time to heat. It was so hot when he burned the *A B Bar* on the heifer's fat ribs, it sizzled through her sleek hair like an ice skate. When he let her go, she was a maverick no more. He hoped Campana and his gang would see her and know what he'd done with them in sight.

He rode up another wash to get close to Moose without being seen. He reached the bank below the horse. Moose was hobbled, his lead rope trailing by his side close to the edge. Ben dismounted, took off his hat, and crept over the bank on his belly. He unhobbled Moose, took the lead rope, and led him slowly to the bank.

He hoped Moose would amble down into the wash after him, but the old fart balked when it was time to step down; he braced his front feet, sat back, raised his head, rolled his eyes, and showed the whole world that someone was trying to pull him down into the wash. Ben could almost reach Prim's reins without letting go of Moose, but Moose would not give him the last inch.

Ben let go of Moose, jumped on Prim, and spurred him up the bank in full view of the VOs. The gang was a mile and a half away and very surprised to see him. Their horses jumped as though under one spur, and out came the rifles.

Old Moose acted so scared of Ben, rolling his eyes, backing up, and keeping his lead rope out of reach, that Ben laughed at himself. Who else but Ben Cowden would be so dumb that he would risk his life to retrieve an ungrateful reprobate like Moose? The first shot sounded as he caught Moose, dallied his head close to his saddle horn, and spurred Prim into the wash. He hit the bottom running, a full volley whining over his head.

He passed the spot where he had earmarked the calf and turned sharply up the wash, gambling that the gang might follow the tracks he'd made chasing the heifer down the wash. Down was the most likely way anyone would flee, the line of least resistance.

The footing was good toward the head of the wash. Rainwater ran fast there, and the ground was not sandy. When he left the wash, the gang was still out of sight. He dived into another wash and made more time toward the San Bernardinos. When next they tried to shoot him, he had gained another half-mile, and he was clear out of range. He turned his face to them and whooped.

He stopped and let Prim Pete blow before he began his

ascent into the mountains. The gang was slow because it stayed together, but Ben knew he could not keep up this pace without giving Prim a rest. He considered switching loads with Moose, riding him and leading Prim. He could cover his panniers and bed with the manta, hide it off the trail, and come back and get it when nobody was chasing him. He climbed to a high point and looked back.

The VOs were no longer in a mood to come on. He wished he could shoot at them, but he did not want to sacrifice his lead to get in range. He would like to see if he could shoot somebody's hat off. He would not mind if his bullet struck low if he missed the hat. That would discourage them because they would find out he hit low when he shot at their hats. They would want him to be a better shot if he was only shooting at them to scare them. He decided he would rather outrun them than shoot them.

Darkness was three hours away. The gang was in Mexico now, out of its jurisdiction. Somebody was bound to complain that the gang was pushing too hard for nothing. Ben counted on Campana having the sense to turn back while he had some daylight to find the trail home. He would not want to come after Ben in mountains after dark.

He watched them try to come on. They knew they were tracking too slowly to worry Ben now. Finally, a pair of them rode off the trail into a canyon to water their horses. Two more followed, and the first two dismounted and took off their hats, finished for the day. The rest of the gang passed the word up the trail, and one by one, they turned back to dismount and water their horses. That was the end of the chase.

The gang could not tell if Ben was headed for Santa Cruz, Cananea, or deepest, darkest Mexico to stay forever. Ben watched them mount and head back to their bunkhouse on the VO. They would antagonize the cook by waking him at midnight and have the only fight they would be able to say they were in that day.

Ben smoked his pipe and watched them go. When they were all the way down off the mountain, he rode up the trail another hour and then headed off the San Bernardinos. He reached bottom at La Acequia, a camp belonging to Don Juan Pedro Elias. He used the last hour and a half of light riding to the Macarena ranch.

Don Juan Pedro Elias came out the front door in answer to

his greeting. Ben was not going to get off his horse this time unless he was damned sure he was welcome.

"Get down, Benjamin, son," Don Juan Pedro said, and he smiled.

CHAPTER 19

Don Juan Pedro called a *mozo*, a groom, to unsaddle Ben's horses, feed them, water them, and rub them down. Ben was happy to let somebody else do it. He was dragging his tracks.

He walked under the archway through which horses and wagons entered the fortlike hacienda, his spurs dragging on the worn brick floor. He stood his rifle against a pillar under the ramada. The ramada encircled the inner patio and sheltered the walkways and doorways. He removed his spurs and leggings, and laid them on a bench. He sat down and did not want to get up.

Don Juan Pedro's four daughters were beautiful. The youngest was sixteen. Margarita, the widow who had been with Don Juan Pedro in Tombstone, the oldest, came to him with a decanter of mescal, a glass, a saucer of salt, and lime from a tree that grew inside the patio. Another daughter, Juana, brought him a tray with strong coffee and sweet cakes. Another, Estela, brought him a cool wet towel for wiping his face and a carafe of water with a clay drinking cup.

He was never given that much attention when he visited there with his brothers. The girls liked his brothers too.

Another daughter, Rosa, brought a chair for her father, and he sat down with Ben under a side of the ramada where the hacienda's saddles were lined up on hardwood horses along the wall. The pillars, eaves, and roof of the ramada were covered by a jungle of broad-leafed grapevines, shrubs, and fruit trees.

The worn, scuffed brick deck had been swept and sprinkled with water.

Acting as the lady of the house, Margarita brought a chair and sat with him too. Ben should have been collapsing with fatigue, but he always revived quickly when these people attended him. The Elias's attention and beauty could revive anyone who had not been dead a full ten days. Ben always felt at home with this family. He liked seeing their open faces after running from every other face in the country for so long. No one at Macarena ever raised a voice or even looked at a visitor in a manner that was not completely splendid.

A white-haired woman came and shook Ben's hand. She was Elena, Magdalena Machuca, called La Secuestrada, The Kidnapped One. The lady had been a captive of Apaches for twelve years and had seldom spoken in the six years since she returned to her family. Ben stood up and embraced her. Her face was full of peace and good humor. She concealed her mouth behind a hand when the sight of Ben forced her to smile.

"You'll never believe who was here to visit Doña Elena," Don Juan Pedro said.

"Yes, I'll believe you, Don Juan Pedro," Ben said.

Margarita's and Don Juan Pedro's eyes seemed full of light. Ben rubbed his own eyes, thinking his judgment must be affected by too much sun or fatigue. The faces of these people were so healthy and untroubled, they seemed unreal. People who did not have to use them day and night running horseback to escape their enemies must have eyes like that.

"Doña Elena's son came to see her," Don Juan Pedro said.

"Her Apache son?" asked Ben.

"Yes, he is Apache of the fiercest kind, a seventeen-year-old brave."

Ben had been fifteen years old and riding with his uncle John Porter and Don Juan Pedro when they and a crew of cowboys and vaqueros had surprised an encampment of the Apaches and liberated Doña Elena. She had not wanted to come with them and had run under a graythorn bush, hugged the trunk, and held on like a wild animal. Ben was left in charge of her while Don Juan Pedro, Uncle John, and the crew scattered the Apache warriors away from the encampment. Doña Elena had been with her family a year before revealing that she had left an eleven-year-old son with the Apaches.

"He appeared like a ghost down on the river where Doña Elena was washing clothes," Don Juan Pedro said.

"Did you see him too?" Ben asked.

"He was here, sitting where you are."

"How did you get him to come in?"

"He came in readily, fearlessly, as though he was accustomed to being among Christians. He strode past my vaqueros as though they were fence-posts upon which he could land like an eagle and use as a perch. He speaks good Spanish and seemed to be completely at ease."

Ben hugged Doña Elena. "That was much for a lady to endure. How long was he here?"

"He showed himself at the river at sunup," Margarita said. "He left when you called at the front door."

"How did he find his mother?"

"He has searched for her all his life. He says his chief uses him as a spy and whenever he has to deal with Christians," Don Juan pedro said.

"What band is he with?"

"The Yawner's. He has questioned captives to find out if they knew his mother. He told us he always did his best to relieve their suffering. Understand me, he is a savage, but his mother taught him the difference between good and bad, the difference between savagery and compassion. He did not say how he relieved the suffering of the captives though. I imagine the things he did would be hard for us to accept."

"The Apache tortures his captives and takes pleasure in their suffering. The only compassionate thing a man could do would be to kill a captive quickly, with one thrust of a lance or one blow of a club," Ben said.

"Exactly."

"Doña Elena has always been grateful for your help in freeing her, Ben," Margarita said.

"Why?" Ben asked. "She seemed inconsolable the day she was rescued."

"She often asks about you. She mentions how softly you spoke to her. You reminded her of her Christian family. You made her remember the kindness of gentle people."

"She was afraid. She tried to run away with the Apache women. I didn't think she understood a thing I said."

"She trusted you because of your *mirada*."

"My gaze? Why did she trust my gaze?"

"Because it was not black, like an Apache's. It was blue, like her mother's."

"Ah, a happy circumstance," Ben said.

Ben spoke directly to Doña Elena, and that made her speak for herself. "The color of your eyes was not the only thing that made me remember my family," she said. She had never spoken to Ben before. "It was the *way* you looked at me that made me remember my mother and father, *mis padres*."

"I was only a boy. I was as afraid as you were. The Yawner killed more people than yellow fever that year. We couldn't go out to work cattle without a fight."

"No, you were not afraid. I remember that too," Doña Elena said. "I knew you were good. I had not seen a good person in a long time. Even the Apaches knew you were good. They called you the colt."

"Ah, I long for those days, when my reputation was good." Ben laughed.

"Your reputation is good here, Benjamin," Don Juan Pedro said. "Evidently it's still good with the Apaches too, not as a good man, but as a good foe. They call you the horseman now."

"I know that," Ben said. "I had a confrontation with one a few weeks ago. He called me Jinete."

"Doña Elena's son calls you El Jinete too. He knew you were kind to his mother. He hid and watched the day we rescued her, and he has always remembered you. He keeps track of you."

"What is his name, Mother?" Ben asked Doña Elena, but he already knew the name of the Apache who sometimes passed for a Mexican and was audacious enough to walk into a store and borrow a dime for jawbreakers.

"*Jesús*," she said.

"They call him Che Che," Don Juan Pedro said.

Ya vez como son las cosas del mundo? Ben said to himself, laughing. "Now do you see how things are in the world?"

"Tell us how things are in your world," Margarita said.

"I will." Ben began to tell them what he knew about Che Che.

Paula Mary watched Frank Marshall act charming. He thought the Cowden women were completely enthralled by him. He would never win Paula Mary but probably figured he did not need her; she was of no consequence. No big self-important dude like Marshall ever cared much about little kids. However, all was not lost. Marshall was falling more under Betty's spell every minute. He was now paying court to her. He had probably never known a good, decent girl like Betty before, never tried to woo and win any young girl. Now that he had discovered a good girl, he did not know how to control his feelings. His face showed greed and lust when he only wanted it to show charm.

Paula Mary figured every time Marshall looked at Betty, he saw a marriage contract being set to type. If he could win Betty, he could take over the whole Cowden outfit, now that its men were scattered.

Paula Mary was not so dumb. She might still be little enough to have fun climbing trees and playing with dolls but, she had two smart-looking eligible sisters, and this big dude was not the first to come here on business and stay to sniff around for a wife and property. After the suitors took stock of everything Papa owned, liked the horses, saw how nice Viney's flower beds were and how gentle, kind, pretty, and probably dumb Betty and Eileen were, they got greedy.

Plenty of suitors came calling. The country did not produce many girls. Girls learned a thing or two about their worth when good men and bad came sniffing around them to see what they could do about bettering themselves.

Paula Mary was worried because her sisters had begun calling Marshall by his first name. He had been entertaining them at El Durazno for an hour while he had supper with them. Betty and Eileen were already in the habit of nodding yes to help him punctuate his sentences. Paula Mary knew he would be needing to get down to business now that he had them doing that, so she was not surprised when he said, "Now, ladies, I have to switch to an unpleasant subject. Where did you say Mr. Cowden went?"

"Mr. Cowden is in Phoenix on business," Viney said.

"Well, I wish he could be here for what I have to say about the new developments in Ben's case. Since he is not, I'll try to impart everything to you just as gently as a member of the family—a brother, a father, or a husband—would."

"Ha, ha, ha," said Paula Mary. "That one's almost as funny as the last story you tried to make us believe."

Marshall gave her the same look he would give a mosquito he intended to mash all over the wall if he ever got the chance.

"Hush, Paula Mary," Viney said.

"I assure you, ladies, this is not a funny story. This is on the territorial records."

"Is it on the records that you want to make yourself part of our family by becoming our father, or brother, or maybe even husband?" Paula Mary asked sweetly.

Marshall's face turned red. "No, little girl, the records show that the charges against your brother are being substantiated in spite of all I've tried to do to disprove them."

"How are you trying to disprove the charges against my son, Captain Marshall?" Viney asked. She was sewing and seemed relaxed, but Paula Mary could see a tremor in her fingers that would not have been there if Frank Marshall had not been bothering her.

"For example, he's been formally charged with the murder of Hoozier Briggs, even though I offered my testimony as proof that Judge Dunn exonerated him at the inquest. He's also charged with the murder of the younger Briggs boy, even though I tried to convince them that he killed that boy in self-defense."

"Pshaw!" Paula Mary said, imitating her friend Maudy.

"That kind of proof would be impossible to find," Viney said. "Because Teddy Briggs is alive. The Farley boys saw him and spoke to him at the Briggs mine near the Mowry. You'd do better to dig up the sack of manure or whatever it was they buried in his place if you're trying to prove my son's innocence."

"Hmmm, that's an interesting idea," Marshall said stiffly.

"Hmmm," Paula Mary said. She leaned forward, her elbows on the parlor table and her chin in her hands, and leveled a stare at Marshall.

"Paula Mary, will you subside?" Betty said crossly.

"Well, why?" asked Paula Mary. "Everybody in the country knows the Briggs boy's at their mine. Isn't Captain Marshall supposed to be a special detective agent, or something? How come he's the last one to find out these things?"

"That's enough of your smart talk," Betty said.

"Go outside and play so Captain Marshall can finish what he's trying to tell us," Eileen said.

"It's dark outside," Paula Mary said.

"You can take a pie to Bill Knox and Gordo. You're bothering our guest. While you're down at the barn, try to remember your manners."

Paula Mary wished she could show everybody how really

mad she was and how far she would go to get rid of this big snake-in-the-grass. She ought to come right out and say that she believed Frank Marshall was lying about trying to help Ben.

Paula Mary remembered when Ben had popped Marshall in the nose. Her brother did not do that unless his target was lying, sneaky, and common. The big dude wanted to get a hold on her family. She did not want anybody to think he could make her give up harassing him and desert the field of battle. She gave Marshall a look that admitted she might be a bothersome mosquito, but if she was a mosquito, Frank Marshall was fly spray.

Paula Mary skimmed the peach pie off the sideboard and slammed out the back door. Lately she'd been scared to death when she had to go to the barn in the dark. She held the pie tightly and ran, kicking extra high with each step to keep from stumbling on the path she had traveled every day of her life. She remembered to calm down and walk before she appeared at the door. No wrath could match the anger of Bill Knox when some little kid charged in and scared a horse he was working on.

Bill and Gordo were forging new horseshoes. Paula Mary held the pie up on the tips of her fingers and put her other hand on her hip, waltzed in close to the forge, passed the pie underneath the noses of the two workingmen, made a turn away from them, then moved in and passed it by them again.

Bill Knox was sweating from head to toe. A big drop of sweat, red with the glow of the forge, dangled on the end of his nose. He did not say a thing or look at her, only grunted each time he dropped his hammer on the iron.

That was all right. Paula Mary knew Bill Knox was busy, and when he was busy, everybody who came within a quarter-mile of him better pull up and find something useful to do.

"I brought you a peach pie, but I need to talk to you, Bill," she said. "Keep right on doing what you're doing, but I sure need your advice."

She paused for effect. Bill Knox was laying on with the hammer, shaping the red-hot chunk of iron. His thoughts were as far away as the Mexican War.

Paula Mary went in the stall Gordo and Bill used for quarters and laid the pie on their table. She went back and watched Bill work awhile longer, decided he was too busy to talk, and went out. She walked away slowly, too worried to remember she was scared of the stretch of darkness to the house. She was not in a hurry to go back and watch her sisters nod their heads while Frank Marshall lied to them.

Marshall and Betty were sitting on the back porch talking and did not hear Paula Mary coming. She stopped. Marshall was sitting in the chair Ben liked to use in the evening when he smoked his pipe. The chair was handmade, of mesquite limbs held together with rawhide strips, so old that peoples' fannies had worn the hair off the rawhide. Ben was always careful when he sat in the chair, but he said it was the most comfortable seat on the ranch. Marshall's tonnage was testing it to its limits, and it creaked with misery every time he moved his fat rump.

Betty and the dude were on the far end of the porch, talking so low that Paula could not hear what they were saying. She hurried around the front of the house and through the soft turf of the peach orchard, and sat down behind a tree close to them. She was so comfortable in this wrongdoing, had such a nice seat and the evening so dark, that a thrill of devilishness shot through her gizzards. Now she could hear every single thing they said, and they never in a hundred years would know she was there.

"I'm about to wind up this case, you know," Marshall said. "Have you given any thought to the offers I've made you?"

"Offers? I don't know of any offers you've made, Frank," Betty said.

Well, at least she wasn't in his arms snuggling with him. Paula Mary could see Marshall's face in the light of the kitchen window. There was no mistaking that pitiful look. He was smitten by the dolts.

"I have confided in you, Betty. I think I've made my intentions clear. I'm ready to marry and have a family. I can see that you are too. I want you to make up your mind about that. I'm ready to make a large investment in ranching. I want to raise my family on a ranch. You'd like that, wouldn't you?"

"All those things you want don't seem like offers to me. Why don't you come right out and ask me what you want from me? Then I'll know how to answer you, if an answer is what you want."

"Well, Betty, I'm offering myself as your . . . uh . . . hus . . . uh . . . band."

"My what?"

"Your . . . er . . . husband."

Betty was silent for over a minute. Paula Mary wiggled her legs on the ground with delight. Betty had finally made Marshall come out and state his intentions, and he sure had not wanted to do that. She made him decide to plunge in and ask her to marry him, in his fashion, and now she could say no and be done with him. Marshall had not known how far he would go to get Betty, so she showed him. He probably didn't think he wanted to be anybody's husband, any more than Paula Mary wanted to be a jailer. Now he was at Betty's mercy, where she always managed to maneuver every dude who thought he was high-powered enough to strike a spark in her.

"What's your answer, Betty? I can make you happy because I'm a man who is going a long way in this territory. With you as my helpmate, there's no limit to the great things I can do."

"What do you need me for?"

"I need a partner who will stand by me, be loyal to me, back me up. Everything I've accomplished, I've done all alone."

"What *have* you accomplished?"

"Betty, my accomplishments are too many and too great to recount in one evening, but let me tell you, I've come a long, long way in my short life."

"Well, I don't know that much about a city man's accomplishments. What can you do?"

"I—uh, what kind of a question is that?"

"What are you good at doing? My brothers are great horsemen, great ropers and fighters. They know cattle better than most men. Their horses are famous for what they can do. My brothers are gentlemen who never quit until a job is done or a fight is finished. My father is known as an honest man who is fair and compassionate. On the other hand, all I've ever heard about you is that you follow Duncan Vincent around faithfully, kind of like his personal hound. Now you tell me you've accomplished great things. I hope you don't count your currying favor with Duncan Vincent as one of your accomplishments?"

"Well, no . . . but . . ."

"What *can* you do?"

"Like I told you, my accomplishments are too many to—"

"Can you stop a bronc, put a whoa on one?"

"Well, I don't know . . ."

"You can't, then. If you could stop one, you'd know it. What are you, a football player or something?"

"No, but I'm a wrestler. It was my wrestling that brought me to the attention of Senator Vincent and got me this job. You see, everything I do is for a purpose. I don't waste any effort. I go for the championship every time."

"Well, I doubt being a wrestler will get you a ranch, and I know it won't make you any more attractive to my papa when you ask him for my hand."

Marshall laughed. "I don't intend to ask your father for anything."

"How did you think you'd get to be my husband, then?"

"Betty, I want you to elope with me. I don't think your parents would understand my suit."

"And I guess you think I do?"

"I assume you do."

"Well, for a man who wants people to believe he is so accomplished, you sure have made a mistake about me. If your accomplishments are based on your assumptions, they must be few indeed."

Marshall was silent for a moment. Finally he said, "I'm very, very disappointed in you, Betty. You led me to believe you were of an adventurous spirit. I'll wait a while longer, because I don't give up easily. Sooner or later, you'll see it my way, I promise you."

Betty laughed good-naturedly at that. "You're an accomplished promiser, I'll say that for you."

That encouraged Marshall and disappointed Paula Mary. Paula Mary wanted her sister to make the man beg, then put him in the breeze. She didn't want her *laughing* with him.

Marshall caught Betty in a bear hug. "I'm a real good kisser too, girl." He was breathing like a bear in a hurry to scratch off his itchy winter fur.

Betty stiffened like a post, but did not try to get away. Paula Mary started backing out of the orchard, going for help. Then Betty said, "You have bad breath, Frank. You ought not to get too close to people."

Marshall uncoiled and moved away from Betty in a hurry. "Why, you little lynx, how can a man be good to you? I can see you'll have to be taught a thing or . . ."

Paula Mary backed into something that snuffed hot air on her neck and flinched away. She jumped and saw she had backed into the muzzle of a bridled horse. She looked up into the darkness and saw a rider on the horse.

"Who are you?" Paula Mary asked loudly and clearly.

The dark horse disappeared into the orchard.

"There's somebody out here," Paula Mary yelled.

"What are you *doing* out there, Paula Mary?" Betty yelled.

"There's a rider out here on a big horse." Paula Mary looked to see if anybody was coming to help her. "Somebody come out here."

"Frank," Betty said.

"The hell with Paula Mary Cowden," Marshall said.

CHAPTER 20

Margarita was unable to sleep. She was lonely and wanted to talk to a man who was not her father, her uncle, or her brother. She wanted that talk to begin politely and develop into intimacy, tonight.

Margarita did not want to be her father's widowed daughter in charge of his household the rest of her life. She wanted her own household and her own man. She did not think the longing she had for Ben Cowden was a sin and did not think his love was too much to ask for.

In the days Ben had been at Macarena, Margarita had spent a lot of time with him. They both liked it when she indulged in *coquetiadas*, the games of quick looks and touches, and gentle, playful, whimsical talk. After five days with him, she knew she was still pretty and desirable.

She took a warm bath, dried herself, and slipped on her nightgown. She brushed her hair and stepped out of the room on clean bare feet.

She was quiet and carried no light. She did not want to make a sound that would arouse someone who could stop her before she reached Ben's room. She did not care what kind of scandal anyone wanted to make of it afterward.

She opened Ben's door and stepped inside. The room was so dark she could not see her own hands. The man was sleeping silently. She moved quickly to the bed, felt for room to lie beside him, slipped off her gown, and slid under the cotton sheet.

Smiling, she reached to touch him and did not find him. She reached out farther and searched for him. He was not in the bed, though the mattress was still warm where he had been lying. "*Benjamin*," she said softly, but he did not answer. She struck a match and saw that he was gone, though his bedroll and other gear were still in the room. He was gone, but he would be back. Margarita relaxed and lay down to wait.

A little while before sunup, Ben Cowden rode into the yard of Maudy's house at La Noria with a wagonload of *mariachis*, musicians, from Santa Cruz. He unloaded everyone as quietly as he could and led them around to the back of the main house and through a door in the *tapia*, the eight-foot wall that enclosed the backyard. The patio inside the wall was fragrant with Maudy's flowers.

When they were all formed, the mariachis began playing and singing "Las Mañanitas," the song of celebration for Maudy's birthday. Someone in the house jumped up and shouted, and overturned a tub that went *bong* on the floor. The back door opened, and Will Pendleton came out with a shotgun in his hands. Someone showed his head over the top of the tapia at the corner of the house; another head appeared over the wall at the other corner. Rifle barrels bristled.

Ben lit a *tizón*, a pitch torch, from a bundle on the patio and held it up so Will and his sons could see who was bringing the music. The face of one of the brothers at the corner of the house smiled and disappeared. That was Bob. Pete, the other brother, walked into the patio through the tapia door.

"Where's Maudy?" Ben asked Pete after the first song was finished. Pete pointed to the top of the house. Maudy's bed was on the roof, and she was peering over the parapet. Ben climbed up to join her. Maudy sat on the parapet, her bare feet dangling. Ben sat beside her, kissed her, and held her hand while the mariachis serenaded her. They played "*Cuatro Milpas*," "*La Golondrina*," "*Cuatro Vidas*," and other songs that ranchers liked. Ben asked them to play the "*Guapango, Torero*" that he called "*El Toro Fiado, The Bull Who Was Bought on Credit*," because it was his favorite and he often had asked these men to play it on credit after his money ran out during a party.

"How come you waited until the first of October to bring me my serenade?" Maudy asked.

"It's your birthday, isn't it?" Ben asked, joking.

"Pshaw!" When Maudy said that word to him, she always pursed her lips softly and gave out a little puff of air before she said the rest of the word in a most irreverent manner. "You know my birthday is the eleventh of September."

"Yes, but I was detained that day."

"I know how detained you were, tomcat. You were probably anchored to Doris Vincent or some other hungry female."

At sunup, Will and his sons came out on the patio to set up a table and chairs for breakfast. When they brought out coffee, biscuits, jerky gravy, bacon, eggs, and hotcakes, Maudy ran and dressed for breakfast.

While Ben and the Pendletons were eating breakfast with the musicians, Les and Mark Cowden walked through the tapia door. Ben was sitting with his back to the house and was the first to see them. They were lean and baked from their work on the roundup and looked fit and happy.

"We heard the mariachis from up the river and thought you were having a wedding," Les said.

"No wedding, yet," Will said. He stood up and offered them chairs. The music had taken the stuffiness out of him. Les and Mark took off their hats, spurs, and leggings, and washed at a stand in a grape arbor by the back door.

When they sat down to eat, Les said, "We're surprised to find anyone here. We were on our way to Macarena, looking for Ben. Didn't you know the Yawner massacred everybody at San Lazaro day before yesterday?"

"How could that be? I was at Macarena only a few miles away, and I didn't hear about a massacre."

"The Yawner fell on them at daybreak, killed everybody, and ran off with the using horses and the fresh cows the rancher was milking."

"How did you find out about it and not me?" Ben asked.

"Kosterlinsky telegraphed Patagonia to report the raid and to warn us the Apaches were headed north again," Les said.

"That's not right," Ben said. "I saw the Yawner go south. He wouldn't take fresh cows if he planned to raid the states, only if he was headed south to hole up."

"That's what everybody thought, but then he hit the Sopori mine yesterday and killed the superintendent."

"He had to cross the Buena Vista to do that," Ben said. "We were working cattle over there and sure didn't see him." He turned to the mariachis. "Did you know the Yawner killed everybody at San Lazaro the other day?"

"Yes, we heard he did," Chayo the trumpet player said.

"You didn't tell me," Ben said.

"You might not have hired us. We needed the work."

"Huh! You're not afraid of the Yawner? I bet he could have more fun with a wagonload of mariachis than we could. He could make you play music while he made you cry and strung your skins up to dry."

"Well, in that case we would be dead," Chayo said. "Dead, we wouldn't need the work."

The Cowdens and the Pendletons agreed that Kosterlinsky could not be trusted to tell the truth or take action against the Apaches. The raid on the Sopori could have been done by the mutineers, and if they would raid a mine, they would raid a ranch. Will Pendleton decided to move his daughter, his sons, and his horses to Harshaw and send Juan Heredia and his family to Santa Cruz with the mariachis.

The Pendletons began to pack, and Ben mounted his horse to return with the mariachis. Les and Mark came out to the wagon.

"Papa and Mama want you to come home, now, Ben," Mark said. "Papa says Frank Marshall has to leave you alone now. You've been granted amnesty by the governor."

"That won't mean anything," Ben said. "Marshall will come to the house anyway, and I'll have to fight and endanger Mama and the girls, or give up. It's better if I stay away from home. I want Marshall to come after me out here in the open."

"Marshall has to respect your amnesty, Ben," Les said. "Papa showed him the governor's order yesterday. He's madder than hell, but he's staying in the hotel and keeping his mouth shut."

"Well, I guess I better go home then," Ben said.

The Pendletons and the Cowdens rode into the barnyard at El Durazno at sundown. Paula Mary came running down the path from the house, her head bobbing up to see who was coming. When she saw Ben, she put her head down and sprinted the rest of the way to the barn. She was swingfooted as old Lemon, the Cowden's kid horse. She jumped into Ben's arms when he stepped off Prim Pete.

"Mama and Betty and Eileen are in the orchard cutting lamb's quarters," Paula Mary said. "Let's go, Maudy."

Ben helped Maudy down from the spring wagon, and she turned toward Paula Mary with her arm around Ben's waist.

"You never did that before," Paula Mary said.

"Never did what, Paula Mary?" Maudy asked.

"You never needed help from anybody to come down off the wagon before, and I never saw you put your arm around my brother like that."

Maudy moved away from Ben and he laughed. "Sorry, Paula Mary," he said.

"Is Maudy still your sweetheart?"

"I think you can say that."

"Then I have awful bad news for you."

"Oh, oh," Ben said, as though he did not believe the news could be too bad. "What's wrong now?"

"I'm sorry to tell you this, but Lorrie Briggs was here, and she has to see you in the worst way."

"Did she say what she wanted?"

"Not to me, but I heard her tell Papa what her trouble was."

"What is her trouble, Paula Mary?"

"She told Papa she wanted to see you because she's in the family way."

"That *is* bad news," Ben said.

Maudy thought the news was so bad that she turned her back and headed for the house with her father.

Les and Mark and the Pendleton brothers were unsaddling and unharnessing horses a few steps away. Les laughed at the look on Ben's face. "It's a good thing you got home when you did," he said. "Look at the business you've been neglecting."

"I'm not sure I want any business with Lorrie after she shot me in the toe."

"You better go see her," Les said. "She's made life so exciting for you, I don't see how you can wait another minute."

Ben looked after Maudy. "Where's Papa?" he asked.

"He's been in Harshaw all day with the sheriff," Paula Mary said. "Do you think Papa will be undersheriff again?"

"No, Paula Mary," Ben said. "I hope not, anyway."

Ben helped his brothers put the horses away, and then he caught Toots and led him toward the barn. Les and Mark caught fresh horses too.

"Where do you two think you're going?" Ben asked.

"We're going with you," Les said. "Where are you going?"

"I'm only going to Harshaw."

"We need to go to Harshaw too."

Ben knew it was useless to try to make his brothers stay home. He saddled and waited for them.

The homes and businesses in Harshaw were lighted, and a haze of woodsmoke from the supper fires hung over the town. They circled the pond in the center of town and saw A. B.'s buggy horse tied in front of the hotel.

They rode through the cottonwoods of the park and past the jail. Ben found a trail on the edge of town where he had walked Lorrie Briggs home in happier times. How long since he'd walked this trail with her? Remembering made him lonesome. Would he ever get to stay home? Every time he thought he was at peace, Lorrie sicked the dogs on him or put him to flight.

"Going to Lorrie's?" Les asked.

"Well, yes. You suppose she still wants to shoot me?"

Les stopped his horse on the dark trail. "Wait. Let's think about it a minute."

Ben stopped with his brothers and listened to the music and laughter from the saloons, the children shouting at play. They were cut off from the town by a willow thicket.

"What is it, Les?" Ben asked. He felt he had to answer this summons of Lorrie's. She had been his friend before his trouble with her brothers, and if she needed his help, he would give it to her.

"Are you going in the house, Ben?" Les asked.

"Yes."

"Don't you think this could be a trap?"

"Yes, but what can she do, turn me in? I've been granted amnesty."

"Your enemies haven't become your friends just because you've been granted amnesty."

"I guess that's right, but what can Lorrie do to me?"

"Murder you."

"She's not a good shot."

"No, but she might be luring you out here so Vincent can have you murdered."

"I have an idea she's not Vincent's friend anymore, Les. It might be worth risking a trap to talk to her."

"Did you ever stop to think she might shoot you for getting her in the family way?"

"I guarantee you, I'm not the daddy. The closest I ever got to her was at the schoolhouse dance with everybody in the county watching."

"She's laying a trap then."

"She probably is, but the way I look at it, the best way to avoid falling in traps is to find them and spring them."

"Then me and Mark will stay out here and watch the bushes for deadfalls."

"Suit yourself. I'm going in there to see what she's trying to pull this time."

Ben went on and tied Toots behind Lorrie's house. He could not hear a sound from inside. He walked around to the front door and knocked.

"Who is it?" Lorrie asked.

"Ben Cowden." The house fell absolutely silent. He waited a long time and was about to leave when the door opened. Lorrie Briggs showed no surprise at finding him on her stoop.

"Come in," she said, and stepped back.

Ben had never been in the house. The place was nicely furnished. Ben smiled to himself. Everything in the place had been hauled there over dangerous roads. Any road to Lorrie's lair must be dangerous to travel.

Ben took off his hat and walked into the parlor. Lorrie showed him where to sit. She sat down in profile to him so he could see how beautiful she was. Her face and hands were pale and transparent. Her shiny auburn curls were disarranged but thick and pretty. Her eyes were pale blue, and their expression childlike and vulnerable. She had already prepared for bed and was wearing a housecoat over nightgown and slippers. This was unusual because she liked to play every night, all night. Maybe she was not having all the fun she wanted as Vincent's mistress anymore.

"Why are you here, Ben?" she asked.

"Paula Mary told me you were looking for me," Ben said.

"She did?"

"Yes, Lorrie. Are you out of humor for it now?"

"I don't think I know how to talk to you, Ben."

"You want to cuss me out because your brothers are dead, like you did before? Get started."

"No, I'm not sure of that anymore. Did you kill my brothers?"

"No, Lorrie, and your little brother is alive, though you let Marshall advertise that he's dead. Who did you bury in the cemetery?"

"You have to understand, that was all Frank Marshall's idea. I didn't mind, though. I did it to help Duncan."

"Did you ask me to come here to help Duncan, too?"

"No, Ben, believe me, I didn't."

"Why do you want to see me, Lorrie?"

"Duncan has me in a family way."

"Well, I'm happy for you."

"Happy for me? I thought you were my friend?"

"My lord, your *friend*? I'd hate to be your enemy if I'm your friend. You called me everything but a cowboy and shot off my little toe. What do you do to your enemies?"

"In spite of everything, I know you're a decent, loyal man. You don't take advantage of women. You stand by your friends. We were good friends. You'll help me if I ask you to, won't you?"

"I'm willing, if you'll come to El Durazno and tell me what you want me to do in front of my family. I'm not stepping into your trap like I did in Patagonia."

"I'm *sorry* that happened, but Duncan made me do it."

Ben stood up to leave. "Well, Lorrie, Duncan runs your life now, so why ask me to help you? I don't want to take his place. I'd appreciate it if you didn't run to my parents every time you get pregnant. You're wasting your time. You and I never got close enough to each other to make babies, and never will."

"Oh no?" Lorrie arched an eyebrow at him. "I could have had you anytime I wanted you, and still can."

"Dream on, little fairy." Ben headed for the door.

"Don't go." Lorrie ran in front of him and hung on his neck. "I didn't mean that. It's really the other way around. I need you, Ben. Please stay with me tonight."

"Come on, Lorrie, all you need is somebody to take you away and pay your hotel bills. Find yourself another Duncan. You've got me too busy watching my back to take you seriously."

"Kiss me one more time?"

"No, Lorrie. Turn me loose."

Lorrie finally put her feet on the floor and stepped back. "At least do me the favor any decent man would do."

"And what's that?"

"Tell Judge Dunn you know I was living in that Tombstone hotel with Duncan. With your testimony, I can make him support me and the child."

"Count me out. I ain't that decent."

"Just tell the truth of what you saw and heard when you were staying in the room next door to me."

"That's a hell of a deal, trying to make me a part of that so you can get money out of Vincent. All you had to do was stick with him, and he would have taken care of you until your hair turned gray."

"He found out you came in the room with me while he was gone. He's insanely jealous of you. He threw me out."

"Yeah, I went in there and looked at his boots under your bed and the packages you'd bought with his money. You had everything your own way. You were having your own way when you invited me in there to gloat over your new prosperity. But he didn't throw you out because of me. You were too smart to let him find out about me unless it suited you. He threw you out because his wife caught him with you and put the almighty fear of God in him."

"Well, that too. I handled everything wrong. I didn't love him enough. If you want to know the truth, I always loved you. Every time he touched me, I worried what you were going to think. I couldn't stay with him. I wanted Doris to find out about us so I could get away from him, but that was before I found out I was in the family way."

"Well, I'm not going to help you, Lorrie. You damned sure handled me wrong when you shot off my little toe."

Lorrie laughed. "I shot off your little toe?"

"You damned sure did."

"I didn't think I could hit a thing with a six-shooter. I'll start practicing again. I must be a better shot than I thought I was."

Ben smiled. "Don't try to tell me you're just a helpless little tart all alone in the world. You'll do all right."

"Look, Ben. I need a stake, and Duncan owes it to me. You're the only witness I have to the plain fact that I was cohabitating with the man when I got pregnant."

"No, I'm not."

"Yes, you are. Who else would be decent enough to help me out?"

"Doris Vincent's a decent person. She ought to be pretty damned mad at Vincent. Maybe she'll help you."

"She's still loyal to Duncan. You're not. Wouldn't you like to see him squirm and pay me money?"

"No. I like Doris. She wants to keep it quiet, or she'd divorce him."

"You like Doris? That's *right*. You carried her off into the hills, didn't you? How was that?"

"That was a lot of trouble," Ben said.

"That was against the law." Frank Marshall strolled in from the kitchen with a shotgun on his hip and his finger on the triggers. "And you're under arrest."

Ben stepped away from Lorrie to protect her, but saw she was grinning at him. She was downright gleeful.

"You dumb bastard," she said. "You never learn, do you."

"I guess not." Ben drew his pistol and fired at Marshall's face. Marshall had made the mistake of giving Ben a mean look to intimidate him before he pulled the triggers on his shotgun. His triggers would have closed the trap on Ben for good, and all the Vincent faction would have had to do was clean up the mess. However, among shooters of weapons, some like to gloat in the faces of their victims before they shoot them, and others pull the triggers first and then look at the faces. Marshall was too much a bully to be a good shooter.

Ben's bullet missed Marshall, but the explosion of the .45 sent him stumbling backwards. He fell and slid across the floor, and his shotgun went off into the ceiling. That scared Lorrie so bad she ran blindly into the front door. She bounced back as Campana and Billy Stiles opened it to come in.

Ben kicked Marshall in the head and ran for the back door. He met Marshall's Irishmen as they came in with drawn pistols. He slammed his shoulder into the chest of one, butted his head under the chin of the other, and ran over the top of them out the door.

He turned and ran back into the house over the Irishmen, banging his pistol against their heads and kicking and stomping like a bronc stampeding through a gate. Marshall was on his hands and knees, his shotgun's breach unlocked, fishing in his pocket for shells. Ben kicked him between the eyes with his bootheel.

Campana and Stiles tangled with Lorrie as they tried to get inside her place and she tried to get out. Ben let a round fly at Campana's head, and he fell on his face at Lorrie's feet with both hands over his ears. Stiles looked up at Ben like a child, raised his hands over his head, and dropped his pistol. Lorrie ran for the brush outside.

Dick Martin and George Smiley came in the back door, already disarmed. Mark Cowden was behind them with his pistol.

Les came in the front door holding up a handful of Lorrie Briggs's hair. He grinned, marveling at something that was not a bit funny to him. "Look what I got," he said. "I didn't want her that bad. She came flying at my face; I just put up my hand to turn her away, and it tangled in her hair. She was going so damned fast her hair came off."

Marshall sat up in the corner of the kitchen with a tough look on his face, as though he had been in a fight. Both his eyes were swelling. Ben snatched at his head, and he covered his eyes with his hands. Ben took him by a handful of hair and dragged him into Lorrie's parlor.

Campana was squatting in a corner with his hands in front of his face, as though he needed to protect it at all cost.

Marshall was heavy, but Ben was crazy with anger, and he dragged his hulk into the parlor by the hair like a heavy sack of feed. He dropped Marshall's head and stomped him between the shoulders to flatten him against the floor. He searched through his pockets and disarmed him of a hideaway revolver. He came up with Black Beauty, smiled at it, and backhanded Marshall's ear with it. Marshall's skull gave softly under the blackjack. Marshall collapsed against the floor. Ben examined him to see if he had killed him, but he was drooling deliciously, and that only showed he was content.

Ben rolled Marshall over on his back. Two half-dry tears were stuck trying to get away from the corners of the man's eyes. Ben decided he was not completely unconscious. He dropped Black Beauty on the bridge of his nose and saw he was right. Marshall rolled away from him, sat up, and held his nose with both hands.

Ben said, "Now, I'm going to change your face so your own mother won't look at you, let alone my sister."

He dropped the sap on Marshall's front teeth and made him hide his face in the corner.

"I know how you feel. I hated it when you did that to me. I bet you could stand a little painkiller." Ben dropped the sap on the base of Marshall's skull and stunned him; he jerked him down on his back by the hair and whacked his front teeth again, then whacked him in the same place again to make sure they were loose enough to fall out later by themselves.

"Look at the paws on you," Ben said. Marshall was lying on his back with both hands outstretched. Ben pounded the sap into the palm of one hand, and when Marshall rolled away, he followed him, measured him, and slapped the blackjack against the back of the other hand. He still did not have the full use of his own hands from trying to ward off Marshall's beatings.

"For the love of God, man," Dick Martin said. "You've already ruined his face. Do you want to cripple him for life?"

"No. If I wanted to do that, I'd pound on his knees, the way he did mine." Ben whacked Marshall's thumbs. "He's meaner at hitting with this thing than I am. He never stunned me. He made sure I felt every blow."

"He's had enough," Dick Martin said.

"I'm almost through with him, now." Ben took out his knife and split Black Beauty open. "Open your mouth, you sonofa-bitch." He dropped on Marshall's chest, straddled him, and held him in place by the throat. Marshall opened his mouth, and Ben filled it with the shot out of Black Beauty's bowels. "Swallow," he ordered.

Marshall tried to roll over so the shot would roll out. "Swallow." Ben slid his pistol out of the holster and pushed the barrel into his eye. "Or by God, I'll blow your brains all over the floor."

Marshall could not swallow, and his mouth was so full he could not close it. He closed his eyes. Mark set a bucket of water with a dipper floating in it by his head. Ben dippered water into Marshall's mouth. "Now, you sonofabitch, swallow or drown."

Marshall swallowed the shot. Ben stood up. "I'm through with you now."

He inspected Marshall's gang. "Campana," he said. "This is the third time you've been part of a trap the VO's laid for me. You and the rest of these gunsels better not do what this man orders you to do anymore. I won't make you eat beebees like I did him. I'll kill you."

Then the Cowden brothers left.

CHAPTER 21

Ben was worn out. He was glad his horse was fresh. He had freshened him some more with an amphora of mescal shared with Les on his way home. He would not have made it home if his horse had been as tired as he.

A. B.'s buggy was parked in the barn when the brothers arrived home. Mark unsaddled Ben's horse for him and made him go to the house. Ben stumbled up the path, feeling like a ghost who would never be able to live at El Durazno again, did not belong in any place that good. His steps were loud in his ears and jarred his every bone.

The lamps were out in the kitchen, and the back of the house was dark. Ben went straight to the demijohn A. B. kept on the back porch and poured himself a full cup of JPS Brown Kentucky whiskey. Nobody ever touched that whiskey without an invitation from A. B., but Ben hoped he would not be discovered. He raised the cup—and saw the glow of A. B.'s cigar in the corner of the porch.

"Good evening, Papa," Ben said softly. "Can I please have a snort of your whiskey?"

A. B. laughed as quietly. "I don't see any reason to stop you, since you already have it in your hand."

Ben drank it all in five big swallows. "Want to have one with me, Papa?"

"You go again, son. I've had my quota for today."

Ben carried another cup of whiskey to the dark corner and sat down on the bench beside his father.

"I'm glad you made it back, son."

"I'm not back to stay. I have to find out what happened to the steers we turned out on the Buena Vista. I've been through there with Don Juan Pedro, and there's no sign of the cattle we turned out in June."

"Oh, you have more important things to do than that, son." The smell of A. B.'s cigar was strong now. Ben wondered why he had not noticed the smell when he walked on the porch. He could have avoided being caught with his snoot in the mash. "You have to serve the country, now that you've been granted amnesty," A. B. said.

"What am I supposed to do, Papa?"

"The governor was ready for me when I went to see him about you. He asked me if you would help the army find the Yawner. When I told him you would, he drafted your bill of amnesty in his own hand and signed it. He granted you a complete pardon for your escape from the Rillito jail and all other assaults and misdemeanors you were supposed to have committed."

"Did you have to go all the way to Prescott to see the governor, Papa?"

"I did. I told everybody in the country I was going to Phoenix to find work for my wagons and teams, and I did that. I also telegraphed the governor for an appointment and went up there to talk to him about you."

"Good. Now we can bring charges of our own against Duncan Vincent."

"Son, Vincent has powerful friends in Washington. We'll never be able to hurt him legally. If we ever lose the friendship of the governor, Vincent will be able to do as he pleases with us again."

"How can we ever win this war, then?"

"Well, we know we can't gain anything by allowing you to go to jail, don't we. I doubt Marshall would have allowed you to go to trial until all the evidence and all the members of the court were against you. They had custody of your life. I never again want to go through the worry I suffered when you were in that jail."

"I told you, Papa."

"I know you did, son. I'm a lawman—or was—so I thought the law would stop the dirty fighting, you would be exonerated, and proper charges would be brought against Vincent. I sure was wrong."

"Can we do it my way now?"

"What is your way, son?"

"We fight a war. We hit them in the pocketbook and make fair game of their livestock, their cowboys, and their thugs."

"The Vincent faction is well organized and well financed by a syndicate that is worldwide and accustomed to success. The only people we can count on to help us are the Porter family and the Mexican families who neighbor with us. All the rest of the Anglo families are too careful to fight Vincent, so don't count on them. That includes the Pendletons."

"I already found that out, Papa," Ben said.

Mark and Les came to the porch and paused by the demijohn. A. B. told them to go right in the kitchen—their supper was ready. He did not ask them to have a drink of whiskey because Les was too wild to drink and Mark did not like whiskey.

"Did you by chance see Frank Marshall in town?" A. B. asked Ben. "I was at the hotel and saw you and your brothers ride by, so I know you were in town for awhile."

"We had a run-in with him when I went to see Lorrie Briggs. He was hiding in her bedroom."

"Did he tell you he's seen the order for your amnesty?"

"No, Papa, he didn't."

"I showed it to him as soon as I got back from Phoenix. He had been telling your mama and sisters he was trying to get it, but he was lying. He's one hundred percent an employee of Vincent's and has not done one thing to help you. Tell me about this trouble Lorrie Briggs is having."

"She's going to have Duncan Vincent's baby, but it's no trouble for her. She and Vincent are strongly attached to one another. She came here and told everybody she was in the family way to get me over there and trap me like she did in Patagonia."

"What did she have to do with your arrest in Patagonia?"

"She asked me to follow her into the thicket behind Los Parados—where Marshall was waiting for me with his black-jack."

"Marshall was there?"

"I thought you knew that, Papa. Lorrie lured me to him, and he and two others worked me over."

"I certainly didn't know it. We've been putting up with Marshall because your mother and sisters thought he might help you. They've fed him supper here, and he's been trying to pay court to Betty."

"I knew something like that was going on when I saw him with you in Tombstone, but I trusted he wouldn't fool the ladies. It was better for us to let him be friendly with them than worry about his harassing them while you and I and my brothers were gone."

"Papa, Marshall almost killed me with that blackjack. He and that Bib Taylor beat me every day for so long I lost track of the time. Didn't Felizardo, the swamper in the jail, tell you what they were doing?"

"No, I only saw Felizardo once, the day we got you out of jail. I saw Marshall several times in Tucson though. I had no idea he was tormenting you. He told me he was trying to help me find you."

"He was the whole source of my trouble, Papa. He told me he intended to split up my family, take over this ranch, and make Betty give him a dozen kids."

"What shall we do about him, son?"

"He's been handled. I don't think he'll bother us anymore."

"You haven't killed him, have you?"

"No. I fed him his blackjack though."

The lamps were on in the kitchen, and Viney called Ben and A. B. inside. Ben kissed his mother and sisters, the first time in his life that he'd kissed them with whiskey on his breath. After swallowing two big cups of whiskey and sharing the amphora of mescal with Les, he did not much care what he smelled like. They could not care much either; A. B. drank a lot of whiskey, and he kissed them all the time.

The table was set, and the family sat down together. The meal was not taken with pleasure. The men were only there to fuel themselves. The women had taken their supper earlier. The family was together more for a war council than a supper. Ben would be gone again before dawn to find the nearest troop of cavalry that was chasing the Yawner.

After the meal, Ben told his family about Marshall's hand in his jailing and beatings. He told them in a matter-of-fact way. They could see he had survived it. He tried to keep his broken hands out of sight. He did not whimper, and he did not whine. He told the plain facts so everyone would clearly see the kind of enemies Frank Marshall and Duncan Vincent were.

He was answering his family's questions when he noticed that Betty was on the verge of tears. She was not one to show

how she felt. She was usually able to contain her emotions. Now her big eyes filled with tears, and Ben was moved. The girl was not trying to get attention. She did not run to her room to hide her feelings, either; she just sat at the table with her family and tried to keep from crying.

The Cowdens' way was to care when a Cowden's feelings were hurt but not to show they noticed. They did not want to make her any sadder by saying something to her and looked away so as not to embarrass her.

"Mama, Betty's crying," Paula Mary said.

"Hush, Paula Mary," Viney said. "Don't you want to bring your brothers some coffee?"

"But why is Betty crying?" The little girl got up from the table. "Is it because she likes that big dude with the big rump after all?"

Betty smiled then and wiped her eyes with the palms of her hands. Mark was her best friend, so he put his arm over her shoulders and gave her a handkerchief wadded and soiled and stuck together with hard adobes he had snorted into it on the trail that day. Betty held it up and looked at it, then looked into her brother's eyes and bowed her head over it. Her shoulders started to shake.

Mark looked to Eileen for help. Eileen separated Betty's hands, looked into her face, and said. "She's all right; she's *laughing*."

A. B. cleared his throat. Poker playing was almost a religion with him. He was so against any display of emotion, he only allowed himself laughter once in a great while. Now and then he allowed himself a calm display of anger. His wife and children could show any kind of emotion they wanted to and he felt deeply for them, but he did not think emotion should be displayed in a reckless or prolonged manner. Consequently, out of respect for A. B., his family showed their feelings around their own house less than they did when they were away.

Betty was coming out of it now.

"Oh, sister," Eileen said. "Did you like Frank Marshall? Was he your friend?"

"I didn't *like* him," Betty said. "I couldn't *stand* the thug."

"Then why are you crying, honey?"

"I'm so *relieved*. I thought everybody wanted me to be nice to him because he was helping my brother." She laughed. "I'm

so happy my brothers put him in the breeze and I don't have
to put up with him anymore."

"Well I *never* put up with him," Paula Mary said. "I wish
I'd been meaner to him than I was."

"Hush, Paula Mary," Viney said, smiling. "You sure are
mean."

Ben and his brothers loaded their horses on the train and
rode it to Cibuta in Sonora to join a troop of the U.S. Fourth
Cavalry. Ben took Prim Pete and Snake to ride, his brothers
their top horses. Ben was not allowed to leave his brothers home.
A. B. and Viney sent them with him to be sure he returned.

Ben had admitted acting as a road agent, and his family was
not altogether sure he was completely innocent of wrongdoing. He never told them about the spoils he had taken, and
they respected him too much to ask about it. Even Paula Mary
kept her mouth shut about it.

The Cowden brothers were jumping their horses out of the
boxcar at Cibuta when Sergeant Dodge of A Company, Fourth
Cavalry, rode up to meet them. He was riding a tall, sleek
black horse who was still plenty fresh at sunset. That meant the
troop might be a long way from home at Fort Huachuca, but
it could still go a long way more.

As the brothers rode to the bivouac, Sergeant Dodge told
them he was still on the same patrol Ben had seen from Hijo
de Pedro Peak. The patrol had turned away from the Huachucas after cutting for sign on the foothills. It had not patrolled
the Huachucas for the Yawner at all. Ben handed his horses to
his brothers and went into the tent of the troop's leader,
Lieutenant Bill Buck.

Lieutenant Buck was a lean and wiry man, Ben's age and
size. His troopers called him the Greyhound because he was
untiring in his pursuit of the Yawner.

"I was on Hijo de Pedro Peak the day you left the post,
Lieutenant Buck," Ben said. "I saw you coming. You flushed
me and the Yawner out of the Huachucas. The Yawner passed
close enough to me that afternoon to count my ears. I saw him
cross into Mexico at Los Metates."

"That verifies what Colonel Kosterlinsky told us," Lieutenant Buck said.

"You can believe that part. But I bet the Yawner raided San
Lazaro on his way south and did not go back north to raid the

Sopori. It's fall now. He wouldn't take milk cows from San Lazaro if he was coming back to raid in the north."

"Why would Colonel Kosterlinsky lie about it, then?"

"Because he's responsible for the Sopori raid."

"You mean the rurales raided the Sopori?"

"Probably not, but the mutineers did, and he told everybody he'd executed them all."

"You're trying to tell me there are still some of those mutineers loose in the country, Mr. Cowden?"

"Yes, I am. I saw them hit Kosterlinsky's coach on the Santa Cruz. I'm pretty sure they were camped in the Huachucas at the same time I was."

"Why would he lie about that?"

"He told his superiors he gave all the mutineers ley de fuga and shot them when they ran. He was either too softhearted to kill them and let them get away, or they made a fool of him and escaped. He and I both saw his mutineers raid Vincent's coach on the Santa Cruz.

"Also, he's not interested in going after the Yawner. He's scared to death of him. He's got you looking for his mutineers. What would you do if you ran into them?"

"I have orders to take bandits into custody, but I wouldn't want to do it. I'm after the Yawner."

"Then let's make a night march to San Lazaro. Give me two Apache scouts, and I'll go ahead from there. I'll use my brothers as messengers. You come up to me every night, and we might catch the old Yawner before the week is over."

"How do you think we'll catch him?"

"He hasn't had to hurry since Kosterlinsky took over the rurales. General Carbo is busy trying to exterminate the Yaquis at Guaymas. We'll either catch up to the Yawner in a week, or we'll take back his milk cows. He can't hurry and drive milk cows at the same time."

"We have a troop of the Tenth Cavalry under Lieutenant Bode scouting between us and Sasabe with his buffalo soldiers."

"Can you get a message to him?"

"Yes. We're using a new method of communication called the heliograph."

"What the hell is a heliograph?" Ben asked.

"Mirrors."

"You can send a message with mirrors?"

"Sure. We use Morse code with a shutter on the mirror's reflection of the sun."

Ben walked out with Buck and looked at the sunset.

"It's time for us to signal Lieutenant Bode," Buck said.

"Tell him to head straight south to Los Molinos tonight and wait there," Ben said. "Tonight we'll go to San Lazaro, and I'll start tracking tomorrow morning. I'll send one of my brothers back to you so you'll know where to bring your troop tomorrow evening. I need two Indians and two messengers, and then all I need to do is find the old Yawner's tracks."

Ben, his brothers, and two Hualapai Apaches named Ben Tom and Juan Pablo picked up the Yawner's tracks at San Lazaro the next day and followed him. As Ben expected, the Yawner could not be blamed for the Sopori raid. He had flown south.

Ben tracked the Yawner five days. He sent one of his brothers back to Lieutenant Buck every afternoon to lead the troop up at night. Juan Pablo brought the brother back to Ben every morning.

Ben did his tracking on Prim Pete because the horse was quiet and not a whinnier. Les and Mark kept the other five Cowden horses aired out traveling the country between Ben and Lieutenant Buck. The Cowden horses were proving themselves again, and the Cowden men were not getting any sleep. Messages from Lieutenant Buck assured Ben that the buffalo soldiers were staying abreast of them to the west.

On the fifth day, Ben knew the Yawner would stop. His cows were footsore and hungry. The Yawner's herdsmen and herdswomen were cutting branches out of the cottonwoods to feed the leaves to their cattle and horses. This high plain of Sonora was bare from the drouth. The Apaches would have to feed their cattle that way if they wanted to take them farther south. Their route was along the Rio Alisos on the east side of the Magdalena Mountains.

The evening of that fifth day, Ben caught up to the herdsmen and saw them drive the cows out of the brush of the river and into the foothills. Ben and the Apache scouts staked their horses in a thick grove of sycamores, left Mark to guard them, and climbed to a ridge above the Yawner's cow camp in the twilight. After dark, they followed the ridge and climbed higher until they saw the Yawner's fires under the peak of Magdalena Mountain. The Yawner was not careful now. He probably thought every Christian soul within a hundred miles was afraid enough of him to stay out of his way.

From the spot where Ben, Ben Tom, and Juan Pablo rested, they could see a long way in all directions. Ben Tom and Ben called each other *tocayo*, namesake, and Ben spoke Spanish with both scouts. They sat in the twilight after the hard climb on the ridge and quietly shared their knowledge of the country.

The Altar Valley stretched away to the west from the foot of the Magdalenas, a desert valley that was two hundred miles wide and three hundred miles long, with hardly a hill on it—long and flat and covered with mesquite, palo verde, palo fierro, sahuaro, pitahaya, and ten thousand other varieties of trees, cactus, and brush, and almost a mile lower than the plateau east of the Magdalenas.

Ben and his tocayo figured the Yawner was probably planning to stay on top of the Magdalenas to rest and cool off before he crossed more desert. He probably wanted to make jerky and teguas, the Apache footware, before he moved on.

Ben and Ben Tom left Juan Pablo on the ridge to keep watch on the Yawner and went back to meet the troop. If Lieutenant Buck signaled the buffalo soldiers to move into sight on the west side of the Magdalenas, he could lay an ambush for the Apaches when they moved their cattle away on the east side.

Lieutenant Buck moved his troop of forty-eight men down the Rio Alisos that night, prepared the ambuscade, and waited. The soldiers were positioned on both sides of a canyon called, *Los Bultos*, The Apparitions. They settled into their places in the dark. Ben ordered Mark to stay down in the canyon with the horses, out of sight and out of range of the shooting. Les had made friends with Sergeant Dodge, and when Ben tried to tell him to stay with Mark, he only smiled and said he wanted to stay with the sergeant's squad.

On Ben's and Ben Tom's advice, Lieutenant Buck counted on superstition to channel the Apaches into the soldiers' positions. The Apaches would not pass through the canyon on the floor because it was considered by Mexicans and Apaches to be a deadly place.

People considered the place haunted by previous victims of ambush because of some bustlike white rocks that rimmed both sides of the canyon. These rocks seemed to waver and move on nights when shadows cast by moonlight played through the branches and leaves of the sycamores. Other vicious men were said to have waited there in ambuscade to murder for profit, and those white shapes were said to be the ghosts of their victims. The place was perfect for an ambush.

The main body of the Apaches would ordinarily never go through the bottom of the canyon because it was such deadly ground, but they could hurry their cattle no other way. Someone would have to drive the cattle through on the floor, but the warriors and the rest of the Yawner's band would go over one side or the other of the canyon. Half of Lieutenant Buck's men held high ground over the trail on one side, and half held the high ground on the other side.

The trails that wound through the rocks on both sides of the canyon were beneath the soldiers. The soldiers positioned themselves in ranks along the trails. If the Yawner came that way, they would let his leaders go past the first rank and catch him in a crossfire from both sides of the canyon when the rearguard of the band appeared.

Ben sat in the dark and wished he could smoke his pipe, but a breeze would carry the odor of tobacco into the canyon and warn the Yawner as surely as a bugle call. He figured the Yawner would come to Lieutenant Buck this time. Ben had been dodging, chasing, and laying traps for Apaches, ladino cattle, and wild horses all his life; Apaches could be trapped whenever they could be channeled the same as any wild animal. They were much harder to snare, but they would go where an ambuscade wanted them to go if they thought they were getting away. Even the smartest, craftiest old ladinos fell into traps when they were led to believe they were getting away.

Ben always felt sorry for the old ladinos when he'd trapped them. He did not consider himself smarter than they were. They were quick, wise, and crafty, but unless they could fly, their avenues for escape were few. They usually chose the way they most wanted to go, the way their hearts and their wild needs led them, toward their *querencias*, the haunts they loved best. They believed they would rather be dead than go to country they did not like, somewhere they did not love. That was why Ben believed the Yawner would come this way, with his cattle or without them. The Yawner wanted to be at peace in the southern Sierra this winter, and this canyon was on a straight line to his favorite winter place.

The Yawner came long before he was expected. Ben was

about to check the loads in his weapons again because the light was better. He brought up his rifle, and at that moment the rocks below him moved. The rocks were Apaches. He was so surprised, he felt a shout rise in his throat. He knew he was the first to see them.

He was afraid to lower his rifle, afraid the movement would give away the ambush. He froze with his bald face out in the open. He had taken off his hat, but his face was showing.

Ben watched the Apaches move through the trap. They were alike as javalinas. They even moved down close to the ground, with a husky, swift lumbering of their shoulders and a quick, trim shifting of their legs, like javalina. They moved through rock like rock come alive, and he could see they were the same as the earth, air, and brush through which they moved. He was intimidated by their silent power and grace. If they affected the rest of the troop the way they affected him, they would escape. The soldiers only had a few seconds to fire before the leaders would be gone.

The first shots came simultaneously from two rifles on the other side of the canyon. Apaches scurried off the trail toward Ben. Some of them were smiling, as if a big joke had been played on them and they were a little tickled that they had fallen for it. Then the soldiers on both sides of the canyon poured fire into the trail.

The horses being ridden at the tail end of the Apache column raised their heads out of the rocks, whirled, and carried their riders into the river brush. A heavy volley of fire met them like a scythe. Some crafty sergeant had positioned his squad there with murderous intent, probably Sergeant Dodge.

The Apaches gave little answering fire. Ricochets in the crossfire were more dangerous to the soldiers than answering fire from the Apaches. Not many bullets ricocheted. Nearly all the Apaches were cut down in the first volley.

The Yawner was given no chance to fight and no chance to run. He was killed like a rattlesnake, in a merciless frenzy in reaction to the fear he inspired.

Ben found himself mounting Prim Pete. When he was aboard, he noticed his rifle was hot. He checked it and found it was fully loaded, though he did not remember firing and reloading. All the chambers in his pistol had been fired, and the empty cartridges were still in the cylinders. He reloaded

and followed Ben Tom down into the canyon in pursuit of the
Apache horsemen.

Most of the horsemen had fallen in the river brush. Dead
and wounded Apaches and horses lay on the bed of yellow
sycamore leaves. Ben saw the rumps of two horses running
upriver through the brush. He and Ben Tom loped after them.

Ben Tom stopped and slid off his horse beside the body of
an Apache. Ben waited for him and saw Mark's mare Sally
lying a few feet away. She raised her head, recognized Prim
Pete, and nickered. She tried to get up, but her hind legs were
lying dead as posts beneath her.

"Poor Sally," Ben whispered, and he noticed his throat
ached. He rode around in front of her and shot her on the
cavalrymen's mark, the spot where imaginary lines from the
ears to the opposite eyes cross high on the forehead. She died
so quickly her head bounced off the ground.

The Apache on the ground was the Yawner. He looked into
Ben Tom's eyes but did not say anything. The scout shoul-
dered his rifle and aimed at the Yawner's face. The chief had
been shot through the hips. His wide mouth was stretched
thin, almost in a smile. His eyes were smiling.

Ben turned away before Ben Tom fired. He had led the killers
of these people here and helped lay the ambush. The sound of
the bullet buffeting the Yawner's skull muffled the report of the
rifle.

Ben hurried on. The Yawner's cattle ran and dodged away
from him, poking their heads in the brush, intent on finding a
place to hide. He rode past two riderless horses and on until he
saw no stock and no tracks. He pulled up then, knowing he was
a good mark for a sniper.

He started back to see if his brothers were still alive and
found his horse Star. Prim and the brown horse nickered low
to each other in the manner of veterans.

Ben rode to Star, afraid he would have to shoot him too. He
was standing groundhitched to his long reins. His head was
covered with wet sand from the river bottom, and his front end
was slick with mud and moss. He had fallen, but he was not
dinked or wounded.

Ben caught Star's reins and saw Che Che pointing his rifle
at him from inside a willow thicket a few feet away.

"Jinete," Che Che said in a low voice. He lowered the rifle
and lay flat on the ground.

"Are you wounded, Che Che?" Ben asked.

"I am dead, Jinete. And *El Bostezador*?"

"Dead."

"Like me."

"No. I'm taking you to your mother." Ben knelt beside him. "Show me where you're hit."

"I'm not hit. You kill me, Jinete."

"Did your horse fall with you?"

"I think so."

Ben held up two fingers. "How many fingers?"

Che Che held up two fingers.

Ben looked in his face. "Can you stand up?"

"I think so." Che Che nodded his head.

"Come on," Ben said. "Your mama wants you."

CHAPTER 22

Paula Mary, Betty, and Maudy were in the horse pasture gathering acorns. The harvest was good in that part of the country, in spite of the drouth. The girls did not have to go far from the house to fill a bucket. Viney and Eileen could look out the window and keep them in sight, though every once in a while, they disappeared in the trees. They stayed by the road where the ore wagons passed. The day was fresh with the cool snap of fall, a good day to be out gathering *bellotas*.

Paula Mary's knees were getting sore from romping on the ground. All three girls were under the same tree with their heads close together, laughing and talking and cracking acorn shells with their teeth.

Paula Mary was kidding Maudy Jane about Ben. She did not feel as close to her, now that she was Ben's sweetheart. Paula Mary wanted to know why everything had to be so different now that Ben and Maudy l-o-oved each other.

"You know, I'm really getting worried," Paula Mary said. "We don't know if our brothers will *ever* come back. That old Yawner is hard to find, and Papa says nobody who ever catches up to him is glad he did."

"I expect they'll be all right, won't they?" Maudy said. "The old Yawner's about finished, isn't he?"

"That's the trouble. Whenever people think he's finished, he catches girls like us out in a pasture and cuts their throats."

"Pshaw!" said Maudy. "He's too old to catch anyone who's as fast on her feet as you are, Paula Mary. I know he'd have to be an awful fast runner to catch me, and you'd be in the house before I even got started."

"You'd be easy to catch." Paula Mary laughed. "My brother Ben caught you, and he's not handy at all when he's afoot."

"That's something I can't understand. When your brother looks at me, I turn into a pillar of stone."

Betty raised up to rub her knees and looked down the road toward Patagonia. "Frank Marshall's coming."

Marshall was with Dick Martin and the two Irishmen who had insulted Betty on the street in Harshaw.

The girls turned back to their business. "Don't look up," Betty said. "Maybe he'll go on by."

They listened to the horses walk up—and stop.

"Good morning, girls," Dick Martin said. "I thought you were three little *chula* does there, grubbing for bellotas. The coatimundis crawl after acorns with their tails up, like you."

Maudy sat back on her legs to hide her tail and smiled at Martin. "Good morning, Dick," she said.

Marshall glared at Maudy. Dick Martin seemed happy Maudy answered him though. Paula Mary thought Dick sure was dumb to run with Frank Marshall.

"That cheerful one's Ben Cowden's girlfriend, isn't she?" Marshall said.

Dick Martin did not answer. The Cowdens knew he liked to partner with people like Marshall, but he was too decent to understand Marshall's evil thinking.

"We have here Cowden's girlfriend and two of Cowden's sisters," Marshall said. "Accessories to his crimes." He stepped off his horse, handed his reins to Martin, and walked toward the girls.

None of the girls knew what it was like to take a beating. They were not afraid of grown-ups. Their feelings could easily be hurt by people they respected, but they did not respect Frank Marshall.

Marshall did not mind beating up girls if it served his purpose. He liked to whip on anyone who would not fight back.

He stopped directly over their bowed heads. "Which one of you is going to tell me where Ben Cowden hid the money he robbed from Duncan Vincent's coach?"

Maudy's expression was as innocent as a girl's could be. That was the best defense against a bully like Marshall. She believed he was too much a coward to hurt someone who was looking right at him unless she was shackled.

Betty moved the acorn bucket by the handle. Marshall stepped around, grabbed her by the hair, and jerked her to her feet. "Stand up and look at an officer of the law and answer him when he's talking to you," he ordered. He pulled Betty's head back, and his grip was so tight, anyone but Betty would have whimpered.

That was all Paula Mary needed. She jumped up and stamped on his right foot, hoping he still had a sore place on it. Marshall swatted her away with the back of his hand and knocked all the good sense out of her head. She bounced up, lowered her head, and butted him in the balls. He was so big and solid, she felt she had run into a wall. She had no idea she could do any damage that way. She had certainly never butted anyone before, and she did not know the sensitive nature of her target. She did it instinctively, like a calf.

That butt made Marshall's feet dance a little jig of agony. He turned loose his grip on Betty's hair, doubled over, and turned toward the Irishmen, frowning with pain. "That little one butted me right in the . . ."

That was as far as he got. Betty swung the bucket of acorns at his head, caught him under the ear with the sharp bottom rim, and knocked his nose in the dirt. The girls ran all the way to the house without looking back.

A. B. was standing inside the door of his barn when Marshall and his thugs rode up, Marshall holding a bloody handkerchief against the back of his head.

"Your goddam kids damned near crippled me, Cowden," Marshall growled.

"They're mean little dickenses when their hair is being pulled," A. B. said. He kept a straight face.

"Well, I'm going to explain a few things to you." Marshall leaned over his saddle horn and pointed a finger at A. B. "I'm not here on a social call this time. Up until now, your women have enjoyed good treatment from me, but from now on, I'm strictly an officer of the law where they or anybody else is concerned."

"Your skulking around here hasn't fooled my ladies a bit, Marshall."

Marshall dismounted, walked up to A. B., and extended his hand, as though in friendship. A. B. reached for it reluctantly, and Marshall slapped him with it.

Marshall said, "I want you"—he slapped the old man again—"to listen"—he slapped him again—"when"—again—"an officer of the territory"—again—"is talking to you." A. B. fell to his knees.

"My Lord, Marshall, you just did the worst damn thing anyone in the whole world could have done," Dick Martin said.

Gordo Soto, the small manurey stableboy, charged out of the barn behind a pitchfork, aiming the tines at Marshall's throat. Marshall drew his pistol, shot him down, and turned back to A. B.

"You're under arrest, you sonofabitch," Marshall said. "Martin, get my rangers in there and saddle a horse for this prisoner."

Dick Martin knelt beside Gordo and turned him over. "This boy isn't dead," he said. He picked up A. B.'s hat and offered it to him. "This is awful, Mr. Cowden."

A. B.'s gray hair was in his eyes. He ignored the hat and bent over Gordo.

"Shut up," Marshall said. "Saddle a horse for the sonofabitch like I told you to."

"I'm carrying this boy to the house so Mrs. Cowden can help him," Martin said. "Then I'm hitching a buggy so we can get him to a doctor."

A. B. took his hat and pressed the brim against the wound in Gordo's back, then pressed his handkerchief against the one in his breast.

"Help him? What for?" Marshall walked over to Gordo with his pistol drawn and looked down into his eyes. Gordo reached weakly for the pitchfork. A. B. grabbed for the pistol. Marshall brushed him aside and shot Gordo again, then again.

"For God's sake, Marshall," Martin said quietly.

"Yeah? Don't you like it, Constable? You want to live? Get your ass to saddling a horse for this goddamned squatter, or I'll put you down beside that Meskin with a bullet in your head."

Dick Martin turned his back and mounted his horse. Marshall shook his pistol barrel at him. "I mean it, Martin."

Martin started riding away. "I'm telegraphing the sheriff about this," he said. "Enough is just enough."

Marshall shot him off his horse. "Enough *is* enough, isn't it." He fished in Martin's pocket until he found a key-ring. He took it, straightened, and left Martin for dead.

Marshall and his Irishmen, with A. B. in custody, were

around a bend in the road out of sight of El Durazno when they heard the first wail that meant the Cowden women had discovered Gordo Soto and Dick Martin.

Marshall grinned. "Sounds like she's sorry about something." The Irishmen were not amused. "However, I doubt they even come to visit this old bastard in jail. That's the coldest bunch of females I've ever known."

Marshall rode up beside A. B. "Cheer up, old man. All you have to do is tell me what your kid did with that money Mr. Vincent gave Kosterlinsky, and you can go back to that covey of battle-axes you're breeding."

A. B. did not say a word. His face showed no sign of pain or anger. He was looking way off, like an old ladino.

"Did that slapping I gave you hurt, old fellow? That wasn't anything. I'm real good at managing pain. I won't *hurt* you until I get you in jail. I was careful not to hit you too hard. When I go to work on you in earnest, I'll use Black Beauty Number One. That's an old sap a police chief in New York gave me. Your son ruined my other one, the one that fit in my pocket. This one is a foot long, and it's right here in my saddlebag. It's a little scuffed, but it's survived every beating it's ever given."

Marshall slapped A. B., knocking his hat to the road. One of the Irishmen stopped to pick it up.

"Leave it," Marshall said. "He won't need it. Before this day is out, he won't know the difference between sunshine and shade. You know, Cowden, that little wildcat of yours butted me in the testicles. A man's testicles are his most precious parts, and it's unfair to hit him there."

"I can understand why you believe your privates are your most precious parts," A. B. finally said.

"Oh, you can? Well, you've bred a nest of vipers with yours, and you ought to be ashamed of yourself."

"You believe your nuts are so precious because you're all member and no manhood, Marshall."

"Well, I'm going to fix yours and make you pay for siring a nest of snakes, you old bastard."

A. B. looked Marshall in the eye. "No matter what you do to me now, the men I've sired will make you wish you'd never been born."

Marshall paled when A. B. said that. He did not say anything more until he pushed A. B. into the Harshaw jail and told the Irishmen to watch the door. Then he went inside with his blackjack. The Irishmen heard the sounds of the blows but did not hear a sound from the old man during the fifteen-minute beating. Marshall came out and walked away to the hotel, mopping his neck with a handkerchief.

The Irishmen found A. B. unconscious and bleeding from cuts over both eyes. He lay with his hands between his legs and his knees tucked to his chest.

Maher probed him with the toe of his shoe. "He's breathing," he said.

"Sure, he has but a few knots on his head. He'll get over it," Langley said.

They stepped outside to face a group of townsmen. Dr. Bill Tucker, carrying his medicine bag, stepped forward. "What did that man do to A. B.? Let me in there," he demanded.

The Irishmen did not move out of the way.

Lieutenant Bill Buck was waiting in the lobby of the hotel when Marshall walked in. "Captain Marshall, Judge Dunn tells me you are the special agent of the Interior Department in charge of the Ben Cowden case," he said after introducing himself.

"You've come to the right man, Lieutenant," Marshall said.

"I have the army's letter of commendation for Ben, and I want it forwarded to the governor so it can be used in the matter of his amnesty."

"Ben Cowden's getting a letter of commendation? What for?"

"All three brothers have been awarded letters for their service at the battle of Los Bultos."

"Lieutenant, I'll be honored to take your letter to the governor."

Lieutenant Buck handed Marshall an envelope. "Cowden's a fine man and deserves our official praise and personal gratitude."

"I appreciate this, Lieutenant," Marshall said, beaming proudly.

Lieutenant Buck thanked Marshall and went out to the street. Sergeant Dodge was mounted, holding his horse and waiting for him. The sergeant could not help glancing longingly at Vince Farley's saloon.

Lieutenant Buck saw the look and tied his horse to the hitchrail. "Sergeant Dodge, would you like a pitcher of beer and some good heavy lunch with pickles and mustard before we head for the fort?"

"I do if you do, sir," Sergeant Dodge said.

Marshall watched the soldiers tie their horses in front of the first saloon in the line. He smiled encouragingly and saluted them as they went inside. He looked across the town pond and saw Viney Cowden hurrying into town in a buggy. Her daughters Eileen and Paula Mary were holding Dick Martin between them in the backseat.

Betty was alone at the ranch. Old man Cowden and the Mexican had evidently been the only men there today. Was Mama Cowden dumb enough to run away and leave Betty at the ranch alone? Did she figure Ben Cowden's redheaded girlfriend would protect her? Where was the blacksmith?"

Marshall walked to Farley's saloon and looked in. Bill Knox was drinking at the bar by himself. He sometimes spent days in the bar, staying drunk day and night, sleeping in the keg room when he was too full to stand. Had he just come in, or was he about to go back to his barn at the Cowdens'? That didn't matter. Marshall could be finished with his business out there before Knox even thought of giving up his place at the bar.

Marshall went over to the town hall and drafted a report for Judge Dunn about the shootings of Gordo Soto and Dick Martin, and his arrest of A. B. Cowden. He had seen Judge Dunn in Vince Farley's saloon. He left the report on the judge's desk and went to the stable behind the hotel for his horse.

He stayed off the Harshaw Canyon road, skirted a hill on the west side of the ranch, went through the Cowdens' horse-pasture gate, and rode into the ranch from the orchard side. Leaving his horse tied in the orchard, he stopped on the edge of the trees a moment and listened. This was Mexican siesta time on these ranches, the time everybody laid their little heads down after "dinner."

Marshall smiled to himself. He was a rapist and had never been caught. If Betty was alone at the ranch, he was about to mash her all over, like a flower in a book. He'd spent a good amount of time setting her up for this. He would go in and get her, be through with her in no time at all, then wait and see if he was lucky enough for Brother Ben to come home.

This was his shortcut to owning the Cowden outfit. Betty would not tell a soul she'd been raped. If she got pregnant,

Marshall would marry her. Once he had Betty, he'd have the Cowdens. A. B. was not going to live through this arrest. The sons would be fair game when they came running to free the father.

He walked to the back porch. Horses in the corrals switched flies and nodded in the sun. He could not hear a sound on the place. The house was his—and everything in it.

He stepped through the screendoor to the back porch; the thing made a homey creak as he passed through. The Cowdens often heard that door announce the step of a loved one. If Betty was in the house, she would think one of her sisters, or maybe her brother Ben, was coming. She did not have any idea the man who would deflower her was on his way.

Paula Mary's dog, Gyp, bounded out from under a cot and charged Marshall in a frenzy of barking. Marshall laughed, stepped inside the kitchen, and closed the door in the furious face, his heart thumping. The expected creature on the place wanted his blood now.

He went through the kitchen quickly but not silently. The hardwood floor could not be crossed quietly, like the door on the porch. The people who shared the house were so many and so close that creaky doors and floors were not noticed. Stealth was never used here.

He stopped at A. B.'s desk to listen. He opened the lid of the desk and searched quickly and expertly for a record of the whereabouts of $40,000 dollars worth of gold coin this family was hiding. He turned away to look somewhere else and heard a rustle of bedclothes and the creak of a spring close in the silent house.

Marshall had been around this home enough to know the sound came from the bedroom shared by the three girls. Boldy, he walked to the open doorway.

Betty was lying with her face to the window on a corner bed, having a cool, delicious nap. A breeze stirred the curtains by her face. Marshall stopped at the edge of the bed.

She certainly was lovely. Her dark lashes adorned her cheek. She had a fine nose, small and regular but very distinct with its slight bulge on the bridge. Her nose was usually tilted at a haughty angle. Now, it was letting out her breath in little sleepy puffs with a dream.

The girl wore a light blouse over a long skirt. Her legs and feet were bare. Her dark hair lay away from her head, except for a few strands over her ear and bare neck. She exuded a sleeping girl's smell, the warm and light musky perfume of her slumber. Marshall bent over the girl's feet. The toes were immobile, lying together in perfect symmetry, perfect toes with little rosy conches for nails. He could see that every detail of her beauty happened naturally for her, with no effort, no grooming on her part. This was good stock. A pity her heart had turned black against him.

Marshall knelt on the edge of the bed carefully and unbuttoned the fly of his loose-fitting trousers. She was turned away from him, her legs doubled up, her blouse had risen above her skirt, baring a section of her back.

He moved a hand toward her mouth. He would take the whole face in his hand to stop the cries. When she kicked, he would slide in close between the legs and jam her into the corner.

His hand was halfway to the face. Certainly his hand moving through the air made no sound, but she became aware of it, opened her eyes, saw it coming, reacted instantly, screamed and kicked.

Then a terrible thing happened. Both her feet caught inside his open fly. Betty was a strong girl, and when she tried to pull her feet out of his pants, she pulled him toward herself. Then her legs coiled, and she kicked him with both feet in his most precious place.

Marshall grunted like a boar and tried to twist free. Betty hissed and growled, and kicked him again. He lunged for her throat. She lifted him over her head on both feet and rammed his head into the corner, slid out from under him, and ran out of the room.

He burst out after her with no idea which way she had gone. He ran past A. B.'s bedroom, and hot air blasted across the back of his head, fire from the muzzle of A. B.'s shotgun. If he had turned into that bedroom, she would have blown him in two.

He hesitated a moment before he went through the door after her. He was not sure she had fired both barrels. Maybe one barrel was still charged. Then Betty ran out of the room, across the parlor, and out the front door.

Marshall was proud of his prowess as a footracer. No female in the world could outrun him. He flew out of the house after her. She ran around the corner of the house and headed for the barn. He rounded the corner and collided with Maudy Jane, who was standing with an armload of flowers watching Betty.

Marshall leveled her on the stone walk, rolled free, and kept running.

He pulled up in the open back door of the barn and held his breath to listen for the sound of Betty's breathing. "Betty-y-y," he cooed. "I've got you now-w." He stepped inside and looked up at the hayloft in time to see Betty stretching her arms above her head to spear a pitchfork into him.

She caught him so flat-footed, he could not dodge it; he only had time to turn his back. The pitchfork grazed by, and one tine snagged him through the fat on his ribs.

Marshall let out a howl that made horses run and dodge in the corral. The heavy pitchfork swung on its hold in his precious fat and skin. He would have followed it anyplace it wanted to go. The tine was stitched in six inches of his fat, and the weight of the handle twisted and wrenched at him, causing great pain. He went to the ground with it to keep it from pulling on him.

The entire surface of Marshall's skin turned cold. Betty stood on the edge of the hayloft with a healthy glow on her face and watched the effect her pitchfork was having on Marshall's capacity for rape.

"You *got* me, Betty," he gasped. "I don't think I can get it out by myself. Help me. Please."

Betty disappeared over the edge of the loft. Marshall made himself sit absolutely still. She would climb down now. If she came close enough, he would mash her all over the floor of this barn, even if he had to break her neck first, even if he had to twist her head off.

Betty appeared on the edge of the loft, carrying an armload of used horseshoes. She hefted one and winged it end-over-end at Marshall's skull. He tried to duck, but the shoe rang off the back of his head. The pitchfork quivered in his flesh.

Marshall held the handle of the pitchfork and scurried on his knees across the floor. Another horseshoe jounced through the air at him. That was all the help he needed for ridding himself of the pitchfork. He stood up, straightened the handle, and jerked it. His fat followed in the direction of the jerk and made him howl again. Another horseshoe came winging at his head, and he ran inside A. B.'s office, banging the handle against the doorsill. This time he held his fat and skin in place while he pulled out the tine.

He drew his pistol and peeked out the door—Betty was not

in sight. She was making him peer around doorsills now. He had not come here to shoot anybody; love had been on his mind. Sure, his ardor scared the girl, but if he could have held her still and finished the act, she wouldn't be so damned mean now. Now he would be forced to use his pistol to keep her from killing him.

He stepped out into the middle of the barn. "Come on down now, Betty, and take your medicine. You know, you can't tease a man as long as you've been teasing me and not expect to eventually open up and put out. You have to admit, I've been patient. Come on down." He heard movement in a stall under the loft. That was clever. She'd climbed down and hidden under the loft, expecting him to climb up after her.

"Are you already down?" he asked. He walked to the stall, swung the door open, and looked inside. Gordo Soto's body was sprawled on its back, its head turned toward the door, its eyes staring. The stall was a living quarters. The corpse was blocking the door, and Marshall did not want to step over it.

He heard a noise in the loft again. He stepped up to the ladder. "I'm coming up with my pistol drawn, Betty. If you throw another horseshoe at me, I'm gonna shoot you. Give me what I want, and I'll go away and leave you alone."

"All right, I give up," a small voice said.

Marshall holstered his pistol and opened his shirt to see where the pitchfork had stuck him. The two holes where the tine had gone in and out were like the stitch of a big needle, the flesh between them turning purple. The wound was bleeding, but hardly any of the blood was coming out.

"You got any more pitchforks up there?" Marshall climbed three steps and was distracted by movement below him. Bill Knox was teetering toward him on a wave of whiskey. Marshall lifted a foot to kick him away and was snatched off the ladder like a dirty rag. He hit the ground on the back of his head. Knox still held his foot. Marshall tried to kick the man again, but Knox made him miss by twisting his foot and rolling him on his face.

The blacksmith caught his free foot, swung him off the ground, and bashed his head against the wall. He had never been manhandled like that. He made it to his feet as Knox stumbled toward him to take hold of him again. The man was sluggish, off-balance from drink, but the strength in his hands was terrible. Marshall knew he could not hurt him with a punch, so he went for his eyes with his fingernails.

Knox took his head in a hammerlock and jerked him down to his knees so suddenly and with such force that his neck, nose, and skull cracked. Then his skull began to contract as the blacksmith squeezed the sides of his head together. He swooned away to a place where he would not know what happened next.

When he awoke, no one was around. Knox had left him for dead. He was so sore from the buffeting, crowning, kicking, squeezing, blackjacking, and spearing that he had taken in the past two days from the Cowdens that he was in a furious hurry to leave that place before another Cowden came after him with more serious intent. He picked up a bridle, staggered out to the corral, and caught the first horse that stood still for him; he mounted bareback and headed for Harshaw.

Betty and Maudy, hiding in Viney's flower bed, watched Marshall ride away on Toots. Maudy's face was bloody from being mauled against the flagstones of the walk by Marshall. Betty was pale and angry. Bill Knox was lying dead in the flower bed between the two girls. He had staggered there and died of the heart attack that seized him before he could finish killing Marshall. The girls were still in the flower bed with Bill when the Cowden brothers rode in from Patagonia.

CHAPTER 23

While Betty told him what Marshall had done, Ben carried Maudy into the house and laid her on a bed so they could doctor the cut on her forehead. Mark reloaded the shotgun and added a loaded six-shooter to Betty's arsenal.

The brothers ate sandwiches of biscuits and bacon while they went out to catch fresh horses. After the horses were saddled and ready to go, they went back to the house to make sure Betty and Maudy felt safe enough to be left alone. Then they stood by the olla on the back porch and took turns drinking their fill of water. When that was done, they headed for town.

On the road to Harshaw, Mark stepped off his horse and slid down the bank beside the road to pick something up. When he climbed back, he was carrying A. B.'s hat. Mark was the best of the three brothers at hiding his anger, using it to his own best ends, and keeping his own counsel about the way he felt, but his face was not hiding his anger now.

He handed the bloody hat to Ben. A cowman would never leave his hat by the side of the road unless he was dead—or too busy saving his life to retrieve it.

The Cowden brothers rode to the edge of town without saying a word. Ben stopped and indicated the way he wanted Mark to go by pointing with his chin. Les stayed with Ben.

Mark rode behind the saloons to the hotel livery. He stopped outside the barn doors and waited for the liveryman to look up from his forge. Mark did not like this man. The man kept this livery by doing business in stolen stock with thugs and thieves. He seemed to think he should act sullen when the Cowdens came to do business with him. Mark did not know how he was crosswise with the Cowdens, but he bet he might find out today because Toots was standing tied under a big alamo outside the livery barn.

The liveryman's name was Eddie Newton. Everybody called him Eddie the Newt, because he was dwarfy, bug-eyed, and devious, and he always contracted his business inside the barn, as though he detested the sunshine. He was trying to stay in the same business as A. B.'s by underbidding and underselling him. He was the kind of competitor who would sell cheap to steal business, then steal from the buyer before he was through with him. He could make a horseshoe and tack it on a horse because he was more a carpenter than a horseman, not because he knew a thing about the care of a horse. He did not know a saddle horse from a sawhorse, though he professed to know everything there was to know about saddle horses, draft horses, and carriage horses. He once even professed to know which kind of mules threw the best progeny until he found out that mules were the hybrid cross between horses and burros and could not procreate.

Now he was keeping his head down over his forge, even though he knew Mark was waiting to speak to him. He was too busy for anybody at that moment, especially since he was sure Mark wanted to know what Toots was doing under his tree.

Mark was usually patient with him, but today he was charged by his family with finding out everything he could about their enemies in a war. His father was a prisoner, and he was mad enough to drag Eddie the Newt through a cholla patch.

"Eddie," he said.

Eddie pounded on a piece of hot iron to drown Mark's voice. Mark timed it so Eddie could hear him between hammerings if he wanted to. "Eddie . . . Eddie," he said, without raising his voice.

Eddie kept pounding on the iron.

Mark made a well-extended flourish of drawing his rifle from its scabbard. That made Eddie look up.

Mark aimed his rifle at Eddie the Newt's boot. Eddie showed great alarm. "Here, now!" he exclaimed. "What do you think you're doing?"

Mark looked up from his sights.

"Don't *ever* aim a rifle at a man unless you intend to shoot him," Eddie the Newt said imperiously.

Mark aimed at Eddie's hat and tightened all the slack out of the trigger.

"What're you *doing*?" Eddie said.

"You said it yourself," Mark said. "I'm gonna shoot off your head." His horse Gus's ears lolled like a mule's. Gus turned to look at Eddie's head as though waiting to see how true Mark's aim was going to be.

"What in the—" Eddie dropped his hammer and backed up.

"*Stand fast*, you sonofabitch," Mark said. "You run, and I'll shoot you. I don't have time to *mess* with you."

"I'm standing, Mark."

"Where's Marshall?"

"Why ask me?"

"Didn't he ride in on that horse you've got tied under the tree?"

"Well, yes, I expect he did. So what?"

"He stole that horse from us, or can't you read brands?"

Eddie the Newt relaxed. "Well now, you must be wrong there, Mark. Captain Marshall's an officer of the law. He don't have to steal. He can just take any horse he wants."

"Where is he?"

"He's usually in the hotel. That's the way he headed when he left here."

"Don't let anybody but a Cowden use that horse. Do you understand?"

"Except Captain Marshall, you mean."

Mark gave the man a moment to think. "You're not hard of hearing are you, Eddie?"

"No."

"Do you understand what I said?"

"Yes."

"Then that horse better be here when we come for him."

Mark rode through the barn and saw the mounts of Campana, Stiles, George Smiley, and the Irishmen. He rode to the back of the hotel, tied his horse, and went inside. He walked through the lobby and saw Campana, Stiles, and Smiley sitting on the hotel's veranda, enjoying the sights. Marshall, Vincent, and Kosterlinsky were sitting in the dining room together. He went out and rode to the jailhouse.

The jail was on the edge of the town park, away from town;

the Catholic Church on the extreme edge of town, beyond the jail. The Irishmen were sitting on a bench by the jail's steel door, smoking their pipes and enjoying the shade. Mark stopped his horse close to them.

The Irishmen were big athletic men who had built their strength with years of work on the railroad and were used to settling disputes with their bare hands. They did not mind shooting a man, but they were like Marshall—they would rather whip him with their fists. Out of habit, they always sized up an opponent's muscles before they thought of shooting him.

All three of the Cowdens shot everybody when it was time to shoot—the big strong ones or the little skinny ones. They did not settle their disputes with their fists. A fistfight never ended a dispute for them, and they never forgot a beating to themselves or to someone they loved. These Irishmen had helped Marshall administer beatings to Mark's family. Those beatings were gone and forgotten as far as the Irishmen were concerned, but Mark was ready to kill them for their participation.

The Irishmen lolled on the bench and did not move when Mark stopped his horse over their heads. They were not afraid of Mark. He did not look strong enough to carry a crosstie or old enough to do a full day's work. He was just a cowboy.

"I always thought Clougherty was a good sort," Maher said, looking at Mark but talking to his partner. "I was surprised we never heard another word from him when he went home. I would have liked some word from the old country."

"Clougherty's an ass. We'll never hear from him again," Langley said. He looked in Mark's direction, but his eyes did not focus on the boy.

"What is it, boy?" Maher asked. "What do you want?"

"I've come to take my papa home," Mark said.

"Yes, and pigs fly," Langley said.

"Your papa can't go home; he's in jail. He'll be in a jail a long time," Maher said.

Out of the corner of his eye, Mark could see Ben riding toward him from the church. "Open the door," Mark said, his pistol in his hand.

Maher straightened on the bench. Langley was watching Les ride up behind Mark. The Farley twins were coming behind Les in a spring wagon. Mark blocked Langley's view of Ben and Maher's view of Les.

"Move your horse back and put up your pistol, boy,"

Maher said. "I don't want to shoot you." He did not reach for the rifle that was propped against the bench by his side.

Mark backed his horse away. Ben and Les rode up beside him at the same moment.

"Open the door," Mark said. He was not going to wait another minute. He was afraid his father was hurt and he wanted to take him home.

"Get that out of your head. We're not opening the door because we don't have the key," Maher said.

"If we had the key, we wouldn't open the door," Langley said.

Mark raised his pistol and aimed it at Maher's knee.

"Wait a minute, Mark," Ben said. "Give them a chance to think about it. They'll open it if you give them a chance."

"Yes, we will, and pigs fly," Langley said. "I'll tell you. I have the key. Why don't you get off your horse and take it away from me."

"When I said a chance, I meant only one chance," Ben said.

Mark shot Maher through the leg above his kneecap, breaking it in two. Maher jumped up, and the leg collapsed, doubling out with the foot in front of him. He fell, screaming, on his face, and his foot lay beside it. He crawled around the leg, clawing the dirt and digging with the toe of his good foot.

Langley rolled him on his back so the leg would lie straight and stared defiantly at the Cowdens.

"Aren't you going to open the door?" Ben said.

"No, by God. You'll have to kill me to get in that jail." Langley remembered his pistol then, but he could not draw it because he was sitting on it. He looked up at the Cowden brothers again. "You'll have to kill us both."

Les roped him around the neck. "No, we won't. We'll just let strangulation change your mind." He turned his horse, jerked Langley away from his partner, and dragged him into the road toward the church. Langley held on to the reata to keep from having his head pulled off. His elbows plowed furrows in the hard road. When he could not stand that anymore, he rolled over on his back, held on to the reata, and tried to keep his head off the ground.

Les dragged Langley to the church before Ben could stop him. Only a strong man with a bull neck could have survived that dragging. He was still conscious and able to move his limbs.

"I don't like doing this," Les told Langley. "But I want that key. After I see how my papa is, I'll either apologize or drag you until your head comes off."

"Get on your feet," Ben ordered. "Unless you want Les to drag you back to the jail."

Langley scrambled to his feet. "I'll give you the key."

"No, you'll open the door," Ben said. "Move."

The Farley twins were holding a compress on Maher's bleeding thigh. Mark was still on his horse. Some miners and townsmen had gathered at the jail to watch. Dr. Tucker hurried through them to help Maher.

Langley opened the door, and the Farleys went inside to bring A. B. out.

Les took one look at A. B., spurred his horse away and jerked Langley over backward. This time, he tried to tear the man's head off. Ben sideswiped him with his horse to stop him. Langley looked dead. Ben stepped off his horse, took Les's reata from him, and put one of Langley's arms through the loop so it would not tighten around his neck; he remounted and dragged him back to the jail.

Mark and the twins helped the doctor load A. B. in the spring wagon. Ben and Les climbed into the wagon to look into their father's face. The doctor ordered the twins to drive to their home, and Ben and Les climbed down and remounted their horses.

Ben asked the townsmen to carry the Irishmen into the jail, lock them in, and give him the key. The townsmen did it readily.

As the brothers rode back into town, Ben threw the key to the jail into the middle of the Harshaw pond. "This time, by God, we'll know those two sonsabitches aren't standing behind a door ready to grab one of us or running up to join a posse that's chasing us."

"How'll they get out?" Les asked.

"They by God won't," Mark said.

Ben led his brothers to the front door of the hotel. The town was quiet. Everyone knew the Cowdens were coming after Marshall. The street was empty of horses, rigs, and people.

Mark wanted to ride around the back, in case Marshall's gang flushed out that way, but Ben would not let him. He wanted Marshall and his gang to run out into the open. He did not want a fight in the hotel. Marshall couldn't get away; he was surrounded by water: the Arctic ocean in the north, the Antarctic in the south, the Atlantic in the east, and the Pacific in the west.

The brothers tied their horses in front of the hotel and went in, walked through the lobby, the dining room, and the bar. The whole ground floor was empty, even the kitchen. They banged up the stairs to Vincent's office and found it empty too. Ben was happy. Marshall had flushed, and he thought he was getting away. Ben signed for his brothers to stay back, kicked down the door to Duncan Vincent's room, and went in.

Vincent was sitting in his shirtsleeves in a corner, his hands in front of him so Ben could see he was unarmed. He was never armed. He bragged there was not a man in the country who would shoot an unarmed man, no matter how angry or mean he was. Doris was sitting on the bed.

"What happened to your crew, Vincent?" Ben asked. "Let's put an end to the war today."

"As far as I'm concerned, the war was over when the governor granted you amnesty," Vincent said. "I can't fight a cow thief if the governor lets him off every time he gets caught. I give up."

"Don't call me a cow thief again, Vincent," Ben said.

"Well, what will you do about it, Cowden? I'm unarmed."

"Your mouth is mean as a cannon. That's reason enough to kill you."

"Well, I'll take that as a threat and figure you'll carry it out. You've won the war, Cowden. I don't want to die. You've cuckolded me with my wife, run off my hired help, stolen all my money, branded all my cattle. I can stand to sacrifice all that. Wives, money, hired hands, and livestock can be replaced. I can't stand to die though. A man doesn't come back from a thing like that."

"Why don't you have a seat, Ben?" Doris said. "Let the poor man tell you his troubles."

"You're responsible for the worst thing that ever happened to me," Vincent said to Doris. "I'll never get over your running away with this man."

Doris laughed musically. "Oh, if that were only true. Ben, would you take me somewhere, please? Please, Ben."

"Don't beg him in front of me, Doris," Vincent said. "Have some decency."

"You damned hypocrite. What do you know about decency? You left all your decency between Lorrie Briggs's legs, and when you go where she keeps it, you don't go to get it back."

"That's a lie. I'm not keeping anybody. All I ever did was help that girl when this man killed her brother. Hoozy was my employee and her only support."

"Hah! You're a liar too. You even lied to defend your decency, you damned hypocrite."

"Show me some loyalty. Don't accuse me in front of my enemy. I have enough to worry about without you shaming me in front of Ben Cowden."

"Are you worried because I got that gold you stole from Jarboe?" Ben asked. "You've been stealing our steers, Vincent, so just consider us even."

"I will if you pay Jarboe that money, since you say I owe it to him."

"*He* says you owe him. I say you owe me, so I'm keeping it."

"That's all I can expect from a road agent and kidnapper, I guess."

"Expect to pay more. The war's not over. My whole family's been hurt now. You and your henchmen have to pay for that."

"I don't understand how you can act so violated about your family, Cowden. At the beginning of this fight, when you declared war, you told me your whole family would be fighting me. If you'll remember, I tried to exclude our families. I wanted to leave out the womenfolk, but you said your women wanted to hurt me too. Then you kidnapped and seduced my wife. I'm sorry Marshall was such a mad dog, but what did you expect? How did you expect me to react when you kidnapped my wife?"

"I returned your wife unharmed. I treated her with respect. You're accusing a good woman of something she would never think of doing. Your man committed murder and tried to commit rape in my home. My father was beaten half to death. I'm going after Marshall now. Write him off as a dead man. After that, I'll decide what to do with you. Let me tell you, before I'm through with you, you will arm yourself. Now tell me where Marshall's gone."

"I won't do any such a thing. Go to hell."

"Ben, he's with Kosterlinsky, on his way to Mexico with Campana, Stiles, and Smiley," Doris said. "They're headed for

Guaymas to catch a ship for California. Let them go. Don't take any more risks. You've won."

"Thank you, Doris," Ben said. "But the sonofagun could not have accommodated me more. He's exactly where I want him to be. He thinks he's getting away."

CHAPTER 24

The Cowden brothers figured they would catch Marshall by dark unless his ass began to hurt and he decided to get off his horse and fight sooner. He was not likely to fight. Kosterlinsky and Campana would not want to stop and face the Cowdens. Marshall would have to stay with Kosterlinsky because he needed his help and influence to escape through Mexico.

Marshall would be easy to catch in Sonora. The Cowdens were as Sonoran as the Sonorans. They had friends and relatives on ranches where they could rest and change horses all the way to Guaymas.

Marshall would have to pay exorbitantly for everything he needed on his way to Guaymas. Kosterlinsky would probably quit him in Nogales. Kosterlinsky was helping Vincent get Marshall out of the country. Vincent probably did not care what the Cowdens did to Marshall as long as they did not bring him back for trial.

Kosterlinsky would give Marshall a rural policeman for a guide and kick him loose in Nogales, Sonora. With that kind of guide, Marshall would be unwelcome at every ranch all the way to Guaymas. The Cowdens were not worried he would get any farther than Nogales, though. He was too soft and dependent on his comforts. He was not quick enough, smart enough, or adapted enough to the country to escape them now.

The brothers were tired though. They had seen too much country. The did not think they would ever be able to ride fast enough to deal with Marshall as quickly as he deserved. They were patient men and angry enough to keep going, but the country was big, and Marshall was still ahead of them. They had the heart to go one more day, but four hours on the trail after they left Vincent sitting comfortably in his hotel room, they were having trouble keeping their spines vertical on their horses. They wondered if they were really winning the war if they had to keep riding and fighting while Vincent could retire to the hotel dining room with his beautiful wife and have a drink and a steak.

Ben was the tiredest of the three. He had rested well at the María Macarena ranch, but the night he'd spent riding to Santa Cruz and freighting the music to Maudy Jane Pendleton was telling on him. He had been out one night in one hundred for fun, and now he couldn't stay on his horse. This spending his youth with music and drinks was just going to have to stop.

He smiled to himself. That was more or less what Maudy said to him before he left El Durazno. She wanted the Cowdens to postpone the war for at least one day so Ben could rest.

Sometimes Ben thought the Pendletons had more sense than the Cowdens. They were never angry. Will was Duncan Vincent's closest neighbor, and he knew the kind of trouble the Cowdens were having and sympathized with them, but Vincent never bothered him unless a Cowden was around.

At sundown, the brothers stopped at the *garita*, the American customhouse on the Mexican border in Nogales. Clay Coughonour, a uniformed customs inspector who was a friend of the Cowdens, came out to say hello.

"Have you seen Gabriel Kosterlinsky today, Clay?" Ben asked. The gang's tracks were wiped out when they reached the Camino Real, the main road into Nogales.

"He crossed a half hour ago with three or four Americans," Coughonour said. "You looking for him, Ben?"

"I'll say," Ben said softly.

"One of the Americans was riding a tall sorrel horse with A. B.'s brand on his hip," Coughonour said. "He looked *rendido*—tired, hungry, thirsty, and mad."

"Mad, huh?"

"Yeah. The big one on the Cowden horse asked me what time the train left for Guaymas."

"What time does it leave?"

"Tonight or tomorrow morning."

The gate was closed to Mexico. Ben kept waiting for Coughonour to open it. Finally he said, "We have to cross, Clay."

"But this gate's closed, Ben. Been closed twenty minutes."

"Clay, are you going to make us ride all the way out of town to the end of the fence so we can cross?"

"Ain't it the shits? I can't help it, but that's the rules. This gate is closed until six tomorrow morning."

"Clay, I'm tired enough to fall over in a faint, unless you open that gate and let us through."

Coughonour grinned. "That's all right. I'm off duty. I'll get Escalada's wagon and take you home with me if you do that. You look like a drink of whiskey, a big supper, and a good night's sleep would do you good."

"We'll take you up on that—on the way back."

"Do these Americans have anything to do with the trouble you've been having, Ben? I know Kosterlinsky's trouble."

"I'll say," Ben said. The Cowdens turned their horses to start up the fence.

"Say," Coughonour called after them. "If you won't let me give you the supper, I can give you a drink of whiskey."

The Cowdens turned back. The man unlocked the gate, swung it open, and stepped inside the garita. Ben and his brothers rode through and did not look back.

Kosterlinsky kept his horses at the end of a box canyon close to the line. People's houses were built on the ridges and cliffs above the canyon on any space that could be leveled enough to support them. They were not houses; they were *viviendas*, places to live. The Cowdens could hear music as they rode into Sonora, guitars they had been unable to hear when they stood at the gate on the American side.

As they rode up the canyon, Les sniffed the air at the aroma of *carne asada*, beefsteak broiling on mesquite coals. "Ah," said he. "For a piece of that meat with plenty of salt, some salza on top, wrapped in a flour tortilla big as my hat, I'd sell myself to another expedition."

Ben saw Toots in the corral at the end of the canyon. "This expedition is damned near over," he said.

The brothers were too tired to dismount. Their horses would have to carry them into this battle. Horses would not be the primary targets because the fight would be at close quarters and everybody would be shooting at everybody else's eyes.

The Cowdens drew their weapons and rode up to the corral. Campana, Stiles, and Smiley were celebrating the end of the day with a fire and a jug of mescal. They did not see the Cowdens until they appeared at the corral.

The Cowdens were ready to shoot at the first sight of Marshall, but he was not in sight. They did not want to start a battle until they knew where he was. If he was not with his minions, the sound of a fight would run him off, and the Cowdens did not want to be held in a fight while Marshall escaped. They had not discussed this, or who they needed to shoot first, but they were not here to waste motion. They wanted Marshall first.

The brothers' eyes met with their enemies', and they never looked away. Les rode around the corral one way, Ben the other, and Mark stayed behind the corral with his rifle drawn. Ben was the talker, the reasoner; Les the quickest and meanest. They left Mark behind because he was the youngest. He was also the most deliberate and the best rifleman.

Campana was the only one of Marshall's men who looked scared. He knew the Cowdens were there to fight. He started moving away from Stiles and Smiley. Ben and Les had spared his life twice in this war. He would not be spared again.

Stiles and Smiley stood up, drew their pistols, and let them hang by their sides as the brothers came in range. Smiley moved away from the fire on Ben's right, in front of Les. Campana moved to Ben's front. Stiles stood his ground by the fire.

Ben said, "We won't kill you if you tell us where Marshall is."

"*Está en las cavernas con Kosterlinsky*. He's in the caverns with Kosterlinsky," Campana said. "I don't want to fight with you, Benjamin."

"You don't have to fight, Campana," Ben said. "But you'll have to leave the country now."

"Who says he don't have to fight," Stiles said. "Of course he has to fight. We're all gonna fight."

"Wait!" Campana said. "Don't start shooting, Benjamin. I told you where Marshall was."

Ben looked at Stiles, giving him the first move.

"That's right, stand and fight, Cowden," Stiles said. "Let's get this over with so some of us can go have a beer."

Ben smiled at him. "All right," he said. He raised his pistol and fired at Stiles, then rode Snake over the top of Campana.

Les spurred his horse past Smiley so the boy would have to turn away from Ben to shoot at him. Ben pulled up on top of Campana and exchanged shots with Stiles. Four or five shots went off in front of Les, enveloping him in smoke and gunfire. Afraid for him, Ben extended his arm like a target shooter and knocked Smiley down.

Stiles was rolling back and forth on the ground, his boots in the fire. Campana was hollering under Snake's hooves. Smiley was lying still on the ground. Les was upright on his horse, whole and sound. Ben rode Snake off Campana. "Get up and pull your partner out of the fire before he burns up," he said.

Campana kept his eyes on Ben as he halfheartedly stretched Stiles' shirt and vest, and lifted his head but left his boots in the fire.

"*Burro!*" Ben said. "Stand away from him and use both hands so you can drag him out of the *fire.*"

"Pardon me," Campana said, "but I have never been good at pulling or dragging."

Ben kept himself from laughing. Les shook his head and smiled. Ben said, "Campana, you drag that boy out of the fire right now, or I swear to God I'll shoot you too."

Campana put his back into the chore, dragged Stiles's smoking feet out of the fire, and dumped him next to Smiley. He looked up to see if anyone was watching, as though he did not want to be caught performing charitable acts for boys who lost gun battles. "Let me go now," he said.

"You're not through. Throw their pistols and yours on top of the ramada."

Campana did that and took hold of his shoulder as though it hurt. "Now I want to go."

"You can't go, because we're going," Ben said. "You have to find a doctor for these boys."

"They're dead."

"Bury them, then, but do whatever has to be done. After that, you better leave the country. Don't let us catch you on our tracks again."

"Sí, Benjamin. I assure you, I'm leaving this time."

"Don't assure me of anything," Ben said. "That makes me think you'll shoot me in the back as soon as I turn away."

"No, please be assured."

"All right, Campana." Ben and Les turned and started toward Mark. He saw Mark raise his rifle and point it toward Campana. He turned back and saw Campana raise his hands in

the air and back away from Smiley as though from a coiled
rattlesnake. "No! No!" Campana shouted.

Smiley did not raise his head off the ground. He pointed a
pistol along the ground at Ben. The boy had drawn it out of his
boot. His boot-top was uncovered, his trouser leg pulled up,
and part of his leg was showing.

The .45 slug struck Ben in the back, grazed his shoulder
blade, and tore out through the muscle at the top of his
shoulder. The bullet smacked all the breath out of him,
knocked him headfirst off his horse, and whipped his pistol
away into the middle of the corral. His hat cushioned his head
when it struck the ground.

Les emptied his pistol at Smiley. Ben regained his feet and
tried to draw his rifle out of the scabbard on his saddle, but
Snake spun away from him to see what was going on behind
him. He pulled Snake around to use him for cover while he
drew the rifle, but the horse would not stand still, and Ben's
right arm would not work for him. He turned loose all holds
and let himself fall into a ditch.

The shooting was soon over. This time, Mark did not spare
Campana. All three members of the Marshall gang were
bleeding in one heap. Mark and Les hurried to look into the
ditch where Ben was lying.

"Get that look off your faces and help me up," Ben said. "If
Kosterlinsky catches me like this, I'm dead. I can't move my
arm."

"Can you ride?" Les asked.

"I'd have to be *dead* not to be able to ride."

Les and Mark tore their shirts and tied a compress on the
holes in Ben's back. The bullet had torn a long furrow in and
out of his back. He imagined his blood was running loose and
filling the wrong places inside him. Les held Snake's head
while Mark helped Ben climb back on.

As the Cowdens left the corrals, Kosterlinsky rode into the
bottom of the canyon with a squad of his rurales. The brothers
looked for a quick way out of the canyon, but they were boxed
in. To escape, they would have to ride across the roofs of the
houses perched on cliffs above their heads.

"I'm sorry, brothers, but I won't let him take me to jail,"
Ben said.

"We won't either, brother," Les said.

"Spread out, then."

As Mark and Les moved away, Kosterlinsky raised his

hand. "No *fighting*, Cowdens." The urgency of the call made his voice break. "We are not here to *fight* you."

Ben tried to answer him, but he did not have the breath to raise his voice. Besides that, he was about to faint.

"Stop there, Gabriel," Les said. "Talk if you want to, but stay down there and don't come closer."

"Don't worry. I don't want to die, and neither do these men with me."

"Then stand aside and let us through," Les said.

"Who is hurt up there?" Kosterlinsky asked. "I've sent for a doctor."

"Ben's hurt. One of your friends shot him in the back."

"Let me come up there. Only me."

"All right, Gabriel, you come on," Les said. Softly, he said, "Hooray, he can keep us company when we ride out."

Kosterlinsky stopped his white horse in front of Ben. He was a good actor; he seemed concerned. "You're hit, Ben. Is it bad? The doctor is coming."

"He'll be all right until we get him to Dr. Noon," Les said.

"But we have doctors *here*, too. Dr. Karem is coming. How badly hurt are those other men?"

Les looked back. Campana was sitting up, bending over his leg moaning in agony.

"Let me bring up two men to help them," Kosterlinsky said. He did not wait for an answer. He ordered the men to come up and give Campana first aid. They hurried to the boys, and one twisted a tourniquet on Campana's thigh while the other examined Stiles and Smiley.

"*Este todavía vive*," the man who examined Stiles said. "This one's still alive." He rolled Smiley over and looked at his eyes. He turned to Kosterlinsky. "This one is dead though."

"Help the other one. The doctor is coming."

Les looked fearfully at Ben's face. "We're going now, Gabriel. We're taking Ben across the line. You're coming with us. Lead the way."

"But, what do you want with me?"

"Safe passage. You ride ahead of us."

Ben slumped in his saddle, but he stayed on board.

Clay Coughonour was still at the garita gate. "I heard the shooting and came back," he said. "I figured you might need sanctuary on this side. I thought you'd be coming faster, though."

"Well, we have an escort who wants us to make it out safely," Les said. "Isn't that right, Gabriel?"

"Most assuredly," Kosterlinsky said.

Kosterlinsky could have turned back then, but he went on to Dr. Noon's office with the brothers. He stood by as the doctor washed Ben and prepared him so he could remove the bullet.

Ben said, "I thought I'd be sorry I let you go at La Noria, Gabriel, but you always do something to redeem yourself with me."

"But why, Ben? I'm your friend, and you have all my money." Kosterlinsky grinned at him.

"You'll never get your money now, Gabriel," Ben said. "You lost your only chance to get it back when you didn't take me in the canyon. They say that dungeon you have back in the cavern gives up a lot of secrets. You might have made me tell you where I hid the alazanas."

"I didn't want to fight you in the canyon, Ben."

"Why not? You had me outnumbered."

"I didn't want to *die*, Ben."

"Where's Marshall, Gabriel?"

Right then a train whistle blew. "There, maybe." Kosterlinsky nodded in the direction of the train.

"He's on that train?" Les asked.

"I think so."

Les and Mark ran out of the office.

"What do they think they're doing?" Kosterlinsky asked.

"Hell, they *want* that sonofabitch," Ben said. "They don't want to have to ride all the way to Guaymas to get him."

"But that train doesn't go all the way to Guaymas, Ben."

"Where to, then—Hermosillo? What's the difference?"

"That train goes to Tucson. The whistle you heard was the engineer's *don't-run-you've-already-missed-this-train* whistle. He's going full speed by now."

"Gabriel, I knew I should have shot you at La Noria."

"You have to shut up now, Ben," Dr. Noon said. "I'm giving you ether."

CHAPTER 25

The Farley twins were drunk, but not drunk enough to suit themselves. After they took A. B. out to El Durazno and carried him to his bed, they took his demijohn of whiskey to the office in the barn. Their father wanted them to stay with the Cowdens until Ben, Les, and Mark came back. That was just right for the twins, as long as they had whiskey.

A. B. had recovered enough in Harshaw to demand to be taken home. He was now comfortable in his bed after a light supper.

The twins tried to get drunk every night. This was unacceptable to their family, so they always took themselves far enough away so they would not bother anyone but close enough so their family could find them and cover them up or drag them out of the way of trampling horses until they slept it off.

They were seventeen years old, and the only time they ever went to bed sober was when they were out working a cow camp. They kept their wits about them when they worked in the haunts of murderers. They dreaded having their skulls smashed while they lay unconscious from gluttony. The nervous state they suffered the first few nights they stayed off the whiskey in their cow camp helped keep them alive.

They could not stand prosperity, though. They thought the availability of whiskey was an excuse for drinking all they could hold.

They heard Dr. Tucker coming back from the house. His

buggy horse was tied in front of the barn. The twins heard him and for a moment tried to think of a place to hide the jug, but they were too slow. The doctor came into the office.

"What are you youngsters up to?" the doctor said. "Oh, you've got A. B.'s *garrafón* down here. Any left?"

"Sure, Doc," Danny said. He poured a heavy splash of spirits into the cup for the doctor.

"Whoa! I can't have those fat drinks you pour for yourselves." He sipped the whiskey and savored it. "That's good stuff. How many of those fat ones have you fellers had?"

"Oh, we been doing chores," Danny said. "We only drank a little one. We're going to supper in a minute."

The doctor was in a hurry. He drank the rest of the whiskey. "Awful good. Put the lid on it and go have supper." He set the cup down on A. B.'s desk. "I mean it. Put it away, now, before your livers shrivel up and fall off."

The twins walked out to the doctor's buggy with him. They backed his horse away from the hitchrail, turned him around toward town, and held him while the doctor climbed in and took the lines. "Put a lid on it, now, until the Cowden boys get home," the doctor said. "Do right for a change."

"Right, Doc," Danny said.

"Aunt Viney said we could only have one drink," Donny said.

"That's all right," the doctor said. "But one's enough."

The twins watched him cross Harshaw creek and head up the road. They turned head-to-head and raced back to the office. They wrestled over the jug but were careful not to upset it. The cork was on the desk. Danny pushed Donny away and raised the jug to his mouth. That posture was inviolate, and Donny stepped away to let him drink.

Danny offered the jug to the rafters, toasting. "Enough is never less than two." He took a swallow. "Or more than four hundred." He handed the precious jug to Donny. There was only one thing he hated more than seeing his brother have more whiskey than he, and that was not being able to share a drink with him.

Frank Marshall stood in the darkness outside the door with a shotgun, listening to them. He had never seen the Farley twins sober. He knew if he waited thirty minutes, they would be so drunk they would not know Frank Marshall from their mother. He was not that patient though.

He stepped into A. B.'s office. The twins were too conented to jump up and reach for their pistols. They remained sprawled on their rumps, gaping at him. He pressed the barrel of the shotgun into the nearest twin's chest, cocked it, and said, "I'd as soon kill you as spit on you. If you don't pay attention to what I say, you're dead. You're only gonna live because I'm gonna use you for billboards. Stand up."

Marshall walked them out into the barn. A block and tackle was set up on the main rafter for hoisting hay into the loft. He made the twins tie their feet to the rope and hoisted them off the floor. He tied their hands behind their backs and gagged them, then hoisted them all the way up against the rafter.

He stood under them, looked into their big round eyes, and said, "You'll be happier this way, you like whiskey so much. It can all run back into your heads now instead of wasting time in your stomachs.

"When the Cowdens come, you tell them to load Kosterlinsky's gold on a packhorse, saddle me two good horses, and bring them to the house.

"If you don't tell them right, I'll kill a woman. I'll probably kill the old lady first by cutting her throat. You tell them, after I kill the others, I'll still have Betty.

"It won't mean a thing to me to kill this family. I'm gonna get that gold, or I'm gonna have more fun with those women than I've ever had in my life. Remember, I told you to pay attention to me? Nod if you understand."

The twins nodded. Marshall took a rope off the wall and stepped outside the barn. The sky was clear, the moon was full. He walked up the path to the house and stood outside a front-room window to watch the Cowden women. Betty and the little one took turns running in and out of the old man's bedroom, fussing over him. Betty finally came out and shut the door. The oldest sister was setting the kitchen table. The old lady was cooking.

Marshall waited until all the women were in the kitchen before he went in, through the living room. He leaned a chair under the knob of the old man's bedroom door to bar his interference. Marshall was not worried that he would have trouble with A. B. After the beating Marshall had given him with Black Beauty Number One, the old goat would be lucky if the doctors didn't have to castrate him to save his life. Marshall had almost worn out his arm on him and had kicked him in the groin so many times his toe got tired.

He walked into the kitchen behind the shotgun and shut

the door behind him. The women all became aware of him at once. Eileen shrieked, and Viney dropped a teakettle on the stove; the water sloshed out and danced and sizzled on the hot lid. Betty saw the gun was pointed at her mother, turned pale, caught Paula Mary in her arms, and sat down by the back door.

"Now, ladies, this is a business visit," Marshall said. "But, as you well know, I am a murderous fella. You have not endeared yourselves to me, so be careful what you do. You will only be able to stay alive as long as you don't make me tired."

"What do you want?" Viney asked.

"I want that Kosterlinsky gold. If you can tell me where it is, I'll let you live. If you don't tell me where it is and I have to wait until Ben Cowden comes homes, I'll probably kill you all."

"We won't help you," Viney said.

"You seem so sure of that, Mrs. Cowden. I'm just as sure I'm capable of killing your whole brood."

"I am no more afraid of you now than I was when I sat you down in my front room and gave you tea. A snake is a snake, whether he is coiled so he can strike, as you are now, or trying to mesmerize us so he can swallow us, as you were then."

"All right, all of you come with me into the front room so I can swallow you if I want to. Come on."

This was not the first time the Cowden women had been in danger of losing their lives. They knew the look of hate in Apache and coontail-rattler eyes. They knew the panic of being taken alive by a runaway horse. The look in Marshall's eyes did not faze them. They knew he would give them plenty of chances to stop him before he pulled his triggers. For weeks they had studied him as he maneuvered his big butt into their chairs, making himself comfortable and keeping himself soft.

He was not the man who could slaughter the four Cowden women, tough as he might think he was. He was mean enough but not man enough to get the best of them. Besides that, they were angry enough at him to draw and quarter him. Not one of them would falter at chopping off his head the way they would a rooster who had spent his days crowing in their barnyard.

As the Cowden women started out of the kitchen, Paula Mary broke away and ran out the back door. Marshall stopped the rest of them and went to the door. "You better come back in here," he yelled. "Don't make me come out and get you."

He turned back inside. "Betty, you tell her to come in, or I'll kill her mother."

"Do as you please with us," Viney said. "You won't get Paula Mary now, no matter what you do."

"Oh no? Just watch me." Marshall tied Viney's hands behind her, than made Eileen stand behind her and reach around so he could tie her hands in front of Viney. He tied their necks together, then their feet, pushed them down on the floor, and gagged them with strips of cloth from Viney's sewing basket. "Isn't this fun, ladies? Wait until I rope you all in a daisy chain. Then watch me get what I want."

He tied Betty's hands in front of her, then put a loop around her neck and pushed her out the back door onto the porch. "I've got your sister by the throat, Paula Mary," he yelled. "I'll keep choking her until you come down here. I know where you are."

He pushed Betty out the screendoor. He stepped up and hugged her close to himself, wiggled behind her and whispered in her ear, "This is really fun, isn't it? Bend over, honey." He reached down and pulled up Betty's dress. *"Bend over, I said!"* He shoved her head down and pulled her dress all the way up over her head.

Betty obliged him and leaned all the way over, then kicked the heel of her foot up between his legs.

"Ohhh!" Marshall said fearfully, but then he realized the kick had done no damage. "Oh-oh-oh. You almost didn't miss, little miss. Don't ruin it for me, honey."

A rock hummed by Marshall's head so close the air brushed his ear in its wake. "You better leave my sister alone," Paula Mary shouted.

Marshall put his arms around Betty's waist and carried her toward the orchard. She kicked him with both heels so hard he had to set her down. Then a rock struck him on the ankle and made him dance and cuss and limp in a circle. Betty started running, and he jerked her down with the rope. Another rock struck him square in the middle of the back.

He tied Betty's throat-latch high on a peach tree. He opened his pocketknife and started up the hill toward Paula Mary's cave. He did not want to fire his shotgun in this canyon. It might be heard in Harshaw on this clear, still night.

He walked up into the shadows of big oaks on a shoulder of the hill. He preferred the dark; he was not so plain a target now. The sounds of his steps and breathing were loud in his ears.

He saw the girl sitting, as small as she could make herself, in the shadow of her cave. He held his shotgun in his left hand, his knife in his right. He had it all his way now. All he had to do was hem her in against the rock wall and slice her up. If he couldn't knife her, he would have to blast her little butt off the hill with the gun.

"*Aaaiii, aaaiii, aaaiii!*" The scream was so close and shrill, it rattled Marshall's ear as a great solid shadow rushed down on his head. The shadow became a big horse that rammed him backward off the hill. He rolled down the hill at the point of the horse's hooves and landed on his back in front of the horse at the bottom. He cocked the shotgun, looked up, and saw the lance upraised in the hand of a man on the horse.

The light of the moon glinted along the worn shaft of the lance as it plunged toward his heart and he let go both barrels of the shotgun into the man.

The lance pierced Marshall beside the throat in the hollow above his collarbone and felled him. The blow so overpowered him that for a moment he thought he was pinned to the ground. He managed to lift himself, but when he tried to stand, he drove the butt of the lance into the hill and fell down screaming.

He heard the screendoor of the house open. He reached into his pocket for new shells to reload the gun. He turned away from the hill so the lance would allow him to rise to his knees. The weight was not more than he could carry, so he held the lance steady until he regained his feet. He broke open the shotgun, the burden of the lance waggling heavily, he dropped the shells into the chambers and heard the satisfying stoppering noise they made when they landed snugly home.

He looked up at the dark form of A. B. Cowden shambling toward him. He knew he should have looked in the bedroom and made sure the old man was in his bed. A white wraithlike figure seemed to be helping the old man along.

"Help me," Marshall said, and he snapped the shotgun's breeches closed. The last thing he remembered in his life was that the gun was too heavy for him to raise. Then both barrels of A. B. Cowden's shotgun went off in his face.

Paula Mary came down the hill and knelt by the form of the man who had been on the horse, the man who had stood his horse and himself between Paula Mary and the murderer. The moonlight was on the man's face, but Paula Mary did not recognize him. He smiled when he saw her beside him.

"Do you still have the *anillo*, Little Wren?" he asked in Spanish.

Paula Mary remembered the ring on the chain around her neck. She pulled it out so he could see it. "Sí," she said.

"I got it for you, no?"

"Yes, thank you." She thought, what's his name, what's his name? "Che Che," she said as he died.

She knew he was dead. She stumbled away and buried her head against her papa's pajamas. Maudy Jane untied Betty. The three girls held on to A. B. and took him back in the house.

CHAPTER 26

From this valley they say you are going.
How I'll miss your bright eyes and sweet smile,
For they say you are taking the sunshine
That has brightened our path for awhile.

Come and sit by my side little darlin'.
Do not hasten to bid me adieu,
But remember the Red River Valley
And the cowgirl that loved you so true.

Maudy's singing awakened Ben, and he saw he was home. He did not know how long he had been unconscious. He remembered boarding the train in Nogales and passing out from pain when the car started moving and not caring if he ever came to.

Lately, he had been trying to regain consciousness, and he finally made it.

He was alone in the room he shared with his brothers at El Durazno after Maudy's clear voice had awakened him with his favorite song. He was comfortable, his carcass felt scrubbed, and his bedclothes smelled good.

After awhile, Maudy opened the door, peeked in, saw he was awake, and sat on the edge of the bed.

"I heard you singing, Snider," Ben said. He sometimes called her Snider to tease her about a cowboy name Snider who had asked her to marry him. "When are you going to sing again so I can be sure and listen?"

"Every day of your life, darlin'," Maudy said. She kissed him, then straightened and looked over her shoulder toward the door.

"What's the matter, afraid somebody's gonna catch you?" Ben laughed.

"Yeah. There's a whole lot of women around here want to kiss you, and I'm getting mine out of turn." Maudy counted women on her fingers. "Six hungry women have been waiting for you to wake up."

"That many?"

"Your mother and sisters are four."

"And you."

"Don't count me. I've already stolen way over my quota when nobody was looking."

"When?"

"Hah! All the time. I've had you all to myself. Your mama made me your nurse and herself your papa's. She said too many nurses was as bad as too many cooks. So I've had you where I wanted you for five days."

"I've been out five days?"

"Five days and six nights, but you've been comfortable, so the doctor said you were just sleeping and resting."

"Five days. God, I have to get up from here."

"Ben, Marshall's dead. He came out here to get even, and your papa killed him." Maudy told Ben the story about Marshall going out after Paula Mary and the way Che Che waited for him and lanced him to protect her.

"How in the world did Marshall miss you and Papa in the house?"

"I was still sick in bed from the time he knocked me down in the yard. I hid under the bed when I heard him in the kitchen, but I don't think he ever thought of me. Your papa was on his throne in the bathroom."

El Durazno was graced with the only indoor toilet in the country, and A. B.'s time on his pot was sacred. No one ever went near the door when he was in there. No one let on they even noticed when he went in or when he came out.

"Marshall thought A. B. was in his bed and stuck a chair under the doorknob to keep him in. A. B., I guess, has the hearing of a horse and knew Marshall's step when he crossed the front room. He stayed in the bathroom and waited for his chance to come out.

"When I heard Marshall go outside with Betty, I untied Viney and Eileen so they could scoot out the front door. I helped A. B. go out the back with his shotgun. Your papa sure is brave. He was really hurting, but he didn't see any sense in peeking around corners or wasting steps. He went out there to shoot Marshall or get shot and only lived through it because the Apache had already stuck his lance in Marshall's throat."

"It seems to me Papa wasn't the only brave one," Ben said. "You were brave, too, Snider."

"Viney said she didn't think Marshall even knew the Cowdens had an indoor pot. No one ever mentioned it to him when he was here visiting. No one invited him to use it, that's for sure."

"So the great man lost his miserable life because my papa outmaneuvered him in an indoor privy. That was just right for him."

"Do you feel like talking to your visitors?"

"Who's here?"

"You'll see." Maudy sat up close to him and brushed his hair into place. He could feel her warmth along his side. It started with her touch on his head and her breath on his ear. "There, handsome. I already shaved you when you were asleep. Now I'm going to bring in your girlfriends, one at a time."

Maudy went out and brought in Don Juan Pedro Elias and Margarita. Margarita kissed Ben quickly and happily. Don Juan wanted to talk about cattle and the range he shared with the Cowdens.

Margarita kept her eyes on Ben's. He gazed back into hers. She probably thought more like Ben than Maudy did. She liked the same Mexican music that Ben did, and her body temperature was more like Ben's. Maudy and he could touch each other a lot, and did, because Maudy's heat was altogether, strictly chaste. Margarita's heat was respectable but would have a falling-down runaway at the first warm touch. Margarita was ready for shortcuts to warm touches.

Don Juan Pedro approved of Margarita's friendship with Ben, so when Ben reached for her hand, she took it in both of hers. When she said good-bye and started walking toward the door, she felt so good she waggled her tail for him, then turned back and gave him a look that she did not want anyone but Ben to see. She became her formal self again when she turned back with her father to wave at the door.

Doris Vincent came in, smiling broadly with big tears in her eyes. She started telling Ben about how worried everyone had been for him but clouded up and put her face in a handkerchief.

"Aw, Doris, cheer up," Ben said. "I'm just glad you're not holding a grudge for that long ride I took you on."

Doris raised her head, laughed, and patted the back of his hand. "I'll never forget that, Ben. You and your jerky gravy and mescal made that ride more enjoyable for me than a trip to Paris. I never had a better time in my life."

"Well, we got home, didn't we?"

"You're darn right we did."

"Where to from here, Doris?"

"We're going back to New York for a while, to recoup."

"You and Dorothy?"

"And Duncan." She included her husband in a tone that said she would never, at any time, consider going anyplace without Duncan Vincent.

"Well, there's a lot happening in New York too," Ben said.

"Not like on Hijo de Pedro Peak, but my family is out there. I'll have a nice visit with my people, I suppose."

"Huh! You'll make things happen wherever you go, Doris. All you have to do is walk through the lobby of the biggest hotel, and everybody'll know you're back in town. If that don't arouse them enough to suit you, shoot at Duncan with your six-shooter like you did in Tombstone."

"That's a good idea. Well, I better go now. Maudy tells me you still need a lot of rest."

"Maudy doesn't mean it."

"Maudy's a dandy girl. You're both darned lucky." Doris's tears marched forth again.

Ben patted her hand. "I'm lucky you're such a fine woman, Doris. I'd be in a lot of trouble if you weren't. What if you had decided to set the law on me, too?"

Doris recovered and laughed. "I thought of that, don't think I didn't. For a time, I would have done anything to get your attention back. I almost sent the U.S. Cavalry after you. I even rehearsed what I would say when you were brought back and thrown at my feet."

Ben laughed. "Tell me what you were going to say."

"Nobly, I would have ordered them to release you. Then,

when you came to thank me, I would have ravished you."
Doris laughed and patted his other hand.

"That's a helluva notion."

"Look at you. I've embarrassed you. I'm really going now."
Doris stood up. "Good-bye, Ben." She bent over and kissed
him softly. She smelled like roses. Her breasts brushed across
the back of his hand. "You're a good man."

"Good-bye, Doris."

She was only gone a second before Maudy came back in.
"Well, you know the only decent thing you can do now is put
on a sweet face and die the death," she said sternly. "Because
I don't know if I'm ever going to forget the looks on the faces
of those two females you just turned out. How will I ever be
able to win you away from those kinds of ladies and their looks?
I'm only the one who has to change your didies when you're
out cold from your adventures."

"Where are my mama and sisters? How come they're not
here pestering?"

"They're out for a drive with your papa. First drive he's
taken since he's been on his feet."

"Come here and give me kisses if you want to know how to
beat out those ladies."

"I'm probably not as hot a kisser as those ladies, and you're
always out cold when I cry over you. I never have a chance to
get all dressed up for you, either."

"Well, come here and we'll practice all those things if you
want to."

"All right, but I warn you, I won't blubber over you like
your other women."

"No, we'll just practice until the mamas and the sisters and
whatever other girlfriends who've been worrying about me
want to come in."

"You're not sick at all. You sure you haven't been faking a
coma?"

As soon as Ben was able to get out of bed, Sheriff Perkins,
Judge Dunn, and Lieutenant Bill Buck came out to El
Durazno together. Sheriff Perkins handed Ben a letter exon-
erating him of any wrongdoing in the altercations at Los
Parados in Patagonia and the Rillito jail in Tucson, and all other
alleged highway robberies and attendant infractions of the law.
Judge Dunn handed him a document that guaranteed him the
governor's amnesty for the cattle theft and title fraud of which

he had been accused. Lieutenant Buck presented all three brothers with letters of commendation from the United States Army for meritorious service against the Yawner at Los Bultos.

After the official moment was over, A. B. brought forward a band of seven Mexican musicians and a hundred friends for a party in honor of his three sons. That party on November 1, 1885, was also the occasion for the announcement of the engagement of Benjamin Joseph Cowden and Maude Jane Pendleton.

J.P.S. Brown

has been one of the most respected writers of the American Southwest for the past two decades. If you enjoyed THE ARIZONA SAGA Book 2: THE HORSE-MAN, you will want to read the third book in this exciting series by J.P.S. Brown

THE ARIZONA SAGA
Book 3:
LADINO

Turn the page for a dynamic preview
from LADINO, on sale April, 1991,
wherever Bantam Books are sold.

In the mountain country of southern Arizona in 1885 lived a wild man named Ben Cowden. Everybody wanted to tame him. Even his sisters wanted him tamed and they were almost as wild. He was wild, but good people loved him because he was a gentle man from gentle people.

He had been pushed to wildness. People were trying to take away his father's land and livestock. The Cowdens were husbandmen in a range war.

Ben Cowden's two brothers were like him. They wanted to be gentlemen, but this did not work well for them. A syndicate made up of New York oil, railroad, and mining interests was trying to eliminate them.

Ben was twenty-one and the oldest of the three brothers. Les was a year and a half younger and Mark was two years younger than Les. On a day in early December 1885 they were on horseback moving cattle across a range called the Buena Vista on the Santa Cruz River near the Mexican border. The country was in a drouth and their cattle, and the cattle of other ranchers who shared that range, were dying. The brothers worked the country a quarter mile apart, gathered the weak cattle and drove them south toward the headquarters of the Maria Macarena ranch in Sonora. They were there to gather all the cattle of the outfits who shared that range with the Cowdens; the Vincents, Romeros, Salazars and Eliases.

Mark was behind the drive, leading a packhorse and letting the cattle drift. Ben and Les threw cattle to him from the flanks. The pace was slow, for the cattle were weak and had a long way to go. The brothers hoped to reach a camp called La Acequia before dark and the sun was just coming up.

Ben was riding a stocky, floppy-eared sorrel he called *Topo*, Gopher. On a steep slope, he rode onto a two year old maverick bull. The animal was lying so still in a cedar thicket that Ben almost rode by without seeing him. Cattle did not jump and run away at the sight of a rider, or move much at all that December. When they found something to eat, they tried to stay until it was all gone. The brown and white maverick bull reverted to his calfhood and lay as still and flat as he could with his chin on the ground, his tail tucked alongside him. He did not twitch an ear or blink an eye.

Ben took stock of him. His backbone did not stick out. His hair was bright and slick. He was doing better than the other cattle. He must have found a high, lonesome place with enough feed to keep himself healthy, got lonesome, and decided to come down and look for company.

The bull's head was turned away from Ben. Ben rode across his front and he lowered his long, white eyelashes as Ben rode past. His horns were long and black at the tips. He was a *granizo*, his dark brown and merle coat studded with small white spots like hailstones. He had clean, brown lines under each eye and a rich, merle cape over his shoulders. His sides were white with dark studs and he had a wide, solid, dark stripe down his backbone.

Ben was recovering from being shot in the back and he could not throw any kind of an overhand loop to catch the bull. He acted as though he did not see the bull, rode on by, then dropped a loop across his chest to the near side of his horse and caught the bull cleanly around the horns. The bull bawled and jumped straight into the air, his tail winding, and when the *reata* took hold of him he bucked and bellowed as though a lion was riding him.

Ben laughed and let the reata burn on his horn so the bull would not jerk and tire his horse. He was fifty feet away before Ben tightened the reata and stopped him.

The bull was too fine an animal to be left a maverick. If Ben took him to the Maria Macarena, someone else might claim him. He gave Ben his full attention now, backed to the end of the reata, shook his horns and glared at Ben, blew strings of slobbers in the air and armed himself for a fight.

These cattle fought when they were cornered or caught. The man did not have a great advantage by being tied to the bull. His reata would not stand a sudden jerk by a 500-pound animal. He rode toward the bull and invited him to charge. The bull blew out a rush of wind and came on with his head up, looking straight into Ben's eyes. Ben quartered around his side and stayed close to him, not enough to make him whirl in place, but enough to keep him running in a close circle, to tire him.

The bull stopped, rested a moment, and charged again. Ben quartered him again, kept him one quarter off center all the time so he could not bracket Ben's horse evenly with his horns, or reach him with his hooking horn. The bull could not drive his weight toward Ben evenly behind his horns, and he could not do anything but stretch and reach and hook the air with the horn nearest the horse.

The bull kept resting and charging. After his eighth charge Ben said, "Dammit, ain't you ever going to stop?" but he charged three more times before he finally pulled up and was still, so mad the pupils of his eyes had turned red.

When the bull was finally fixed in place and refused to untrack, Ben quartered him again and let his reata trail along his side and rode around behind him. He held the reata above the bull's hocks and rode around in front of him, wound the reata below the bull's knees, and rode off. The reata tripped under the bull's front legs and looped around the hocks and down he went with his head trussed to his hind legs. He was so winded he did not even grunt.

Ben coiled his reata as he rode back to him, tied off when he was close to him, stepped off and let Topo hold him down. He tied the bull's front and hind legs together, then built a fire to heat his running iron.

He carved bullet holes in both ears to earmark him. He whacked off the bottom half of the scrotum and took hold of the first nut. The bull did not stir, or make a sound. His eyes were half closed. He was either resting or dying, but Ben did not think he was dying, because his breathing was subsiding and he was calm. Ben sliced down through the outer skin on the nut until the organ popped out, separated the outer skin from the nut, pushed it high up the cord and cut the cord where it was thinnest. Granizo bled about forty drops. After all, they were in a drouth.

Ben searched for the other nut. It had run for cover way up in Granizo's belly. Ben pushed gently on his belly to get it down, but he couldn't even find it. He knew better than to carve or fumble for it. The nut might have been injured in calfhood and turned into scar tissue, but he saw no sign of that. The nut was hiding and Ben would never find it that day. Lucky Granizo would have to remain a bull.

Ben branded with his own brand, a 7X on the left hip. He went to the cutoff boot top on the back of his saddle and took out his screw worm dope, a mixture of chloroform, mezcal, and pine tar, and smeared it on the brand and scrotum to keep off the blowflies and their progeny, the screw worm.

He took his reata off the bull, rolled him on his back and untied him, but held on to the crossed legs. A small dribble of blood, only about as much as a double shot, dropped freely out of the scrotum. Good, he probably wouldn't swell and he was strong enough to fight off the blow flies while the wound dried up.

Granizo's tail was still, his eyes closed. He acted dead as a carcass. Ben grabbed a horn and turned his head over so both horns were stuck in the ground and his clean white throat and a mole on his jaw were bare to the whole world, and he still did not resist.

"Are you alive, Granizo?" Ben asked. He knew from long, long, experience that he better not believe this bull was dead after eleven charges and a good rest. He let

go the legs and stepped up on Topo almost before they settled to the ground. Granizo's horns were still stuck in the ground, his head upside down, his body on its side.

"Well, you might as well get up. I'm going to leave you here, anyway," Ben said. "I'm not going to take you into a roundup so my neighbors can see you fresh branded. You're strong enough to stay out here until next year."

Ben rode Topo close to the bull and whacked the root of his tail with the reata.

No response.

Ben snagged Granizo's nose in the loop of his reata and rolled his horns out of the dirt so he could raise his head. The head flopped on the ground as though it had been cut off and dropped on a slaughterhouse floor.

Ben started to ride away and all of a sudden the bull's eyes glared open and the horns raised up. The bull speared toward Topo quick as a lizard. He scraped Topo's butt with the tips of both horns before Ben could spur the horse away. Topo bucked and kicked at the bull and stampeded off the hill.

Ben stopped Topo at the bottom and looked back. Granizo was silhouetted on top the hill with his head high and the sun at his back. He tossed his horns as if to say, "You hurt me. Don't come back here again, because I'll be ready for you."

Ben dismounted and looked at the scrapes Granizo's horns had made on Topo's butt. Topo rolled an eye at him, as if to ask, "Is it very bad?"

Ben laughed. "We've dammit been put to flight, Topito, but you'll be all right. That's the cheapest lesson you'll ever learn. Now, for the rest of your life you'll know what a bull's horns can do, and I bet you never let them get that close again."

Ben mounted and admired Granizo a moment longer. He thought, now you've done it, Cowden. That gentleman'll be a lot harder to catch next time. He's smart as a jaguar and now he's been turned loose after being trussed up, knifed, and hurt. From now on he'll be hard to see, let alone catch. Sure as hell, he'll become another famous *ladino* and give us cowboys lots of trouble. Before his horns ever get stuck in the dirt again he'll be called El Ladino Granizo and be known to every *vaquero* in this country. I'll bet a new hat on that. Now, he'll be a ladino just like me, running from the law and getting smarter about it every day.

The brothers penned the cattle at La Acequia at twilight and left them with vaqueros who had worked the roundup from other sides. They reached the headquarters of the Maria Macarena ranch long after dark and could see no light in the main house. They rode behind the main house and were heartened by the sight of a fire in front of Chapito Cano's house. Chapito was the ranch's *mayordomo*. They sat their horses in the firelight. Everyone on the place had already gone to bed.

"Chapitooo," Ben growled in a low voice.

"*Et,*" shouted Chapito as he awakened. After a while he came to the door pulling up his pants and recognized the three horsemen. "*Dios Mio*, the fire, the plague, and the flood have arrived and the drouth is already with us. Get down from there, Horsemen." He turned back over his shoulder. "Luz, send the boy to wake up the main house. The Horsemen are here."

People began to stir and a lamp was lit inside Chapito's house. A sleepy headed boy came out barefooted, skirted the fire and the horsemen, and headed for the main house. Ben recognized Pepe, the owner Don Juan Pedro Elias's grandson. The boy had seen his father and uncle killed by Apaches in June of that year at La Acequia.

The brothers followed Chapito to a shed row where they unsaddled and fed and stabled their horses. They unsheathed their rifles, took blanket rolls off their saddles and followed him toward the main house. They met Pepe as he was returning.

"*Quehubole, Pepito*," Ben said. "How's my friend?"

The boy stopped and shook Ben's hand, then shook the hands of Les and Mark and looked them in the eye.

"You must be working full time as a vaquero, now," Ben said. "Is that why you're living with Chapo?"

"Yes," the boy said.

"Are you making a hand?"

"*Saaabe*. Who knows?"

"He's making a top hand," Chapito said.

"I better go sleep, now," the boy said.

"Correct."

"*Buena noche*."

"Buena noche," the brothers said.

The boy hurried on.

"He's young to wean, but I know he's a good vaquero," Les said. "Can you imagine us weaning our little sister Paula Mary and putting her to work at that age?"

"That is absolutely beyond my imagination," Mark said.

"That's not it," Chapito said as he led the way toward the back door of the main house. "He's not living with me by choice."

"How could that be?" Les said. "You mean he's been run out of the house?"

"You'll see."

The brothers followed Chapito through the back door and a long, narrow passageway to the open patio in the center of the house. The house was built like a fort. The front and back doors were its most vulnerable places. The back door was reinforced by iron straps and studs. The front entrance was wide enough to accommodate a wagon and team, but two iron gates and an iron reinforced door were locked across it at night or when the hacienda was under siege.

Margarita, the person Ben most wanted to see, crossed the patio to meet them. She was a good friend of Ben's, but when he stepped forward to see it in her eyes, she only turned her cheek to him and went on to shake hands with his brothers. Ben thought Margarita was the most beautiful woman he had ever seen, but that night she looked old and dry. Her hair had been cut short and she looked used and sad.

Margarita was Pepe's mother. She had been in mourning since June, but Ben had seen her enjoy a visit to Tombstone on the 16th of September. Though still wearing her weeds, she had been vibrant, pretty, and coquettish. Later, when Ben laid up at home with his wound she and her father Don Juan Pedro came to see him and she, by God, flirted with Ben. He could not understand why she looked so mournful now.

"Please take your *mochilas* to the room you always use and then seat yourselves in the dining room. I'll bring you supper," she said and went away to the kitchen. The brothers did as they were told, ducking their heads when they passed through the door to their room. A lamp was already lit there and they laid their blanket rolls down and drank water from clay pitchers and clay cups at their bedsides.

Chapito excused himself and went home. The brothers washed at a basin on the patio and trooped into the dining room. Ben turned into the kitchen. Margarita kept her back to him.

"Margarita, what happened to your hair?" Ben asked.

"I had a fever and it fell out."

"When were you sick? I didn't know."

"Last month." She turned with a trace of the fresh

smile Ben remembered. "I think it's coming back. Do you think so? Please say you do."

"Of course it is. It is only curious looking, not unattractive."

"Thank you for that."

"You must have been very sick."

"I almost died."

"Is that why Pepito is living with the Canos?"

"Oh, yes."

"What caused your fever?"

"I got married."

"You got *married*? Who did you marry, an ogre?"

"He's not so bad. Yes he is. He's old, stern and cruel and believes the touch of a woman is evil."

Ben decided he might as well believe what he heard, but it sure was not any of his business. He straightened in the doorway and saw a tall figure standing in the shadows on the patio. The figure stepped forward into the light, a long, bony white man in his trousers and undershirt. His hands were huge and brown on thick boned wrists. His big feet were bare under his trouser cuffs. His long forehead was white, his big nose burned red, his small, close set, blue eyes round and staring. Ben stared back.

"*Quien eres tu*? Who are you?" the man said, his deep voice booming inside the kitchen.

Margarita flinched as though popped by a whip. "My husband, Jack Odoms," she said.

Ben did not offer his hand and neither did Odoms.

"What is this man here for?" the man demanded.

"For his supper. For the roundup. Why would anyone visit here these days except to work?" Margarita said.

Odoms looked into the dining room at Les and Mark,

then looked closely into Ben's face. "You're Ben Cowden?"

"*A sus ordenes, señor*. At your service."

"Yeah, you'll think 'at my service'." The man was a giant, mostly bone and very little flesh and blood.

Ben could see Margarita was afraid of him. She kept her mouth so tightly closed that the corners turned down. She owned the darkest brown eyes Ben had ever seen, so dark the pupils could not be seen unless she was out in the sun. They were wide open with fear now.

"I'm Jack Odoms of the Texas Rangers," the man said.

"Never heard of you," Ben said.

"Well, so you'll know, I've been hired by the Vincents and the Pima County Livestock Association, to police this area against cowthieves. That's my wife there fixing your supper. Keep in mind, she's mine and I want her back as soon as you've been fed." Odoms turned and walked hugely and soundlessly away, his big hands swinging with their palms toward Ben, the soles of his big feet showing white in the kitchen light.

Margarita sat at the table while the brothers ate supper. Les and Mark had not heard what she said about her marriage. She did not talk about Odoms again and the longer she sat with the brothers the more she brightened up. By the time the meal was over she was their friend Margarita again. The last time Ben had seen her she gave him a long, wet, warm kiss and then wiggled her hips when she left the room to make him feel good.

When his brothers went on to bed, Ben stayed to help Margarita clear the dishes off the table. As he stood up from his chair, he bumped her accidentally with his hip. Then he reached for a dish and accidentally grabbed her hand. "Ah, *perdón*, he said, when she recoiled.

She turned and found something to do away from him and seemed not to appreciate being touched.

"Sorry, I almost knocked you down," he said.

With a serious face and at arm's length, Margarita handed him a stack of dishes.

"Excuse me, Margarita. I'm too accustomed to my sisters. We're always bumping and grabbing each other."

"Don't worry."

"You sure have changed."

"In what way?"

"You remember how we used to dance at the fiestas, how close we used to get when we were having fun?"

"I'm married now."

"You were married to Pepe's father, the musician, then, too."

"Ah, but Pepe's father was not a Texas Ranger. Pepe's father handled a woman on a featherweight rein."

"And this one?"

"*A golpes*. By blows. *A puñaladas*. With his fists. And sometimes at the point of a pistol and sometimes even with the blows of a pistol."

"He pistol-whips you?"

"Sometimes, but only after he has come to the fresh conclusion that I am a whore and a slut."

Ben had never in his life heard a woman say those words, not even the Campana girls in Santa Cruz who entertained men in their home. *He* never said those words. He could not imagine anyone deserving to be called that. He suddenly realized he was in the wrong place at the wrong time, not the situation to which any cowpuncher aspired.

"How nice it would be to be touched again," Margarita said. "I want to be touched and rubbed and kissed again. Let me tell you, Ben, if a woman can't look forward to that, her life is over."

"Ah, Margarita." Ben sighed. He had no idea how the woman could resolve her problem.

"You, Ben. Will you be my lover? I've always loved you."

"But you're married, Margarita, and I'm engaged to Maudy Jane Pendleton. What would you do with Maudy and your husband?"

"I told you, I need to be touched. Don't you?"

"Everybody needs that."

"Just think about it, won't you?"

In all truth, what answer could a gentleman give? "Yes, I will," he said.

"That's all I'm asking you to do."

Ben looked up and saw that Les and Mark had turned back to wait for him. Their faces were stern and angry. He knew they could not have heard what he and Margarita said, but they could guess the nature of it and were giving him identically disapproving looks.

ELMER KELTON

☐	27713	THE MAN WHO RODE MIDNIGHT	$3.50
☐	25658	AFTER THE BUGLES	$2.95
☐	27351	HORSEHEAD CROSSING	$2.95
☐	27119	LLANO RIVER	$2.95
☐	27218	MANHUNTERS	$2.95
☐	27620	HANGING JUDGE	$2.95
☐	27467	WAGONTONGUE	$2.95
☐	25629	BOWIE'S MINE	$2.95
☐	26999	MASSACRE AT GOLIAD	$2.95
☐	25651	EYES OF THE HAWK	$2.95
☐	26042	JOE PEPPER	$2.95
☐	26105	DARK THICKET	$2.95
☐	26449	LONG WAY TO TEXAS	$2.95
☐	25740	THE WOLF AND THE BUFFALO	$3.95